HIGHLAND FIRE

A tremor of want tore through Tavig. Wrapping his arms around Moira, he pulled her down onto their meager bed. He cupped her face in his hands he kissed her, savoring the heated sweetness of her mouth. The way she shyly bandied the strokes of his tongue, the way she pressed against him, told him she was willing. Tavig knew it was going to be hard to go slowly, gently. His desire for her was fierce and greedy.

Moira felt her nervousness and hint of fear smoothed away with each stroke of Tavig's tongue, each touch of his hand. This was what she wanted. She had no doubts about it. She also knew she would have no regrets. For ten long years she had known no happiness and no affection. Tavig had made her blood burn. She was certain this would be as close to love as she would ever get and she intended to enjoy it to the fullest. After facing death in Craigmoordun, she knew any consequences she might face for being so free with her favors would never equal the regret she would suffer for continuing to say no to Tavig.

"Loving, ye feel so bonnie. Like warm silk." Tavig gently traced the shape of her face with soft kisses.

"Ye feel rather bonnie yourself," she whispered, tentatively running her hands over his broad, smooth back.

"There is still time to stop, sweet Moira."

"Nay, I dinna wish to stop. I want this and for the first time in a verra long time I will do what *I* want . . ."

Books by Hannah Howell

Published by Zebra Books

HIGHLAND FIRE

HANNAH HOWELL

ZEBRA BOOKS
Kensington Publishing Corp.
www.kensingtonbooks.com

ZEBRA BOOKS are published by

Kensington Publishing Corp.
850 Third Avenue
New York, NY 10022

All Kensington titles, imprints, and distributed lines are available at special quantity discounts for bulk purchases for sales promotion, premiums, fund-raising, educational, or institutional use.

Special book excerpts or customized printings can also be created to fit specific needs. For details, write or phone the office of the Kensington Special Sales Manager: Attn. Special Sales Department. Kensington Publishing Corp., 850 Third Avenue, New York, NY I0022. Phone: 1-800-221-2647.

Zebra and the Z logo Reg. U.S. Pat. & TM Off.

ISBN-13: 978-0-8217-7429-8
ISBN-10: 0-8217-7429-8

Previously published by Jove Books under the pseudonym Anna Jennet and the title *Fire*.
First Zebra Mass Market Paperback Printing: June 2008

10 9 8 7 6 5 4 3 2 1

Printed in the United States of America

Chapter One

Northwest Coast of Scotland—August 1400

"Come, lass, surely my flattery deserves at least a wee smile."

Moira stole a glance at the man speaking to her. He had been watching her since she had boarded the ship three days before. Crooked Annie, her sharp tongued watchdog, had grumbled about the man and sternly warned Moira to avoid him. That was not easy to do on such a small ship.

He made her uneasy. His black hair was heavily streaked with gray, and his middle was very thick, causing his doublet to fit oddly. His black beard was straggly, and he wore his hat so low she could not really see his eyes.

Everything about him indicated an aging, somewhat unclean man, yet she noticed a few things that sharply contradicted that image. The tight sleeves of his elegant black doublet revealed strong, slender arms. His equally black hose fit snugly over long, well-shaped legs. His voice was deep and rich, the voice of a vibrant young man. He moved with a lithe grace that belied his apparent age and overfed condition. Then he smiled at her, and Moira was convinced he was not what he appeared to be. The revelation made her even more nervous. Glancing around for Crooked Annie,

she was a little annoyed to see the gnarled old woman cozening up to an equally gnarled old sailor.

"She will be over to scold ye and hurry ye away soon
enough," the man said.

"I believe I will go and join her." She uttered a soft gasp
of surprise when he caught her by the hand and held her in
place.

"Now, lass, ye dinnae wish to ruin the old crone's
chance for a wee bit of loving, do ye?"

Moira was shocked by his blunt words. The thought of
Annie doing any loving at all was almost as unsettling as
being touched by the strange man. He started to grin, then
frowned. She realized he could read the fear she was
unable to hide. Her guardian had taught her well to fear
men. It was unfair, but the moment the man grabbed her
by the hand, she tensed for a blow.

"Ah, my poor, sweet, timid bairn, ye have no need to
fear old George Fraser."

It stung to hear this man call her a baby, and she quickly
regained some of her lost courage, yanking free of his
hold. "As I see it, Master Fraser, a 'bairn' ought to be verra
concerned when a mon thrice her age cozens up to her."

"*Thrice* her age?" George gasped then fiddled with the
front of his doublet for a moment before shrugging. "Age
doesnae stop a mon from appreciating the sight of a
bonnie wee lass."

"Then perhaps your wife ought to."

"She would have, save that she is no longer with us." He
sighed, slumping against the railing. "My sainted Margaret
caught a fever and coughed her last but three years ago."

"Oh, I am so sorry, sir." She patted his arm, her sympathy waning a little when she felt how strong and slender that
arm was. "I did not mean to stir any painful memories."

"Here now, ye keep your old eyes off this bairn," snapped
Crooked Annie, snatching Moira's hand off his arm just as
he was about to cover it with his own.

"We were just discussing his wife," Moira protested, trying

to struggle free of Annie's iron grip, but the woman's weathered hand was wrapped around her wrist like a manacle.

"Weel, she ought to box the rogue's ears for being such a lecherous bastard."

"Annie," Moira said with a gasp, blushing a little over Annie's coarse language. "His wife died."

"Humph. He probably sent her to her deathbed with all his philandering about."

"I am sorry, sir." Moira's apology faltered a little, for she was sure the man was suppressing a grin.

"Come on, lass." Annie yanked her away from the man, continuing to pull her along as she headed for the ship's tiny cabins. "Ye dinnae want old Bearnard to catch ye talking to a mon, do ye?"

The mere thought of her guardian sent a chill coursing down Moira's spine, immediately ending her attempts to resist Crooked Annie's insistent tug upon her hand. "Nay, I shouldnae like that at all."

Tavig MacAlpin watched the scowling Crooked Annie drag Moira away and sighed. He leaned against the railing, checking to be sure no one was watching him as he carefully adjusted the thick padding around his middle. Ever since he had set eyes on Moira Robertson his disguise as the graying George Fraser had become a curse, even though he knew it was saving his life. The ransom offered for his capture was big enough to tempt even the most principled of men. There were none of those on the small ship.

It had taken him three long days to grab a chance to speak to Moira, but he wondered why he had been so intent on doing so. He had watched her avidly as she strolled the deck with her bent, gray-haired nurse. Moira's coppery hair was always braided tightly, but soft curls forever slipped free to frame her small oval face. Whenever he was fortunate enough to get a closer look at her, he marveled at how few freckles colored her soft white skin. He could clearly recall how startled he had been when he stole his first look into her eyes. Tavig had expected brown ones or even green ones, but never the rich, clear blue eyes she possessed. And such big eyes, too, he mused, smiling faintly. He admitted to himself with a soft laugh that he did whatever he could to get her to look his way so that he could see those huge eyes with their long, thick dark lashes.

A chuckle escaped him. It was possible he remembered her face so well because there was not much else of her to see. She was a tiny, too-thin lass. She had a woman's soft curves, but they were also tiny. She was certainly not his usual fare, yet Tavig had to concede that she had captured his full attention.

He cursed as he recalled the fear that had flashed in her beautiful eyes when he had touched her. That fear had returned in force when Crooked Annie had mentioned Moira's guardian's name. Even some of the color in Moira's high-boned cheeks had faded. Moira's guardian Sir Bearnard Robertson was a bully. Tavig had seen that from the start. Although Bearnard had not yet struck Moira, Tavig was certain that the possibility existed. He prayed Bearnard would not touch the girl, at least not until Tavig was within running distance of his cousin Mungan's keep and safety. He knew that if Bearnard Robertson raised a hand against Moira, he would rush to her rescue. A good tussle with a man the size of Robertson could easily ruin his disguise. Tavig knew that would mean being dragged back to his treacherous cousin Iver. And there awaited a hangman's noose for murders he had not committed.

A sudden chill wind swept over him. Tavig cursed again and shivered, pulling his heavy black cloak fighter around himself. He scowled up at the sky. Mixed in with the usual evening clouds that forecast the approaching night were some very ominous black clouds. Another chill wind blew over the deck with far more force than the first. Tavig cursed. A late summer storm was nearly upon them. He would soon have to return to the small cabin he shared with three other men and he dreaded it. Such close confinement with others only increased his chances of being discovered. The rain the storm would bring was far more threatening to his tenuous disguise, however, so he promised himself he would seek shelter at the first hint of rain.

A heavy weight across Moira's chest slowly pulled her out of her dreams. She opened her eyes and hastily swallowed a scream. By the dim light of a lantern dangerously left lit and swinging wildly on its ceiling hook, Moira saw that it was not Crooked Annie sprawled on top of her but Connor, her guardian's man-at-arms. For one long moment she lay still, barely breathing, until she realized Connor was far too drunk to be a threat. Irritation quickly banished her panic.

Moira muttered a curse as she hastily untangled herself from the snoring man. Briefly she considered sleeping on the floor of the crowded cabin, but one look revealed that the wine-soaked people already sprawled there had left little room for her. Pressing against the wall in the hope of keeping away from Connor, who smelled strongly of drink and sweat, Moira cursed the ship. She wondered for the hundredth time why they had not allowed themselves enough time to travel by horse and cart. The ransom demand for her cousin Una had arrived weeks ago. Her guardian could easily have taken a longer, more comfortable route to rescue her. Even the poor roads would not have caused them to suffer such a rough journey. Nor, she thought crossly, would she have had to suffer sleeping in such close quarters with her kinsmen and as many retainers as they could stuff into the tiny cabin.

The ship tossed roughly from side to side again. Moira frowned, listening closely as she gripped the edge of the straw mattress to hold herself away from the loudly snoring Connor. Something was wrong. The tiny ship careened over some very rough seas. Her eyes widened as she heard the wind and rain battering the outer walls of their cabin. They had sailed into a storm and a very fierce one, too, if she was any judge of such things. The rain hit the outside of the ship so hard it sounded like drumbeats. The fierce wind howled as it slammed into the ship's wood, wailing as it tore around the ship.

Annie. Moira felt her heart skip with fear for her aging companion. The old woman was not in the cabin. She suspected Annie had crept off to see the sailor she had flirted with earlier and was now trapped out in the storm. She had to go see if Annie was safe.

Holding her breath, Moira carefully crept to the foot of the bed. She grabbed her cloak, which swung from a nail on the bedpost, and slipped it on. The moment she got out of bed she dropped to her hands and knees. The way the ship was beginning to rock it would be impossible to maneuver on foot through the people cluttering the cabin floor. Although everyone appeared to be deep in a drink-ladened sleep, Moira inched toward the door, tense with fear that someone would wake up and see her. Discovery would mean confronting her guardian Bearnard.

Once outside of the cabin she paused, bracing herself against the wall of the narrow passage. What should she do next? Annie could be safe and dry in some cabin. Moira shook her head. The man Annie had been cozening up to only hours ago was a mere deckhand, a poor lowly sailor of no rank. He would have no private place to take Annie except up on the deck. She simply had to look and assure herself that her old nursemaid was safe.

Her first attempt almost proved to be her last. Moira edged onto the first step leading up to the deck. The ship lurched, the violent motion knocking her off her feet. She slammed into the hard wall. For several moments she clung to the wall, gasping for breath. Her body still aching, she tried again.

When she first emerged onto the deck the wind and the pelting rain nearly drove her back. Moira gritted her teeth and, using anything at hand to hang on to and steady herself, started on her search for Annie. She could not believe Annie was still outside, yet the woman was not in her bed where she belonged, either. The storm had not completely dimmed the light of dawn, but it would still be difficult to find one thin old woman on the rain-washed deck. Moira heartily cursed Annie as she struggled over the pitching deck.

Tavig saw the small figure, bent against the wind and rain, edging her way, along the deck, and cursed. He had spent the last hour trying to get back to his own cabin but, since the crew was a man short, the captain had forced him to help. Tavig knew that missing man was off with Annie. He also knew that his disguise was melting away with every drop of rain, but if he left he could easily be putting everyone's life in danger.

And now Moira was there. He had also spent the last hour praying that he was wrong, that she would not come searching for her randy old nursemaid. This was one time when he desperately wanted his accursed foresight to be proven wrong. The girl was stumbling her way toward a great deal of trouble, and he hated knowing that. He especially hated knowing that somehow he would be the cause. She fell to her knees, gripping the railing but a few feet away from him, and he sighed as he stumbled over to her. Now there was only one life he was concerned with.

"What are ye doing here, lass?" he shouted, fighting to be heard over the fury of the storm. "What few sailors are on deck are all lashed to their posts. The others will soon be wisely huddled below decks. 'Tis where ye should be."

"'Tis where ye should be as weel."

"I had to help batten down the hatches." He frowned, looking up at the sky as the wind suddenly eased and the rain grew almost gentle. "It seems the storm needs to catch its breath."

"Good. Now I can find Annie."

"Annie is off rutting with her sailor." He shook his head when she blushed so brightly even the dark could not hide it.

"That may be true, but she could be in trouble now. Once the storm started she should have returned to the cabin." A gust of wind slapped her, forcing her to cling more tightly to the ship's railing.

Tavig looked at Moira, trying to think of a way to convince her to go back inside, and froze. The cold familiar feeling that he was caught up in circumstances he could not control or change oozed over him. He tried to keep his frustration and fear out of his voice, but knew he was failing even as he spoke.

"Get away from that railing, lass."

Moira frowned. There was an odd, strained note to his voice. She tensed, wondering if Master Fraser was something more dangerous than the aging lecher she had thought him to be.

"I will as soon as the wind eases some more," she replied, trying to decide if she should scurry out of his reach.

"It willnae ease any more," he snapped. "'Tis a cursed gale. This lull willnae last much longer, and the storm will probably come back stronger than before. Now move away from that twice-cursed railing."

Even as she decided to do so in an effort to placate him, she suddenly noticed something that halted her. Master Fraser's hair was no longer the dull color it had been. The gray was seeping out of his shoulder-length hair to settle at the tips in sticky clumps. She stared at him, watching closely as another of the few remaining streaks of gray slithered down his hair. Master Fraser was definitely not what he appeared to be. Curiosity overwhelmed her, and she reached out to touch his hair.

"Your age is washing away in the rain," she murmured, her eyes widening at the curse he spat.

"I kenned that would happen. I have to get out of this rain." He grabbed her so forcefully she fell against him.

"So this is where ye disappeared to—out whoring!"

Moira cried out in surprise and fear as her guardian, Sir Bearnard Robertson, grabbed her by the arm, roughly yanking her to her feet. "Nay, sir, I swear I just came out to look for Crooked Annie."

"In this rogue's arms?" he bellowed, vigorously shaking her. "Dinnae add lying to your sins, ye little slut."

As Bearnard raised his meaty hand to strike her, Moira quickly turned to prepare for the blow. She fought to relax, to banish all tension and resistance from her body. Over the years she had learned that such limpness robbed his blows of some of their strength. She made no sound when he backhanded her across the face, sending her slamming onto the rough wooden deck. Landing on her hands and knees, Moira quickly bowed her head, all the while keeping a covert eye on her guardian. She wanted to be ready to avoid the worst of the pain if he decided to add a few kicks to his brutal reprimand.

An odd sound abruptly interrupted her concentration. She shook her head, but it was not a roar from inside her head, caused by the force of her guardian's blow. A soft, low roar of pure fury erupted from the man calling himself George Fraser. Moira spun around, sitting on the deck to stare at hum. She gaped when he lunged at Bearnard, punching the bigger, heavier man and sending him sprawling onto the deck.

"Such a brave mon ye are, Robertson," he spat. "It takes such courage to strike down a wee, skinny lass."

"'Ware, sir," Bearnard yelled, scrambling to his feet. "A man who scurries after a lass half his age has little right to speak so self-righteously of others. Ye are naught but an old lecher trying to seduce a foolish young lass."

"Even if that charge were true, 'twould still make me a better mon than some slinking cur who beats a wee lass."

A growl of pure rage escaped Bearnard as he charged Master Fraser. Both men fell to the deck with a crash. Moira cried out in dismay. Although she had no idea what she could do, she began moving toward the men. She had to stop the fight she had inadvertently caused.

"Dinnae be an idiot," said a deep voice as she was caught from behind.

"Nicol!" she cried, looking over her shoulder at her cousin. "Where did ye come from?"

"I followed Father when he came looking for you. I must have had a vision that ye were about to do something verra stupid. Sweet Lord, Moira, why would ye want to tryst with that old fool?"

"I wasnae trysting with him. I came looking for Crooked Annie, and Master Fraser was trying to get me to go back to my cabin."

"Ye should never have left it," Nicol muttered then cursed softly. "Your savior's belly has shifted."

Nicol's words made no sense, and Moira looked at the two combatants. They were on their feet again, warily circling as each sought a new opening to attack the other. She stared at Master Fraser and gasped. His soft belly was now an uneven lump protruding from his left side. His doublet was torn open, and she could see something sticking out. After staring hard for a moment she realized what it was. Mister Fraser's soft belly was no more than rolled-up rags.

"His gray hair has washed away, too," she said.

"Aye," agreed Nicol. "The mon isnae what he pretends to be. Curse me, but I think I ken who he is."

Before Moira could ask Nicol to explain, he left her side. Even as he drew near to his father, Bearnard charged Fraser, knocking the smaller man down. Fraser's hat spun off his head to be caught by the wind and flung out to sea. His now completely black hair whipped around his face as he fought to keep Bearnard from putting his meaty hands around his throat. There was no mistaking Fraser as anything other than a young, strong man.

Nicol took a step toward his father as Bearnard froze. The looks on their faces told Moira they now recognized the man and were stunned by his presence on the ship. The expression forming on Fraser's face told her that recognition was the very last thing he wanted. She tensed, suddenly afraid for the man who had so gallantly leapt to her defense.

"Tavig MacAlpin," Bearnard yelled, leaping to his feet and placing his hand on his sword.

"Aye, and what business is it of yours?" Tavig snapped as he cautiously stood up to face the Robertson men.

"'Tis the business of every righteous mon twixt here and London."

"Ye are no righteous mon, Robertson, but a brute who holds sway o'er others with his fists and an inexhaustible well of cruelty. Ye can command no respect or affection so ye instill fear in all those around you." Tavig slowly put his hand on his sword, preparing for the attack he knew was to come. "'Tis a wonder ye have lived so long, that no one has yet cut your fat throat."

"And ye would be a good one to do it, wouldnae ye? Ye like naught better than to creep up from behind a mon and cut his throat. Or their bellies, as ye did to your two friends. Your cousin Iver MacAlpin is offering a handsome sum for ye, and I mean to collect it." Bearnard drew his sword, lunging at Tavig.

"Father," yelled Nicol. "Sir Iver doesnae want the mon dead."

"The bastard deserves killing," snarled Sir Bearnard.

"Come and try," taunted Tavig. "Aye, ye may yet get lucky, but I swear I will gut ye ere I die, ye swine."

Bearnard roared with fury, and his attack became more vicious, but Tavig parried his every blow. He did not wish to die, but he did not want to be taken prisoner, either. If he was returned to his traitorous cousin Iver, he knew he faced a slow, painful death for murders he had not committed. If he could not win the battle against Robertson, then he would make sure the man cut him down.

"Nay, Cousin Bearnard," Moira cried as Tavig faltered and Bearnard raised his sword to strike the death blow.

As Tavig frantically scrambled out of the way of
Bearnard's sword, he saw Moira rush toward her uncle. He
cursed when Bearnard swatted the girl away, hurtling her
back against the railing—the very railing Tavig had
warned her to get away from. Bearnard's attention was
briefly diverted, and Tavig took quick advantage of that.
He charged the man, knocking Bearnard to the ground.
With two swift, furious punches he knocked Bearnard out.
He barely glanced at Bearnard's son Nicol as he leapt to
his feet and ran to Moira.

"Moira, get away from that railing," he demanded, ignoring Nicol, who stood to his right, pointing a sword at him.

Still groggy from Bearnard's blow, Moira did not question
him, but as she moved to obey his hoarse command, the renewed winds worked against her. They slammed into her,
pushing her hard up against the railing. She tried to reach out
for Tavig's outstretched hand, but the howling wind held her
tightly in place, as securely as any chains. Moira felt as if the
breath were being forced from her body. The rough wood
of the railings dug into her as the gale pressed her harder and
harder against them. She could see Tavig start to move
toward her, determinedly fighting the winds, but she could
not move or extend her hand toward him. Then she heard the
ominous sound of wood cracking.

The railing Moira was pinned to gave way even as both
Tavig and Nicol yelled a warning. She clung to it as the
section swung out over the swirling waters. Moira looked
back at the ship to see that the railing she clutched was
attached by only one splintered piece of wood. Carefully
inching her hands along, she tried to make her way back
to the ship, to within reach of Nicol's and Tavig's outstretched hands. She was only a finger's length away from
safety when the section of railing gave up its last tenuous
connection to the ship. She screamed as she plummeted
into the gale-tossed waters.

Tavig bellowed out Moira's name as he clung to the un-
damaged railing. He could barely see the white of her

nightgown. She still held on to the piece of railing, but half her body was submerged beneath the cold, churning water. Tavig knew Moira could not hold on for long, nor would she be able to pull herself out of the water. Soon she would be dragged beneath the high waves. She needed help if she was to have any chance of survival.

"Get me that rope," he ordered Nicol, pointing to a length of hemp knotted to a nearby bollard.

"What can ye do?" asked Nicol, resheathing his sword as he hurried to obey.

"Go after her." Tavig secured the ropes about his arm and moved to the gap in the railing.

Nicol grabbed his arn. "Are ye mad? Ye will be killed."

"Better to die trying to save some skinny red-haired lass than swinging from Iver's rope. And mayhap I willnae die."

As Nicol looked down into the churning waters, he cursed. "Aye, ye will."

"I prefer to think not. All I ken is that I *must* go in after Moira, or she willnae survive this. 'Tis cursed hard to trust that wee voice when it demands I hurl myself in after her, though. I just hope my intuition has the good grace to tell me how or even what will happen after I jump into these dark threatening waters."

"What are ye babbling about, MacAlpin?"

"Fate, laddie. Twice-cursed fate."

With a prayer that his intuitions continued to be correct, he took a deep breath and jumped. For a brief moment after he hit the cold water he panicked. He sank beneath the froth-tipped waves and feared that he would never get back to the surface. Tavig struggled upward, fighting the currents battering him. When he emerged, he took several hearty breaths, more out of relief than need. He looked for Moira and swam toward the white patch of nightgown he could still see.

Tavig cursed the waters as he struggled through the tumultuous waves toward Moira and the section of the ship's railing she clung to so desperately. He hoisted himself up onto her haphazard raft. Tying one piece of rope about his waist, he hastily lashed himself to the wood. As soon as he felt secure, he grabbed Moira by one of her slender wrists, hauling her out of the water, and she collapsed at his side. As the cold water washed over them, he secured one of her hands to the railings as well. He then took her free hand in his. When he pressed his body flat against the sodden wood he found himself nose to nose with Moira.

"Ye are mad," she yelled, coughing as a wave swirled over them, filling her mouth with salty water. "Now we shall both drown."

As another wave rushed over their bodies, Tavig could not help but think that she might be right.

Chapter Two

A hoarse groan grated upon Moira's ears. It took her a moment to realize that the wretched sound was coming from her own mouth. She felt terrible. Her cheek pressed against something both damp and gritty, and she realized she was sprawled facedown on a beach. Her body ached so much that she wanted to weep. She was drenched both inside and out. Suddenly her stomach clenched. Struggling to lift up her head, she became painfully, helplessly ill. A low male voice murmuring some nonsense about how the agony she was enduring was for the best, that she would soon feel better, penetrated her misery. Moira prayed that she would stop being ill just long enough to tell the fool to go to hell and stay there, but she was not sure she could accomplish that goal. Her body was determined to rid itself of whatever ailed it, and that agony held all of her attention.

Tavig smiled wearily when he heard her cursing him. She would be all right. He continued to rub her back as she retched, hating to view her misery, but knowing that it was necessary. The moment she was done, he tugged her away from the place where she had been ill before allowing her to collapse on the sand.

"Here, rinse out your mouth," he urged.

Moira opened her eyes to see him holding out a roughly

carved cup. She propped herself up on one elbow, took the cup, and discovered that it held wine. As she rinsed out her mouth then sipped some of the mildly bitter brew, she glanced around. Slowly she began to remember what had happened and understood why she was sitting on a beach tinted a soft rose by a rising sun. She frowned as she looked at Tavig.

"Where did ye get the wine and the cup? They didnae wash up with us, did they?"

"Nay, there is a fishermon's hut just beyond the shore."

"So there is someone who may help us?"

"I dinnae think so. The hut looks as if no one has used it for a while. Since there are still supplies within and there is no sign of a boat of any kind, I can only think that the poor soul went out fishing and didnae return."

Even as she handed him back the cup, Moira crossed herself. She then collapsed back onto the sand. Tavig's clothes were dirty and ragged, and she wondered why he even bothered to wear what was left of a once fine linen shirt. The tatters that remained of the garment did very little to cover the broad expanse of his smooth, dark chest.

The sad state of his attire started her wondering about her own. A cool morning breeze flowed across the shore. It was touching far more of her skin than it should be if her nightgown and cloak were still whole. Moira knew she ought to at least peek down at herself to be sure that she was decently covered but she was not inclined to move. Every inch of her body felt battered and drained of all strength.

"What happened to your beard?" she asked, thinking that his lean features were too attractive for her peace of mind.

"I scraped it off. Couldnae abide the thing," he replied, sitting more comfortably at her side.

"And your wife who died of a fever?"

"A lie, I fear. Do ye feel any better?"

"Nay, not verra much. I believe I shall just lie here and

finish dying. I am nearly as cold as a corpse already. Ye
had best dig me a grave and prepare my winding sheet."

"I dinnae think that, even between us, we have enough
cloth left for a winding sheet."

"So I, too, am clothed in rags and mayhap indecently
covered."

"Weel—nay. At least, the parts I wouldnae mind having
a wee look at are still hidden."

Moira wondered why she did not blush, did not even
feel outraged, then decided she was simply too weary to
be bothered by his impudence. "Ye are verra impertinent
for a mon condemned to hang."

"Condemned—aye—but free."

"No condemned mon can e'er be free. Ye are but alive.
And so am I. For that I thank ye. I recall enough to ken that
ye leapt in after me. A verra strange thing to do, but I am
grateful for that moment of madness."

"Ye tried to stop your guardian from cleaving me in
twain. That distraction may weel have saved my life. I
could do no less in return. And how could I just stand by
and let the lass I mean to wed be swept away?"

Tavig waited patiently for his statement to be understood. He could read her face so easily. First there was confusion, then slow understanding, which caused her rich
blue eyes to grow very wide. He doubted she would believe
him. She would probably think he was mad. Tavig wondered about that himself. Nevertheless, as he had tended to
her, he had begun to understand why their lives were suddenly so completely intertwined. They were mates. He was
almost certain of it.

It took Moira a little while to be sure she had heard what
she thought she had heard. Even as she began to believe it,
she did not understand. The man had to be mad. Or, she
mused, he was testing her, trying to see if she still had the
wit to recognize the absurdity of what he just said.

"I think ye swallowed so much water it has rotted your
brain, Sir MacAlpin," she said.

"A most unusual response to a proposal," he murmured.

"Proposal? 'Twas nonsense. I thought ye but tested me to see if I was aware enough to recognize it as such."

"Madness and nonsense? I am wounded to the heart."

"Cease your teasing and help me sit up." She held her hand out to him. "Do ye think that the ship itself sank?" she asked as he pulled her up then kept a firm grasp on her hand.

"Nay, I think not. I saw no wreckage upon the beach." He ignored her attempts to extract her hand delicately from his. "I walked a fair distance in both directions whilst I waited for ye to rouse yourself."

With her free hand, Moira tugged her damp, torn cloak over her legs. She was pleased to see that little else was exposed to his obsidian gaze. Their situation was awkward enough without having to concern herself about her modesty as well. She set her mind back on the intricate matter of what she must do next.

"If the ship survived the storm, my kinsmen will look for us," she said. "I think I should just stay here."

"Do ye now?" he drawled.

"I realize that ye have no wish to see them again so I will understand if ye take this chance to flee."

"How kind."

She scowled at him as she ceased trying to be subtle about freeing her hand from his, forcefully yanking it from his firm grasp. "Sir MacAlpin, I begin to think that ye consider my plan a verra poor one."

"I kenned from the start that ye were a clever lass." Tavig could see by her narrowing eyes that he was starting to anger her, and so rushed to explain himself. "If your kinsmen dinnae believe that ye are dead already and actually think that ye might have survived being washed away, there are miles and miles of shoreline they will have to search. 'Twould take them days to find ye, and they dinnae have days, do they?"

Moira cursed softly. He was irritatingly correct. Her

kinsmen did not have the time to search for her even if they thought she might still be alive. They had to ransom her cousin Una by the end of the month. That was only three weeks away. They had wasted too much time trying to bargain with Una's kidnapper and had none to spare now. She was sure whatever ransom was being offered for Sir Tavig MacAlpin would tempt them, but not enough to risk losing Una. Sir Bearnard had some grand plans for his daughter. He intended to enhance his own prestige and fatten his purse through a skillfully arranged marriage for her.

She had to help herself, she decided, glancing at Tavig who sat calmly watching her. She probably could not depend upon him for any more assistance than he had already given. He had his own neck to save. If he stayed with her he could well meet up with her kinsmen again. She was sure the man had no wish to see Sir Bearnard again. Then, too, she decided, how much faith could she put in a man accused of two murders even if that man had risked his life to save her?

"Weel, then I had best go in search of a sheriff or the like," she finally said.

"And do ye really think ye will find much aid here? Ye are now ragged and with no means of proving ye are who ye say ye are. I mean no insult, lass, but right now ye look no more than a poor beggar girl. And, since your tattered clothes are of such a rich material, ye could easily be taken for a thief as weel."

"Do ye have a better plan, then?" she snapped, annoyed at the way he destroyed her schemes with unarguable logic.

"Aye, my ill-tempered bride."

"I am *not* your bride."

Tavig ignored that sulky interruption. "Ye can stay with me, and I shall take ye to a safe place."

"With ye? I heard what my cousin Bearnard said when your disguise wilted away. Ye are headed straight for the gallows. I dinnae think that is a verra safe place."

"The noose isnae around my neck yet, dearling." He stood up, brushed himself off, and held his hand out to her. "Come along. We had best be on our way. 'Tis a long, hard journey that lies ahead of us."

A little warily she allowed him to help her to her feet. "Where do we journey to?"

He started to walk inland, smiling faintly when he heard her hurry to follow him. Tavig was not really hurt by her wary attitude toward him, nor did he blame her for having it. Even though he had saved her life, he was a condemned murderer. Since she did not really know him, she could make no judgment upon the truth of those charges. And she had to think he was just a little mad with his abrupt talk of marriage, he mused, chuckling to himself. In truth, he would have thought she was lacking in wits if she had not shown some hesitancy and mistrust.

"Sir Tavig," Moira said, struggling to follow him as he scrambled up a rocky incline to the moorlands bordering the beach. "*Where* do ye plan to take us?"

"To my cousin's keep." After helping her up the last few inches of the stony rise, he headed toward a tiny thatch-roofed cottage a few yards away. "He will not only aid us, but also find us a priest so that we can be wed."

Moira decided the best thing to do concerning his daft talk of marriage was to ignore it. "Do I have any knowledge of this cousin of yours? I am certain that ye must have several cousins since ye surely cannae mean Sir Iver who hunts ye down. A name would be most helpful."

"Mungan Coll." Tavig heard her stumble to a halt, and turned to look at her.

"The Mungan Coll we were traveling to meet when I was swept into the sea? The Mungan Coll who holds my cousin Una for ransom?"

"The verra same."

"Ye would have me believe that I could find safety with such a mon?"

"Aye, but I can see that ye arenae inclined to do so. Consider this, then—ye will be in a place where your kinsmen are certain to find ye." He took her by the hand, ignoring her slight resistance, and tugged her toward the fisherman's hut.

"Oh, aye—to find me captive right alongside Una. No doubt a wee ransom would be asked for me as weel." That deeply worried her for Moira could not feel sure that her kinsmen would pay anything to free her.

"Nay. Mungan would ne'er ransom my wife."

As he nudged her inside the hut, Moira muttered a curse. She stood just inside the low door while he lit a fire and a few tallow candles. His plan was a terrible one as far as she could see, but much to her annoyance she could not think of a better one.

When there was some light in the nearly windowless house, she sat down on a rough bench next to an equally crudely made wooden table. A little sullenly she watched as Tavig found some food and began to make them porridge. His self-sufficiency irritated her. It all too clearly illustrated the one very good reason why she was stuck with him. She had never, in all of her eighteen years upon the earth, been on her own. Not only did the thought of trying to fend for herself terrify her, but also she greatly doubted that she could survive any long period of enforced hardship.

Her lack of skills was not wholly her fault, she consoled herself. Her parents, nurses, and even her maids had allowed her to do very little. She had not been allowed to continue that pampered life when she had gone to live with Sir Bearnard Robertson and his family, however. She had quickly been put to work weaving and sewing. But neither skill would do her much good now. Crooked Annie, who had taken her under her aging wing two years ago, had begun to teach her a few more useful things. There had not been enough time, however, to learn very much except for a reasonably good skill with a knife.

So, I can protect myself a wee bit, she mused. It was some comfort. She knew it was far from enough. It would not keep her fed or clothed or protected from the harshness of the weather. She needed Tavig MacAlpin, and that galled her. Moira glared at the bowl of porridge he set before her.

"Ah, now, lassie—why so dreary?" Tavig sat down opposite her and began to eat.

"Ye mean aside from the fact that I spent several hours being tossed about in the cold seawater and was nearly drowned?" She had to acknowledge that he could stir up a fine meal of porridge, which did nothing to improve her mood.

"But ye survived. Ye were slapped about some, but ye were still alive when the water spat ye up onto the shore."

"Then what about the fact that I have naught to wear but this tattered nightgown and bedraggled cloak?"

"I was thinking that your clothes survived your ordeal rather weel."

"Were ye, indeed? How about the fact that I have no idea of where we are? I am stuck upon some desolate moorlands with no idea of where to go or how to get there."

"Dinnae worry o'er that, dearling. I will lead ye to safety."

"Aye, and there is another thing," she muttered, scraping the last of the porridge from her bowl with short, clipped movements.

"And what is that other thing?" he asked when she did not continue and simply glared into her now-empty bowl.

"I cannae take care of myself. I cannae do whatever needs to be done to survive this ordeal. I have to depend upon ye to help me to get somewhere safe."

"'Tisnae such a bad thing for a wife to depend upon her husband."

Moira slammed her crude wooden spoon down onto the table. "If we must be together, ye can just cease that foolish talk right now. I dinnae find it at all amusing."

"I am glad to hear it. Marriage isnae something to

chuckle at. 'Tis a verra serious matter." He almost laughed at the thoroughly disgusted look she gave him.

"Why do ye persist?"

It had to be a jest, and she found that a little painful. She had more or less resigned herself to spinsterhood, perhaps spending her days as nursemaid to Una's children. Since no marriage had been arranged for her or even been discussed, she assumed that she had no dowry. That lack combined with her red hair, something many considered an unacceptable color if not a mark of the devil himself, made marriage an unattainable goal. And there was her "gift," her healing touch, which she kept a close secret for it also stirred people's fears. She doubted she could keep it a secret forever from her own husband. That fact made her believe that it was probably for the best if she remained a maid, to forgo marriage forever. Now this man continually teased her about it. It seemed somewhat cruel of him.

"Ye dinnae even ken who I am," she continued. "Our acquaintance is too short a one for ye to be talking about making it a permanent partnership. Not that your life looks to be a verra long one anyway."

"I should remind ye that I am not dead yet, lassie. I dinnae suppose ye would believe me if I told you that I was completely innocent, that I ne'er killed those men," he said, pouring them each some of the wine.

"If ye are innocent then why are ye condemned to hang? Aye, and by your verra own kinsmon? I heard what Cousin Bearnard said, and ye didnae deny a word of it."

"Just because I am condemned to hang doesnae mean I committed the crime. The carcasses of many an innocent mon have dangled from the gallows. I am certain of it. And as for being tried and convicted by my own kinsmon—what better way is there to be rid of the rightful heir to all that ye covet?"

He sounded very sincere. There was a wealth of bitterness in his rich voice which only added veracity to his words. Moira wanted to believe him, but fought to cling tightly to her doubts and wariness. It was a very bad time for her to be too trusting.

"Where were the rest of your kinsmen?" she asked. "Did they all believe this lie? Did none stand up in your defense?" She could see a pained look in his dark eyes, but refused to let sympathy temper or halt her questions. "Did no other stand as your advocate? Did none protest the sentence handed down or argue against the accusation?"

"The answers to all of those questions must be aye, but a tempered aye. The mon who did this to me, my cousin Iver, has many a strong ally. I have some allies, too, but if they had openly come to my aid they would have harmed themselves more than they could e'er have helped me. They have neither the power nor the wealth to stand against Iver and his friends. I couldnae and cannae allow them to risk their verra lives for me. They did what little they could for me, which is why I was able to escape."

"Ye didnae stay free for verra long or ye would have reached Mungan Coll by now." Moira heartily wished that his tale did not sound so very plausible, for it strongly tempted her to believe him.

"True. I fell victim to a bonnie face that hid a black heart."

"A verra pretty way of saying that ye were caught because ye dallied instead of ran."

Tavig grinned. "Aye. A mon can be verra easily diverted by the glint of welcome in a lass's eyes." He reached across the table, gently clasping her hand. "Howbeit, ye willnae have to fear my wandering from the marriage bed. I am a mon who takes a vow verra seriously."

She snatched her hand out of his. "Ye are a mon whose wits are sadly addled."

"Such harsh words."

He looked so ridiculously mournful that Moira almost laughed, then caught herself. It was far from funny. If he was not taunting her because she was so clearly doomed to spinsterhood, then he was mad. There was no cause for laughter in either case. She told herself that she had to try harder to ignore his ridiculous talk of marriage. Since she now faced the enormous task of staying alive until she was back with her kinsmen, Moira told herself that she must concentrate on that task and only that task.

"Why did ye get onto our ship?"

"As I was fleeing my cousin's faithful lackeys, I heard that your ship was sailing to my cousin Mungan's lands. 'Twas risky, but not as risky as staying where I was." He gave her a small smile. "Ye dinnae believe me."

"I must think about it first." She clasped her hands together, trying to effect a stern look. "Now, I think our time would be much better served if we discussed what we must do next."

"I told ye—we are going to my cousin Mungan's keep." He picked up her dishes as well as his own and moved toward a pan of water.

As he started to wash the dishes, Moira briefly contemplated taking over that chore since he had prepared the meal. She knew it was not completely fair to allow him to do all the work, but she did blame him somewhat for the dire circumstances she found herself in. It would serve as a penance of sorts if he had to wait upon her a little bit.

She watched him, idly wondering how he could look so good when he was in such a disreputable state. His clothing was ragged and stained. His thick black hair was tousled and stiffened from the salt water they had floundered in for so long. She could also see bruises and swelling upon his face as well as on the patches of skin peeking through his ragged clothes. Some of those marks could have been caused by the rough treatment of the stormy waves, but she suspected most of his wounds were suffered in his battle with Sir Bearnard. When she began to think rather tenderly of nursing his many injuries, she was startled and a little appalled. The man had not only plunged her life into chaos, but also he was starting to have an alarming effect upon her good sense. Moira forced her errant musings back to the matter of what they needed to do next. That was far more important than how smooth his dark skin was or how well shaped his long legs were.

"Sir Tavig, I hadnae forgotten that ye planned to take us to Mungan Coll's," she hurried to say, hoping that by talking she could clear her mind of all thoughts save how to get to safety.

"Then what else do ye need to be told?"

"*How* do we get there? We are ragged, without horses and without supplies."

"Verra true." He wiped his hands on a dingy rag and sat back down at the table. "I think we can find enough here to start us on our way."

"That would be stealing."

"Lass, the mon who used to abide here is dead, I am fair certain of that. And if by some odd miracle he isnae, then he has fled this place without a thought to what is here. Cease fretting o'er the right and wrong of it all. Whatever happened to the mon, he left everything here to rot or to be taken, and we have a sore need for what little he may have left behind."

"I can understand the reasoning ye are using, and 'tis sound, yet it troubles me to take someone else's things."

"If I had any coin I would leave it in payment, but 'twould only be stolen. To ease your acute conscience, I will swear to either return or have someone else come back here later. If the mon is still alive, he will be paid."

"'Tis verra kind of ye, but ye may not be able to return."

"Then ye can."

"I would, but I fear I have no coin." She felt a mild blush tingle in her cheeks and wondered why she should be embarrassed to confess her poverty to such a man.

"None at all?" Tavig found her discomfort somewhat endearing for it was self-inflicted by her own honesty.

"Nay. My cousin Bearnard says that my father didnae have the skill to hold on to a farthing."

"Ah, weel, I dinnne mind. An heiress would have been a fine thing to have, but I dinnae need the coin so I can be happy taking a poor lass as a wife." He grinned when she glared at him.

Moira told herself that he was not saying such things to be intentionally hurtful. He could not have known about her lack of a dowry before she told him. Neither could he have known how it was one of the many things that doomed her to a spinsterhood she did not really wish to endure, but had been struggling to accept. Even though she could convince herself that he was not intentionally trying to cause her pain, that did not make his cheerful talk of wedding her any less irritating, however.

"'Tis time that ye found yourself a new jest," she muttered.

Tavig shook his head, pulling a mournful face. "Weel, my wee bride, 'tis a good thing we shall be bound together for a fortnight or so because of our circumstances. I can see that ye will take a great deal of wooing."

She ignored the latter part of what he said. "A fortnight or so? Why so long?"

"As ye said—we have no horse."

"Oh. Aye. And we cannae get one?"

"Weel, I have no coin and ye have no coin, and 'tis verra clear that ye arenae amenable to the necessity of stealing. So, nay, we cannae get a horse."

"So how do we get to your cousin's?"

"We walk."

"Walk?"

"Aye, dearling—use those pretty wee feet of yours."

"But your cousin is miles and miles away, isnae he?"

"He is. 'Twill take us a fortnight or more."

Moira stared at him and decided that she should worry less about his being a condemned murderer and more about the fact that he was quite certainly mad.

Chapter Three

"I look even more like a beggar than I did before."

Tavig looked Moira over, struggling not to grin in response to her complaint. He could not think of a good way to deny her accusation, for it was true. They had found a needle and thread and, as they had taken turns cleaning themselves up, they had patched her clothes as well as they could. The mending could easily be seen since the thread was dark and her nightgown was white. The faded blue plaid tied about her waist served as a skirt, but was thin and crudely mended in places. An old, dull brown linsey-woolsey shirt, too large on her slender frame and marred by a few coarse patches, served as her bodice. Only her delicate features and soft white skin hinted at the fact that she was something more than the poorest of beggars.

Glancing down at himself, he almost laughed. With all of the neat dark stitching holding it together, his fine white shirt looked as if it were striped. The rough dark homespun jerkin he wore was old, stained, and smelled faintly of fish. So did the ill-fitting hose he wore. The man whose clothes they had confiscated had clearly not made a very good living at fishing.

"We do make a sad pair," he murmured.

"Are ye certain we should take these things at all?

Mayhap the mon isnae dead, just left home for a wee while." Moira still felt she was stealing and did not like it at all.

"Lass, if ye had seen the condition of the farm animals, few that they were, ye would be as certain as I am that some ill has befallen the mon. No one has tended to those poor beasts for days. I nearly killed them for I thought 'twould be best to simply end their misery. Howbeit, instead I did what little I could for them and then set them loose. They will either feed the wolves, fend for themselves, or be collected up by some poor farmer who can make better use of them. And if by some twist of fate the mon is alive, he deserves to lose his stock for treating it so badly."

"'Tis probably true," she agreed, her reluctance to admit it heavily weighting her voice. "Howbeit, despite all ye have said, I cannae fully shake the feeling that I am stealing."

"And, as I have also said, I would be willing to leave his ghost some recompense, but I am a wee bit short of coin. And I doubt ye had the foresight to fetch your purse ere ye were hurled into the sea." He was not sure he completely believed in her professed poverty although he suspected that she did.

"Such a finely honed wit. There is no need to be so impertinent."

"Lass, your sensibility is to be honored, but I fear 'tis verra misplaced just now. We landed on this harsh shore in naught but rags with no money and no supplies. Since I am nearly certain that the mon who lived here is dead, I consider it fortuitous that the place wasnae already picked clean of all that could be of use to us."

She grimaced. He was right—again. Moira decided that it was a particularly irritating quality of his. She would try harder to overcome her "sensibilities" as he called them. Such fine sentiments were a luxury she could not afford to indulge in at the moment.

"I shallnae speak out again on the way we are forced to

survive," she finally said. "I am sure that ye have far more important things to attend to than constantly assuring me we are doing only what is necessary."

Tavig briefly put his arm about her shoulders, giving her a little hug and ignoring the way she tensed and pulled away. "As I promised, I will do my best to recall where and what we have appropriated for our own use and see that the ones we borrowed from are paid in full."

Moira silently vowed to herself to do the same no matter how difficult it would be for her to get some coin. Although she was finding it increasingly uncomfortable to think of it, there was no ignoring the fact that Tavig was a condemned man. His intention to repay everyone they had to steal from could well be a sincere one, but she could not ignore the possibility that he would be unable to keep his promise. Somehow, some way, she would have to fulfill that promise herself.

"Now why do ye look so sour? Shake away your ill mood, my wee bride, and let us begin our journey." He picked up the bundle of supplies he had gathered and started out of the tiny hut.

"Ye expect me to be gay as I begin what could be a verra long and dangerous walk?" she asked as she followed him. "Only a witless fool could be pleased at the thought of marching o'er Scotland for a fortnight or so with naught but rags and tattered hose to protect his feet."

Tavig glanced back at her woolen-swathed feet then looked at his own boots. He felt a twinge of guilt he knew was unwarranted. There had been nothing to fit her dainty feet within the fisherman's hut. His own battered, salt-stiffened boots were far too large for her. The thick woolen rags wrapped around her feet would have to suffice until he could either steal or beg something else for her to wear.

"I will concede that your poor wee feet arenae too weel protected," he said, helping her hop over a shallow ditch. "I will do my best to correct that lack as soon as I can."

"Ye mean ye will steal me some shoes." She winced as she trod on a small thistle plant.

"A bride shouldnae demean her mon's method of caring for her needs."

"Will ye cease calling me your bride? Why do ye persist with that madness?"

"'Tisnae madness."

"Nay? I cannae think of what else ye might call it." She stumbled over a rock and, when he took her by the hand, she did not pull free for she appreciated that light, steadying touch. "Ye dinnae ken who I am, who my family is, or anything else about me. I am no heiress to be coveted, and our kinsmen havenae made some truce or bargain we are forced to seal with our marriage. I just dinnae understand what has put the idea into your head and why ye hold to it. 'Tisnae as if we are fated or the like."

"Ah, but we *are* fated."

Moira muttered a curse, scowling at his broad back. "I willnae say that I have no belief in fate or destiny. 'Tis hard not to have a wee bit. Howbeit, in this matter any talk of fate or destiny is foolishness."

"I fear that—in this matter—fate and destiny are a verra large part of it all. When that railing broke and ye were dangling over those churning waters, I kenned that our lives were fated to be bound together. I understood why I had been watching ye so closely e'en though ye are such a wee, thin lass."

"Thank ye," she grumbled, nettled by his constant reference to her small stature.

"Dinnae ye think that Fate was working her mischief when suddenly ye paid heed to me and spared a wee moment to talk with me?"

"'Twasnae fate. Ye spoke to me first. I simply answered ye."

"Was it not fate that caused ye to suddenly plunge into the sea?"

"'Twas the storm and rotting railings. That captain should be flogged for keeping such a poor ship."

"It was fate that prompted me to leap into the water after ye, to try and save ye."

"'Twas lunacy, moon madness, 'twas unthinking gallantry of the sort that has buried many a mon."

He stopped, turning toward her and grinning. "Gallantry? Weel, thank ye."

"Ye thank me for calling ye a lunatic?"

"Ye also called me gallant."

"I consider the two quite equal in witlessness." She shook her head when he just winked at her and started walking again, gently tugging her along with him.

"I kenned that our lives were bound together whilst I waited for ye to recover from your wee swim. I looked at ye sprawled upon the sand and, as I tended to ye, 'twas suddenly all verra clear to me."

"Clear? I was spewing up water, covered in sand and sodden rags and cursing. 'Twas no sight to inspire a mon to thoughts of marriage. I was a dripping, wretched mess. 'Tis all ye saw."

"Nay, I saw a great deal more. 'Tis my curse," he murmured.

She frowned at him. "Are ye trying to tell me that ye are gifted with the sight or the like?"

"Nay, not the sight. I dinnae really have visions." He kept his gaze fixed upon the ground, not eager to see her face as he confessed his strange gift. "I just *ken* things, have a deep certainty about what is to occur next in my life and the lives of others. When I first saw ye coming up on deck I was certain it meant naught but trouble. I was sure that ye shouldnae rest against that railing, that it would break."

"That could be naught but simple chance, a guess, a suspicion."

"'Tis much stronger than that. I can see things in my head, but they arenae truly visions. They are more the images born of the certainty that grips me so tightly. The day of the murders I have been accused of committing, I kenned that my two friends were doomed. Even as I hurried to warn them I was certain I would be too late. I could see them dead. In my mind's eye, I could see them murdered. I ne'er have the time to change what is fated, but, that time, the forewarning allowed me to save myself from falling into my cousin's trap."

Moira was not sure what to think about his confession. A part of her scorned the idea of forewarnings, but an equal part of her believed in them. Since she had a strange gift, why could he not have one as well? She was certain, however, that she did not like his particular gift, whether it was fact or just some delusion of his.

"If ye are right *and* if ye arenae jesting with your foolish talk of marriage, ye have just given me another good reason to refuse to be your bride. Besides the fact that ye are condemned to hang, of course," she added.

Tavig stopped and looked at her, hurt that she, like so many others, could not accept his strange talent. "Ye are afraid, just like all the others."

"Fear, and whether I believe ye or not, has little to do with it. Look at me." She pointed to her hair. "Did ye not happen to see what color my hair is? 'Tis red."

"Aye—a glorious red. Bright yet not too bright." He stepped closer, running his hand down her long, thick braid. "A silken curtain of fire. Warm, soft, and of a hue that greatly compliments ye."

She was touched by his flattery and pleasantly unsettled by his nearness, but struggled to keep her mind on what they were discussing. "Dinnae ye ken what is said about red hair? 'Tis the sign of a hot-tempered and choleric disposition. They say 'twas the color of Judas's hair, 'tis the color of a dissembler. A red beard is a token of a vile and cruel disposition. Red is a witch's color. Many believe redheads are witches, fit only for burning. If ye and I were to wed, we probably wouldnae live out the year. Someone would surely cry us witches and set us alight."

"Burned as witches?" He almost laughed, relieved that her horror had not been aimed at him, but caused by the thought of all the difficulties such an odd gift could bring them. "I have had this foresight for my whole life, as no one has yet piled kindling about my feet."

"Weel, mayhaps those whom ye abide with can either accept or avoid ye. They treat me the same way. Howbeit, to put the two of us together could easily be more than anyone could endure." *Especially when it is seen that I, too, have an odd talent.*

"Nay, ye worry o'er naught."

"I do, eh? Are ye saying ye ne'er had anyone who learned of your skill cross themselves or make the sign to ward off evil? Would ye have me believe no one has decided to have as little to do with ye as they can?"

He grimaced as some painful memories of just such reactions passed swiftly though his mind. "There have been a few."

"A few? Ye try to hide the truth, but it cannae be ignored. Ye ken that truth as weel as I do. I have suffered the looks that silently cry me a witch or touched by the hand of the devil. I have had folk avoid me because they feared such superstitions were fact. I have e'en had an old woman cluck o'er how thin I was, o'er how little fat there would be for the taking when I died."

"Fat? What is so important about your fat or lack of it?"

"I would have thought a mon with your gift would be weel aware of each and every superstition held by those around him. The fat of a dead redhead is verra useful in potions."

"That is utter nonsense."

"Of course it is, but the fact that what they believe is utter nonsense has ne'er stopped people from believing it. A part of me says that your claim of foreseeing is utter nonsense, but another part of me believes it and is frightened by it, and I consider myself a verra reasonable person."

"It frightens ye?" He frowned as he studied her, regretting his confession. The very last thing he wished her to feel for him was fear. "There is no need for ye to be frightened."

"Nay? I would wager that it frightens even ye at times." She nodded when a light color flooded his dark, high-boned cheeks. She knew better than most how the fear of one's own gift could grip one from time to time. "No one likes the idea that someone can see what *will* be. There is a great debate o'er whether such a thing is a gift from God or the work of the devil. It could be considered a curse, and that must mean 'tis the devil's unholy work. Howbeit, ye claim it has saved your life and it certainly helped ye save mine, so that must mean 'tis a blessing that makes your foresight a gift from God. Sadly, we both ken that many folk will see anything that they cannae understand as the devil's work."

Tavig cursed softly, running his hand through his hair. "I dinnae wish ye to fear me because of it."

"Weel, I dinnae verra much. It but makes me uneasy. If I was to fear ye, it wouldnae be for that, but because ye are a condemned murderer." Even as she said it Moira knew that she no longer believed he was some vicious killer.

"I didnae kill those men," he snapped and started to walk again, tugging her after him with a touch of force. "I could hear their screams," he said softly, his rapid pace easing as his annoyance died beneath the numbing weight of painful memory.

"Ye were that near to them when they were murdered?"

"Nay. I could hear the screams in my head. 'Twas part of my foretelling of their death—those pain-filled, horrible screams. I was a day's ride or more away, too far away to stop their slaughter. They were hung from a tree by their bound wrists and gutted like newly killed deer. God alone kens how long they must have suffered ere they died."

Moira felt slightly ill over the thought of such a cruel, savage death. Tavig's "gift" was far worse than her own. She could at least comfort herself with the knowledge that she had helped people, had eased their pain.

"And ye found them like that?" she asked.

"Nay. I was halted not far from them by a friend. He warned me of the trap that had been laid for me. My cousin Iver was trying to use my gift against me, to use it to snare me. He was sure that I would, weel, see the deaths of my dear friends and ride to them. He was waiting there with a few men-at-arms to grab me."

"Ah, and claim that ye were caught with bloodied dagger in hand."

"Just so. Avoiding the trap didnae save me, though, neither from seeing my friends hung up like rotting game nor from being accused of their foul murder." He grasped her by the waist, easily lifting her to the top of a stony rise then hopping up after her. "I was caught, dragged before the corpses of my friends to see what I was being accused of, then tossed into the pits of Drumdearg." He clasped her by the hand again and led her along a slowly rising sheep trail.

"Drumdearg?"

"My keep."

"The one your cousin Iver now lays claim to."

"Aye. If I judge where we are correctly, Drumdearg lies a good week's ride north-northwest of here."

"A little closer than ye might like, I suspect."

"Aye—for now. Soon I shall sit in the great hall again— as a free mon."

"Tell me, how is it that your gift of foretelling didnae warn ye of the trap ye were riding into?"

"It did, but I wasnae inclined to heed that part of the vision. I belittled it. Two men were being murdered. I told myself that that was the danger, that it was simply dangerous to go where there was killing being done."

"True, although men do seem to be verra fond of doing just that. 'Tis easily seen in how they flock to a battle."

"'Tis honor that draws them, lass."

"Humph. Honor has put many a mon in his grave. I doubt that it makes his shroud any warmer."

"In part, I am tempted to agree. Howbeit, a mon must hold himself to some code and one of honor is as good as any other."

Moira considered that for a moment as she struggled over the rutted path. Honor *was* a fine thing. Unfortunately too many men used the preservation of honor as an excuse for killing other men. Whenever she was told that a man had "died with honor," she always wondered how the dead man felt about it. Did he wake in heaven, realize that his life was now over, and say, "Oh, weel, I still have my honor"? She heard Tavig chuckle and realized that she had muttered her speculation aloud.

"Ye dinnae have a high regard for a mon's ways, do ye, dearling?" Tavig asked, amused and intrigued by her opinions for they revealed a keen wit.

"I wouldnae say that I have none, but, aye, I do wonder on it all at times. And, at times, I think it is all verra absurd. There are occasions, howsomever, when there can be a great nobility revealed in a mon's acts. Mayhap 'tis just my woman's mind, my womanly heart. I simply dinnae understand. I wasnae trained as a mon is, wasnae taught the knightly ways or rules."

"Nay. Women are trained to give life, to nurture it. Men are trained to take life away." He stopped, facing her and holding out the rough waterskin he had taken from the fisherman's cottage. "Women arenae made to take any life."

After quenching her thirst and handing the waterskin back to him, Moira smiled faintly. "I wouldnae say that. Women may not be trained in the ways of war and deeds, but some still have the stomach for killing. Aye, and I suspect that the ones who do kill can do so with some skill. Women just dinnae do it for such things as honor." She watched him drink, intrigued by the gentle motion in his strong throat as he swallowed.

"Nay?" Tavig wiped his mouth with the back of his hand. "What would make a woman kill?"

"Tis a verra strange conversation we are having."

"True, but now ye have stirred my curiosity. What would make a woman kill someone? Hate?" He dampened a scrap of cloth and gently wiped the dust from her small face.

Although Moira found it a little difficult to keep her mind on what they were discussing, she struggled to reply. "A woman can hate. Mayhaps e'en more adamantly than a mon." Still unsettled by his soft bathing of her face, she watched as he briskly wiped the dust from his own. "Jealousy might prompt a woman, too," she continued, hoping that talk would stop him from noticing how she kept staring at him.

"And greed." He slung the waterskin over his shoulder, took her by the hand, and started walking again.

"Weel—aye—I suppose. And most women would do their utmost to kill anyone who threatened the life of a bairn."

"Aye, a woman *can* grow most fierce when ye endanger her child."

"In truth, I think a woman can be prompted to kill for most of the same reasons a mon can. We just arenae driven to it as often, and some of the things a mon feels are worth dying for or killing for seem verra odd to us."

"They can sometimes seem verra odd to men, too," Tavig murmured, glancing at her. "Another difference is that women can be verra treacherous in the manner of their killing."

"Weel, we cannae always face our enemy eye to eye and sword to sword. We would then become the slain instead of the slayer. Only a fool doesnae recognize his own weaknesses."

"Aye, so ye slip a dirk in their backs in the dark of night whilst they lie asleep in their beds."

There was a hint of bitterness in his voice. Moira puzzled over it, but lacked the courage to ask the reason for it. She then thought of her guardian, of his brutality both subtle and direct. Many a time, as she nursed the bruises he gave her, she thought of the many ways she might kill him. Often she had imagined long, slow deaths that would finally repay him for all of the pain he had caused her. Occasionally she had simply considered cutting his fat throat as he slept, quietly ending his long reign of cruelty and fear.

"And some men deserve no better than a stealthy death," she said in a very quiet voice.

A deep anger shaded her words, and Tavig sensed it was directed at Sir Bearnard. He ached to question her about her life with her guardian, about her feelings, but knew it was not a good time for such an inquisition. She had to grow more accustomed to him, to get to know him much better. The wait would be frustrating, for he was certain that Sir Bearnard's treatment of Moira would cause him some trouble, could even be a wall between them that he would find hard to breach, and yet he could not just charge ahead, demanding the information he wanted. After silently and heartily cursing Sir Bearnard Robertson, Tavig strove for a tighter tone in their conversation.

"Ye are an impertinent wee thing," he teased, frowning when he felt her tense.

Moira shivered as a thrill of fear went through her, lodging in her stomach and knotting it. Impertinent wee thing, Tavig had called her. When she had first gone to live with her guardian, he had often called her that. She had quickly learned the wisdom of controlling her tongue. Any hint of impertinence on her part had always brought about the worst of his beatings.

She covertly studied Tavig, who frowned at her for a moment then shrugged and turned his attention to the rough path they traveled. Tavig did not look ready to strike her. He did not look as if he even considered such an act. Nevertheless, she decided to take his words as a warning. She had learned the thin limits of Sir Bearnard's tolerance and patience and she would learn Tavig's limits. Until now she had not really feared Tavig. She had spoken with an unaccustomed freedom. Too much freedom, she mused. She had let herself forget the unkind ways of men, but she would not do so again. She would remember to weigh her every word and to make sure that she uttered as few words as possible. Silence had proven to be the safest route to follow.

When Moira continued to say nothing, Tavig concentrated on picking out the smoothest path to follow. The brief frightened look she had cast his way had stung him. The almost tangible way she had withdrawn from him, although her hand still rested in his, hurt him. Tavig knew he had a lot of work ahead of him if he was to accomplish what he felt was their destiny—marriage, full and lasting. He did not want a wife who cowered at every turn. He knew there was wit and strength within Moira. Sir Bearnard had beaten down the spirit within her. Tavig vowed that he would free it.

Chapter Four

"Let me have a look at those feet, dearling," Tavig said as he knelt before Moira.

Moira gave a soft cry of surprise. She glanced around, stunned to see that a fire was already built, their meager bedding of thin blankets laid out, and Tavig had already begun preparing the porridge. The last thing she recalled was that they had halted in the clearing, and she had sat down on the rock intending to rest for just a moment before helping him set up their camp. She had unwrapped her aching feet and simply lost any sense of time passing.

"Nay, they are fine," she protested pulling her feet away when he reached for one.

Tavig studied her for a moment, frowning when he saw the hint of nervous fear in her eyes. "Those are the first words ye have said in several hours. I wonder why. Ye werenae so quiet earlier in the day."

"I said all I needed to. I didnae wish to be too impertinent."

"Impertinent? What made ye think ye were being impertinent?"

"Ye said I was. Ye said I was an impertinent wee lass."

"And that made ye grow so quiet and wan? I was but teasing ye." He could see by the wary look on her face that she was not sure she ought to believe him. "Truly. 'Tis no crime to be a wee bit impertinent."

"My guardian thought it was." Moira leaned away from Tavig when his face hardened in an expression of anger.

"I am not your twice-cursed guardian. I willnae knock ye down just because ye say something I may not like." He grasped her by the ankle, pulled her small foot toward him. "'Twill take more than a few impertinent or ill-tempered words ere I would even think of striking a lass. I have no liking for such a thing." He looked at her foot and cursed. "No wonder ye began to limp. Ye have sore abused these pretty wee feet."

"*I* have abused them?"

"Aye. Ye should have watched where ye were stepping instead of sulking just because I called ye impertinent."

Moira clenched her hands into tight fists, fighting the urge to pummel the top of his head. She was not sure if she should believe him when he claimed to have no liking or inclination to strike a woman. A man could spout such fine sentiments in one breath and knock a woman down in the next. Fury had dispelled her fears for the moment, however. She was tired and ached all over. Both conditions added to her anger.

"I wasnae sulking," she snapped. "And I *did* watch where I stepped. Ye have some gall to scold me when 'tis all *your* fault I am sitting here too weary to move and my poor feet fair throbbing with pain."

"*My* fault? Ye *are* fond of flinging out rash, unfounded accusations."

"'Tis your fault. Ye were the one who tried to flirt with me. Ye are the one with the covetous cousin. If not for him, ye wouldnae have been condemned and ye wouldnae have been hiding on board that ship. None of us would have been aboard that ship if not for yet another of your cousins—that hulking kidnapper Mungan Coll. Aye, and if your thrice-cursed kinsmen hadnae placed us all on that thrice-cursed ship with their machinations, Annie wouldnae have met that disreputable little sailor, and I wouldnae have had to go out in the storm to try to find her. That was when we were flung into the sea, tossed up on that barren shore, and left with naught. And 'twas ye who decided we must take this hell-begotten journey. If ye hadnae devised this grand plan to walk to your mad cousin Coll's, I wouldnae be sitting here with aching feet."

"It does appear as if neither of us are blessed in our relations," Tavig murmured. He stared at her for a moment before asking, "Do ye feel better for having said all that?"

"Aye. I do."

Moira realized that was the truth. She did feel better. It had all been nonsense, a litany of blame for things he had not really done and could not change. She would not apologize for that, however. He slowly grinned, and she gave him a weak smile.

"I had meant to help ye set out our camp," she said.

"'Tis your first day of hard travel, lass. Ye are weary. Ye will harden to it soon enough."

"Weel, 'tisnae as if I have been pampered." She gave a sigh of pleasure as he dampened a rag with water from the waterskin and tenderly bathed her feet.

"Nay, ye havenae, have ye?"

Tavig spoke softly as he frowned at her feet. He could not see very well in the dim light of a nearly set sun and the small fire, but he did not need to. Beneath his hands he could feel the calluses. They were not something he should find upon Moira's tiny feet, for she was a wellborn lass.

"Is something wrong?" she asked, unsettled by the dark look upon his face.

"Did your kinsmen ne'er buy ye any shoes, or do ye have a liking for running about barefoot?"

"They fed and clothed me. I had no right to expect too much."

"A pair of shoes isnae too much for your kinsmen to provide."

"They did give me some."

"Ye couldnae have worn them verra often, then."

"Weel, I was only given them last month." She eased the foot he still held of his grasp. She was deeply embarrassed that he found her feet hard and rough. His gentle massage was also beginning to feel uncommonly pleasant. "Crooked Annie had even begun to rub my feet with an oil to soften them."

"It took them so long to realize that ye were roughening your feet?"

Moira shrugged. "They had more important matters to concern themselves with."

"Aye—themselves," Tavig muttered as he rose and walked back to the fire

He sat down and started to cook their porridge. The matter of Moira's shoes was a puzzle. Why would Sir Bearnard deny her shoes for so long then abruptly discard his cruel parsimony and give her some? Why had the man ignored the condition of her feet until just a month or so ago? It made no sense. Neither did Sir Bearnard appear the sort of man who was given to whims of kindness. There had to be a reason why the man suddenly cared about his ward's feet becoming as callused as some common beggar's.

There was another puzzle he had to solve, Tavig thought, briefly glancing at Moira as she sat down across the fire from him. Why had she been on that ship? There was no need for her presence. She could do nothing to help in ransoming Una Robertson. From what little he had been able to learn of Moira's life with the Robertsons, Tavig did not think she was considered a part of that family, but was seen as an annoying burden of familial responsibility. There was, quite simply, no reason for Moira's place in the Robertson entourage.

As he handed Moira a serving of porridge in a battered wooden bowl, Tavig studied her. He doubted she would know why she had been included. Somehow he had to think of the right questions to ask, ones whose answers would add up to a solution of the puzzle.

"Moira?" he asked as they ate their plain but filling meal. "Why were ye on that ship?"

"We were going to ransom Una. I thought ye kenned that."

"Aye, I did. I do. I just wondered why *ye* were going along with the others. Did ye ask to go?"

For a moment Moira used the act of eating her meal to avoid answering him. She was not really sure what to say. Several times she had asked herself the very same question. There really was no good answer. That was not something she wanted to confess to Tavig. It would be admitting that she had no place in the Robertson family. She dreaded such an admission. Silently acknowledging it to herself was painful enough.

"'Twas Robertson business," she finally replied. "Why shouldnae I be there?"

"If naught else but because the journey is a long, arduous, and dangerous one."

"It wasnae verra dangerous until I made the mistake of feeling charitable toward a certain George Fraser."

Tavig ignored that. "Ye could serve no purpose. Settling a ransom demand is men's work."

"Mayhap they thought Una would be in need of a female, one of her own ilk to turn to for comfort after her ordeal."

"Ye and this Una are close friends?"

It was yet another question she did not really want to answer. The man had a particular skill for asking such awkward questions, Moira thought as she rubbed out her empty bowl with dirt. This time her hesitation did not work to hide the truth. When he took her bowl from her to rinse it with a little water, she realized she would have to tell the full unpleasant truth.

"Nay, Una and I arenae friends," she muttered. "We arenae enemies, either. She was ne'er unkind to me. I was ne'er part of her life in truth. She was verra busy being trained and readied for a good marriage."

"And ye were set to work with the maids."

"Aye. 'Tis but fair that I earn my keep."

Although he suspected she was worked very hard, Tavig said nothing as he wiped out their bowls and stuck them back into their sack of supplies. "So why would anyone think that ye could be a comfort to her?"

"We are of an age and both maids. There is a great deal we have in common. Why do ye ask? In truth, what does it matter? I can see no reason for your curiosity." That was not the whole truth, for Moira did see the puzzle, but she did not understand why it should stir Tavig's interest.

"Everything that concerns ye is of interest to me. A mon likes to learn all he can about the lass he will marry."

The warmth she felt over his first statement faded abruptly with his second. "Ye *are* mad. Just as I begin to think ye are a reasonable mon, ye talk like a fool again. Weel, I have had my fill of your nonsense for the day. I need some rest." She scowled toward the bedding he had spread out. "Ye prepared only one place to sleep?"

"Aye, my sweet Moira. Only one. The fishermon lived alone, I think."

"How sad," she murmured as she stood up, carefully brushing herself off.

"True. It must have been a lonely life for him."

"Oh. Aye. My thought was that if he truly is dead, there is no one to grieve for him. A person ought to have a few tears shed for him when his life is ended. Someone should miss ye when ye are gone, or 'tis as if ye werenae here at all. 'Tis a verra sad thought."

"And do ye have folk who would miss ye?" Tavig was curious about what other kinsmon she had, perhaps some a little less swinish and brutal than Sir Bearnard.

Moira inwardly winced, for she knew there would be few, if any, and their sense of loss would be fleeting. She struggled to shrug with an air of nonchalance. "There are a few."

"Ah, poor wee Moira," he said in a soft voice, easily seeing through her lie. "*I* will weep for ye."

The thought that he might actually do so touched Moira in a way that made her nervous and she frowned at him. "Ye are a verra silly mon. Ye dinnae e'en ken who I am, have barely kenned me for a full day. For all ye can tell, I could be one of those people most folk would wish an early death on. And as far as ye being able to weep for me, I would have to succumb to the Grim Reaper's touch verra quickly, indeed, to be sure that ye are still alive to do so. The hangmon waits for ye, Tavig MacAlpin."

"A fact I am not apt to forget. If I meet my fate ere ye do, will ye shed a tear for me as I sway from the gallows tree?"

"This is a verra foolish conversation," she grumbled, walking to their bed of blankets.

Tavig smiled faintly as he watched her settle down on their meager bed. He was beginning to understand Moira. She had not answered his question. That meant that she could not give him a firm nay. Moira would be upset if he was taken by the hangman, although she might not fully understand why.

He banked the fire, leaving a smaller and safer flame to flicker during the night. It would not give them much warmth, but it would serve to ward off any curious or dangerous animals. He moved to the bedding they would have to share, sat down, and tugged off his boots. After slipping beneath the blanket, he placed the ill-made sword he had acquired in the fisherman's hut close by his side. He tucked his knife just under the edge of the blanket beneath him. Tavig turned on his side, smiling at Moira, who pointedly kept her back toward him. He slipped his arm around her tiny waist.

Moira pushed his arm away, alarmed at how nice it felt as Tavig eased it around her. "There will be none of that. Ye can stay to your own side."

"A mon ought to be able to cuddle with his bride."

A warm, subtly intoxicating feeling caused by his

closeness had been seeping over Moira, but it abruptly fled at his words. It occurred to her that his constant talk of marriage could have some cunning purpose. After all, she mused, if he made her believe they were to be wed, she might grow lax in protecting her chastity. She turned onto her side and glared at him, silently cursing the shadows that disguised his expression.

"Is that your game, then?" she demanded.

"My game?" Tavig could hear the anger in her husky voice and wondered how he had stepped wrong this time.

"Aye—your game. Ye try to deceive me into acting like some tavern wench. Ye want me to believe all your babble about being wed, about being your bride, so that I will think 'tis no great sin to allow ye to bed me."

"Ah, now I see what twisted path your thoughts are taking. Ye had me a wee bit confused for a moment. Lass, if all I sought was a good rutting I would ne'er speak the words 'marriage' or 'bride.' I would be verra careful not to give ye any claim to me." He tugged her into his arms, holding her just tight enough to mute her struggles. "I would just seduce you."

"Such arrogance." Moira gave up struggling, but remained tense, silently protesting his hold and fighting how right, how good, it felt to be so close to him. "Not every lass can be seduced."

"Aye, I ken it. I wouldnae try to seduce ye, lass." He inwardly asked forgiveness for that lie for he had every intention of trying to coax her into being his lover. "I have no need to. We are mates, a fated match. Destiny has paired us."

"Ye talk such complete nonsense."

"Do I? Can ye not feel it, fair Moira?"

"Feel what?"

"The bond between us."

Moira could feel something, but she was not sure she should call it a bond. He was warming the curve of her neck from her shoulder to her earlobe with soft kisses, and that warmth rippled through her body. That gentle yet pervasive heat also curled through her mind, melting away all her suspicions and anger. She considered a bond to be something steadfast, built over the years by familiarity and trust which made a person feel calm, confident, and safe. What Tavig was stirring inside of her was hot, fierce, new, and frightening. He *was* seducing her. He spoke of bonds and matrimony yet what he was pulling from her, what Moira was certain he was intending to stir within her, was the basest of hungers. Moira was afraid of the strength of that hunger and of her own weakness.

"'Tis unfair of ye to play your lecher's games with me," she protested, a little surprised at how soft and husky her voice was. "I am a weelborn maid, not some light-moraled wench."

"Now, lassie, whilst I will admit that ye make me feel verra lecherous, I play no game here." He began to brush light, teasing kisses over her small face, stirred by the signs of passion he could sense in her. "How can ye not feel the bond destiny has set between us? Do ye think I speak of marriage to every sodden lass I find sprawled upon the shore?"

"How should I ken what ye tell the lasses? I only started to speak to ye but yesterday."

"True, but I have forgiven ye for behaving so coldly toward me."

"Ye are a jester. Ye should wear the belled cap so that all may ken your wit."

"Now, Moira, what have I done to make ye mistrust me so?"

"Other than being condemned to hang for the murder of two men?"

Tavig looked at her for a moment then smiled. "Ye ken that I didnae do that."

Moira decided that the way he could just look at her and know how she felt was not only intimidating but annoying.

"I havenae decided if I believe your tale of innocence or not."

"Aye, ye have." He kissed the hollow by her ear.

She trembled. "Ye are a verra arrogant fellow." She clung to the front of his shirt, struggling vainly to regain her wits enough to push him away. "Ye should have more respect for a woman's innocence and her desire to keep it."

"Lass, I begin to think that ye could merrily rut with every mon the length and breadth of Scotland and still be innocent. A wee bit of loving from a mon who wishes to wed ye cannae steal it away."

"I have decided to ignore all your mad talk of wedding me."

"Have ye now?" He feathered soft kisses over her cheeks, edging ever closer to her full, tempting mouth.

"Aye, and now I demand that ye release me."

"Free yourself," he murmured, lightly brushing his lips over hers.

Moira really did not want to. A sharp flicker of resentment cut through the heat flowing through her. He should accept her refusal to play his game no matter how half-hearted it was. Her irritation was short-lived, however. The desire rushing through her body was too strong. She had never been kissed before and she desperately wanted to know what it would be like to be kissed by the darkly handsome man holding her. She promised herself that she would allow only one kiss.

Tavig sensed her acquiescence, and covered her soft mouth with his. She curled her slender arms around his neck. He held her close, heartily savoring the sweet innocence of her mouth. The promise of a fiery passion was there, and he ached to uncover it, but he knew he could not rush her. Life with Sir Bearnard had left her wounded. Tavig knew he would need a very gentle hand to smooth away those scars.

He moved his hands down her sides, lightly tracing her slender shape. When she pressed against him, her body trembling beneath his touch, he knew it would be difficult to proceed as carefully as he needed to. Only the thought of how easily he could destroy the very passion he ached to taste held him to his vow to move slowly.

When he lifted his head and looked at her, his breath caught in his throat. Even in the dim moonlight he could see the flush of passion in her cheeks. Her beautiful eyes were heavy-lidded. Her full lips glistened from the moisture of his kiss. He could feel her small, taut breasts moving against his chest in a quickened rhythm.

"Part those bonnie lips," he whispered.

"Why?"

"Do it and ye will soon ken why."

Moira hesitated only a moment. He had done nothing frightening yet. When she parted her lips and he uttered a low moan, she began to have doubts. He allowed her no time to consider them. He pressed his warm mouth against hers, easing his tongue between her lips. She clutched at him as he stroked the inside of her mouth, each movement of his tongue sending fire through her veins. Moira lost all sense of time and place, her mind rapidly filling with nothing but the thought of how good Tavig MacAlpin was making her feel.

When he silently urged her down onto their rough bed, covering her body with his, his touch growing bolder, she began to regain her senses. She fought a stern battle with her own desire. It felt so wonderful she wanted to continue, but, innocent though she was, she knew things had gone too far. In her head she could hear Crooked Annie's raspy voice saying, "Dinnae let a mon cover ye, lass." She had let Tavig do so and must put a stop to it.

Just as she was about to try to say something to push him away when every part of her wanted to hold him close, he stopped. He pressed his forehead against hers for a moment as he took several long, unsteady breaths. A minute later, he rolled onto his side, but kept her tucked up against him.

"I believe that is enough of that, lass," he said, his voice soft and husky.

"Aye, it certainly is." Moira realized even the sound of his voice, roughened by desire, was making it difficult to rein in her passion.

"I shouldnae have let ye tempt me so. Ye shall have to behave yourself better, loving, if ye mean to hold fast to your chastity."

It took Moira a minute to understand what he was saying and then to believe that she was hearing him correctly. She muttered one of the many curse words Crooked Annie was so fond of. When he laughed, she grew even more agitated and swatted him. Her hand had barely brushed against his arm when she realized what she was doing. Moira gasped, a tremor of fear banishing the last of her desire, and she hastily pulled away from him.

"I am sorry," she whispered, tensing with the certainty that he would reciprocate with far more force than she had used.

"For what, lass? I deserved a wee slap." He frowned. "Do ye now expect me to knock ye on your arse?"

There was a hint of anger in his voice that confused her. It was clearly aimed at what she expected him to do and not at what she had done. "Nay, of course not. And ye cannae do it anyway, for I am already on my arse." She clapped a hand over her mouth, astounded and a little shocked at her own words. "Oh! Listen to me. Ye are a poor influence, Tavig MacAlpin."

Tavig laughed, gently kissing her on the forehead. "Nay. What harm in a wee bit of wit even if it is faintly coarse? Aye, and it shows that ye can be at ease with me. There is no harm in that."

"Nay? I would think that growing at ease with a mon accused of two murders isnae verra clever at all."

"How ye wound me."

"I doubt that much can pierce your thick hide." She yawned, not resisting when he tucked her up close to his side. "I believe I really must go to sleep, Sir Tavig," she murmured even as she closed her eyes

Tavig waited for her to wish him a good sleep, but after a moment of silence, he looked at her. It was evident she had gone to sleep within a heartbeat of speaking. He smiled, nestling her slim form more comfortably against him. His smile widened when she murmured, cuddling up to him as if it were already a habit.

"Ah, lass, ye will soon see that we are destined. Aye, I just have to soothe those hurts that bastard Sir Bearnard inflicted upon ye." He sighed, kissing the top of her head. "I just pray that I have the patience and skill to do it."

Chapter Five

"I dinnae suppose ye will believe me if I say I found this growing wild in the field."

Moira looked at the bread Tavig held, then at him. "Nay, I dinnae think I would."

After two days of trudging north over the rougher, emptier parts of Scotland, Moira had begun to believe she had convinced the man not to steal anything. The bread he tempted her with was solid proof that she had been naïve. What she hated most about it was how it forced her to face conflicting emotions within herself. She knew Tavig MacAlpin was a good man yet he could obviously steal with ease and success. The idea of stealing anything was repugnant to her, yet she knew she wanted and would heartily enjoy, some of that bread. Hunger was rapidly blurring her morals.

Tavig sighed, sitting down beside her, taking out his knife and cutting off a piece of bread. "Ye wouldnae believe it was a miracle either, would ye? That it just appeared in my hands because God understood our need?"

"Ye blaspheme. I had hoped we could make this journey without stealing anything."

"Weel, dearling, I regret dashing your hopes, but they were unreasonable ones. Even if we continue to each eat just two small bowls of porridge a day, we will be without food by the week's end." He smiled faintly when she crossly snatched up the piece of bread he held out to her. "Neither of us is accustomed to such a long, arduous march, either."

The bread was delicious, which irritated Moira. "And that makes a difference, does it?"

"Oh, aye. 'Twill be a struggle requiring all of our strength. One must needs eat weel when enduring such a trial."

"Ye make some verra pretty excuses."

"Not excuses—facts."

"Mayhap, but whilst we fill our bellies, the owner of this bread goes hungry."

"Nay. I couldnae and wouldnae take food from those who might starve without it."

"And how can ye be so sure that they didnae need it?"

"Because I took it from the kitchens of a verra fine house a few miles to the west of us. 'Twas one of five loaves, and the meal being prepared showed me that there was no lack of food in the place."

Moira frowned when he put his arm around her, but she was too curious to waste time scolding him over his familiarity. "Are ye saying that ye just ambled into some wealthy laird's kitchens, helped yourself to a loaf of his bread and sauntered away?" She absently accepted a second piece of bread.

"It wasnae *that* easy. I didnae have to do much creeping about or lying, though." He shook his head. "When my troubles are at an end, I shall have to tell that laird how weak his guard is. He must be a good mon, for his people are a happy, trusting lot. Too trusting. I could easily have been some enemy surveying the mon's strengths and weaknesses. I shall repay him for this bread by letting him ken how easily he could be taken. Sad to say, a mon cannae allow himself or his people to be too welcoming. Aye, hospitality is the mark of a good knight, but this mon's keep was as open and vulnerable as a monastery."

"Ye are right. 'Tis sad that he could be hurt because he lives so openly and trustingly."

"Aye, and 'twill come, for 'tis clear to anyone who takes a moment to look that he also lives weel."

"And eventually someone will come along who wishes to take that away." She frowned up at the sky. "'Tis growing late, only a few hours of light remaining."

"True. We will travel on in a moment."

He tucked the remaining bread into his sack, then, smiling faintly, pulled her into his arms. Moira tried to look stern, but it grew more difficult to resist him with each hour she spent in his company. She placed her hands against his chest, intending to push him away. That intention was swiftly banished by the touch of his lips on hers. His mouth was gentle and warm. Good sense and morality told her to resist the temptation they represented, but, as with the bread, she found she was too weak to refuse something she wanted so badly.

She curled her arms around his neck as he teased her lips with small, nibbling kisses. After a moment she pressed closer, silently requesting the fuller kiss he held back. A soft groan escaped her when he readily answered her plea. The heat that both frightened and enthralled her raced through her body, its strength centering low in her abdomen. On occasion Moira had heard one of the maids speak of how she burned for a particular man. Now Moira knew what that maid had been talking about. She knew that she burned for Tavig MacAlpin, ached for him. It was the worst and the best thing that had ever happened to her.

"Ah, lass, ye have the sweetest mouth I have e'er tasted," he murmured against her throat, tracing her frantic pulse with little kisses.

"Yours isnae so bad, either." She grimaced when he laughed softly.

"Such flattery."

His long fingers brushed over the curve of her breast, and Moira shuddered from the force of the desire ripping through her body. Gritting her teeth, she squirmed out of his hold. She hastily stood up, silently praying he could not see how unsteady she was. Somehow she was going to have to find the strength to fight his allure, much more strength than she was showing now.

"We had better be on our way," she said, inwardly cursing the huskiness infecting her voice.

"Ye cannae keep running away." Tavig picked up their supplies and began to walk.

"I dinnae ken what ye are talking about," Moira protested, hurrying after him.

"Aye, ye do. We are fated, Moira. Ye feel that each time I touch you. Ye feel it in your blood, in how it heats with desire."

"What arrogance."

Tavig ignored her muttered interruption. "Ye have been so sheltered ye dinnae understand what your body and your heart are telling you, so ye fight it, pushing me away. I am a patient mon, though. I can wait until ye do see the truth."

Moira glared at his back, wondering how she could ache to tumble about in the heather with him one minute and desperately want to kick him in his too attractive backside the next. She knew what irritated her the most was his knowledge of how she felt. As she grudgingly accepted his help over some moss-covered rocks, she briefly feared he could read her mind. She easily shrugged away that fear. If Tavig could read minds, right now he would either be laughing at her or getting out of the reach of her foot.

He just knows me too well or has a knack for reading the expressions on my face, she mused. If she was to retain any emotional secrets from the man, she was going to have to learn a few new tricks. She had learned to hide her fear and anger from Sir Bearnard. Now she would learn how to hide her feelings, thoughts, and emotional turmoil from Tavig.

* * *

"I suppose it had to rain at some time during our journey," Moira grumbled, trying to huddle farther back beneath the crude branch-and-blanket shelter Tavig had made for them.

"Aye. 'Tis a shame it does so during our resting time, though. We willnae have a comfortable sleep." He cut her a slice of bread from the dwindling loaf he had stolen that afternoon. "This is all we shall have for food tonight as I cannae light a fire without dry wood and kindling."

"Do ye think that will make me less concerned that ye stole this?" She wrapped her blanket more tightly around herself as she nibbled on the bread.

"Nay. I ken that ye have the strength to cling tightly to your disapproval."

"But not so tightly that I refuse to eat this ill-gotten bounty. Ye need not keep that thought to yourself. I swear I can hear ye thinking the words." She sighed, rubbing her aching feet.

"Why dinnae ye unwrap the rags from your feet and stick them out in the rain for a wee while?"

"But they will get wet. Most likely cold as weel."

"'Twill soothe that aching ye are trying so hard to hide." He met her disbelieving look with a smile. "Trust me, dearling. There was a time or two when I had to walk long miles in ill-made boots or bare feet. I ken weel that hot aching that can afflict one's feet. I found naught that was as soothing as bathing them in cool water. There isnae a stream or pool about, only what falls from the sky. Try it. It cannae hurt."

"Nay, mayhap not."

With his help she unwrapped her feet. Cautiously she edged closer to the opening of their shelter until her feet protruded beyond its somewhat weak protection. Moira hated to admit it, but the cool spray did feel good. Just exposing her tender feet to the cooler night air had felt good.

The rain washing over her feet made her sigh with relief. She scowled at a grinning Tavig. The man did not have to look so smug.

"Aye, it helps some," she muttered.

Tavig laughed and shook his head. "Ye are a stubborn lass, Moira Robertson."

Moira knew her sudden, instinctive flash of fear had been seen by him, for his laughter abruptly faded, and he scowled at her. In her years with Bearnard Robertson, being called a stubborn lass had always been followed by a beating or one of Sir Bearnard's many other cruel punishments. Although she had been with Tavig only a short while, she knew he would never treat her as her guardian had. Her fears could not yet make that distinction, however.

"I wish I kenned what I must do to get ye to cease fearing me," Tavig said, cutting her another slice of bread.

"I dinnae fear you, Tavig," she said quietly.

"Nay? 'Twas stark fear I just saw in your face, loving."

"Aye, ye probably did see that. Howbeit, it wasnae a fear of you. 'Twas fear of a memory."

"A memory?"

"Aye, a memory. Ye called me a stubborn lass, and the words stirred a harsh, frightening memory. That was what my fear was born of, not ye or anything ye have done."

"Must I weigh every word I utter then?"

She shook her head. "That wouldnae be fair to you, nor would it help me. I must learn that just because someone says the same thing Sir Bearnard once said, it doesnae mean he will now act as my guardian did. Ye meant the words as a tease, not a scold or a threat. I must learn to hear more than the words. I must listen to the way they are spoken. There was no anger or warning in your voice. That is what I must teach myself to heed."

"Aye, for I begin to think Sir Bearnard said little that wasnae followed by some act of brutality."

"Sometimes he said nothing at all. He was at his most dangerous then." She shivered, trying to shake away bad memories. "The rain grows more chilling than soothing," she murmured, pulling her feet back inside their shelter.

As he helped her rub her feet dry and rewrap them, Tavig studied her. She never talked long about Sir Bearnard and her life with the man. There would be one or two faint allusions to what she had endured, then she would grow silent and withdraw, just as she had now. It left him feeling as if she had retreated from him, yet he knew that was not truly the case. He could not help but wonder, however, how long the shadow of Sir Bearnard would hang over them.

"Not every mon is like your guardian," he said, huddling back in the shelter and gently tugging her to his side.

"I ken it. Tavig, I am sorry if the way I act sometimes offends you."

He lightly kissed her mouth, stopping her words. "No need to apologize. As ye must learn to heed how the words are spoken, and not just the words themselves, so I must learn to cease thinking that every flash of fear or instinctive cringe is directed at me. Sir Bearnard taught ye those harsh lessons. Ye just need time to learn when and with whom they are needed. Although I intend to insure that ye never have to live that way again."

"Oh, and how do ye plan to do that?"

"By convincing ye to stay with me."

"Aye? Your fate isnae too certain, my fine knight. I cannae see that sharing a gallows with you is better than living with Sir Bearnard."

"And I dinnae intend to swing from Iver's gallows."

"I cannae say I wish that to happen either, but I dinnae understand how ye can be so verra sure that it willnae."

"Once I reach my cousin Mungan I will have the aid I need to fight it out with Iver."

"That willnae prove your innocence." She yawned, leaning more heavily against him.

"True, but no one believes I killed those men. Every one of my people at Drumdearg kens exactly who is the murderer. Howbeit, I shall try to get some proof of my innocence, mayhap some confession, so that others will believe it, too." He shook his head. "I have thought of little else besides getting back what has been stolen from me and of making Iver pay for his crimes. Ye are right, though. That willnae prove my innocence, and since Iver has spread his baseless accusations far and wide, I must look to the matter of clearing that black mark from my name."

"Ye may never be able to fully clear it."

"Ye are a veritable well of cheer, arenae ye?" he grumbled, then smiled when she giggled sleepily. "And ye are right about that as weel, although I curse the unfairness of it. Nevertheless, the people that matter will ken the truth. Most of them do already."

"And ye are verra sure that your cousin Mungan will believe your tale and not hand ye over to Iver?"

"Verra sure. Mungan has always loathed and mistrusted Iver." He touched a kiss to the top of her head. "Dinnae worry, lass. We will be safe at Mungan's, *and* I will find out what game he plays by snatching your cousin."

"Ye dinnae suppose he saw her from afar, fell in love with her, and had to try to make her his?"

Tavig thought about that for a moment then replied with confidence, "Nay, not Mungan. He isnae given to such feelings. He is a good mon, and I am certain your cousin is safe and unharmed, but Mungan isnae a romantic sort of fellow. When he decides to take a wife he will be good to her, care for her, and be unswervingly faithful, but she will have to accept that she willnae hear much flattery, sweet words, or declarations of heartfelt sentiment. Then, too, if by some miracle Mungan has been seized by a romantic urge, why has he asked a ransom for her?"

"He could have lost his romantic urge when he discovered that my cousin Una didnae and wouldnae feel the same."

"Mayhap, but I truly doubt it. Mungan just isnae that type of mon. He once hanged a minstrel up by his feet, dangled the poor fellow over the head table because the mon wouldnae sing anything but songs of love. Ye see, Mungan wished to hear a few rousing tunes about battles won and lost. Mostly won, though, *and* won by the Scots."

Although her eyelids were weighted by her need to sleep, Moira managed one last long look at Tavig. "And ye think we shall find safety with such a madmon?"

He laughed as he leaned more comfortably against the tree trunk he had used to help support their meager shelter. "He didnae kill the minstrel, did he? Nay, nor did he dangle the mon long enough for the poor terrified fool to be injured. Mungan is, weel, odd, but harmless. At least toward those he counts as his friends. I swear to ye, ye will be safe with the mon. Mungan has ne'er hurt a woman or a child."

Moira could not fully suppress a wide yawn. "Ye have a verra odd family, Tavig MacAlpin."

"Ye dinnae ken the half of it, dearling. Go to sleep. Ye need your rest. We still have a long way to go."

A moment later he felt her grow lax and heavy in his arms. He glanced at her feet, sighing over the discomfort she had to be suffering. Tavig wished he could carry her all the way to Mungan's keep. As he gently brushed a few damp strands of hair from her face, he also wished he knew how to make her trust him, to love him and want to stay with him. There were ten, perhaps twelve, days left before they reached Mungan's keep. Despite the fact that they would have to walk every mile, it suddenly looked to be far too short a time.

Moira groaned softly, curling her arms around Tavig's neck as his lips warmed hers. His kiss stole the cold invading her body as well as all her aches and pains. Her discomfort was quickly replaced by passion. She pressed her body closer to his, soaking up his heat and savoring the feel of his long, sinewy body.

He traced her shape with his skilled hands. Moira shuddered with delight when he curved his hands over her backside, pressing her loins against his. She could feel the hard proof of his desire. It enthralled her. She gasped with pleasure when he slid his hand up her side to cup her breast. For a full minute she blindly arched into his touch, then a tiny shaft of reason broke through the haze of passion clouding her mind. With a soft curse, she scrambled out of his hold and got up on her knees, her head brushing the top of their shelter. She glared at Tavig.

"I dinnae suppose ye could just say 'good morn, lass,'" she snapped and, seeing dawn's light brightening the sky, crawled out from beneath the tiny shelter.

"I thought that was what I was doing," Tavig said, crawling out and standing up for a leisurely stretch.

"What ye were doing was trying to catch me unawares so that ye could have your way with me."

"*My* way? It felt like it might be your way as weel, lass."

"I dinnae think so, Sir Tavig."

She decided to ignore his impudent grin, striding off to the shelter of the trees to relieve herself. As she readjusted her clothes she realized that, although the cool rain had helped, her feet still ached. Moira thought it extremely unfair that she could not use her healing hands to cure her own pain. Even if she tried, she risked Tavig discovering her strange gift. From past experience she knew she would leave herself so completely drained, so utterly weakened, that, even if Tavig did not guess that she could heal with a touch, he would certainly be dangerously curious over how her feet were so much better but she could not walk a step.

Moira shook her head as she returned to camp, finding that Tavig had already taken down their shelter and started their meal. She dearly wished she understood her strange skill better. Mayhap then she would not be so afraid of others finding out about it. Sadly she admitted her gift was enough of a mystery to herself, almost frightening at times, and she could easily see how deeply it would frighten others. Even though Tavig suffered with a gift that could rouse superstitions, she could easily envision him being afraid of hers. Moira realized that one reason she did not confide her secret to Tavig was that she dreaded seeing that wariness enter his eyes, dreaded the thought that he would pull away from her and shun her.

"Now, dearling, ye arenae still sulking o'er my giving ye a wee morning kiss, are ye?" he asked her as she sat down across the fire from him.

"Nay, and I dinnae ken how ye can call what ye did no more than a wee morning kiss. Aye, and look so sweetly innocent as ye do so."

"Ye think I am sweetly innocent, do ye?"

"Jester. Ye ken verra weel I dinnae think that. I just said ye looked so." She accepted the bowl of porridge he gave her, muttering, "Thank ye, rogue."

"Your opinion of me rises and falls with startling rapidity."

"And ye are vain if ye think I trouble myself to form any opinion of ye at all."

He chuckled, and Moira smiled faintly. She was startled at how easily and quickly she had returned to her old ways, to that sharp tongue her guardian had found so infuriating. What her father had always lovingly referred to as her spirit had never fully died, simply retreated, softened, and grown quiet. Although she was not really surprised that Bearnard had not beaten it out of her, despite how she had feared that at times, she was amazed at how swiftly it had reasserted itself.

As she cleaned out their dishes and put them away, she decided she liked how it felt. There was danger and definitely discomfort in the situation she found herself in now, yet she had never felt so free, almost lighthearted. It was going to be hard to return to life with Sir Bearnard, a life filled with fear and wariness. She shivered with apprehension at the mere thought of it.

She glanced at Tavig, who was making certain the fire

had completely gone out. There was a danger in thinking too much about her life with Sir Bearnard. It would make her increasingly susceptible to Tavig's talk of staying with him, of marriage, fate, and destiny. Life with the Robertsons was so miserable that she could easily forget all the good reasons for staying away from Tavig and not grabbing what he offered her. Now that she knew how much better she could feel when out from beneath the shadow of Bearnard's heavy fists, it would be even easier to cast aside common sense and stay with Tavig. With far more regularity, she was going to have to remind herself why a match between them would be dangerous.

For the short while she was with him, however, she intended to enjoy her newfound freedom. She knew all too well that she might never taste it again. Tavig probably had no idea of the gift he had given her, but she was deeply grateful.

"Are ye ready to go yet, lass?" he asked as he picked up their supplies.

"Aye." She sighed a little dramatically as she followed him. "'Tis a shame we cannae find a shorter way or learn how to fly. I dinnae suppose ye have a cousin who lives nearer."

"Nay." He glanced up at the sky then flashed her a smile. "'Twould be nice to fly. Easier on the feet."

"Much easier. Tavig, since ye live near here and Mungan lives to the north, what were ye doing so far south?"

"I had the foolish idea of going to speak to the king. Although I didnae meet with the king himself I did talk with one of his men, a mon close enough to the king to ken what I would be told. He said I should go home, gain what aid I can from my other kinsmen and take care of the matter myself."

"Ye would think the king would be interested in seeing that such feuds and battles ne'er got started."

"He has too much to deal with already. All of his attention is fixed upon the border lairds and the English. 'Tis a contentious area. As I was headed back, planning to go to Mungan, I was nearly caught by Iver's men and then discovered your ship. I felt I would be safe out at sea as long as I remained disguised."

"And then Sir Bearnard and I came along to ruin your escape."

"Nay, ye didnae ruin it. Mayhap added a few days, but no more. I told ye—we are fated. I just wish fate had thought of a gentler way for us to meet."

Moira frowned when he briefly looked her way. "I fear I dinnae hold as strong a belief in fate as ye do."

The look of amused disbelief he cast her way irritated her. He was right to feel she was making an empty boast, but he did not have to be so openly cocky about it. In this case, however, fate had made a very large mistake in throwing her and Tavig together. Fate did not always arrange a happy ending for the people whose lives it directed, either. Since she had not told Tavig about her own special "gift," he could blissfully accept the workings of fate. Somehow she was going to have to maintain the strength to fight what Tavig kept saying was their destiny.

Chapter Six

A soft cry of fear and surprise escaped Moira when Tavig suddenly appeared at her side. In the week they had been together, she had not yet grown accustomed to his ability to move so quietly. He had left her hidden in the tangled shrubs at the edge of the wood while he went ahead to reconnoiter the village they approached. Moira knew the hour or so she had spent alone had increased her nervousness. She had just been envisioning Tavig suffering a horrible slow death when he arrived. A hint of relief tempered her annoyance over how he had startled her.

"Can we go into the village?" she asked, frowning when he sat down very close to her and draped his arm around her shoulders.

"Aye, it looks safe although 'tis a poor place, and the people look as if life has treated them poorly. I am not sure we will gain much. Not shoes for your poor wee feet or any new clothes, leastwise. One of us may be able to work for a meal, howbeit, mayhap e'en a sheltered corner to spend the night." He touched a kiss to the soft curve of her neck, grinning when she hunched her shoulders. "So cold to your husband," he murmured and gave her an exaggeratedly mournful face.

"Ye arenae my husband."

"I shall call myself that, and ye shall agree with me whilst we are in this village."

"Oh? Shall I now?"

"Aye, my wee bride, ye shall. These folk look to be a dour pious lot. They will act more kindly toward us if they believe we are properly wed."

"Cannae we just be kinsmen? Cousins? Or brother and sister?"

"We dinnae look at all alike, lass."

"Cousins need not look much alike."

"Nay, but cousins can be lovers, and I believe these villagers willnae abide any hint of sin."

Moira decided to accept his judgments but gave him as stern a look as she could manage. "Then we shall play the game of mon and wife but dinnae ye try to play it too seriously."

"Ah, I see." He slipped his other arm about her waist, turning her toward him to touch his lips lightly to hers. "No stolen kisses?"

"Nay," Moira whispered, held firmly in place by a weakening heat engendered by his touch and the warmth of his obsidian gaze.

"And no holding ye too closely." he murmured, slowly tracing the shape of her full mouth with the tip of his tongue. "Not e'en as we sleep beneath the same blanket."

"Aye. None of that."

It occurred to Moira that Tavig was attempting to seduce her again and, yet again, she was not doing a very good job of pushing him away. He nibbled at her mouth. She trembled with pleasure, her eyes weighted into closing. She allowed him to draw her more securely into his strong arms. Tavig deepened his kiss and she opened her mouth to welcome the enticing strokes of his tongue. As she curled her arms about his neck a snide voice in her mind told her she was doing a pathetic job of resisting his advances, of giving her constant nays much strength of conviction. She promised herself she could allow no more than one sweet stolen kiss.

He gave her a long, slow kiss and she savored every heated moment. The way her blood warmed as he moved his hands up and down her back made her almost regret her decision to resist the temptation he presented her with. She could not forget that her maidenhead was her only dowry, however. Although her chances of an honest, reasonable marriage proposal were distressingly slim, she would not toss that meager dowry away for a brief moment of passion. She just wished the passion Tavig could stir within her was not such a fierce and heady thing. At times, when she felt the heat of his body next to hers in the night, she found herself questioning the wisdom of her decision to cling to her chastity.

"Shouldnae we be getting to the village ere they all cease work for the day?" she managed to choke out when he released her mouth to dot her throat with soft, teasing kisses.

"Aye, ye are right." Tavig released her and stood up, brushing himself off. "Ye must cease distracting me, lass."

Silently muttering every curse she could think of, she ignored his offered hand and stood up to brush herself off also. The man could be so irritating. It was no wonder there were people who wanted him dead. His cousin Iver probably did not care about Tavig's holdings much at all; he simply could no longer abide Tavig's teasing and nonsense. Then she hastily, if silently, apologized for making light of Tavig's desperate situation.

When he took her by the hand to lead her to the village, she almost jerked her hand free. He led her much the same as he would lead a horse. Moira recalled that they were to behave as husband and wife, however. Tavig had already proven that he was a clever survivor. She decided it would be wise to do exactly what he told her to. She would just make sure that he did not try to twist their circumstances to his advantage. It had not taken her long to see how good he was at that, too.

Tavig strode into the village with a cockiness that stunned Moira. He seemed to forget that he was a hunted man. She wondered how he could be so cheerfully oblivious to the hard, wary looks sent their way. There was no welcome from the people they saw. Moira began to think it was far more than a hard life that soured these people. She glanced toward the laird's tower that sat on a rise at the far end of the village.

"'Tis a dark, forbidding place, isnae it?" murmured Tavig.

"Aye. I shouldnae like to have to look at that every day of my life."

She glanced around at the poor houses huddled side by side along the rutted, muddy road. They showed as little life as the people scurrying in and out of them. The laird's tower cast its long shadow over everything and everyone beneath it. She shivered. The similarity to the people living under the brutal Sir Bearnard was too close to ignore. A lot of her old fears rushed back, and she realized how gently Tavig had smoothed them away. Even he could not tease away the fear and unhappiness that soaked the air around the little village, however.

When Tavig stopped at a tiny inn, she kept close by his side. The innkeeper, a fat balding man with a deeply lined face, sat on a worn bench outside his too quiet establishment. A sour smile crossed his face when Tavig spoke of earning a bed and a meal.

"If it was of my choosing, laddie," the innkeeper said in a rough voice, "I would put ye and your lass in my finest room right now. 'Twould be a fine thing to have some custom again, even poor ragged children like ye who cannae pay for it. I swear the old laird can hear the ropes on my beds creak when a guest beds down, howbeit. He will swoop down here in a winking and demand his share of the tally."

"Is there *no* work to be had in the village?" asked Tavig.

"Nay, I fear not, lad. No one passes through here if they can find another route."

"Why dinnae ye leave here?" asked Moira.

"We are bound to our laird." The man shrugged his bulky shoulders. "And even those of us who feel he has broken his bond with us dare not leave. The mon has made enemies of all who live about us. We are encircled by those who hate us. If one of us is found outside of the laird's lands, we risk being murdered. Ye keep on walking. Get away ere someone begins to think ye are one of us or deal with us. There are spies aplenty round here."

"I had hoped to get my wife something to put on her feet and mayhap just a wee bowl of porridge," Tavig said, looking up and down the road.

"Weel, ye could try the widow Giorsal. She abides in the last hovel on this side of the road. She had but one child, a son, and he was killed by the laird last Michaelmas. She may need something done for her. She willnae ask it of us for she feels 'twould be done in charity, and her pride willnae allow that. She has no coin either, but she would have a bed and a wee bit of food."

"Thank ye, sir."

"No thanks be needed, son. A last warning—dinnae show your bonnie face or that of your wee bride too freely. 'Twas having too fine a face that got the widow Giorsal's lad murdered, and dinnae let anyone try to tell ye elsewise. Aye, and my sister's prettiest girl child was dragged up to yonder tower after the last harvest and hasnae been seen since. A bonnie face can be a curse in this land."

As they walked away from the man, Moira whispered, "Mayhap we should leave."

"Let us try to gain a meal and a bed from the widow first. Ye need both. Aye, and so do I."

Their progress was slowed by a knot of people outside a small church. A young woman shook her head as people mournfully told her how lovely her tiny daughter was.

Tavig started to shake his head over the oddity of it all, then looked at the little girl in question and tensed. She was a healthy, beautiful child with golden curls and a rosy complexion. As she stepped into the road, he felt the chill of premonition streak down his spine. The little child waved at a lanky young man across the road and started to toddle over to him. Tavig was not sure why, but he knew he had to keep the little girl out of the road.

"Nay, child," he said, grabbing the sweet-faced child by one dimpled arm. "Stay here."

"Papa," she cried, vigorously trying to pull free. "I go see me papa."

"Nay. Ye must stay here."

The mother rushed to Tavig's side. "Let my bairn go. Are ye one of that devil's men? Cannae ye at least let her grow into a woman ere ye steal her away?" She reached for the child.

Tavig yanked the girl into his arms, holding the squirming child out of her mother's reach. "Nay, I dinnae try to steal her. But wait a moment. I cannae tell ye why, but the child must stay out of the road."

"Are ye mad, then? She wants to go to her father."

At that moment the lanky young man arrived and began to struggle with Tavig, who clung to the little girl. He could see Moira's face through the gathering crowd. She was pale and clearly afraid, but she moved to try to keep people away from him. By doing so she showed that she believed in his foretelling ability no matter how much she disliked it. Tavig knew she could never understand how much that meant to him.

Just as he feared he would lose his grip on the now-screaming child, a low thunderous sound began to steal people's attention away from him. Even the child's parents although still keeping their hands on their daughter, turned to look in the direction of the sound. A large troop of heavily armed men galloped down the road from the laird's tower. They rode heedlessly through town, kicking up clouds of dust and slowing for nothing in their way. An old man was knocked aside, and several chickens were trampled beneath the hooves of the men's horses. Tavig knew why he had felt compelled to keep the child out of the road. She would never have made it to the other side in time, and the scowling men-at-arms would have ridden right over her.

The men rode out of the village, disappearing into the surrounding wood. For one long, tense moment after they were out of sight no one said a word. Everyone slowly turned to stare at him. Tavig released the child to her parents and felt Moira slip her hand into his. He saw the suspicion and fear begin to settle on the people's faces. He heartily wished he had never brought Moira into the village.

"Witch," whispered one old woman.

"Nay," snapped Moira. "Ye old fool, he but saw the men riding this way."

"He kenned what was to happen," said a plump, graying woman, pointing an accusatory finger at Tavig. "No one else saw those men. He is a witch."

"Get out of here, Moira," Tavig ordered, nudging her away from his side. "Run, lass."

"I cannae leave ye," she protested.

"Run for your life, ye fool lass," he snapped, but, even as he spoke, he knew it was too late. "The woman has naught to do with it," he cried as the people swarmed around them, grabbing Moira as well as him. "Let her go."

He fought to break free of the two men holding him, but two more moved to help them. The sight of Moira being roughly restrained by a burly man enraged him, and he struggled all the harder. When he saw one of his captors raise a thick club, Tavig braced for the blow.

Moira screamed when the man hit Tavig on the head. Tavig slumped in the arms of his captors, blood trickling down the side of his face. Moira tried to wriggle free of the huge man who had her pinned in his arms, but he just tightened his grip.

"Be still, witch, or ye will get the same as your mon," her captor growled in her ear.

There was no doubt in Moira's mind that the man meant exactly what he said. She went very still, barely breathing. A youth pulled forward an officious-looking little man who decided she and Tavig should be kept in the storage hole at the inn until the priest could judge them. As she and Tavig were dragged to the inn, she listened closely to what the people were saying. Moira bit back a cry of horror when a man said the priest was not due to pass through the village for a fortnight or more.

The innkeeper would not meet her eyes as he opened the hatch in the floor of his tavern. The people crowded around her did not even wait for him to lower the ladder, callously pushing her into the hole. Moira hit the packed dirt floor hard. Winded and unsure of how badly she was hurt, she scrambled out of the way as they tossed the unconscious Tavig in after her. She cried out a protest as the hatch was shut, leaving her and Tavig in complete darkness, but no one paid her any heed.

Fighting a stomach-knotting panic, Moira took a moment to examine herself as best she could in the dark. She breathed a sigh of relief. She was only bruised and battered; no bones were broken. She groped her way through the blackness until she felt Tavig's limp form. It was difficult, but she slowly, carefully, ran her hands over his body until she felt certain that he had no broken bones, either. The wound on his head felt sticky with blood, but she could not feel any new blood flowing from it. She prayed she was guessing correctly that it was only a small wound and he would soon wake up.

A soft scurrying sound echoed in the dark, and she shuddered. She hated rats. She particularly hated when she could hear them but not see them. It surprised her that she was not terrified. Her guardian was fond of locking her in places for days at a time which had left her with a deep dread of such dark places. Fear was a bitter taste in her mouth, but she still possessed all her senses. She decided it was because she was not alone.

Moira took Tavig's limp hand in hers, huddling closer to him. It was going to be a long, frightening time while she waited for him to wake up.

Tavig clawed his way back to consciousness, groaning and cursing. Although his head rested on something soft, it was throbbing badly with pain. He felt a cool, faintly callused little hand gently caressing his forehead. Again he cursed, suddenly recalling what had happened. He opened his eyes to look at Moira and saw only blackness. He was momentarily alarmed. It took a minute for him to realize his eyesight had not been affected by the blow to his head; he was simply in a very dark place. He started to move, then stayed where he was, a little startled at how soothing Moira's touch was, each stroke of her fingers lessening his pain.

"I should have let the twice-cursed bairn toddle to her death," he muttered.

"Nay," Moira said. "She would have been killed, and ye would have ached with guilt kenning that ye could have stopped it. How is your head?"

"It feels as if it has been split clean apart." He frowned. "Although the throbbing already begins to ease."

"Dinnae fret. 'Tis still in one piece. E'en a thick club cannae break such a hard pate."

"Thank ye. Where are we? For a moment I feared I had been blinded for when I opened my eyes, I saw nothing. 'Tis cursed dark in here."

"We have been tossed into a storage hole beneath the inn. I fear we are to be kept secured here until a priest can judge us. From what was said, that willnae happen for a fortnight or so." She shuddered, and Tavig groped in the dark until he held her hand in his. "I think there are rats in here," she whispered.

"Verra likely, sweeting. They will do naught if one of us remains awake. If this is where the innkeeper stores things, they probably have enough to eat without trying to have a wee nibble on us."

"Dinnae say such things!" She glanced around even though she could see nothing.

"Weel, I got us a roof o'er our heads for the night." He grimaced as he slowly tried to sit up then relaxed, surprised that the movement did not increase throbbing in his head. "A poor jest. Sorry, lass."

"Most of your jests have been poor ones," she murmured without any animosity or anger, frowning up toward the hatch they had been tossed through. "Do ye think they will feed and water us?"

"Oh, aye, though it may not be as much as we would like. They will wish us to be alive to face the priest's godly judgment, howbeit. But of course there is always the chance that the much-feared laird of theirs will hear of all this and seek to judge us for himself."

"Ye dinnae sound as if ye think that will be a good thing." He draped his arm around her shoulders, and she leaned against him. "A priest might be harder in his judgment than some laird."

He rested his head against the top of hers. "True, but mayhap not this time. Recall what was said about this laird." He felt her tremble and briefly tightened his hold on her. "I wish I could say something to lift your spirits."

"Nay, I prefer the truth no matter how dire it is. I just wish it wasnae quite so dark."

Tavig pressed a kiss to her hair. He could hear the fear in her voice, felt it rippling through her body, but she was fighting it. It fed his sense of guilt even as he felt a wave of tenderness wash over him. The need to get her to safety gnawed at him, but he could see no chance of rescue for either of them. Yet, he could not believe that the fate his foretelling skill had urged him to reach for was that he and Moira would die together before they had even become lovers. He was certain the destiny he had sensed was not an early grave.

"Ye should have run when I told ye to, dearling," he said.

"That would have been verra cowardly of me. *And* if ye could leap into the storm-tossed sea to aid me, I could certainly try to get ye free from the grasp of superstitious village fools. There is also the verra practical matter that I have to stay with ye. Ye are the one who kens how to get to your cousin's. I have no idea of where I am, of where to go, and of how to survive long enough to get there."

"Ah, and here I was cherishing the thought that ye had come to care for me."

"Ye shouldnae let your vanity place such lies into your head."

He smiled against her soft hair at her tart response. She did care for him. It had been there to see in her face as the crowd had turned against him. It had also been there in her cry when he had been struck down. Her regard for him might not be the deep, enduring emotion he sought, but she did have some feeling for him beyond the desire he could stir within her.

"Not that it does ye any good now, ye great oaf," he grumbled.

"What?" she asked.

"Nothing, lass. I just curse my stupidity."

"Ye couldnae ken that ye would be tossed into a hole in the ground for saving a child's life. The ingratitude those people showed is truly appalling." She felt him move away, and his absence quickly intensified her fears. "Where are ye going?"

"Not far. There isnae the room here, anyway, I think. The throbbing in my head has eased sooner than I expected, and I thought I would stumble about our prison to see if there is anything of use here. Ye didnae see anything before they closed the door, did ye?"

"Nay, I was too busy falling. I didnae think to see what

they threw us into." She gave a start of surprise when he suddenly took her hand in his, wondering how he could find her in the dark.

"They *threw* us into this pit?"

"Aye. Like sacks of grain."

"Are ye hurt, lass?"

"Nay. A few bruises. No more. Ye landed far more heavily than I did."

"Ah, now I understand why my body aches so much. I thought 'twas from the rough handling I must have received after they knocked me on the head." He released her hand, moving away again.

Moira heard him give a cry of surprise a moment later and tensed. "Are ye all right, Tavig?"

"Aye, loving. I found a keg of ale. Poor quality, but it should sustain us for a wee while. I think there are a few cheeses hanging here, too. They cannae starve us leastwise."

"Nay, we can be fat and drunk when they tie us to the stake." She jumped a little when he brushed against her side. "Do ye see in the dark?" she complained when he sat down at her side, tugging her into his arms.

"We arenae going to die at the stake," he said in a firm voice as he kissed her cheeks.

"Have ye seen that?" she asked, feeling her first flicker of hope since they had been accused of being witches. She realized that she believed in his ability to foretell what was to happen.

"I wish I could say I have clearly seen a swift and successful escape, but, nay, I havenae seen anything." He felt her slump a little in his grasp. "'Tis just that I cannae believe all that has happened to us was for naught but this. I ken 'tis weak comfort, but cannae believe this was to be our destiny. Look at the paths we have been forced along. I was warned of Iver's trap. I was warned of your fate and rushed to follow ye into those cold waters. Why would fate or God keep plucking us from the jaws of death only to lead us to this?"

Moira had no answer for that question. She suspected every person facing death asked it, especially when they were innocent of any wrong as she and Tavig were. For a moment she tried to convince herself that they could be proclaimed innocent and set free, but failed. They had been called witches, and such an accusation was as good as a death sentence. They had no advocates to cry them innocent or money to buy their freedom. Tavig could not even let the people know that he was a knight and a laird, for such information would surely put him back in the murderous hands of his cousin Iver. When she found herself praying that he did not think of that as a way to save her life, she realized how much he had begun to mean to her.

That disturbing revelation was still clear in her mind when he touched his lips to hers. Moira curled her arms around his neck, meeting his kiss with a fierce mixture of passion and desperation. Tavig groaned softly, pushing her down onto the cold, hard dirt. She offered no resistance, welcoming the bold strokes of his hands on her body. If she was to die, she was not going to do so without having known the fullness of the desire they shared.

Chapter Seven

"Here now, laddie, that be enough of that."

It took Tavig a moment to realize he was hearing a voice. It took another moment to realize that he could savor the look of passion on Moira's face because there was now light in their prison. Even as he saw her eyes widen with a look of embarrassment and a touch of hope, he shook away the last of passion's blinding grip, easing his body off hers. Blinking rapidly as his eyes adjusted to the sudden light, he turned to look up. He was both glad and annoyed that he had not had the time to remove any of their clothing. Moira had been ready to make love, he was certain of it. Although he welcomed the opportunity for escape, he wished it had come much later.

"Ye best have a verra good reason for this visit," he grumbled, recognizing the burly innkeeper looking down at them.

The innkeeper laughed as he lowered a rope ladder. "Ye and your wife can finish your loving elsewhere."

Tavig was not so sure Moira would be willing once they were safe, but he quickly got to his feet, pulling Moira to hers. "Ye are letting us go?"

"Aye, laddie. Oh, I think ye did have a vision or the like," he continued as Tavig urged Moira up the ladder, "but I dinnae consider the sight such a bad thing. Nay, especially not when it saved the life of my own wee grandchild." He grasped Moira by the wrist, tugging her up out of the hatchway.

Moira gasped when she saw six other people in the inn gathered around the opening to her and Tavig's prison. She only relaxed a little when she recognized two of them as the little girl's parents. When Tavig got out, he quickly moved to her side, and she stepped closer to him, her trepidation easing somewhat when he put his arm around her shoulders. It was a little hard to believe they were going to be released, but they were out of that hole. It was enough to give her hope.

"Why did ye let them drag us away?" she asked, not sure she trusted this sudden change of heart.

"I am sorry for that," replied the child's mother. "We were confused, stunned, in truth. We had thought your mon was stealing our child, but then saw that he had saved her life. Ere we had time to understand what had happened, the folk were crying witch, and what followed was past stopping. We made the quick decision that 'twould be safer for all of us if we waited and then helped ye creep away from Craigmoordun."

"That could put ye in danger," said Tavig. "Have ye planned a good explanation for why we were able to flee?"

"Aye," the innkeeper assured him. "In truth, I think ye would have found a way yourself, laddie. There is more than enough in that storage room to have aided ye and, given time, I am sure ye would have put it to good use. We will drag one of the ale kegs over and set it beneath the hatch, then shatter the door. There is a heavy mallet down there to show folk how ye could have done it. I will be given a wee knock to the jaw so I can say ye overpowered me. Dinnae fret, I willnae cry ye gone until I have to. I hope that willnae be till many an hour has passed, but ye should move fast, laddie. Get as far away as ye can. Get off Craigmoordun land. Once ye do ye will be safe."

"How do I ken when I am off Craigmoordun land?"

"Ye head north, and when ye cross a wee brook ye have left this accursed place. I would go a few miles beyond that just to be safe, although I doubt anyone will cross after ye. As I told ye, we are surrounded by foes." The innkeeper returned Tavig's weapons as he spoke.

"Would it not be better to wait until dark?"

"Aye, but the folk have chosen a guard for you. Believing I would wish to rest, they have chosen a burly lad to sit here all through the night. Ye must leave now."

"Show me which door to creep out of, then. I thank ye for giving us this chance." As Tavig grabbed Moira by the hand and started to follow the innkeeper, the little girl's mother thrust two sacks at him. "What is this?" he asked as he took one, Moira warily accepting the other.

"Food for your journey," the woman answered. "I also put in a pair of shoes and a few bits of clothing for your wife. I think they will fit her." The woman briefly frowned at the delicate Moira. "'Twas hard to find something in such a small size."

The way the woman began to study Moira closely made Tavig uneasy. Too careful an inspection would tell the woman Moira was no ragged pauper despite her attire. Moira might have callouses on her hands and feet, but everything else about her bespoke quality. Tavig did not want any more questions or suspicions roused.

"Thank ye, mistress. We have a dire need of all those things, ill-fitting or not. We must go now, Moira," he said, tugging sharply at Moira's hand and waving the innkeeper on. He scowled at her when she resisted his pull, freeing her hand.

"Thank ye, mistress." Moira echoed Tavig and, setting down her sack, briefly clasped the woman's hand.

The moment her hands enclosed the woman's, Moira realized she had made a mistake, perhaps even a fatal one. The calloused hand she held was knotted with pain. The woman's tired eyes widened as Moira's touch began to work its magic. Silently, trying to put all of her own fear and a plea for secrecy into her expression, Moira held the woman's gaze as she finished the work she had inadvertently begun. As soon as she was certain her gift could do no more, she released the woman's hand, picked up her sack, and followed Tavig.

Flora Dunn stared after the couple as they hurried away, then stared at her hand. She closed it into a fist and opened it again and again until she realized the rest of her family was staring at her. Without a word she reached out, grasping her husband's hand and squeezing. There was no pain. Her husband's eyes also widened, and she felt hers sting with tears. One by one she clasped the hands of the rest of her family until they all stared at her with a mixture of wonder and confusion.

"What miracle has cured your hand, child?" asked her father, the innkeeper in a hoarse voice, taking her now straight and limber hand in his.

"That tiny woman but held it for a moment, 'tis all. She enfolded my crippled hand between both of hers, and 'twas as if all the knots within my hand eased apart."

An old woman shuffled forward to touch Flora's hand timidly. "Then they *were* witches."

"Nay," snapped the innkeeper. "Mother, when have witches e'er done a kind thing? My child's hand is now strong and straight instead of cramped and gnarled with pain. My wee bonnie grandchild is alive instead of trampled beneath the hooves of our laird's warhorses. Nay, that lad but has the sight and his wee lass has the healing touch. God preserve them, they have blessed us twice."

"I dinnae think he kens she has the gift of healing," murmured Flora. "In her eyes was a plea for silence."

"Weel, the path they are taking is a treacherous one. He will soon ken her secret as the time will come for her to use it on him. I fear trouble stalks those two."

* * *

"Tavig, cannae we rest yet?" Moira asked. But she did not slow down as she followed Tavig's swift progress through the heather and treacherous patches of thistle. "I need to catch my breath."

It felt to Moira as if they had been moving at a steady lope for hours. She was not sure she could trot another mile. Her feet hurt, and the sack she carried began to feel as if it were filled with bricks.

"Not yet, lass. I think that wee burn we must cross is just ahead. I can hear the sound of tumbling water."

She listened carefully for a moment and nodded. "Aye, I can hear it, too."

Cursing herself for being a coward, she looked behind her for what she was sure was the hundredth time. The woman whose hand she had healed had made no outcry, but Moira still feared their rescuers would suffer a change of heart and come after them. She cursed herself again for not having been more careful, for not having looked at the woman closely before impulsively enfolding her hand in her own. If she had been more cautious she would have seen that the woman had a crippled hand. In that one moment of impulsiveness she could have ruined everything—exposed her secret or, worse, put a swift end to all chance of escape for herself and Tavig.

She had risked enough while she and Tavig had been prisoners. Tavig could have guessed that she had eased his pain with her touch. It had been impossible just to sit by and leave him in pain, however. She had decided to take the risk that her special gift would be revealed. The fact that Tavig had been unconscious during most of her work had helped her maintain her secret. The woman had been a complete mistake, however. Moira prayed that the fear she had been gripped with then as she had faced possible exposure would be enough to remind her of the important need to be cautious.

"There it is, loving," Tavig announced, dropping her hand and bounding ahead to study the brook they would have to cross.

Moira walked up to stand at his side, frowning at the rapidly flowing water. It was clear enough for her to see the rocky bottom, but she could not judge its depth accurately. Neither could she see a way to cross it without getting extremely wet.

"It looks deep, cold, and it runs too swiftly," she muttered. "I dinnae suppose we can find a way to walk around it."

"Nay, sweeting. Straight across."

"Weel, ye shall get verra wet carrying those sacks and me."

Tavig laughed, stepping into the water and yanking her along after him, "'Tis not enough to drown you."

A small screech escaped her as the bitter cold of the water cut through her clothes. She quickly put the small sack she carried on top of her head, holding it there with one hand. She muttered complaints and curses all the way across, ignoring Tavig's amusement. Complaining helped her control her fear when, in the middle of the little river, the swift water rose up to her waist, chilling her to the bone as it pulled at her.

"There, on land again and safe," he said, helping her climb up the mossy bank.

"Aye, but chilled to the bone." She set down her sack to squeeze the cold water from her skirts.

"It was a wee bit brisk."

"Brisk! 'Twas ice that forgot to grow hard. We shall both catch the fever and die."

"Nay, the sun is warm, and the sky is clear of clouds. We will be dry again soon enough."

He took her hand, starting up a low, rocky rise leading into a thick wood. It had not taken him long to see that Moira's complaints were but a way to hide her fear. She never faltered and was proving to have a surprising strength. That had certainly been revealed back in the village when, instead of fleeing, she had tried to help him. Her talk of fever did worry him, however, even though he knew she was fond of predicting their deaths at every new obstacle they faced.

The moment he had felt the bite of that cold water, he had been concerned about what it would do to her. Despite the fortitude Moira had revealed, she was a delicate woman, reed-slim and small. Tavig wanted to get her to a place where they could camp as fast as possible. He needed to build a fire to warm her and dry her clothes. He wished he had been able to steal them a horse so that they could make the rest of their journey in some comfort and with a little more speed, but fleeing in the midst of a sun-drenched afternoon had been risky enough. On foot it would be another hour or so before it would be safe to camp. By then the chill of the water could be settling into Moira far more firmly than was healthy.

Nearly two hours passed before Tavig found a spot where they could camp for the night. The sun was beginning to set, its warmth rapidly diminishing. The small clearing in the midst of the thick wood had a clear path to the rocky hills just to the north. It was almost perfect. If they were spotted by anyone, they had a chance, a very good chance, of making it into the hills where pursuit would become extremely difficult. Tavig wasted no time in digging a shallow pit and starting their fire for, despite her attempts to hide it, Moira was shivering.

"Take those wet clothes off, lass," he ordered, taking out his flint, crouching by the pile of sticks he had made and striking a spark. He carefully nursed the small spark he made in the dry kindling.

"Take my clothes off?" Moira frowned at him as she set down her sack. "I cannae do that here."

"There is no one about to see you, dearling. We are quite alone."

"Ye are still here."

"I willnae look." He stood up, extracting a thin blanket from the pack he had made up at the fisherman's cottage. He advanced on Moira. "Here, I will hold this up as ye take those wet clothes off then ye can wrap this around yourself." When she still hesitated, he cursed. "Ye need to get warm and dry, loving, and ye cannae do so standing about in those sodden clothes." He turned his face away. "Get 'em off."

Tavig did his best to keep his eyes averted, but decided it was more than should be asked of any man. The soft rustle she made as she slipped out of her clothes could not be ignored. Even as he looked he hoped she would not consider it too large a breach of her trust. He did not want to ruin what few gains he had made in easing her wariness simply because he could not resist temptation.

When he glanced her way he drew his breath in so sharply he was briefly afraid that he had already given himself away. She was easing off the thin remains of her nightgown which served as her chemise, slowly revealing herself. He knew it was going to be very difficult to continue to woo her gently and slowly draw out her passion now that he had seen all he hungered for.

Her breasts were small and perfectly shaped, the honey-colored tips hardened by the chill of the air. His mouth watered as he imagined how they would taste. There was no excess flesh on her delicate frame. She reminded him of a young colt, sleek and limber. Her waist was tiny, her hips gently rounded. Despite her lack of height, her slender, beautifully shaped legs were long. Her skin was a soft white, and his hands tingled as he thought of how that skin would feel beneath his touch. As she dropped her chemise, he quickly turned away, praying that she would not see how aroused he was, for she would be sure to guess that he had been spying on her.

Moira gave a little tug on the blanket, and Tavig immediately released it. He flashed her a brief, strained smile and quickly moved back to the fire. Wrapping the blanket around herself, she sat down across from him, but he paid her no attention. He concentrated on mixing up some porridge. He remained tensely silent as they ate, but could not shake the image of her slender form from his mind. It was painfully easy to imagine her lithe body curled around him as he made her his lover. He found it impossible to dismiss the thought, even though it made him ache uncomfortably with need.

As soon as they had finished eating, he moved to find a store of firewood. He found some sticks to drape her damp clothes on, taking them down from the tree branches she had hung them on. Tavig prayed that keeping busy might ease the hunger for her which was knotting up his insides.

"The nearer they are to the fire the faster they will dry," he muttered in explanation and, not waiting for an answer, began to set out their bedding.

Moira clutched her blanket around her, glanced at the clothing the village woman had given her, and then looked at Tavig. The clothes would be big, but they would serve. They were of such a rough homespun, however. She dreaded donning them without putting on her nightgown as a chemise to protect her skin. Still watching Tavig, who was taking far more than his usual care in spreading out their bed, she tried to hitch the blanket more securely around herself. It, too, was itchy, but not nearly as rough as the clothes.

What concerned her far more than what she was or was not wearing was the way Tavig was acting. He had barely spoken to her, and she had been prepared for a slew of teasing remarks. The man loved to make her blush. She scrubbed out their battered wooden bowls with a little water and sand as she tried to ignore his odd mood, but the menial chore failed to distract her fully.

Another look Tavig's way revealed him scowling at their bedding as he knelt beside it.

Moira grew nervous. Tavig looked angry. Angry men were dangerous men. She prepared herself to be as silent and unobtrusive as possible, but suddenly she felt that was not the right thing to do. Moira realized she wanted to know what troubled Tavig. She was willing to suffer any of the consequences that could result from intruding on his black mood. She took a deep breath, cautiously approached him, and knelt beside him.

"Tavig? Have I done something to anger you?"

When he whirled to look at her, she instinctively flinched, huddling away from him. He cursed, and she trembled. Despite her best intentions to be brave and resolute, she tensed, cringing inside when he grasped her by the shoulders and gave her a slight shaking. Moira realized that she was not afraid of the pain he might inflict, but that *he* would be the one to inflict it. She desperately wanted him to be different.

"Sweet Mary, lass, dinnae cringe from me."

"Ye are angry."

"Nay, I am not angry. But what matter if I was? Think, my wee timid Moira. What have ye done that would give me the right to be angry at you?"

She frowned as she stared at him, then said, "Naught. I have done naught." She relaxed a little, her fear easing as annoyance crept over her. "So why *are* ye angry, then?"

"Weel, I am *not* angry. 'Tis something else that causes my dark mood. That woman's clothes will fit ye?"

His gaze left her face. She frowned a little over how abruptly he had changed the subject. When she felt him move his hands over her bare shoulders in a light caress, she began to lean toward him. A moment later she noticed that he was staring intently at where the blanket was cinched beneath her arms and lightly tucked around her breasts. There was a look on his face she had come to recognize well over the last week. Tavig's desire was running hot. A searing memory of the passionate embraces they had shared while in their prison tore through her mind. She felt her desire for him sweeping through her.

Tavig wanted her—badly. Moira found the knowledge intoxicating. She wanted him now as desperately as she had when they had been held captive, facing the often gruesome death meted out to condemned witches. Suddenly Moira knew that clinging to her innocence might be the right thing to do, the wisest thing to do, but she no longer wanted to be right or wise. She no longer wanted to hold herself in righteous purity for a marriage that might never come or would be arranged without any consideration for her feelings. She wanted Tavig, she wanted to know the fullness of the passion his kisses stirred within her. And she no longer cared if she would have to pay some penalty later for giving in to that greed.

"Tavig?" She briefly touched his thick hair, causing him to look at her.

Tavig cursed softly, abruptly releasing her. "Sorry, lass. I willnae do anything ye dinnae want, so ye need not look so worried." He sat down and yanked off his boots. "We had best get some sleep, lass."

She frowned and remained kneeling by their meager bed as he stripped down to his hose. "But I thought—"

"Thought what? That I hungered for ye? Aye, I have since I first set eyes on ye. And right now, seeing ye sitting there wearing naught but a thin blanket, the firelight kissing your bonnie shoulders, I am twisted up inside with hunger for you. But ye need not fret. Aye, I willnae stop trying to woo ye into my arms, but I willnae try to take what I want. So lie ye down and let us get some twice-cursed sleep," he grumbled as he sprawled on his back.

Moira almost smiled when she heard the sulkiness in his voice. He was behaving honorably, but he was not enjoying it at all. She then frowned, wondering how she could let him know he did not have to be a gentleman any longer. It would require a boldness she was not sure she could muster. There was the lurking fear that by acting boldly, she could make him think poorly of her or, worse, discover she had misjudged the depth of his desire for her.

She took a deep breath to strengthen her resolve and, in a soft, somewhat timid voice, said, "Mayhap ye need not woo me so gently anymore." A soft cry of surprise escaped her when, in one clean, swift move, he was kneeling in front her.

"What did ye just say? I want to be sure I heard ye correctly, lass."

Although she could feel a blush burning in her cheeks, she repeated, "I said mayhap ye need not woo me so gently now."

His hands unsteady, he reached out to draw her thick braid forward over her shoulder and began to unravel it. "There will be no turning back, dearling. I cannae return what I will take from ye if we become lovers."

"I ken it. I have decided I"—She cleared her throat—"I want ye to have it as I have no wish to die still clutching my purity and, if I wed, I willnae have a choice in whom I give it to." When he did nothing more than unbraid her hair and comb his fingers through it, she grew uneasy, unsure of herself. "Why do ye hesitate?"

"Ye have so much fear in ye, loving. I need to be verra sure ye ken what ye ask for, because I dinnae wish to move too swiftly or step wrong. Then I would do naught but add to your fears."

Moira was not sure how much more she could do to convince him that she knew exactly what she wanted. She had said aye. She had confessed to wanting him. She had declared that she did not wish to cling to her purity any longer. What else could she say? Then instinct told her that words would not be enough. She had to act. Astounded at her boldness, she slowly unhitched the blanket, allowing it to fall in a heap around her hips.

Chapter Eight

Tavig groaned softly as he stared at her. The feelings rushing through him were so strong they held him motionless. Moira was freely offering him everything he ached for. Suddenly he was terrified he would do something wrong. She needed to be treated so carefully. Did he have the skills needed?

"Tavig?" she whispered, reaching for the blanket.

"Nay." He stopped her from covering herself again, smiling at her. "I but suffer from cowardice."

"Cowardice? I dinnae understand."

"Ah, lass, ye are so innocent." He traced the shape of her full mouth with one fingertip. "Ye are so delicate. For years ye have seen only the worst of men. I but fear to step wrong, to fail to please you, and mayhap just add to your own fears."

"I dinnae fear ye, Tavig. I ken I sometimes flinch or cower, but 'tis more out of habit than fear." She took a deep breath, slipping her arms around his neck and pressing close to him. "I also have the wit to ken that I have asked for this. If it isnae to my liking, ye need not fear I will blame you. But," she said with a smile, brushing her lips over his, "I wouldnae ask if I didnae think I would like it just fine."

A tremor of want tore through Tavig. Wrapping his arms around Moira, he pulled her down onto their meager bed. He cupped her face in his hands as he kissed her, savoring the heated sweetness of her mouth. The way she shyly bandied the strokes of his tongue, the way she pressed against him, told him she was willing. Tavig knew it was going to be hard to go slowly, gently. His desire for her was fierce and greedy.

Moira felt her nervousness and hint of fear smoothed away with each stroke of his tongue, each touch of his hand. This was what she wanted. She had no doubts about it. She also knew she would have no regrets. For ten long years she had known no happiness and no affection. Tavig had made no mention of love, but he was kind, gentle, and he made her blood burn. Moira was certain this would be as close to love as she would ever get, and she intended to enjoy it to the fullest. After facing death in Craigmoordun, she knew any consequences she might face for being so free with her favors would never equal the regret she would suffer for continuing to say no to Tavig.

She blushed as Tavig tugged away the blanket caught around her hips. He crouched over her, staring at her, and she knew some of the color burning in her cheeks was caused by her own desire. It was exciting to be looked at so passionately by a man like Tavig MacAlpin. Moira did not doubt that Tavig wanted her. It was clear to read in the taut lines of his face. But she still found it hard to believe.

"Ah, lass, ye hold a lot of beauty in this tiny body," Tavig murmured, shedding the last of his clothes.

A man's body was not unfamiliar to Moira. Sir Bearnard's men were not modest, and complete privacy was often an unattainable luxury. She had never seen one to match Tavig's, however. The few glimpses she had caught of other men had never caused her heart to pound so hard it echoed in her ears or stole her breath away. As he lowered his lean, strong, body onto her, she reached out to pull him close, shuddering when their flesh met.

"Loving, ye feel so bonnie. Like warm silk." Tavig gently traced the shape of her face with soft kisses.

"Ye feel rather bonnie yourself," she whispered, tentatively running her hands over his broad, smooth back.

"There is still time to stop, sweet Moira."

"Nay, I dinnae wish to stop." She could feel the hard proof of his desire for her pressing against her, enticing her. "I want this and for the first time in a verra long time I will do what *I* want. Is that so wrong?"

"Ye cannae expect a fair answer from me, lassie. Not when we lie naked in each other's arms. Yet, nay, 'tisnae wrong. From what little I saw and what little ye tell me, ye are deserving of a wee bit of pleasure. I but pray I can give it to ye. I am no green lad, but I have ne'er bedded down with a lass like you, Moira Robertson."

"If it ends as weel as it starts, I believe I will be verra well pleased, Sir MacAlpin."

She eagerly welcomed his hungry kiss. He felt so good beneath her hands. His skin was warm and taut over smooth, hard muscle. The hair on his long legs felt rough against her skin, yet that, too, excited her. The light calloses on his hands aroused her as he stroked her. When he slid his hands up her sides to cup her breasts, she arched eagerly into his touch. Tangling her hands in his thick hair, she held him close as he covered her breasts with hot kisses. A soft cry of delight escaped her when he lathed the hardened tips with his tongue. She thought she had never felt anything so pleasurable, and then he drew the taut nipple deep into his mouth, suckling greedily. Moira sank beneath waves of pure feeling, the heat of passion flowing rapidly through her body.

Tavig reveled in the passion Moira was revealing. His own desire was running so hot and wild he found control difficult. He caressed her with his hands and body, enflamed by the way she shifted against him, her body clearly expressing her eagerness for him. Slowly he slid his hand upward along her inner thigh and gently stroked the bright curls hiding the treasure he so desperately sought. A moment before he realized she had tensed beneath his intimate touch.

"Be easy, dearling," he said, brushing his lips over hers. "I do no wrong."

"Nay?" Moira asked even as she opened to his touch.

"Aye, give yourself o'er to me, sweeting. Dinnae shy from this or from anything that can bring us pleasure. I but seek to make ye more welcoming."

"I dinnae think I can be much more welcoming."

He laughed softly against the side of her neck as he trailed his increasingly feverish kisses back toward her breasts. "Such heat, such sweet fire. How can ye keep denying that we are destined?"

"'Tis the kinder thing to do—for both of us." She clutched at his broad shoulders, wrapping her legs around him as a tightening in her body urged her to draw him closer. "Tavig," she called, yet could not think of the words to describe what she was feeling.

"Ye are ready, sweet bonnie Moira. I fear I must hurt ye a wee bit, now."

"I ken it. That much I do ken." She grew still as she felt him probe for entry into her body.

"I dinnae wish to hurt ye," he whispered, pressing his forehead against hers.

"Then mayhap 'tis best to do it quickly."

Her eyes widening, she held him tightly as she felt him ease into her. Even in the shadowy light from the moon and the banked fire she could see the tension in his face. The light glistened off beads of sweat on his upper lip. Then suddenly he grasped her by the hips and pushed into her. A sharp tearing pain caused her to gasp and close her eyes, but it quickly became insignificant compared to the feeling of their bodies uniting. His heavy breaths heated her ear. He moved his hands over her body lightly, gently.

So caught up was she in savoring the feeling of his being inside of her, of their being one, it was a moment before she realized he was not moving. She opened her eyes to find him staring at her.

"Is something wrong?" she asked barely able to recognize the soft, husky voice as her own.

"I hurt ye. Ye cried out in pain."

"'Twas but a wee hurt, already forgotten."

She trailed her fingers down the backs of his thighs. He jerked and trembled beneath her touch, his body moving inside of her. Moira gasped, the slight stroking movement causing her desire to flare up so intensely it was almost painful. Moira knew that the last things she wanted Tavig to be right now were still and gentle. Watching him closely, she slid her hands up the backs of his thighs until she cupped his taut backside. She pulled him closer, deeper. She savored his groan, his shudder, for she knew they were born of passion.

"Lass, if ye keep tormenting me so, I willnae be able to go slowly, mayhap not even gently," he said in a raspy voice, his words broken by his strained breathing.

"I believe I dinnae want ye to be either, Tavig Mac-Alpin."

Kissing him lightly, she wrapped her body more tightly around his. She teased his lips with her tongue, and that was all the added incentive he needed. He kissed her hungrily and began to move. Moira quickly learned to parry his increasingly feverish thrusts. The strokes of his tongue matched the rhythm of his body. The pleasurable tightening she had felt before her passion had been checked by the loss of her maidenhead returned in full force. It grew until she groaned beneath the weight of it, then shattered. Moira cried out as she was engulfed by a pleasure that stole all thought, all sense of where she was. She clung to Tavig as his movements grew briefly frantic, then he cried out her name, his hands clenching her hips as he pressed deep inside of her. Still tingling and dazed, she held him close when he collapsed in her arms.

Moira was not sure how long she lay there savoring the feelings that lingered throughout her body, but suddenly she began to be aware of other things. The hard ground began to impress itself upon her back. Her neck was growing hot and moist where Tavig was pressing his face against it. She tried to call back the intoxicating feelings, but they continued to fade.

"I didnae realize it could go away," she murmured.

Easing the intimacy of their embrace, Tavig propped himself up on one elbow to look at her. "What went away, sweet Moira?"

"I am not sure what to call it." Blushing and unable to meet his gaze, she admitted, "'Twas a feeling. 'Twas verra nice, but it didnae stay as long as I would have liked it to." She heard him chuckle and looked at him, feeling the sting of embarrassment. "I have said something foolish."

"Nay, loving." He cupped her face in his hands, giving her a gentle kiss. "Ye are all sweetness and fire. My laugh is born of hearing ye say ye felt pleasure. I heard ye cry out, felt your body thrash around mine, but I fear I was so lost in my own hungers by then, I couldnae be sure of what I felt."

When he rose from their bed, Moira frowned, tugging the discarded blanket over her suddenly chilled body. He returned a moment later with a wet cloth. Moira blushed furiously as he yanked her covering away, washed her off, and held the cool cloth between her legs for several moments. That felt good, but his grin at her embarrassment kept her scowling at him. Just like a man, she mused, tugging the blanket back over herself when he finished tending her. No appreciation for even the simplest of modesties.

Tavig laughed softly, tossing the cloth aside. Moira's sudden concern over her nakedness amused him as did her irritation over his amusement. That touch of modesty did not hinder her passion in any way so he found it endearing. Checking to be sure his sword and dagger were close at hand, he slipped beneath the blanket and tugged her into his arms. The feel of her soft skin against his immediately restirred his desire, but he forcibly quelled it. Her first time had brought her pleasure, but he knew it had also brought her pain. He would let her have some time to recover from that.

"Now ye are mine, Moira," he murmured, combing his fingers through her lightly tangled hair.

"Are ye going to start that mad talk of marriage again?"

"Most women wouldnae consider it mad."

"I might not, either, had ye not started speaking of it from the first day we met. And, as I have told ye, verra clearly and verra often, 'twould be pure lunacy for us to marry. Ye dinnae have to wed me because of this, either."

"Wedded or not, ye are still mine." He smiled when she leaned back a little to send him a cross look.

"Ye are verra particular about that, I see."

"Aye. I am. I thought it only fair to tell ye how I feel about it."

"Humph." She settled herself comfortably back in his arms. "Ye are an arrogant mon, Tavig MacAlpin."

"So I have often been told. And, after what we have just shared, I feel I have some right to my arrogance."

"It was *shared,* was it? Ye felt there was something different, did ye?"

"Oh, aye, loving. Mightily different. I have kent my share of lovers—"

"I dinnae think I wish to ken this part of your past," she muttered.

He laughed, kissing the top of her head and briefly hugging her. "It pleases me to hear that hint of jealousy." Tavig ignored her grumbled denial of such an emotion. "None of those other women has given me what ye have tonight. None of them has fired my blood as ye have. What we share is what every mon with any wit has a hunger for. 'Twas no

simple rutting. *That* is what I had in the past. Nay, with ye
'twas blinding heat and fierce, compelling passion."

But not love, Moira thought, inwardly sighing. She
wanted Tavig to love her. The moment their bodies had
united, Moira knew she loved him, deeply and incurably.
She wanted him to feel the same. She did not wish to hear
any more pretty words about passion, fate, or destiny. She
wanted Tavig to shout out that he loved her.

She then cursed herself for her selfishness. Making him
fall in love with her would be cruel even if she could accomplish such a task. She could not marry him without
bringing the full dangerous weight of people's superstitions down on their heads. It was kinder to leave him believing her to be one of his more enjoyable lovers. Then
only she would suffer when they had to part. To draw out
his love would only serve to stroke her vanity.

"I—" She gave a muffled cry of surprise when Tavig
suddenly covered her mouth with his hand.

"Get your clothes on, lass," he ordered in a whisper,
snatching up their blanket and using it to smother their
fire.

Moira obeyed him without hesitation. Fear gripping her
tightly by the throat, her mind a confusing whirl of questions, she silently and hastily dressed. Collecting up their
bedding and her sack, she followed Tavig into the surrounding wood. She headed for the rocky hills where
Tavig had said they would hide, but, while still within
sight of their camp, he veered to the right. Moira stopped,
staring after him in confusion. He reached out, grasped her
by the arm and pulled her along after him. When they
reached a tight knot of trees half encircled by a thick un-
dergrowth, he set their things down.

"I thought we were running away from something," she
whispered, crouching down at Tavig's side.

"Aye, we were and we will continue to do so as soon as
I ken who we are running from."

"Someone is coming?" she asked, hearing the approach

of horses even as she spoke. "Do ye think they search for us?"

"The innkeeper didnae think anyone from Craigmoor-dun would dare cross that water, and I dinnae see any reason to question his judgment. Still, 'twould be best to ken who trails us. We may have need to change our course."

Six burly men rode into the clearing, and Moira huddled closer to Tavig. The leader dismounted and knelt by the remains of their fire. He yanked off his gauntlet, gingerly touching the still-warm ashes.

"They cannae have been gone but a few minutes," he said.

"They must ken that we are near, Tavig," Moira said, speaking close to his ear.

"Aye. I think these are the men the innkeeper fears so much. 'Tis also clear they have kenned that we are on their lands and rode in here to find us." He picked up his things. "I think we had better leave, dearling."

"I think ye and your dearling had better come with me," drawled a deep voice,

Tavig whirled, clasping the hilt of his sword. Moira wriggled back when he swung his arm to push her behind him. The man who spoke was huge, wearing only his plaid. His long sword was pointed at Tavig, as were the swords of his two smaller and grinning companions. Moira was sure that they were about to die.

"Now, laddie," said the man, "do ye really want to cross swords with three men whilst *dearling* is here? Up now. We will go and talk to Old Colin, eh? I will have those weapons of yours first, though."

Cursing softly, Tavig stood up and handed the man his weapons. He kept an eye on the three grinning men as he picked up his and Moira's belongings. Putting his arm around a faintly trembling Moira's shoulders, he allowed himself to be led back to the clearing. His mind worked feverishly over ways to ensure Moira's safety.

He faced the man poking idly at the relit fire. Since his

captors had nudged him and Moira toward the man, Tavig knew this had to be Old Colin. Except for the white streaking the man's long, shaggy dark hair, Tavig saw little sign of age in this hard-muscled man closely studying him and Moira. Old Colin looked impressively wild in his plaid and his wolfskin cape. Tavig relaxed a little as he met the man's steady gaze, for he could find nothing to fear there. He prayed that his confidence was born of his instincts and not false hope.

"Now, laddie," Old Colin said, "I think ye should tell me why ye are roaming across my lands."

"I think they be that pair that fled Craigmoordun," said the largest of their three captors.

"Aye, Lachlan, they are. What I want to hear is why they fled that wee village as if the devil's hounds were nipping at their heels. Do ye have a good answer for that?" Colin asked Tavig.

"I saved a wee child's life," Tavig answered, smiling grimly at Colin's narrow-eyed stare. "Aye, 'tis all. I saw that she would be trampled by the laird's men-at-arms so I pulled her out of the road. No one else saw the danger, so felt I must have used some devil's trick. They cried me a witch." Feeling Moira tremble at the mere mention of the word, he hugged her a little closer to his side. "My wife tried to intervene and was also accused."

"So why arenae ye waiting for the priest to pile kindling about your feet and strike his flint?"

"The family of the child decided that roasting us wasnae the proper way to thank us for their child's life."

"And your names?"

"Tavig and Moira."

"Ye have no clan, no laird?"

"Not at this moment." Tavig was a little surprised when the man grinned.

"And where are ye traveling to?"

"North, to my cousin Sir Mungan Coll."

"Ah, a fine mon. Honorable, a good warrior, and a staunch ally if ye can win him to your side. A wee bit odd."

"Ye ken my cousin weel, do ye?" Several more fires had been lit, and the smell of roasting venison was making his mouth water, but Tavig fought to hide it.

"His fool of a father gifted me with a wee scrap of land ere Mungan was old enough to curb the old mon's vagaries. Last year Mungan got that scrap back."

"Ye fought with my cousin?"

"Nay. The land wasnae worth a battle, and Mungan Coll isnae a mon I care to have snarling at my back. And your cunning cousin Iver was turning his evil eye toward it."

Tavig tensed although he did not sense any real threat from Colin. "Ye ken exactly who I am, dinnae ye?"

"Aye, laddie. Now, ye and your woman can sit down and have a wee bit of venison and ale. Dinnae fear," he added as Moira and Tavig sat down, facing him across the fire. "I willnae be handing ye over to Sir Iver MacAlpin though he does offer a handsome purse for your capture and return. I want no dealing with a mon as sly as Iver. Aye, and Mungan spoke only good of ye whilst warning me to beware of Iver. A back-gnawing rat, he called him."

"Then ye will let us go on our way?"

"Aye. I wish I could give ye a horse to help ye, but I dinnae have enough for my own men. A sickness took o'er half my stable this past spring. 'Tis verra slow work to steal back what I need from the folks in Craigmoordun."

Courtesy demanded that he keep up his part of the conversation, but Tavig found it difficult when he and Moira were given a plate of venison and a tankard of ale to share. "The people in Craigmoordun are terrified of ye. They say ye will murder anyone who steps onto your land." Colin and his men laughed. Frowning, Tavig took advantage of the brief diversion to savor the freshly roasted meat and hearty ale.

"Half the men ye see here were once Craigmoordun men. Aye, and Craigmoordun was once mine." Colin shook a half-gnawed bone at Tavig. "The leader Duncan MacBean, what squats in that tower, has sucked all the life out of that wee village and its good people. He stole Craigmoordun from my father through deceit and murder. I tried to retain what was mine, but my father built that thrice-cursed tower weel. Many a good mon has died at its walls. Being slaughtered at the foot of that lump of stone gains me naught."

"I cannae believe ye have given up."

"Nay, 'twas your cousin Mungan who told me how to regain it. Steal it, he said. Steal it back mon by mon, woman by woman, horse by horse. One day that bastard Duncan will wake up to find that he has naught but empty fields, empty stables, and only a handful of men too scared or too stupid to leave him. Then I can retake that tower. Whenever we face a MacBean we offer him a chance to join our cause. Aye, some die, for they choose to fight. Many are glad to shake off the yoke of Duncan, feeling the vow of loyalty they gave him was forced from them and thus not binding and heartfelt. If I trust their word, they become part of my clan. Some return to be my eyes and ears within the village. MacBean's sergeant-at-arms is one of my men. 'Tisnae as glorious as battle, but 'tis working."

"And most of your men and kinsmen will be alive to share in the success."

"Exactly. So when ye see that great hulking cousin of yours, tell him that his idea has worked. He may wish to use it himself someday."

For hours Tavig and Old Colin talked. The man was eager for any information his visitor had about events and changes in the world outside his lands. Tavig did not realize how long he and Colin had talked until Moira slumped against him, sleeping soundly.

"Poor lassie," murmured Colin. "'Tis a wonder that any kin of Bearnard Robertson's could be so sweet of face."

Tavig slowly smiled at Colin. "Is there anything that remains a secret to you?"

"Aye, but I try verra hard not to let there be too many

secrets and that they dinnae stay secret for too long. 'Tis no great feat of cunning to ken who she is. My cousin visits with me now, and he saw Robertson's ship limping into harbor three days south of here. The tale of how ye and she were swept away was much told. 'Tis said that Robertson wasnae suffering much grief, but that he was annoyed. Aye, enraged. The lass will fare better out of his reach. Robertson has long been named a brutish mon. My men have spread out your bedding o'er there beneath that tree."

"Thank ye for your kindness, sir," Tavig said, gently picking Moira up in his arms as he stood up.

"And I thank ye, laddie. Ye have given me more information than I have gathered in a twelvemonth. Dinnae let Robertson get his fat hands on the wee lass."

"'Tis a deed already done, sir. When she fell out of that ship, Robertson lost all claim to her. I but need to make her understand that." Tavig smiled as Colin laughed.

Chapter Nine

Moira woke to hot, fierce passion rushing through her body. She arched beneath Tavig's stroking hands. Threading her fingers through his hair she pulled his mouth down to hers, hungrily kissing him, groaning softly with eagerness when he met and equaled the desire he had roused in her. She wrapped her limbs around him, crying out in soft welcome as he joined their bodies. She rose up to meet him as his thrusting body took her to the engulfing release she craved. He quickly joined her in that blinding fall into passion's heady whirlpool, their cries of pleasure echoing in the wood.

She was savoring the tingling vestiges of her release, enjoying the way Tavig lethargically stroked her body and nuzzled her neck, when she recalled what had been going on just before she fell asleep. A cry of horror escaped her, and she pushed Tavig away. Sitting up, she clutched a blanket to her chest and looked around.

"Where is everyone?" she asked, ignoring Tavig's muttered curses as he brushed dirt and leaves off his backside.

"Did ye think I would be loving ye with a dozen men looking on?" he asked and laughed, shaking his head.

"Weel, nay, I didnae really think that." She shrugged, smiling at him. "I dinnae ken what I was thinking. I just suddenly recalled that there had been a crowd of people here when I fell asleep. Where did they go?"

"Back to Colin's keep. We met up with them because they had been chasing some Craigmoordun men back home. The same lot of men who nearly rode over that child." He tossed her her clothes, then began to dress.

"I was afraid he would take ye back to your cousin Iver." She slipped on her chemise.

"Aye, so was I for a moment. Old Colin was a wee bit tempted, but he couldnae stomach dealing with Iver. 'Tis the first time my cousin's blackheartedness has done me some good. A shame we couldnae get a horse, though."

"Weel, we are half the way there."

"And we have even more food plus an extra blanket," he said, standing and pointing to their new supplies. "I will make some porridge, lass. We dinnae want to linger here too long."

Groaning inwardly, Moira finished dressing and packed up their bedding. She dreaded another day of walking, but consoled herself with the fact that she now had shoes. The woman in Craigmoordun had judged her size almost exactly, and the shoes were soft and comfortable. Moira hoped they would continue to suit her after she had walked a few miles.

"We will reach a village by day's end," Tavig said as Moira sat down to eat.

"How can ye even think of going into another village?" she asked, accepting the bowl of porridge he served her.

"We will be safe in this one."

"Ye must have thought we would be safe in the last one or ye never would have entered it."

"Aye, but I didnae ken any of the people there. I have a friend or two in the next village."

Taking the waterskin he held out to her, she washed down the porridge then frowned at him. "These friends will ken who ye are. If Old Colin has heard that ye are accused of murder and your cousin Iver is offering a goodly sum of coin for your capture, then the people in this village will have heard about it, too. Old Colin said the ransom offered for you sorely tempted him. Dinnae ye think it will tempt some of the people in the village?"

"Nay. Ye need not worry about that, loving."

"Ye cannae believe that. I wasnae suggesting that your friends would betray you, but that some of the villagers may do so. Unless—do ye plan to creep into the village to seek your friends' aid?"

"I shall march into the village as boldly as I did into Craigmoordun."

"Aye, and look what that gained us. Ye are mad." Moira could not believe Tavig would act so foolishly, not when it could risk both their lives, and she began to eye him with suspicion. "Or ye are teasing me."

Tavig laughed, leaning over to kiss her cheek. "Aye, I tease you. I *do* have friends in the village, but they dinnae ken me as Tavig MacAlpin."

"Oh, ye arenae going to don that wretched disguise again. Are ye?"

"Wretched? I thought I made a verra fine George Fraser."

"Aye, until it rained. It rains a lot in Scotland."

"True enough. Nay, no disguises. To the friends we will meet at the end of this day's journey in the wee village of Dalnasith, I am Tomas de Mornay, the bastard son of a fine Scottish warrior and a wee French maiden. A small reminder of his glorious battles against the English in France. For a long time I have kenned that my cousin Iver has sought to harm me. Over the last few years I made certain that there are places I might go where none would ken me as Tavig MacAlpin. At times I disguise myself, but in Dalnasith I only play a poor mon wearing ragged clothing and appearing untidy."

"Ah, so that is why ye havenae scraped the beard growth from your face," she murmured, reaching out to brush her hand lightly over the coarse stubble on his cheeks.

He took her hand in his, kissing her palm. "I dinnae hurt your fine soft skin this morning, did I?"

Moira blushed at his reference to their lovemaking. She had been so concerned that Old Colin and his men might be near at hand, she had not given much thought to the fact that they had been making love in the bright morning sun. Now that she had time to think about it, she was shocked. What was it about Tavig MacAlpin that made her act so brazenly?

"Nay, ye didnae hurt me," she mumbled as she concentrated on cleaning out their bowls.

Passion, she decided, had no respect for a person's more delicate feelings. She was going to have to be more careful. She did not want to let her passion rule her and make her weak. Moira had done enough bending to people and things more powerful than she was. Suddenly she knew she could not allow some feeling inside of her to rule her no matter how sweet it was. It was a small rebellion, one that only she would know about, but the decision gave her strength.

A soft groan escaped Moira as she sat down on the soft, mossy ground. She glanced back at the rocky hill they had spent all morning trudging over. Seeing it from a level place, she was surprised they had crossed it so quickly. Looking to the other side of the thin valley Tavig had chosen for their noon respite, she saw more low but rocky hills and groaned again.

"Here, lassie, a wee sip of wine will revive you," Tavig said, sitting by her side and holding out the skin.

Moira took a hearty drink of the sweet wine, then accepted the bread and cheese Tavig gave her. "How many more mountains do we have to climb?" she asked.

He grinned at her. "Ye cannae call those wee hills mountains, lass."

"Aye, I can. They certainly feel like mountains when we are scrambling o'er them."

"The lot of hills ahead of us are smaller and right at the foot of them lies Dalnasith. Now, I havenae been there in a long while, so they will believe I could have been wed in the interim. Ye can be my wife again."

"Oh? It didnae keep us verra safe in Craigmoordun, did it?"

"Moira, it isnae wise for ye to be traveling about with a mon. Ye ken how folk frown on such things and how they would treat ye if they thought ye were just my leman."

"They have no right to think that I *am* your leman."

"Nay, but they will, and weel ye ken it. By claiming that ye are my wife, we avoid all of that irritation and trouble. I fear I cannae do much to avoid trouble I dinnae see coming, trouble of the kind we met in Craigmoordun."

"I was wondering why ye didnae sense it was there waiting for us."

Tavig doused the fire with water and dirt. "I fear my gift isnae constant. 'Tis actually quite a fickle thing. And the closer the danger is to me and mine, the more fickle it becomes." He shrugged, shaking his head. "Mayhap there were just too many things I needed to be worried about. My gift chose to warn me about the bairn instead."

"She was the one of us least able to help herself," Moira said. "Mayhap that is how your gift chooses to work."

"'Twould be nice if there was such reason behind it, but I fear 'tis just a temperamental thing." He picked up his sack and their rolled-up bedding. "I get no *feelings* about Dalnasith, but I cannae promise ye that it will be completely safe."

"Is there a chance of getting a hot bath and a soft bed?" she asked, picking up her sack.

"Aye, and a hot meal, fresh bread, and some fine ale or sweet cider."

"Then why do we continue to cool our heels here?"

Tavig laughed, starting toward the hills. Moira quickly

fell into step beside him. For a hot bath she would scramble over the rocky hills with the speed and ease of a goat. The brief icy wetting she had gotten while crossing the small river had rinsed off some of the travel dust she had collected, but she craved a long soak in hot water. With scented soap, she mused with a sigh.

A soft bed would also be welcome, she decided, silently cursing the rocks that prodded her feet through the soft bottoms of her boots. She would be grateful for any bed besides the hard ground. Her life with Sir Bearnard had been far from easy, but on the nights she was not being punished in some way, she had at least had a bed to go to when her work was done.

The thought of Sir Bearnard made her shiver. She looked over her shoulder, almost surprised not to find him looming behind her, his meaty fists raised to strike. The man and his treatment of her had become a canker in her heart, mind, and soul. She wondered if she would ever be free of him and the fears he had beaten into her.

"He isnae here, dearling," Tavig said, his voice soft and comforting.

Moira gasped softly and stared at him as he helped her up a steep, sheer incline. "Do ye see into my mind?" The thought that Tavig could do so was a chilling one. She did not like the idea of being so completely exposed.

"Nay, lass, not truly." He stopped when they reached an easier part of the path through the hills, turning to trace her cheekbone lightly with his fingertips. "I but caught a certain look on your face."

"A look? What sort of look?"

"That haunted look ye get whenever ye see, hear, or think of that bastard Sir Bearnard Robertson. A deep fear clouds your bonnie eyes, and your face tightens. I *will* make that slinking cur pay for putting that look into your eyes."

"'Tis my fault, too. I am a coward. I gave up fighting."

"Fool. Ye have survived. That takes both strength and

courage. Ye are no mon, battle-hardened and able to face down a mon like Bearnard. Ye are but a wee lass, and were naught but a bairn when ye first came under Robertson's fists. Aye, ye have scars, but ye didnae break, and I have naught but admiration for that."

Moira did not know what to say. He spoke only the truth as he saw it. She could see it in his eyes. All his flattery about her eyes, her hair, or whatever attractive attributes he felt she had had been easy to shrug off or treat as a man's nonsense. This compliment struck deep into her heart. She felt her much-abused pride stir to life, but swiftly quelled its rebirth. Pride was an emotion that often got her into trouble.

"Weel, I dinnae think I am such a grand person, but thank ye."

"Mayhap ye just need to see others who have lived beneath the fist of some brute. Then ye will see how weel ye have survived. In truth, ye already have seen such folk. The people of Craigmoordun showed ye how others act when their lives are ruled by fear and brutality." When Moira said nothing, he shrugged, starting on his way again. "I cannae make ye see your own strengths with just words. 'Tis something ye must learn by yourself. *Ye* have to banish your fears and Robertson's ugly specter from your heart."

Scrambling after him, Moira silently agreed with him. She was not sure how she could accomplish it, however. And what good would it do her anyhow? She would soon be returning to life under Bearnard Robertson's brutal rule. If she strengthened her spirit and restructured her pride he would quickly beat them back into submission. What use was it to shake off his ghost when in a week she would be face-to-face with the man himself? In fact, it was a little cruel of Tavig to try to inspire her to regain her spirit and pride. He had to know that such a return to her old ways would only gain her more pain in the end.

She was still puzzling over the matter as they reached the top of the hill. Below them was a village similar to Craigmoordun except that there was no ominous tower house casting a shadow over it. There was, however, a small stone church. Moira shivered, idly rubbing her arms in reaction to a sudden inner chill. If anyone decided to accuse them of witchcraft, this time there could be men of God near at hand to render a swift sentence. She looked at Tavig, who stood by her side and frowned down at the village.

"Dalnasith has a church," she murmured.

"Now, lass, ye arenae feeling an urge to confess, are ye?" Tavig grinned, kissing her cheek.

"Nay, although I should be making my penitent way to yonder church on my knees."

"I should wait until we are beyond all these rocks."

Moira ignored his irreverence. "If there is a church, there is probably a priest residing there. Not every church is left deserted like the one in Craigmoordun. If there had been a priest there, we never would have lived long enough to escape. Priests mete out a swift and fatal justice to those they believe are in league with the devil."

"We willnae be cried witches down there."

"So confident. Ye felt we would be safe in Craig-moordun."

"And so we would have been, had I been more cautious. I fear I acted without thought when I kenned the child was in danger. There are ways to act upon my warnings without being so dangerously obvious."

"I didnae mean to criticize. Ye did what ye had to. 'Tis just that, after what happened in Craigmoordun, I fear I am reluctant to enter another village." She smiled faintly, a little embarrassed by her timidity. "The chance of gaining a bed and a hot bath is verra tempting, though. It kept me clawing my awkward way over those twice-cursed hills. I but falter a wee bit now."

"'Tis understandable." He took her hand in his, touching a soft kiss to her palm. "Now, remember, ye are a de Mornay, Moira de Mornay, wife to Tomas de Mornay."

"I hope we arenae asked too many questions. I have ne'er been verra skilled at weaving lies."

"They ken me, lass. They willnae press ye hard. Most folk in these tiny villages arenae interested in some traveler's past, but in what he has seen or heard in his travels. We shall just divert their curiosity with tales of the world outside the confines of Dalnasith."

"I am sure ye are verra skilled at telling tales," she murmured as he led her down the hill.

"It has been said that I have a clever tongue."

"I am sure it has. Clever, smooth, and sweet."

"Ah, ye think I am sweet, do ye?" He laughed at her repressive look. "It ne'er hurts to be able to talk away trouble. Fewer people are hurt. Careful, dearling, the trail grows steep and rocky here."

Moira did not see that as much of a change, but did not say so. She concentrated on maintaining a steady footing as she and Tavig made their way down the hill. Three men stood guard at the edge of the village, but made no move toward them to either help or stop them. Moira wondered if Tavig had paused at the top of the path, in full view of the village, in order to let the guards know that only a man and a woman approached. When the men laughed at the clumsy way she and Tavig negotiated the last few yards of the steep trail, she knew the men did not see them as a threat.

"I thought it was ye, Tomas," a burly man said as he stepped forward to shake Tavig's hand "The lass?"

Blushing a little as all three guards stared at her, Moira elbowed Tavig to hurry his answer. She was afraid to say much, certain she would call him by the wrong name. Tomas was close to Tavig, and she was a poor liar.

Tavig put his arm around Moira's shoulders, tugging her closer. "My wife, Moira. Moira, this brute is Robert."

"Ye are wed?" Robert laughed heartily, slapping his knee and shaking his head. "That news willnae please everyone."

"What does he mean?" Moira demanded of Tavig.

"He but jests, dearling." Tavig slapped Robert on the arm. "He just ne'er expected a rogue like me to marry."

Tavig was staring hard at his friend. Moira got the distinct impression Tavig was silently telling Robert to shut his mouth. Robert cast her a nervous glance from beneath his thick graying brows. There was some secret between the men, something Tavig did not want her to know.

Moira smiled, deciding to pretend ignorance. As far as she knew, Tavig had been honest with her thus far. She could not believe that he now kept some large, important secret from her. Curiosity nibbled at her, but she subdued it. It was Tavig's place to tell her about whatever it was he was trying to hide. She just hoped he would not leave her ignorant too long and thus vulnerable to some unpleasant surprise.

"Weel." Robert cleared his throat and smiled at Moira, his teeth gleaming white through his thick, ill-trimmed gray and black beard. "Ye found yourself a bonnie lass, Tomas."

"Thank ye," Moira said quietly, her gratitude for the compliment echoed by Tavig.

"My wife, Mary, will be glad of a visitor," Robert continued. "Now she can hear some of the news from afar that a lady likes to hear. Go on down to my home, laddie. I will be done here come sunset, and we can share some ale."

"Ye are a good mon, Robert. I thank ye," Tavig said, taking Moira's hand and leading her down the road that ran straight through the village. "I will try to save ye some ale," Tavig called over his shoulder, grinning when Robert laughed.

"Are ye sure he can afford to be so hospitable?" asked Moira. "His clothes mark him as a poor mon."

"Aye, he isnae as poor as some, but, as with many who live their whole lives in these wee villages, he doesnae have much." He glanced at her, smiling faintly at her frown. "That troubles ye, does it?"

"If he is poor, asking him to give us a bed and food may be unkind. He may not have it to spare, but courtesy requires him to offer it."

"He has enough to feed us and give us a bed for the night." He kissed her cheek. "And he will be weel rewarded for the kindness he has shown me o'er the years. When my troubles are cleared away, I mean to improve Robert's circumstances greatly." He watched her closely, slowly smiling when she said nothing. "What? No reminder of my impending doom?"

"I see no need to keep repeating myself," Moira said, ignoring his soft laughter.

She knew why she had stopped constantly mentioning the hangman's noose that awaited Tavig. Moira was sure that he knew why as well, but she ignored his wide grin. The thought of Tavig hanging had troubled her from the start. Now it made her almost physically ill, her stomach knotting and her heart pounding painfully with fear. Her feelings for Tavig had reached a depth that compelled her to try to share his hopeful outlook on the future. It was difficult, however. Since the death of her parents and her long years under the brutal guardianship of Sir Bearnard, her optimism had grown very weak.

Tavig stopped before a tidy thatch-roofed house. A plump woman with graying brown hair and bright brown eyes cheerfully greeted him. Moira shyly returned Mary's hearty greeting when Tavig introduced her to the woman as his wife. She felt a little guilty for lying to this woman who so cordially welcomed them into her home, proudly introducing her five children. It seemed an unkind way to repay the woman's kindness. Moira allowed Tavig to do most of the talking, knowing she could not lie as smoothly as he could.

For a moment, as Mary served them ale, bread, and cheese, Moira wondered if that particular skill of Tavig's ought to worry her more. He was spinning a tale of their meeting and their marriage with ease, almost as if he believed it himself. Despite that, she did believe the things he told her. If he declared something was the truth, she accepted it as such. Moira decided he saw the lying he indulged in now as just another way to keep them safe. She just hoped she was not being foolishly blind, letting her heart and their perilous circumstances mislead her.

Tavig asked Mary for a bath and, before Moira could protest, Mary agreed. Moira was briefly torn between refusing the bath because she did not want to add to Mary's work and aching for a long hot soak. Even as she apologized for the inconvenience, Moira finally accepted the offer. She did not even mind that she would have to take her bath in an old wooden vat in the cow shed. It was private and sheltered from the wind. Moira began to shed her clothes even as Mary walked out of the shed.

The sound of Moira humming a ballad in a soft, sweet voice greeted Tavig as he entered the cow shed. He smiled as he quietly approached the vat. She was soaking in the hot, soapy water, her head resting on the rim and her wet hair hanging down the outside of the tub. He found her intense pleasure in something as simple as a hot bath delightful.

Her eyes were closed, allowing him to reach her side unseen. His desire for her rose swiftly as he watched her, even though the soapy water hid most of her slim form from his gaze. Grinning, he dipped his hand into the water, and splashed a little of it on her face. Tavig laughed when she screeched softly with surprise, crossing her arms over her chest and sinking deeper into the water. A moment later she scowled at him.

"If ye try to tell me ye are here to milk the cows," she said, "I willnae believe you."

"I would at least make sure the beasties were in here ere I tried that lie." He trailed his fingers through the water, observing her blushes with ill-hidden amusement. "I have already bathed and dressed. Dinnae ye think ye have been soaking in that vat long enough? Ye will wrinkle like some old shirt."

"That minor affliction will be weel hidden by my clothes." She shivered, cursing inwardly over her water choosing such an awkward moment to cool. "Now that ye have assured yourself that I havenae drowned in this tub, could ye please leave? I need to dry myself and get dressed."

"I thought ye might need some help getting out of the tub and in drying off," he said as he held up her drying cloth. "It could be awkward for ye to climb out safely when ye are slick with water."

"I believe I can accomplish that without your kind assistance."

Tavig leaned closer, kissing her lightly on the mouth. "I can stand here waiting a lot longer than ye can abide sitting in that chilling water."

"Rogue," she muttered, knowing he was right. She was already tired of soaking in the water. "I dinnae suppose I can trust ye to close your eyes?"

"Nay, I dinnae suppose ye can. 'Tis too much to ask of any mon, loving."

"I was just asking ye to behave like a gentlemon."

When he just grinned, she cursed softly. Since they were lovers, she was not sure why she was feeling so modest. She decided that standing up with only the dim shadowy light in the cow shed to hide her nakedness was a little bold for her tastes. It was clear that Tavig was not going to allow her to succumb to that pinch of modesty. Taking a deep breath, she slowly stood up.

Chapter Ten

As Moira stood up, Tavig felt his breath catch in his throat. Even the irritation on her face could not dim her beauty. The water gave her soft skin an inviting sheen. He did not want to hide any of her with the large drying cloth he held. She was a feast for his eyes, and he savored the way his body responded with desire for her. When she shivered slightly, he pulled himself out of his fascination and wrapped the cloth around her. He picked her out of the vat, pulling her into his arms.

"This isnae the way to get dry," she murmured as he brushed his lips over hers.

"Mayhap not, but it will help ye get warm." He traced her collarbone with light kisses. "'Tis certainly making me all asweat."

She giggled, slipping her arms around his neck. Tavig groaned softly as he kissed her, lifting her in his arms and carrying her to a soft mound of hay. Tossing the large drying cloth over the hay, he eased her down on top of it, then covered her body with his. The way she welcomed him into her arms told him she wanted him as much as he wanted her. He hastily yanked off his shirt, murmuring his pleasure as their flesh met.

"Tomas!"

Tavig barely acknowledged the shrill female voice calling out his assumed name. Moira's gasp of shock and the sudden tensing of her body warned him that they had been interrupted. He sat up, turning to look toward the door of the cow shed. Cursing inwardly as Moira frantically wrapped herself in the drying cloth, Tavig glared at the woman who had so rudely put a halt to their passion. He sat up straighter, shielding a blushing Moira from view.

"What are ye doing in here, Jeanne?" he demanded, furious that the voluptuous brunette had appeared before he could warn Moira about her.

"Word spread swiftly that ye had returned to the village." She strode over to him, her hands on her full hips. "Mary wouldnae tell me where ye were, so I decided to look around meself."

"So, ye found me. Glad to see that ye are still hale and hearty. So am I. Fareweel."

"How can ye speak to me so dismissively? After all we have been to each other? And who is this slut?"

"This *woman* is my wife." Tavig spoke through gritted teeth, only a distaste for striking a woman keeping him from slapping Jeanne for insulting Moira.

"Your wife!" Jeanne clenched her fists, taking a step closer, a wild look of pure fury in her hazel eyes. "Oh, aye, when I asked after ye, that fool Mary said something about ye being taken, but I ne'er thought she referred to a wife. How could ye marry someone else after all that has passed between us? Tell me this is a cruel jest, that ye havenae scorned my love and insulted me so gravely."

"I dinnae ken what ye are ranting about, woman." Tavig stood up to face Jeanne as Moira scurried behind the vat to get dressed. "Aye, we were lovers, but no more. Ye have no right or cause to stand here acting the injured, cast-aside maiden. Ye were weel trained in the act of loving ere I even bedded down with ye, and I gave ye no promises. I took what ye offered—no more."

"Ye bastard!" Jeanne swung at Tavig, but he caught her by the wrist, stopping her blow.

"I think ye had best leave, Jeanne. If ye thought to catch me as a husband, ye have lost that game. Cease wasting your time here. I am wed now, and we will play no more games. Find yourself another mon."

Moira winced as Jeanne colorfully cursed Tavig. She was finding the confrontation between Tavig and his old lover as painful as it was embarrassing. Although she was not so stupid as to think him as virginal as herself, she detested seeing one of the many women he had bedded. Especially when that woman was lovely and curvaceous, she mused with a sigh as she finished dressing. She stood up, nervously finger-combing her hair and watching Tavig push a still-cursing Jeanne out of the cow shed. Jeanne's fury made Moira uneasy. She was not sure what the woman could do to them, but it was unsettling to have so much fury and hatred aimed at her.

Jeanne pulled free of Tavig's grip of her arm, pausing in the low doorway of the shed. "Aye, I will leave. Enjoy your child bride while ye can. I dinnae take such insults lightly, Tomas. I will see that ye dinnae rest in her bone-thin arms for too long."

Tavig cursed, watching Jeanne flounce away and wondering how seriously he ought to take her threats. He turned to look at Moira, cursing again when he saw that she was dressed. There would be no returning to the sweet passion Jeanne had so rudely ended, at least not for a while. He had hoped that Jeanne would possess the pride and dignity to stay away once she heard that he was married or saw him with Moira. It had been a foolish hope, one certainly not based on what he knew about the woman. Tavig just wished he knew what emotions had Moira looking so solemn.

"Sorry about that, loving," he said as he walked over to her. "I had meant to warn ye about her." He took her hand, tugging her closer and brushing a kiss over her mouth. "Ye need not worry o'er her."

"Nay? She was verra angry. She hates both of us. Ye could see it in her face. She wants revenge."

"She has naught to get revenge for. I promised her nothing except for a fine time atween the sheets." He sighed when she winced slightly. "Sorry, lass."

"Ye dinnae have to keep apologizing, Tavig. Ye have done nothing wrong. I dinnae think we should completely ignore her threats, though. We are in no position to be so carefree."

"What can she do, Moira? She doesnae ken who I am. And no one will heed her rantings. They all ken that she has no call to claim that she has been misused or betrayed. God's bones, she has bedded nearly every mon in the village, and they all ken that she wasnae faithful to me when I wasnae here. Sometimes not even when I was here. She will gain no allies."

"Mayhap I am just being a coward, but although your words make sense, I still feel uneasy."

"We will be gone come the morning." He draped his arm around her shoulders and started out of the shed. "In truth, if anyone has a right to vengeance, 'tis me. She destroyed what promised to be a verra pleasing afternoon." He laughed softly when she blushed.

"Ye must not let that whore Jeanne trouble ye," said Mary as she sat down across the rough table from Moira.

Moira gave a start, looking around for Tavig as she accepted the ale Mary served her. The evening meal was done, the children were asleep in the loft, and, to her dismay, she found herself completely alone with the amiable Mary. Tavig sat at the far end of the room helping Robert sharpen his sword and mend his light armor, deep in conversation over what battles, feuds, and raids had occurred since they had last talked. Neither man could hear her or Mary, but Moira still eyed the older woman warily.

"She was sent off so I havenae thought too much about her," Moira said, not surpised when Mary laughed.

"Oh, aye, ye have. I wager ye have thought of nothing else since she found ye and the laddie in the cow shed. Jeanne wouldnae heed me when I told her he wouldnae want to see her. She isnae worth fretting on, child. She is one of those women a mon makes use of ere he decides to settle down."

"And one some men use even after they have—er—settled," Moira said in a quiet voice, needing to voice her fears but not wanting Tavig to hear them.

"True. Sadly true. Not our Tomas, though. He isnae like that."

"How can ye be so certain of that?"

"I feel it here." Mary pointed to her chest. "If I was a lass deciding on which sweet-tongued mon to trust with my heart, I would trust that black-haired bonnie lad. He has heart, courage, and honor." She smiled faintly when Moira blushed. "I ken he holds a secret or two from us. He will tell us what they are when he can."

"Why do ye think he has secrets?"

"Moira, my sweet bairn, I was born poor, raised poor, and wed a poor man. I ken a laird when I see one. That lad o'er there is no poor bastard son. He has led men. He has lived fine. He *is* a laird. Now for some reason he is wandering about pretending to be some vagabond. Kenning the mon he is, my mon Robert and I believe he is hiding. Men with power and wealth often have enemies, men trying to take those things away." She reached across the table to pat Moira's clenched hand. "Dinnae look so afraid, child. We will let him hide here for as long as he is of a mind to do so."

For one brief moment Moira contemplated adamantly denying what Mary said, then decided there was no threat to fear. Mary and Robert clearly liked Tavig and would quietly play his game until he was ready to give it up. Inwardly grimacing, she then worried if Mary had guessed that she and Tavig were not truly husband and wife.

"I am sure he will appreciate that," she murmured. "Now ye can see why Jeanne's threats make me so uneasy."

"What can she do? She doesnae ken who he is so she cannae bring his enemies to our door. I dinnae think her threats are really what has ye looking so sad, however. Ye worry about how she might threaten what ye and your mon share. If ye dinnae wish to speak on it, I will understand. 'Tis just that speaking on such fears can oftimes lessen them."

"That would be nice." She smiled weakly at Mary. "Jeanne is a verra comely woman, comely and lush in body. I am a bone-thin, tiny lass with red hair and freckles. Aye, to be honest, she does worry me. He was angry with her today, but she is a determined woman. I ken it." She sighed. "I shouldnae fret because he says we will leave, yet then I find myself wondering how many other Jeannes clutter his past."

"Aye, his *past*. Jeanne will always be one of those lasses who clutters a mon's past. Ye are a lass who sets the path for a mon's future. Sad to say, few men meet the lass they will wed in as innocent a state as she is. They do their best to shed that innocence, and so women like us have to try to forgive them for tussling about with lasses like Jeanne. That is all they do, though—tussle."

"I ken it and I ken that there is naught to forgive. He didnae ken me then and he isnae tussling with her now. 'Tis foolish, but I just cannae help thinking of how much more she has for him to tussle with." She smiled when Mary laughed.

"Aye, she is a fulsome lass. Most of the lads in town have helped themselves to her freely offered bounty."

"Do ye not think it a wee bit unfair that men condemn her for doing just what they do?"

"Verra unfair, but 'tis the way of it. There are men who can forgive a lass for a past lover. What makes Jeanne different is that she has a whore's soul. 'Tis the heart and mind that make a whore, child, not lying with a mon. 'Tis the rot inside of Jeanne that marks her as a whore. Ye cannae lose your mon to one like her. And, nay, he willnae be a-creeping off to her bed, either. If ye didnae warm his blanket weel, he wouldnae have asked ye to share it with him. I willnae believe ye if ye try to say he doesnae have a muckle lot of desire for ye. I have seen it glistening in those black eyes of his each time he looks your way."

"Truly?" Moira often thought she saw it, too, but then feared she saw only what she wished to, not what was really there.

"Aye, truly. If a mon cares for ye, a good mon like yours, then the fullness of your curves is of no concern."

If a mon cares for ye, Mary had said, and the words pounded in Moira's head. Mary could not know that Tavig had never spoken of caring, of love, or of any feelings deeper than lust. He still mentioned destiny on occasion, but she could not put her faith in that. She also did not want him to stay with her because some voice inside of him told him he should. Moira sadly admitted to herself that she had absolutely no idea how Tavig really felt about her.

"Weel, it doesnae look as if I comforted ye much," Mary said, shaking her head. "I ken your fears weel. I had them when I was a lass and first gave my heart to Robert. If ye will pardon my meddling, I mean to give ye a wee bit of advice. Dinnae plague your mon with your fears, dinnae let your fears make ye accuse him when ye have no proof that he has done any wrong, and dinnae let them blind ye to the truth. Watch him. Heed his words and actions. I will wager that ye will soon see ye have no cause to fear the lasses he once kenned or the ones who try to catch his eye."

"I shall try to remember that."

Mary quickly changed the subject to fashions and gossip. The woman was eager to hear any news Moira had. It was late before she and Tavig retired to the curtained alcove where they would sleep. Mary and Robert went to sleep in the loft with their children, allowing her and Tavig some privacy. Moira hastily stripped to her chemise and climbed into the narrow bed.

"Ye have been verra quiet this evening," Tavig said as he crawled in beside her, gently tugging her into his arms.

"I was afraid I would be caught out in a lie," she murmured, settling a little closer as he smoothed his hands over her back. "'Tis hard to lie to Mary."

"Aye, but I dinnae think that is all that troubles you. Ye havenae said much since Jeanne screamed her poison at us. Lass, ye dinnae think I would try to slip away to her bed, do ye?"

Moira found it a little annoying that everyone seemed to read her fears so easily. "And what makes ye think I would fret myself o'er where ye bed down?" She ached to slap that smile off his face.

Tavig kissed her. "Ye have naught to be jealous of, dearling."

"I am *not* jealous," she protested, but he just kissed her again.

"And ye dinnae need to fear that I cannae be faithful. Why should I reach for another when I hold such a sweet fire in my arms?"

"Because another has a wee bit more to reach for?" She cringed, unable to believe she had spoken the thought aloud.

"Sweet Moira, ye can be a foolish lass."

"How kind."

He laughed, hugging her tightly for a moment, "Aye, ye are as slender as a reed. Ye will probably never have the fulsome shape a woman like Jeanne has. I will be honest, loving. E'en as I ached to hold ye, I often asked myself why, as ye werenae the sort of lass I usually reached for. I didnae ask myself that too often, howbeit, and after we made love, I kenned I would ne'er ask it again." He slowly moved his hand down her side. "Ye have all the curves I need, dearling. Aye, and all the fire any mon could want."

Moira was touched by his words. He made no flowery

speeches or covered her with pretty flatteries. He gave her no vows or promises. The lack of such things made it easier to believe him. Tavig spoke only of their shared passion, and that was also something she believed in. He might not feel it as fiercely or as deeply as she did, but he did feel it.

"I am sorry," she murmured, her voice growing husky as he caressed her. "I fear I have no knowledge of such things. Jeanne had the comely face and shape all the troubadours warble about." She shrugged. "I saw that and—"

"Felt that I, too, would soon start to warble about her."

"Ye did once."

"Nay, I ne'er felt more for her than a base need to rut. Why do ye think I stay here, with Robert and Mary, have always done so when I pass through the town? If Jeanne meant more to me than a quick, easy tumble in the heather, surely I would have bedded down with her. I ne'er have, lass. Aye, I have felt my heart quicken o'er a lass or two in my life, but 'twas a swiftly passing thing, for I was too young to judge what was love and what was lust. Jeanne wasnae but a lusting and, in truth, if she hadnae fairly thrown herself at my feet, I probably would have let her be."

"Why?" she asked, returning his gently hungry kiss. "I dinnae press for some pretty words or the like. I am just curious."

"'Tis difficult to explain. I cannae be certain if 'tis something every mon can sense or if my thrice-cursed gift leads me in such matters. I looked at her and I kenned she would cause me more trouble than she was worth. But I proved as susceptible as any mon to a skilled hand and freely offered favors. She was near and she was easy." He gave her a somewhat guilty smile. "'Tisnae something I am proud of."

"Weel, ye ne'er tried to claim yourself a saint."

Jeanne was no longer a threat. Moira realized her pangs of jealousy and her fears were eased by the dismissive way he spoke of the woman. Jeanne had boldly offered Tavig what any virile young man wants, and he took it. Moira did not really like to think of him and Jeanne bedded down together, but the woman no longer made her jealous.

"Nay," Tavig explained, "I am no saint. If I was, I would-nae have tried so hard to seduce you."

"I suppose I ought to be thoroughly ashamed that ye didnae have to work too hard to draw me into your bed."

"But ye arenae ashamed."

"Not much, leastwise. It pinches a bit from time to time, but 'tis a weak pinch."

"Good, for ye have naught to be ashamed of."

"Ye are the only one who would think so. I am sharing a bed with a mon who isnae my husband." She quickly put her hand over his mouth when he started to speak. "Dinnae start that mad talk about being destined to wed me."

Tavig tugged her hand away. "'Tisnae mad talk. I thought ye believed in my sight. I—"

She frowned when he tensed and stared at the wall behind her. "Tavig?" She cried out in surprise when he suddenly leapt from the bed, pulling her along with him. "What is it? What is wrong?"

"Get dressed," he ordered as he yanked on his clothes. "We must flee."

Even as she obeyed him, she asked, "Have ye seen something?"

"Nay, curse it. I just ken that we have to leave—now. Hurry, lass."

"I am dressing as fast as I can," she muttered as she yanked on her boots. "Should we warn Robert and Mary?"

"Nay, they are in no danger. Curse it to the ground, why doesnae it give me enough time?"

Moira gasped as he drew his sword and faced the front door. She barely had time to blink before several men burst in through the door. Tavig shoved her toward the back door, but that, too, was flung open and blocked by armed men. Moira stayed close to Tavig as he tried to watch both doors and shield her with his body. When Jeanne pushed through the men crowding the front doorway, Moira felt a chill wriggle up her spine. She should have paid more attention to the woman's threats instead of allowing herself to be distracted by her own fears and jealousies.

"There she is," Jeanne cried, pointing at Moira. "Look at her. She kenned we were coming for her and prepares to flee. Ask yourself, how could she ken that unless she is just what I say she is?"

"What goes on here?" demanded Robert, tugging on his jerkin even as he stumbled down from the loft, a pale, wide-eyed Mary at his heels. "Are ye people mad? What makes ye burst into my home in the dead of night?"

"We have come to get the witch," replied a bulky man standing to the right of Jeanne.

"Witch? What are ye babbling about Geordie?"

"Jeanne says the woman is a witch," Geordie said, advancing a step toward Moira only to hastily retreat when Tavig raised his sword. "Ye need not fear for your life, sir," he assured Tavig. "We ken ye have been bewitched into abiding with the lass. Ye, too," he told a gaping Robert.

"That lass is no witch," yelled Robert. "Ye are allowing yourselves to be fooled by that whore." He pointed at Jeanne.

"She is a witch," screamed Jeanne. "I tried to pull Tomas from her evil grip, and she visited her evil upon me. She has afflicted me with a burning rash, and one of my poor goats died, black blood pouring from its mouth. The poor beast wasnae even ill, and I had no marks upon my skin until after *she* cursed me in the cow shed earlier today."

"Ye lying whore," Tavig snapped.

Moira shivered, fear knotting her stomach as she listened to Tavig curse Jeanne, causing the woman to elaborate upon her accusations. Several of the men bellowed their support for Jeanne. There was no escape. Two men kept Robert and Mary captive on the ladder to the loft. Tavig was armed, but could not fight the half dozen men in the cottage. Even if he could defeat them, more huddled outside ready to take their places. It was clear that Tavig intended to fight to protect her, but Moira was coldly certain it would only bring about his death. It was also clear that none of the men was prepared to listen to reason. She knew she had to end the confrontation. She also knew there was only one way to do that, and Tavig was going to be furious.

"I am sorry, Tavig," she whispered and, swinging the bag he had shoved into her arms just before her accusers had arrived, she knocked the sword from his hands.

Tavig gaped at her then lunged for his sword. Geordie and another man moved faster, quickly pinning him in their hold. Another man rushed forward to grab her. She winced as he roughly yanked her arms behind her back and bound her wrists together.

"What did ye do that for, lass?" Tavig asked, staring at her with a mixture of confusion and fear.

"I ken that ye are a good fighter," she replied, smiling sadly. "Ye couldnae win against so many, howbeit."

"Neither can you, dearling."

"Mayhap not, but 'tis only me they are accusing. They would cut ye down to get to me, and I would still be taken. I decided I didnae really want to see ye die in some fruitless display of gallantry."

"Which he may still try," said Jeanne, stepping closer yet being very careful to stay out of a glaring Tavig's reach. "I think he needs to be secured somewhere so that he doesnae try to set her free. She could yet use her spell to draw him back to her."

"What are ye going to do with her?" he demanded as his wrists were tied behind his back.

"We will take her to the priest," replied Geordie. "Father Matthew will ken what to do with her."

Moira glanced toward Mary and Robert. Robert was frowning, and Mary had gone quite pale. It did not seem to Moira that they felt her chances of acquittal were very good. She had the sinking feeling she was about to meet a man who held tightly to superstition. The ease with which Jeanne had convinced the villagers that her wild accusations were true was also worrisome.

"We had best take her to the priest now," Jeanne said. "We cannae risk her using her skills to escape."

"'Tis late," said Geordie. "The priest will be abed. I dinnae think we ought to wake him."

"He will be pleased to be roused for this. Doesnae he always warn us about the devil's allies? Now we can show him how vigilant we are."

"More like what complete fools ye are," said Robert, and he glared at Jeanne. "The priest also warns us to beware of whores, yet we havenae dragged ye before him for judgment yet."

"She has ye all bewitched," screamed Jeanne. "We will take them all to the priest."

Jeanne marched to the door, urging everyone to follow. As Moira was dragged along, she glanced up at the loft. Robert and Mary's five children watched in terror as their parents were toted away, but they obeyed their parents' command to stay put. She then looked at Tavig. He appeared even more furious than the cursing Robert did. Moira knew that, whatever happened, Jeanne would pay for her trickery. She just wished she could find some strength in that knowledge. She had the feeling she would need all the strength she could muster.

Chapter Eleven

One look into Father Matthew's cold gray eyes was all Moira needed to realize she would find no mercy from this man. It was hard to see if he believed any of Jeanne's wild claims, but he was savoring the chance to flex his clerical muscle. Moira had the sinking feeling he saw in her a chance to enhance his prestige within the church.

"Ye cannae believe this foolishness," Tavig cried. "The only one accusing my wife is no credible witness."

"Ye cannae weaken the strength of the charge of witchcraft by attacking the victim of it," the priest replied in a low, emotionless voice as he walked around Moira, his long robes sweeping along the rush-strewn floor of the tiny church.

"The only thing Jeanne is a victim of is her own vanity. She uses ye, all of ye, to wreak vengeance. Ye persecute an innocent to placate a scorned woman's anger."

"And why should Jeanne feel scorned?" Father Matthew asked, barely glancing at Tavig.

"Because I wouldnae take her to bed."

"And ye accuse our Jeanne of vanity? I think ye suffer greatly from that sin." He took a handful of Moira's bright hair and let it slowly fall from his fingers. "Red hair. The mark of the devil."

"That is just more foolishness. Many a person has red hair."

"I have long believed that we are too lax in our vigilance in this land. The devil is allowed too free a rein."

"'Tis Jeanne's vicious tongue that has been allowed too free a rein. For God's sweet sake, think of whom ye are heeding."

As Tavig valiantly tried to discredit Jeanne and thus weaken the validity of her accusations, Moira watched the woman. Jeanne did an excellent job of displaying hurt and shock, as if each truth Tavig uttered about her was no more than vicious slander. Her eyes revealed her true feelings, however. In Jeanne's eyes was the glitter of triumph.

Glancing around at the villagers only raised Moira's hopes a tiny bit. They were heeding Tavig. Many of them began to look uncomfortable, sending Jeanne some very unfriendly glances. Mary had said that Jeanne had bedded nearly every man in the village, and they were obviously recalling that. If the looks on their faces were any indication, they were also recalling a great deal more about the woman they had so blindly followed, things Jeanne probably wished forgotten. No one made an effort to renounce his support of her claim, however. It was clear to the dimmest wits among them that the priest was ready, even eager, to fight a witch. Although they had all begun to change their minds, their fear of the priest kept them silent.

"Silence," Father Matthew yelled, glaring at Tavig. "Ye give me many a reason to doubt Jeanne's word, slandering her with every word ye utter."

"'Tis no slander, but the truth," Tavig snapped.

"Yet ye give me no reason to believe ye o'er Jeanne. Is the accused witch not your wife?"

"Aye, Moira is my wife. That doesnae lessen the truth of what I am saying."

"Nay? Ye would say anything to save her. 'Tis part of the bewitchment. Ye should be more cautious, my lad. Ye have been carnal with a witch. That carries as heavy a penalty as being a witch."

"Moira is no witch," Tavig bellowed.

"Gag him," the priest commanded, nodding when the men holding Tavig hastily obeyed. "Now." He looked at Moira. "What are we to do with you?"

"I believe ye have already decided, so why torment me with your questions?" Moira replied.

"Ye are resigned to your fate?"

"Nay, but I see the futility of arguing my innocence. Ye have all gone deaf to the truth. Ye havenae even checked the truth of what Jeanne claims I have done to her. I willnae add to your macabre fun by pleading for my life."

"My goat is dead," Jeanne said, stepping forward. "I cannae prove how it died, but I can prove how she has afflicted me. I am covered with spots and sores." She yanked up her skirts to reveal a vivid rash on her legs, the red patches broken here and there by ugly open and oozing sores.

"I hope ye didnae have that when ye bedded down with my husband," Moira mumbled.

"Ye gave it to me. It appeared after I tried to aid Tomas, to pull him from your devilish clutches." She rushed forward, yanking up Moira's skirts despite Moira's struggles, and pointing to a small mole just above Moira's knee, said, "And there is the devil's mark. She has others. I saw them in Robert's cow shed, for she was naked."

When Jeanne released her skirts, Moira kicked the woman in the knee. Jeanne screeched with pain, then moved toward Moira again. One of the two men guarding Moira shoved Jeanne away. Geordie curtly ordered another man to hold Jeanne. Moira prayed Jeanne's actions would not prompt a public search for witch's marks. She did have several more moles and birthmarks. Since the priest deemed her guilty already, a search for witch's marks would only serve to embarrass and shame her.

"It seems to me ye have no more than one lass's word against another's," said Robert.

"True," agreed the priest, never taking his gaze from Moira. "I believe we need a test to see who speaks the truth. An ordeal would bring us the truth we need. There are many to choose from." He spared only a brief glance for Tavig who cursed beneath his gag, struggling violently in the hold of his guard.

Moira fought the fear that welled up inside her. Quite often a person put through an ordeal proved his innocence only by dying. Ordeals were always painful, ranging from tossing a bound person into the water, declaring him innocent only if he sank and usually drowned, to holding a piece of red-hot iron on one's hand and needing to come away uninjured to prove one's innocence. The theory was that God would protect the innocent from harm. Moira had always felt that God had far better things to do. She did not really wish to have her somewhat scandalous opinion proved correct.

The way the priest kept staring at her as he mulled the problem over made Moira uneasy, very uneasy. It was difficult to hide her fears with his cold eyes fixed upon her. There was nothing to be read on his thin, angular face and Moira found that lack of expression unsettling.

"We dinnae have the tools to do as we must," he finally said.

"What a shame," Moira drawled, idly wondering when she had become so sharp-tongued.

"I believe we have enough to prepare a reasonably successful ordeal, howbeit."

As she listened to the priest order some of the men to clear a place in front of the church and heat rocks, Moira knew she grew pale. She could feel the blood seep from her face. A quick glance at Tavig showed him looking the same. She was not sure what she was going to be forced to do, but if it included hot rocks or coals, it was not going to be pleasant. Clearly it was going to be one of those ordeals that required her to do something dangerous and somehow come through it unscathed. She knew she was innocent, but had no confidence in an ordeal proving that.

When the priest ordered two men to take off her boots and hose, a soft cry of alarm escaped her despite all of her efforts to be brave. Now she knew why the men were preparing a bed of hot coals and rocks. The hard-eyed Father Matthew wanted her to walk over them to prove her innocence. When she completed her torturous walk and her feet were badly burned, he would be able to have her executed with a clear conscience.

As two men started to drag her out of the church, Moira decided she was tired of pretending to be brave. She struggled, dragged her feet, and called her captors every vile name she had ever heard. The priest walked behind, scolding her in a dull, pious voice for her language and lack of faith. Moira wished she could get free and hit him, then hastily apologized for what might appear to be blasphemy. In her brief prayer for forgiveness, she included the wish that God would have a closer look at one particular priest who did not seem to behave in a very Christian manner.

Once in front of the bed of coals, Moira lost her last grip on her courage. She looked around at the crowd of people in front of the church. Tavig was slumped in the hold of his captors, one of them having struck him over the head with a small club to put an end to his violent struggles. Robert and Mary tried to talk sense to their friends and neighbors. The looks on the faces of the villagers revealed how uncertain they had become, but they still made no protest. Jeanne was clearly savoring every moment.

"Now, witch, ye must walk the length of this," the priest said, pointing to the heated bed of stones.

"'Tis clear that, although ye offer me an ordeal to prove my innocence, ye have already decided on my guilt." Moira shook her head, inwardly hoping that the relatively calm tone of her voice distracted everyone enough so that they would not notice she was awash in sweat. "Ye have already tried and judged me. This is but a way to add to my pain."

"Walk. If ye can get to the other side and your feet reveal no injury, then God has proclaimed ye innocent."

"When God is done proclaiming my innocence, I hope He takes a long look at some of the ones who claim to work in His name."

She took a deep breath, shaking free of her captors' light

hold. A rousing Tavig cried out when she took her first step onto the smoldering path she had to walk. Since her hands were still bound, Moira knew she would risk falling if she moved too swiftly. She suspected the priest would declare the test invalid if she ran and would force her to do it all over again. She kept her gaze fixed resolutely on the end of the red-hot trail.

The heat seeped into the soles of her feet. Moira was amazed that she could feel the heat, suffered from the discomfort of it, yet felt no true pain. She wondered if her mind was somehow refusing to acknowledge the agony her feet had to be suffering.

When she stepped onto the cool dirt at the end of the path, she stared down at her feet. She was surprised to see no smoke. For a moment she wondered if she had imagined the whole thing. A quick look at the bed of rocks and coals revealed that they were indeed hot. The red glow, fed by the fires in the pit beneath the rocks, sent out a frightening light.

She awkwardly sat down even as the priest rushed over to look at her feet. Moira looked with him and nearly gaped. Her feet still felt uncomfortably warm, but there was no sign of an injury. Father Matthew roughly brushed dirt from her feet and looked again. Even as he glared at her, someone untied her wrists. A moment later Tavig was at her side, pulling her into his arms. Mary and Robert also crouched near her, staring at her feet in amazement. Moira realized she had passed the cold-eyed priest's test.

"Her innocence has been proven," said Tavig, glancing at Father Matthew.

"She moved too quickly," the priest said, then glanced around nervously as an angry murmur rose from the crowd.

"The test is done," said Geordie, who then looked at Jeanne. "The mon was right. We were used to soothe a whore's stung vanity."

Moira pulled away from Tavig a little as the anger of the crowd turned on Jeanne. Jeanne protested her innocence, re-iterating her accusations as the villagers encircled her. The priest quickly moved to join in the condemnation. Moira had the chilling feeling that Jeanne's life was in danger.

"Tavig," she said as he helped her to her feet, "I think they mean to kill her."

"There is naught we can do about it," he replied.

"Aye," agreed Robert. "I think ye and the lass would be wise to flee from this place," he advised Tavig.

All four of them started back to Robert's house. A scream from Jeanne caused Moira to hesitate, but Tavig urged her to continue. The moment they were back in Robert's cottage, Mary urged her to sit down, then bathed her feet. Robert helped Tavig collect up their belongings.

"We should have helped her," Moira whispered, looking at her feet one last time before donning her hose and boots which Robert had rescued from the church.

"Some of the woman's own kinsmen were in that crowd," said Robert. "They fled as soon as the fury of the people turned against Jeanne. 'Tisnae right, but the four of us cannae halt them. See to your own safety, lass."

"Jeanne tried to have you killed," Mary reminded her.

"I ken it." Moira shook her head. "I still dinnae understand how I could walk over those things and suffer no more than a stinging from the heat."

"I should like to tell ye that ye have been proven innocent by God Himself," said Tavig.

"But ye cannae." She smiled faintly as she stood, picking up the sack she would carry. "Dinnae worry about saying so. I truly cannae believe God has the time to guard a wee lass's feet."

"Nay, probably not. All I can think of is that the calluses ye were so ashamed of have proven their worth. Ye have tough wee feet, dearling. Aye, and I noticed ye had somehow gained a fine coat of dirt on the bottoms of your feet."

She grimaced. "I was terrified. I was awash in sweat, right down to the soles of my feet. 'Tis odd, I found the dirt clinging to my feet an irritation. I guess it is a good thing that I had neither the time nor the wit to scrape them clean ere I began my walk. At first I thought my mind simply refused to accept my injuries, but I have looked closely, and there are no injuries."

"Nay, none. The dirt and the calluses worked as weel as any boot, mayhap better. We have to go now."

They thanked Robert and Mary even as they hurried out the door. Moira could hear the crowd and started to look back toward the church, but Tavig would not allow it. He pulled her along the road in such haste she had no choice but to keep a very close eye upon where she stepped.

His sense of urgency began to infect her. She felt her insides knot with fear as she stumbled along behind him. As they stepped into the wood at the far northern edge of the village's fields, she began to relax only to cry out softly in fear as a man called out Tavig's assumed name. Tavig pushed her behind him, drew his sword, and turned to face the man in one clean, graceful move. When the shadowy figure moved into the moonlight, Moira began to relax again. It was only one man carrying a bundle and towing a goat. She felt Tavig ease his tense stance and knew she was right to think that there was no threat.

"Iain," Tavig said, nodding curtly at the older man. "I fear your daughter has gotten herself entangled in something she cannae get out of."

"I ken it. She is dead. As I hurried to meet ye I saw her hanging from the tree in the square."

"I am sorry."

"Ye have naught to be sorry about. She tried to have your wife killed. Aye, I will grieve. She was of my flesh, but the lass has spent most of her short life rushing toward just such an ending."

"How did ye ken where to meet me?"

"I was going to Robert's cottage to meet with ye there, but saw ye preparing to flee. I was sure ye wouldnae leave by the road ye came in on so I hurried here. I couldnae let ye disappear again without seeing you."

"But why?"

"To give ye this." Iain held out the bundle he carried, placing it into a frowning Tavig's arms.

Moira did not need to see the stunned look on Tavig's face to know exactly what was swaddled in the bundle of cloth he held. She had already guessed. A small voice in her head told her she did not want to know any more, but as Tavig tugged open the swaddling, she moved closer to get a better look. Although there was only a shadowy light of the moon, she bit back a cry as she looked at the baby's face. The child carried Tavig's mark. Jeanne had borne Tavig a child.

"It cannae be . . ." Tavig began, his voice weakened by shock.

"Aye, it can and it is. 'Tis your son, and I am giving him to you."

"Iain, I mean no insult, nor do I wish to speak ill of the dead, but Jeanne . . ."

"Was a whore. I ken it. She has been so afflicted since her first flux."

"So how can ye be so certain this child is mine?"

"The eyes," Moira whispered.

"Aye," agreed Iain. "Your lassie has the right of it. The boy has those black eyes of yours, lad. When Jeanne birthed him, I waited to see the color of his eyes. I had hoped they would match one of the lads in the village so that I could get her wedded off. There isnae a mon here who has those eyes. That bairn is your son, born of your flesh."

Tavig stared at the child, who stared right back at him. He wanted to deny any kinship, but he could not. Even if the boy did not have his eyes, Tavig's instinct told him that the child was his. The moment he had looked into the baby's face he had been sure of it. He glanced at Moira, silently cursing when she refused to look his way. Although holding his son had already filled him with a strong sense of possession, as well as a vast array of confusing and conflicting emotions, he cursed the fates for bringing him the child now.

"Iain, I am traveling on foot and have at least a week's

journey ahead of me. I cannae take the bairn. He is of your flesh, too."

"I ken it and I will sorely miss the wee lad. He is a good bairn, quiet as weel as strong. I cannae keep him. I have eight of my own, a wife, and her widowed sister's family to feed. I am a poor mon, lad, and weel ye ken it. And, think on this, my Jeanne was his mother. If he stays here he will pay dearly for that as he grows into a mon."

"How old is he?"

"Eight months, nearing nine."

"His name?"

"He doesnae have one, I fear. Jeanne had the mad idea that ye would wed her once ye kenned she had given ye a son, so she was leaving the naming of him for ye to do. I told her ye might take the lad, but that ye would ne'er wed her." He shrugged. "She wouldnae heed me. I wouldnae mind hearing how the laddie fares from time to time."

"Ye will be told. I swear to it."

Iain dragged the goat over to Moira, stuffing the animal's lead into her hand. "The child thrives on the goat's milk. Has since the day he was born. Jeanne wasnae the sort of lass to feed a bairn herself." He handed her a sack. "Ye will find all ye need for him in here. I am sorry to set this trouble in your arms, mistress, but I cannae care for the lad. I swear to ye, he is a good bairn and will give ye little trouble. I pray ye willnae fault him for his mother."

"Nay, sir. I would ne'er do that. No bairn should be made to pay for the sins of his mother." She glanced at Tavig. "Or father. He will be cared for as weel as possible."

"I ken that ye will do your best. Take care. God be with ye, laddie," he murmured, pausing briefly to kiss the baby's cheek before disappearing into the wood.

"Moira," Tavig said quietly as soon as the man was gone.

She grimaced, forcing herself to look at Tavig yet not give in to the emotions tearing at her. Seeing him holding the child, Jeanne's child, made restraint very difficult. She needed time to recover from the shock.

"I thought ye felt it was verra important for us to get as far away from here as we can. Have ye changed your mind about that, then?" she asked.

"Nay, 'tis still important. The villagers kenned that they had been tricked into making false accusations and turned their anger on the one who tricked them. I dinnae want to linger here to see if they might now feel angry that they have been driven to kill one of their own and would like to blame us for that."

"Then we had best be moving along." She adjusted the sacks she had to carry and started to walk.

"'Twill be awkward to walk carrying this bairn."

She stopped, taking a deep breath, and turned back to him. Without saying a word, she made a sling out of one of their blankets, tied it on herself and secured the baby inside it. With the child tucked snugly against her chest, she handed the sacks to Tavig, took hold of the goat's lead, and started on her way again. To her relief, Tavig made no effort to speak to her. She was afraid of what she might say to him while her emotions still ran so hot and were so confused.

Anger was one emotion she easily recognized, but she was not really sure what she was angry about. She had never thought Tavig was as untouched and innocent as she. A bastard child should come as no great surprise. She decided that knowing Tavig had bedded other women was a lot easier to endure than seeing the tangible proof of his past. And there was no more tangible proof than the cooing child pressed against her. She was going to have to convince herself that giving a woman a child was not necessarily a sign of any true affection. Considering the number of illegitimate children cluttering the land, she was a little surprised that she still clung to such a hazily romantic ideal.

There was also jealousy and hurt stirring within her. She did her best to banish those feelings. The babe was nine months old and had taken nine months to be formed. She had not even known who Sir Tavig MacAlpin was eighteen months ago, and he had not known anything about her. It would be the height of foolishness to consider the making of the child as some personal affront. The only thing that should matter to her was how Tavig had and did act while he was with her. In that she had no cause for complaint, jealousy, or hurt.

Yanking the stubborn goat up a steep path, she continued to scold herself for how she was feeling. If nothing else, she wished such ill feelings banished from her heart before the tiny boy she carried could become aware of them and be hurt by them. Tavig did not deserve them, either, she decided, but resisted the urge to look at him. There would be plenty of time to talk when they made camp. Since she could not go to some private place to sort out her emotions, she kept herself private by simply pretending Tavig was not there.

Tavig cursed when, yet again, he failed to catch Moira's eye. She was acting as if he did not exist. Although he could sympathize with how she must feel, it was extremely annoying to be so totally ignored. He wanted to know what she felt and thought, and he wanted to know now. If he did not learn what was stirring in her heart and mind he would be unable to say what was needed to soothe her.

His deepest fear was that the appearance of his illegitimate son had built a wall between them that he might never breach. The workings of fate, he decided, were not only frivolous, but also cruel. Moira was going to be a hard-won prize. The very last thing he needed was yet another obstacle to her heart. He concentrated on finding them a suitable place to camp for what little remained of the night. Once he had her captive in one spot he would make her talk to him.

Chapter Twelve

"The bairn is asleep, we have eaten, and our bed is readied," Tavig said as he stood across the fire and stared at a
still-silent Moira. "Now we can talk."

"What do ye wish to talk about?" Moira asked, deriving
a little pleasure from the glare of irritation he sent her.

"The bairn. Ye havenae said a word to me since Iain
dropped him in my arms. God's tears, ye have barely even
looked at me. I need to ken what is going on in that bonnie
head of yours."

She studied him for a moment and was surprised to see
that he spoke the truth. He *did* need to know what she was
thinking. It was both pleasing and puzzling. It had been a
very long time since anyone had truly wanted to know
what she thought or felt. She was not sure how she could
put it into words.

The true trick would be to speak honestly yet not reveal
too much about how she felt about Tavig. She still believed
that speaking of her love and trying to get him to love her
would be cruel. She could not stay with the man. The terrifying incidents in the villages they had stopped in had
only strengthened her conviction that a union between
them would be very dangerous.

"He is a bonnie child," she finally said. "And ye need to name him. We cannae keep calling him 'the bairn.'"

"Nay, I ken it. I thought to call him Adair. 'Twas my friend's name."

"One of the men your cousin Iver murdered?" When Tavig nodded, she smiled faintly. "'Tis a good name."

"He was a good mon. There—the child is now named. Is there anything else ye wish to try and divert me with ere we begin to talk?"

"I am not sure what ye wish to me say. In truth, what right do I have to say anything?"

He moved to sit by her side, taking her hand in his. "More right than any other. Aye, and we are lovers now. That certainly gives ye the right to say a word or two when I am handed a son born of another woman. I would not be so reticent had someone arrived to give ye a child ye had borne for another mon."

"Nay. I imagine ye would have a great deal to say," she murmured, half smiling, for he had scowled deeply even as he had said the words. "We both ken verra weel that that will ne'er happen, howbeit. He *is* your son. 'Tis seen clearly with but one look at his tiny face. Ye have placed a strong mark upon the boy."

"Aye. I kenned he was mine the moment Iain set him in my arms. I wouldnae wish him gone, but, considering how many men Jeanne romped in the heather with, it seems verra capricious of fate to make my seed take root. Aye, especially when I was so verra careful," he muttered, scowling as he briefly tried to think of what he had done wrong.

"Mayhap 'tis just that she couldnae rid her body of your seed." She blushed when he looked at her in slight surprise. "I ken it is done. The maids at Sir Bearnard's keep are often free with their favors, yet there are few bastards. I am certain that a woman as careless of her chastity as Jeanne was, must have learned how to be rid of an unwanted bairn. Ye just bred a verra strong lad who wouldnae let Jeanne shake him free."

"Ye are probably right. We are now talking, and ye even look at me now and again, but ye still havenae said how ye feel about all of this. Dinnae try and tell me that ye feel naught, for ye neither spoke nor looked at me for hours. I feared ye were angry with me yet I see no sign of that anger."

"I banished it."

"Aha! So ye were angry."

"I dinnae ken why ye should sound so pleased about that."

"I was feeling confused and uncertain. I thought ye were angry, but I couldnae be sure. I just like to be proven right."

She laughed softly. "Dinnae feel too smug, Sir MacAlpin. Anger was but a part of it." She held up her hand when he started to speak. "Nay, dinnae press me. Most of what I felt was such a tangled mess that even I cannae say what it was. 'Twould be impossible to try to explain it all to you."

"Then tell me why ye were angry with me."

"So ye can argue it away? No need. I have done that for myself. I started by reminding myself that the child who stirred my anger had been conceived eighteen long months ago. I didnae ken who ye were that long ago, and ye didnae ken anything about me. 'Twould be foolish to get upset about things that happened ere we even met each other." She laughed when he hugged her. "So pleased. I cannae believe ye would be so concerned about my anger."

"Nay? When Iain set wee Adair in my arms, I saw that poor tiny bairn as a huge wall rapidly being built between us."

Moira leaned back a little to look at him. "Now, why should ye think that, and why should I allow it? Aye, it pinches that Jeanne is the child's mother. After all, the woman tried to kill me." Moira shook her head. "She couldnae even do it with her own hands but tried to rouse others to commit the crime for her. I cannae let that wrong turn me against ye or the bairn. Ye bedded a willing woman. No more. No less." She realized there was the hint of a question behind her words and inwardly grimaced when he smiled, revealing that he had heard it.

"No more. No less. As I told ye last night, all that went on before was little more than rutting. 'Tis hard to say such things for, again, I dinnae wish the lad gone, but I now wish that I had listened more to my intuitions the last time I passed this way." He grimaced and ran a hand through his hair. "Oh, I let my lusts rule me as I too often have in the past, but that time it troubled me." He glanced toward the baby who slept near the bedding he had spread out for himself and Moira. "I should have kept my breeches laced. I dinnae regret the child but I sorely regret that 'twas Jeanne who bore him. Out of every lass I have kenned since I first felt the spark of interest in them, she is the verra last I should have chosen to be a mother to my child. 'Tis a hard thing to say, but 'tis best that she is dead. She willnae have the raising of Adair."

"And she willnae be able to use your own son against you," Moira said. "Enough. We should not speak ill of the dead and, right now, I fear we cannae find it in our hearts to speak of Jeanne with any kindness. Ye shall have to learn how to do so, though, ere Adair becomes old enough to understand what is said and asks questions about her."

"So will ye."

"I willnae be around to see him, will I? My kinsmen will be at your cousin Mungan's when we arrive, or verra soon thereafter, and they will reclaim me."

"Not if we are married."

"Ye arenae going to start that again, are ye?"

"Because of Adair?"

"Nay, and weel ye ken it. *If* I thought I could be your wife, I wouldnae care how many illegitimate children ye had ere ye met me. How far and wide ye had spread your seed ere we wed would not be my greatest concern.

"Nay, 'tis not the bairn or your rutting past. 'Tis still the fact that a union between us could lead straight to the gallows or the pyre. Surely what has occurred in each of the two villages we have stopped in has shown ye the danger. Superstition and the fear it breeds run deep in the people of this land. When 'tis roused, people are hurt or killed."

Tavig cursed when she moved away to clean out their bowls and put their food safely back into their sacks. "Ye cannae cease living your life because of other people's foolish fears."

"I ken it, but to ignore them is equally as foolish. I cannae live a life where each night could be the one where the villagers kick in our door, torches held high, and drag us to our deaths. I cannae live kenning that at any time we will have to hie into the woods, fleeing the cries of 'Witch, witch.'" She stood in front of him, her hands on her hips. "We are both cursed with something that rouses superstition in many a breast. Apart we can probably get through our lives with only a wee bit of trouble. Together 'tis as if we spit in the eye of superstition, and that will certainly get us knocked down. Twice we were nearly killed because of it."

He grabbed her hand, tugging her down onto his lap. "Nay. Once my gift caused us trouble. The other time it was a jealous woman and an ambitious priest."

"Ambitious? What makes ye think that priest was ambitious?"

"Only Jeanne accused you. No other mon, woman, or child stepped forward to claim that ye had done them harm. A good priest would have sent them all home, would have seen that 'twas no more than a whore's stung vanity causing all the trouble. Not this priest. He saw a chance to make his mark. To find and destroy one of Satan's servants? That would win him favor and prestige. Ye were to be his stepping stone to a larger, richer church. Mayhap even higher than that."

"Not a verra godly mon."

"Nay. The priest who serves my people is a verra godly mon."

"And ye are a verra stubborn mon."

"When I am certain of what I want, I work hard to get it."

"I dinnae ken how ye can be so sure of wanting to wed me. We have only been together for a little more than a week."

"Ye must have kenned something of importance for ye became my lover."

Moira turned in his hold so that she sat facing him, moving her legs so that he was gently caged between them. "I kenned that I wanted you," she said softly, curling her arms around his neck and kissing him lightly on the mouth. "I kenned that I would forever regret not satisfying the passion ye could stir within me." She slowly traced the lines of his lean face with soft, gentle kisses.

"Ye are trying to distract me from a talk about marriage," he said, his voice growing hoarse as she trailed kisses over his throat.

"Is it working?"

"Aye, ye wretch. Verra weel."

She laughed as he moved, standing with her in his arms. He carried her over to their rough bed, gently laid her down, and sprawled on top of her. She had not tempted him solely to shut him up. Her need for him was strong. Moira suspected that facing death yet again fed her greedy desire for Tavig. Tasting the passion he could stir within her was the sweetest way to prove to herself that she had indeed cheated death once again.

"Now mayhap we can finish what we have twice started today, only to be interrupted," he muttered as he yanked off her boots then his own. "Aye, and what I feared ye might now be thinking of denying me."

"Because of Adair?" She lifted her hips to aid him in the removal of her skirts and petticoat.

"Aye, I didnae think that when ye grew so distant to me that ye just tried to sort out your thoughts and feelings. I feared ye had grown distant because ye couldnae forgive me. Since I couldnae—aye, and wouldnae—deny that the child was mine, I wasnae sure I could cross that cold distance and pull ye back to me." Tossing aside the last of their clothing, he eased himself into her arms, sighing with a mixture of pleasure and relief. "I feared that we would ne'er lie together again."

"Tavig, I near to threw myself into your arms after kenning ye for but one week. Do ye really think that after breaking every rule so completely and so swiftly, I would leave your bed because ye sired a child ere ye had ever met me?"

"Yet ye are willing to allow the fears of ignorant people to send ye away from me." He watched her closely, brushing a few stray wisps of hair from her face.

"The fear of ignorant people can kill us. A bairn can cause us no harm." She threaded her fingers in his thick hair and pulled his face down to hers. "Ye should be flattered that I am so concerned for your safety."

"I am, and it gives me hope. But 'twould flatter me more if ye cared enough to face those risks at my side."

Before Moira could say a word, he kissed her. She quickly ceased to think, allowing herself to become a creature of only feelings. She wanted to sink into the passion they shared, to forget the fear she had tasted but hours ago. Making love with Tavig made her feel a strange mixture of free, strong, beautiful, and safe.

She matched him kiss for kiss, stroke for stroke. The bolder she grew, the fiercer he became in his passion, and his increasing loss of control heightened her own desire. When he joined their bodies, she greedily welcomed him. Her release was swift and blinding. She was only faintly aware of how he shuddered with his own, hoarsely calling out her name, as she fell headlong into the sweet semiconsciousness of ecstasy.

Her senses slowly returned as she savored the lingering warmth in her body. Tavig made a lethargic effort to leave her, and she tightened her grip on him, using her passion-weighted limb to hold him closer. As the last remnants of her desire left her body, she sighed. She was content, sated, all her lingering fears eased, yet she wished the delicious feelings Tavig stirred within her could last far longer than they did.

"Ye are a wonder, dearling," Tavig murmured, easing the intimacy of their embrace, turning onto his side and tugging her into his arms. "A fast learner, too."

Moira smiled against his shoulder as she idly smoothed her hand over his broad chest. "Is that a good thing?"

"Oh, aye, this mon certainly thinks so. It could be bad for my health, though." He smiled and kissed her forehead when she giggled. "We had best get some sleep. There isnae much left of this night, and we cannae sleep away the day. We still have too many miles to go."

Stretching languorously when he rose to put on his braies, Moira wondered idly if Tavig knew what a fine figure of a man he was. A huge yawn broke her fascination with Tavig's lean form, and she realized how exhausted she was. After slipping on her chemise, she waited for Tavig to return to bed and then curled up in his arms. Even as she relaxed, preparing to go to sleep, a concern tickled at her mind.

"Oh, the bairn," she murmured, sitting up to look at the sleeping child. "Are ye sure 'tis safe to leave him sleeping on the ground like that?"

"We have no other place for him to sleep."

"I think he is old enough to move about, Tavig. He could wake without our kenning it and crawl away."

Tavig sat up frowning and rubbing his chin. "I suppose we could take him into the bed between us. Then we would sense if he began to move about." He sighed, smiling crookedly at her. "Although I much prefer curling up with you in the night."

"And I much prefer you, especially since bairns can be quite damp by the morning. I think we shall have to put him between us, howbeit. He could hurt himself badly

crawling about our camp or the wood without someone
to watch o'er him."

Inwardly cursing then silently apologizing to the tiny
Adair, for it was not the child's fault, Tavig set the sleeping
baby in between him and Moria. As he resettled himself beneath the blanket, Adair turned, snuggling up to Moria.

Tavig frowned at the child, a little ashamed over the
pinch of jealousy that assailed him, then glanced up to
meet Moria grinning at him.

"Like father, like son," Moira said, laughing softly.

"Verra amusing." He lightly touched the child's thick
black curls. "He doesnae enjoy all the benefits his father
does," he drawled, smiling when Moria blushed then tried
to look annoyed. "This is all verra cozy, but I shall be
pleased to get the child into his own bed."

Moira closed her eyes, the need to go to sleep swiftly
grabbing hold of her. "Aye, it wouldnae be good for him to
become too accustomed to this."

Tavig watched her as she fell asleep. He knew she was
not referring to some normal rule of child-rearing but to
the fact that she did not intend to be around much longer.
If little Adair became too attached to her, he would be hurt
when she left. Tavig wondered if she gave any thought to
how *he* would feel, then hastily subdued his flash of anger
at her. She had never said that she would stay, had clearly
stated her reasons for refusing to marry him. He had no
right to be angry with her.

Failure was a bitter taste in his mouth. Moira had become
his lover, but he wanted more—much more. He cursed fate
for having shown him his mate only to thrust them into sit-
uations that convinced Moira they could not marry. It was
as if God and fate were forcing him through some ordeal.

Gently draping his arm around Moira and Adair, he
edged as close to them as he dared without waking them.
Moira had quickly accepted his son. That had to mean that
she cared for him. He was almost afraid to search his heart
and face what he felt for her. The terror he had experienced

when she had been dragged before the priest gave him a painful glimpse of his feelings. So did the cold that seeped through his veins when he thought of her leaving him. Somehow he was going to have to break through her stubborn resistance. He just wished he could shake the feeling that he faced a long, hard fight.

Moira grunted as a weight settled on her stomach and chest. She cautiously opened one eye, exhaustion clouding her vision. Adair's face was but inches from her own. She watched a bubble of drool leave his mouth then winced as it hit her on the nose. A sigh escaped her as she wiped it off and another quickly replaced it. The dim light surrounding them told her that it was barely dawn. She ached to go back to sleep, but the wide, bright obsidian eyes staring down at her told her she would not be allowed that luxury. A fleeting glance revealed that Tavig was still sleeping.

"I didnae suppose it occurred to ye to wake up your father," she whispered, gently moving the child off her and slipping out of bed.

The air was cool enough to make her shiver. She dressed quickly, keeping a close eye on Adair. She had had little to do with small children. There had been a few in and around Sir Bearnard's keep, but the mothers had done their best to keep the children out of sight and very quiet. Moira suspected Sir Bearnard's brutal temper had a great deal to do with that.

"Ye cannae be that hungry, laddie," she murmured, gently taking away a rock before Adair could stuff it into his mouth. "Just be patient whilst I try to get ye your milk."

She changed his wet rags, smiling at the way he played with his feet. He had to be hungry, but he did not fret. Moira started to get the uneasy feeling that, unlike a lot of babies, he just knew that he would be fed. She quickly scolded herself for giving in to foolish superstition. He had his father's eyes, but that did not mean he also had his father's unique gift. Adair was simply a quiet, happy child and, if she did not hurry and get him his milk, he would probably start howling.

By the time she filled Adair's goatskin bottle, Tavig was awake. He grinned at the way she cursed the goat, which was reluctant to give up its milk to her inexperienced hands. Moira picked up Adair, sitting by the fire as Tavig started it. She looked from Adair to Tavig and back again several times as the baby quietly drank his milk.

"He really does look like you," she said with a smile, finding that what had been painful at first now amused her.

"Aye, Jeanne didnae leave her mark on the boy at all. At least, not that we can see now." He began to prepare their porridge.

"Will it trouble ye if he does grow to reveal some hint of his mother?"

"Nay. I but worried that he might carry some of the traits that made her bad. Then I pushed that fear aside as foolish. Jeanne willnae have the raising of him. Iain is a good mon, but his wife oftimes complains about how poor they are. I think Jeanne took those complaints, that unhappiness with her lot, to heart and thought that being a whore would gain her something better. Aye, she did gain a few wee gifts and coin, but she failed to see that that was all she would ever get."

"And Adair willnae suffer that need to have better?" Moira asked as she held the baby against her shoulder, rubbing his back to ease out any air he may have swallowed. She idly wondered if he was already too old for such help then decided he was enjoying the attention, so it could do no real harm.

"I hope Adair will suffer no want at all, but he willnae be taught that unhappiness. He willnae grow to a mon thinking that 'tis right to do *anything* to gain some coin. He likes you," he added abruptly.

Moira shook her head, fully aware of Tavig's ploy. "He is a bairn. Bairns havenae been taught to dislike people.

They are full of trust and love. Ye dinnae really wish to try to hold me through Adair, do ye?" she asked softly. "Ye wouldnae want him caught up in the peril that our marriage could cause."

"I dinnae believe that a marriage between us would cause any more peril than we see each and every day whilst apart from each other. I can see that ye dinnae wish to listen to reason, howbeit."

"I could say the same thing about you, Sir Tavig Mac-Alpin. Ye sink your teeth into an idea and cling to it like a ferret."

"Aye. I have been called persistent."

"Stubborn."

"Determined."

She laughed, shaking her head as she set Adair down next to her and took the bowl of porridge Tavig held out to her. Beneath her laughter was a lingering pain, however. The end of their journey would mark the end of her time with Tavig and this loomed ahead of her like a death sentence. She knew that she had to leave him for both their sakes. She also knew that it would tear her heart out. Halting his talk of marriage would not lessen that pain, so she decided to let him talk. It allowed her to state her reasons for refusing yet again, and perhaps he would eventually accept them. They were very good reasons. He had to see that.

As she allowed Adair to suck a bit of porridge off her spoon, she prayed she could armor herself against the child as she had failed to do against the father. She did not need to pine for yet another MacAlpin. It saddened her already to think of leaving the child, for she knew she would be able to accept him as her own. Many another woman would not be able to do so.

She quickly shook away that thought. It could easily convince her that she needed to stay with Tavig for the child's sake. It was almost laughable. She had just scolded Tavig for his tentative attempt to use the child to hold her to his side, yet she was obviously capable of using the child herself—as an excuse to go against her better judgment and follow her heart. Suddenly afraid he could easily read her thoughts, if only by the expressions on her face, Moira leapt to her feet.

"I have to rinse out the bairn's wet clothes," she said. "Ye will have to watch o'er him." Snatching up the goatskin of water, Moira walked away.

Tavig frowned after her, moving quickly to catch Adair, who started to crawl after her. He held on to the boy as he put out the fire. Although Moira was only a few feet away trying to rinse out Adair s things, Tavig could not shake the chilling feeling that she had just run away from him. A look of something akin to fear had sped across her face just before she had leapt to her feet. As Tavig rubbed their eating utensils clean with a great deal of help from Adair, he carefully sorted out everything that had occurred or been said just before Moira's abrupt retreat.

Suddenly he sat back on his heels and looked at Adair, who was happily chewing on a wooden spoon. Moira had not run from him but from the child. She had suddenly seen how easily she could soften to the boy. That could become a weakness, one that might end her stiff resistance to the idea of marrying him. She had rightfully scolded him for trying to use the child to pull her to his side, only to see that she could also end up using the child as a means to stay with him.

It was only a theory and a wild one at that, but Tavig could not shake the conviction that he was right. He did not want her to stay because of the boy but because her heart told her that he was her true mate. A fortnight might not be enough time to convince her of that, however. Tavig smiled at his son. It might not be the honorable or fair thing to do but it was very comforting to know that if all else failed, he did still hold one last toss of the dice.

Chapter Thirteen

Moira gaped at Tavig as he burst through the trees, running straight toward her. They had stopped so that she could give Adair his afternoon meal. Although they had only had the child with them for two days, Adair was adjusting to the journey with ease. Even he looked startled by Tavig's abrupt arrival, however. Then Moira saw the tense expression on Tavig's dark face, and she felt fear tickle its way down her spine.

"Ye didnae find the rabbit ye were looking for, did ye?" she said, stuffing Adair's things back into his sack in preparation for the order to leave she expected Tavig to give.

"Nay," he replied. "But I did see a pack of wolves and I fear they saw me." He helped her get Adair into the sling she wore across her chest.

"Those are wolves following you?"

"Sorry, dearling, I am being unclear. These wolves are men, hunters sent out by my cousin Iver. Now, I want ye to take the goat, our supplies, and all else ye can carry and go and hide."

"But, Tavig, what are ye going to do? Ye should be trying to find a place to hide as weel."

"They are too close. I am going to lead them away from ye and the bairn. If I dinnae return by the time the sun begins to set, ye are to continue on to Mungan's without me. Straight o'er those hills to the north. Go," he demanded, giving her a slight push. "Ye dinnae want to fall into the hands of these curs, and they cannae find my son, either."

She wanted to argue with him but she could hear the men approaching. Although she could demand to go with him, she no longer had only herself to consider. Tavig was right. His enemies could not be allowed to find Adair. Iver would see Adair as just another impediment to all he coveted. Adair's life was in as much danger as Tavig's.

As Tavig disappeared into the trees she hurried to find a good hiding place. Just as she found a hollow inside a clump of thick shrubs encircling a boulder she heard a cry rise up from Iver's men. Tavig had been spotted. Now all she could do was hide, wait, and pray.

Tavig cursed as he looked over his shoulder. He tried to keep to the thick wood that slowed his mounted pursuers, but they were still gaining on him. Worse, he was approaching a clearing, and they were blocking his way back into the forest. Once out of the wood, they would easily overrun him.

As he broke through the last of the trees and underbrush into the open land, he cursed again. His gift of foresight had failed him miserably this time. It had given him no warning at all. Intent upon finding some meat for their evening meal, he had practically walked into his enemies' hands. All his efforts to elude Iver's dogs were proving useless. He knew that the minute he saw them and they saw him. His only consolation was that Moira and Adair were safe.

Once out into the open field, Iver's men quickly encircled him. Tavig drew his sword, hoping to take down at least a few of the six well-armed men before they captured him. He had no doubt that he would lose the fight, but he wanted them to pay dearly for their victory.

Wounding two of the men proved so easy Tavig felt his hopes rise. Even as he pulled a third man from his saddle, his brief hope of freedom was brutally extinguished. Before Tavig could get on the riderless horse a burly man slammed into him from behind. Tavig hit the ground hard enough to push all the breath from his body. He had no chance to fight back, a flurry of kicks and punches sending him into a helpless, semiconscious state. Although he hated to give Iver's men the satisfaction of knowing they had hurt him, he groaned as he was yanked to his feet, one man roughly bringing his hands behind his back. The man standing before him was Andrew MacBain, and Tavig realized he was in the hands of Iver's mercenaries, men cast out by their own clans who were willing and often eager to do anything for coin.

"Iver will pay us weel for this," Andrew said, stroking his dirty, tangled beard. "He is offering a handsome sum for ye, Tavig."

"So I have been told. If ye trust Iver to pay you, ye are a bigger fool than I was."

"Nay, laddie, dinnae try seeding distrust. We have been duly warned about your clever tongue. Iver will pay us the fee he promised to any mon who brought his murdering cousin to justice."

"Fine words coming from the mon who wielded the knife."

"Ye are the only one who kens that aside from Iver and ourselves. Iver daren't speak the truth, and none of my men will, either. Aye, and *ye* shouldnae speak of it too often." He drew his dagger and idly touched its sharp blade. "'Tisnae so rare for a mon to lose his tongue in battle." After holding Tavig's gaze for a moment, he resheathed his dagger. "How are the wounded?" he asked the man on his right.

"Their wounds arenae bad, but they need bandaging."

"Aye. Weel, we have ridden hard this day so we will camp now. Here is as good a place as any. 'Twill be hard for anyone to creep up on us here." He shoved Tavig back down onto the ground. "Tie his ankles," he ordered a thin, scar-faced man.

Once tied, Tavig was left where he was as the men saw to the wounded and prepared their camp. Wincing over the aches in his body, Tavig edged back against a low bush to escape the wind. August was almost over, and the breeze carried the bite of approaching fall. Weakened by the beating he had endured at the hands of his captors, Tavig decided he would be wise to try to avoid catching a chill.

Unless some miracle happened, Iver had won, and that was a bitter taste in Tavig's mouth—a defeat made all the more bitter by how close he had come to reaching Mungan Coll, aid, and safety. The moment Moira reached Mungan and told him everything that had happened, he was certain Mungan would try to come to his rescue. He was also sure it would be too late. MacBain and his hard-eyed men would get him to Iver before Moira could get to Mungan. Iver would undoubtedly take some time to gloat over his victory, but not enough to allow Mungan to rescue him.

As he thought of Moira, Tavig sighed, saddened by the thought of never seeing her again and angry at himself for not planning for such an inevitability. She was not his wife, nor had he the tools or the time to write down his wishes for her future. She would have no choice but to return to Sir Bearnard's brutal care. Tavig could not shake the feeling that he had failed her—badly.

And his son as well, he realized, cursing viciously at himself. He had not claimed Adair as his own by spoken or written word. That was going to make it very difficult for Adair to claim what was his by birthright, far more his than Iver's. Despite his looks, Adair would have a hard time proving that he was Tavig MacAlpin's son. Worse, when Moira was taken from the child, the boy would truly be orphaned. It was only a small comfort to know Mungan would care for the boy.

At least they are alive, he told himself fiercely. If

Andrew MacBain and his cohorts had captured Moira and
Adair, neither would have survived for long. Worse, Tavig
knew he would have had to live through the hell of watching Moira abused then murdered. The very thought of it
twisted his insides into hard, painful knots of fear. Tavig
prayed that Moira had the good sense to do exactly as he
had ordered.

Moira stared up at the sky as she finished changing
Adair's rags. She could no longer deny that it was sunset,
and Tavig was nowhere to be seen. Setting Adair in his sling,
she used another blanket to set the sacks of supplies like
panniers on the goat's back. Head straight for the hills, Tavig
had told her. Looking down at a peacefully sleeping Adair,
she knew she had no choice but to obey. Her only hope—
and she knew it was a small one—was that she would reach
Mungan Coll in time for him to hie to Tavig's rescue. Not
only did she doubt her ability to get to Mungan's keep with
any great speed, but also she doubted Iver would allow
Tavig to live very long after he got his hands on him.

"He wouldnae let *ye* live verra long either, laddie," she
murmured, winding her way through the trees, fixing her
gaze on the hills she had to cross and dragging the reluctant goat behind her. "Ye are Tavig's son. Ye may not have
been claimed openly by him—save within my hearing—
and ye may have no paper, but ye do have the look of him.
Iver would take one peek at ye and ken exactly who ye are.
He willnae think on how ye have naught to prove your
claim, he will just see Tavig's son and want ye dead. I just
wish that saving your life didnae mean losing all chance to
save Tavig. Not that I could help him anyway,"she grumbled, shoving aside a branch blocking her path.

Adair gurgled sleepily, reaching out to grab her long
braid and tucking it against his cheek as he closed his eyes.
Moira briefly touched his thick black curls and sighed. She
was so afraid for Tavig she ached, yet every instinct told her

to walk away from him, to leave the man and save the child. Moira prayed that when Adair grew up, he would understand not only why she made such a choice, but how hard it was for her to do it.

The colors of sunset were fading to the dull gray of twilight by the time she reached the end of the wood. She frowned toward the hills she was supposed to cross. Between her and them was a wide stretch of open land with only a few wind-contorted shrubs, none of which was big enough to hide her, the baby, and the goat. The grass was long, but it would only hide her if she crawled, and the goat could not be made to do that.

She tied the goat's lead to a low tree branch then edged forward. There was no sign of Tavig's enemies between her and the hills, but she knew that did not mean that they were gone. Cautiously, keeping to the shelter of the trees, she moved to look to the west, relieved to find no signs of people there.

When she looked to the east she froze. A fire was clear to see, as were the six men gathered around it. What held her full attention was the figure on the ground, half-hidden by a low shrub. She was sure she was looking at Tavig's hunters and Tavig himself. The figure on the ground moved slightly, and she breathed a sigh of relief. Tavig was alive.

Adair shifted a little in the sling, and she silently cursed. Knowing Tavig was so close and alive had briefly caused her to forget her priorities.

"But kenning that he is in reach and alive, how can I just walk away?"

And just what do ye think ye can do? asked a snide voice inside her head. She had no answer. As she continued to watch the men she began to have an idea, however. Tavig's captors were clearly not swilling water from the skins they were tipping up to their mouths. Even from where she stood she could hear the increasing rowdiness that indicated inebriation. If the men kept drinking as heavily as they were, Tavig's captors would soon be aware of very little.

She came to a decision, praying that she was not allowing emotion to conquer good sense. Returning to the goat, she untied the animal, gagged him, and started toward the hills. Moira kept looking in the direction of the men's fire but did not see it until she was within a few feet of the rocky base of the hills. She covered those last several feet swiftly, anxious to get within the shelter of the rocks.

Tugging the goat along, she wended her way over the uneven ground until she found a drover's trail. She tied the goat to a windblown shrub then looked for a good place to hide Adair. Although she did not plan to leave him alone for very long, she needed a place that was sheltered from the night air and any animals that might wander by.

There was nothing to meet her requirements, and she slumped against a moss-covered rock. Moira knew she could not just tuck the child away, even for only a little while. If something happened to her, he would die. She was going to have to take him with her. Even as she wondered if she had gone completely mad, she took a knife from Tavig's sack of supplies.

"Adair, ye have been the quietest bairn I have e'er met," she said, lightly touching his cheek and smiling faintly when he smacked his lips in his sleep. "Please, I beg of you, dinnae change your ways now. We are going to try to save your father, or at least give him a second chance to save himself."

Moira took a deep breath and raced back across the clearing, pausing to breathe once she reached the safety of the trees. "If Tavig escapes," she muttered, "he is going to kill me—slowly."

After taking a moment to bolster her courage, she began to make her way through the trees. She could see the light of the fire again and crept along until she was directly across from it. Easing off the sling, she gently placed a still-sleeping Adair on the ground. She could see the bush Tavig huddled near, his long body too big to be completely hidden by it. Once at the very edge of the trees, she clamped the knife between her teeth and dropped to her stomach. Praying that the men were as drunk and half asleep as they appeared, she edged toward Tavig on her belly. All she had to do was cut his bonds and hand him the knife, she told herself over and over as she inched closer to him.

Tavig winced as he tried to shift his cramped body into a more comfortable position. He glared at his captors. The two men he had wounded had already drunk themselves into unconsciousness. Two of the others were sprawled on the ground, soon to join them, and the other two would not be able to stay awake much longer. Their confidence in his inability to escape or threaten them angered Tavig, especially since he knew they had every right to feel that way.

A faint tug on the ropes around his wrists caused him to tense. He resisted the urge to jerk away, his first thought being that some animal was inspecting him for his value as food. The cool touch of steel against his skin told him what was happening—someone was cutting him free. He knew it had to be Moira.

"What in God's sweet name are ye doing here?" he asked in a taut whisper, keeping his gaze fixed upon MacBain and his men.

"What little I am able to do to try to keep ye alive," she whispered back.

"Lass, I told ye to run, to flee."

"Aye, and I was being verra obedient until I saw you. Now, cease talking, or one of those pigs may stagger over here to see why ye are muttering away to yourself."

"Adair," he protested, elated to have a chance to escape, yet furious that she would put herself in danger.

"He is quite safe, and as soon as I cut you loose, we will be scrambling o'er those wee hills. I willnae do any more than cut through your bonds. I cannae. Adair and I are crossing o'er the hills at a point where the forest is closest to the rocks. If ye can get away, that is where ye will be able to find us."

"Dinnae hesitate and try to wait for me to join you."

"I have no intention of doing that. In fact, I intend to move as fast as I dare and get as far away as possible. There," she said as she finished cutting through the ropes binding his ankles. "Take care."

He heard only the faintest of rustles as she left. It surprised him that she could move with such stealth. Still watching his captors, he subtly tried to rub the feeling back into his wrists and ankles. He waited tensely for some outcry that would indicate that Moira had been seen. Minutes crept by, and none of the men even glanced toward the hills. Relieved though he was that she had escaped, Tavig vowed to rebuke her soundly for the risks she had taken. He had to admire her skill, however.

Andrew MacBain was the last man to tumble into a drunken stupor. Tavig closed his eyes. He had been staring so long and so hard at his captors that his eyes burned. After the stinging eased he glanced toward the men again. He had to be certain they were past waking before he attempted his escape. His only chance to remain free was to get as deep into the hills as he could before they realized he was gone. Only briefly did he contemplate stealing one of their horses. The animals were too close to the men. Tavig could not chance rousing them.

It was several more minutes before he felt confident that none of the men could move until morning. Tavig continued to watch them closely, however, as he edged back into the forest. He nearly groaned aloud when he finally stood up. His first steps were awkward and unsettlingly noisy as he wound his way through the dark wood. When he finally reached the rocky base of the hills, he ached to rest, but pressed on.

Tavig was surprised at how long it took him before he caught his first hint that Moira was directly ahead of him.

He had to smile, for he heard her before he saw her. Alone she could creep about like a ghost. Dragging the stubborn goat stole every bit of stealth from her movements. He knew he could walk up beside her and tap her on the shoulder before she would know he was even near at hand. That would frighten her too much to be amusing, however.

"Moira," he called, smiling faintly at the way she gasped, spinning round to gape at him.

"Is that ye, Tavig?"

"Nay, 'tis a spirit that simply sounds like me."

"How verra amusing. I ken it was a foolish question," she said as he walked over to her, "but ye cannae expect a lass's wits to be verra sharp after she has been dragging this cursed beast about all night long."

After lightly rubbing the goat's head, Tavig took the lead from her hands. "He wants to rest. Ye cannae fault him for that." He glanced at the way she had secured their supplies to the goat's back. "A good idea."

"Thank ye. Ye dinnae think it will cause the beast's milk to dry up, do ye?"

"It may, but not before we reach Mungan's." He touched a kiss to her mouth. "Thank ye for saving my fool neck." Tugging on the goat's lead, he started to walk. "Ye shouldnae have done it, though. I thought I had made it clear that ye should take the bairn and run—as far and as fast as ye could."

"Aye, ye made it verra clear," she agreed as she followed him up the rocky slope, glad to hear no real anger in his voice. "I didnae like deserting ye, but I was doing exactly what ye told me to do."

"If ye had been, ye wouldnae have been creeping through the grass and cutting my bonds."

"I meant I was obeying you in the beginning, but once I saw where ye were and that ye were still alive, I *had* to do something."

"Ye put yourself and my son in danger. I wasnae lying when I told ye it would be dangerous for ye and Adair if Iver got his hands on you. As dangerous as it is for me."

"Oh, I believed you. As I said, I was being verra obedient. Then I saw ye, captive but still alive. I also saw how weak your guard was. I had a long talk with myself and decided I couldnae just walk away. 'Twould forever trouble me. Aye, and I thought of how someday your son might ask me about this day. I decided to do just one little thing, to give ye the chance to save yourself. The drunken state of your guards made it easy to slip up through the trees and cut your ropes."

"And what did ye do with the bairn while ye were creeping about?" When she did not answer, he stopped, turning to look at her. "From the guilty look upon your face, I have the feeling ye are about to tell me ye carried my son into the verra heart of the enemy's camp."

"Actually I was trying to think of a way not to tell ye the truth yet not lie to you, either."

"Moira!"

"Weel, I couldnae leave him alone, could I? And it wasnae into the *verra heart* of the enemy's camp, just on the edge." She gave him a weak smile as he stared at her in disbelief for a full moment. "I am sorry, Tavig. I couldnae do nothing when I could *see* you, bound and helpless. If I had left Adair alone and been captured, he would have died anyway. A wee bairn could ne'er survive out here alone. I was sure I could get close enough to cut your bonds without being seen or heard."

"Adair could have made a noise and alerted Iver's men."

"True, but he is such a quiet, contented lad I felt the chance of him remaining quiet was verra good."

Tavig cursed softly, shaking his head as he started walking again. "Ye are mad. Aye, and I must be a wee bit mad myself for I can understand your reasoning. Just where did ye learn to move about with a stealth any soldier would envy? 'Tis not a skill a wee lass usually acquires."

"When ye live with a mon like Bearnard Robertson, ye learn to keep verra quiet and out of sight. The verra last thing I wished to do was to draw his attention, for he seemed to be forever angry with me. 'Tis nice that I could put that skill to a good use, one besides keeping myself safe from Bearnard's anger."

"I really hate to be grateful to that mon for anything, even for teaching you something that worked to save my miserable life."

"Ah, but he didnae teach me. He just inspired me to teach myself." She matched his quick grin with one of her own. "In truth, 'tis not such an unusual skill at Sir Bearnard's keep. Most everyone trapped there learns to move about like a ghost."

"And yet ye are planning to return to that wretched place."

"I have no choice."

Tavig stopped short, spinning round to stare at her so abruptly she took a quick step backward. "Aye, ye do have a choice. I have been offering ye one since the day we woke up on that pitiful beach. Ye just refuse to take it. Considering how much ye just risked to save my life, I understand the reasons for your refusal less and less."

"That is because ye refuse to listen to my reasons or accept how the incidents at those thrice-cursed villages justify them. A match between us will only enflame people's superstitions, thus putting us both in peril. I have said that so often I begin to feel like a child repeating her lessons for a verra demanding tutor."

"Ye are no coward, Moira. Your courage has been proven time and again on this journey. I find it hard to believe ye will run back to Bearnard's brutal care because ye believe our marriage will stir superstition. I find it hard to believe ye would run from superstition at all."

"I dinnae think that I am as brave as ye try to make me," she protested, although flattered by his words. "If I see a danger and still walk toward it, howbeit, is that not foolish? Especially where there *is* a choice of direction? Then, too, did ye not think that I might be doing what is best for ye or whatever children we may have? Mayhap I am simply not brave enough to face what could happen to you or to our bairns because we tried to spit in the eye of superstition."

"My people arenae so blinded by such foolishness. We could be safe amongst them."

"Ye can be safe, but even their tolerance can be pushed too far."

"I think not. There is only one way to prove that to you. Ye must stay with me until ye meet my people. Then ye can decide."

"Why prolong the matter? I cannae see it changing my mind. 'Twould be better to go when my kinsmen come to collect Una."

Moira wished that he would not keep trying to persuade her. It made it harder and harder to say nay. She desperately wanted what he offered even though he never once mentioned love. His persistence kept reminding her of the secret she was keeping from him, something she was feeling increasingly guilty about. As far as she knew, he kept no secrets from her.

Tavig stepped closer, gently grasping her by the shoulders. "Ye can go back to the wretched life Sir Bearnard offers at any time. All I ask is a few more days of your life. Now, promise me ye will stay with me until I have regained all Iver has stolen from me."

"Aye. I promise."

He grinned, gave her a brief but stirring kiss, and took up the goat's lead again. As Moira followed Tavig, she cursed herself as a weakling. She had given him the promise because she did not have the strength to refuse him something he wanted so badly. It was also tempting to accept a few more days with him, to delay the pain of leaving him. She prayed his people were not as tolerant as he thought they were, or she could easily be coerced into staying longer. Moira knew that would be a grave error. She could not hide her gift from him forever.

Chapter Fourteen

"Ye said your cousin's keep was just o'er these hills. Ye didnae say these hills were endless," Moira grumbled as she sat down on a moss-covered rock. "We have been crossing them for two cursed days."

"We had to take a winding route to avoid Iver's men," Tavig reminded her as he finished milking the goat and handed Moira Adair's noon feeding. "If Iver's hired dogs dinnae block our way at every turning, we will reach Mungan's keep by day's end on the morrow."

Frowning at Tavig over the contentedly drinking Adair, Moira said, "I really hadnae thought those men would pursue us with such vigor and determination."

"Iver is offering a heavy purse in ransom for me. Then, too, they dinnae wish to return to Iver without their quarry. Iver isnae one who forgives failures. Since two of the men are now marked with wounds, Iver will easily guess that the men had had me in their grasp but lost me. He willnae believe them if they try to deny it. It could weel be that they see finding me as a matter of life and death."

"That would certainly explain their persistence. Of course, if they keep riding about they will soon have to halt and take time to bury those two wounded men. They cannae survive much longer without rest and care."

"I wouldnae wager on the others stopping to bury anyone." He shrugged when her eyes widened with a hint of shock. "They dinnae possess even that much delicacy of feeling. They fight weel together, but not one of them would exert himself or put himself at risk for another. In truth, if they gained the price Iver offers for me, they would undoubtedly take to killing each other over it. The only thing that binds them together is that they have all been cast out by their own clans."

"They will follow us to Mungan Coll's verra gates, will-nae they?"

"I expect them to be putting themselves between us and Mungan. They have to have guessed that I am traveling there."

"Then I pray I am right in assuming ye have some plan to slip us past them safely."

"One or two—aye. Dinnae worry so, sweet Moira. We do have one advantage."

"Over six armed and mounted men? I should like to hear what it is."

"They willnae want to be seen by Mungan or his men. Mungan will recognize who and what they are and will be eager to cut them down. 'Tis a small advantage, true enough but better a small one than none at all."

Moira nodded but inwardly sighed. She had not given much thought to what Iver's men would do once they discovered their prize was gone. She certainly had not imagined the dogged pursuit she and Tavig had been struggling to evade for two exhausting nights and days. The food they had brought from the last village was nearly gone, for they had not been able to light a fire to cook up their porridge. Even a small fire could be seen by Iver's men and lead them right to her and Tavig.

They had been hunted from the beginning of their long journey, but never like this. Now her fear for Tavig was a constant sour taste in her mouth. She feared for herself and Adair as well, but not as strongly. Moira knew Tavig would do exactly what he had done before, put himself in the hands of his enemy in order to give her and his son a chance to reach safety. She feared that most of all, for she was certain her sense of guilt would become crippling. It was bad enough already, for she knew that caring for her and Adair slowed Tavig down.

"Mayhap ye should leave us here, Tavig, and go onto Mungan alone," she suggested as she set aside Adair's empty feeder and proceeded with the ritual of rubbing his back.

Tavig stared at her, then rolled his eyes. "There are times, lass, when ye say the most foolish things."

"There is nothing foolish about it. Ye cannae deny that Adair and I slow ye down and make ye less, weel, agile. Without us ye could probably slip right past those men."

"And what are ye to do whilst I save myself?"

"We will wait here until ye can get some help to come back for us."

"And what will ye do if Iver's dogs stumble upon ye and the bairn? What if those wolves we have heard in the night come sniffing about? Ye cannae light a fire to ward them off without telling Andrew where ye are. I am not even sure ye ken how to start a fire."

"I have watched ye do it for nearly a fortnight. I am sure I can do it."

Moira inwardly cursed. He was making what had sounded like a good idea appear as foolish as he claimed it was. She had not expected him to be gone long enough for her to face any real danger, but she realized she had not thought far enough ahead. It would undoubtedly take him most of a day. She would be alone for at least one night, and she dreaded the thought—but she could not tell him that.

"I didnae wish to be responsible for your capture once again," she said.

"Ye werenae responsible for my capture."

"Nay? If we hadnae been with you, ye could have easily eluded those men. Instead ye had to put yourself right in their path so that they wouldnae find Adair and me. It could happen again." She frowned when he crouched by her side and kissed her cheek. "What was that for?"

"For ye caring so much about my welfare." He gently poked Adair in the ribs, causing the child to giggle and bounce around in Moira's hold. "We will stay together. Mungan's keep is barely a half day's journey from here."

"Aye, if our hunters dinnae force ye to change direction yet again." She sighed, trying to force down the anxiety that made her temper flare. "I am sorry, Tavig. I grow weary of running and hiding."

"As do I, loving. Howbeit, we have been doing that since we fell off that ship."

"But not like this. We havenae had the hunters nipping at our heels, making us afraid to light even a small fire."

Tavig sat down beside her, slipped his arm about her shoulders, and held her close against his side. He understood what troubled her. The same feeling gnawed at him. Iver's hirelings had never been so close for so long. He felt like a rabbit pursued by a hunter, all the entrances to its lair blocked, so that it ran in circles until it dropped. Mungan and safety were just within reach, yet he and Moira had to take so many twists and turns to elude their pursuers they were adding miles to their journey. At times it was difficult not to do something reckless in a vain attempt to shake free of Iver's mercenaries.

"We *will* get to Mungan's, lass. 'Tis just proving a wee bit more difficult than I had planned for." He ruffled Adair's thick curls. "The lad is done. Shall we continue?"

"Aye, let us try to get a few steps closer." Moira sighed as she put Adair back into his sling and stood up. "Pay me no heed, Tavig. I am in a sour temper."

"No need to apologize, loving. My temper isnae much sweeter." He started down the hill, praying that this time they could stay to their chosen path.

"Ye hide it a great deal better than I do."

"Mayhap. If I could ease my temper with words, though,

ye would be hearing a multitude of them. That wouldnae help soothe the fury twisting my belly, however. I need to act. Right now, I would like to find those hirelings Iver sent after us and kill them—slowly."

Moira's eyes widened as she followed him. There had been a wealth of cold anger in his voice. She now realized there were clear if faint signs of the anger churning inside of Tavig. It was there to see in the taut lines of his face, in the way he moved, even in the way he yanked the goat along, not catering to the animal's obstinance in any way. She felt guilty for having been so caught up in her own feelings of frustration, weariness, and anger that she had paid no heed to how he felt.

She promised herself she would cease to complain. It did make her feel a little better to express her feelings, releasing her emotions with bitter words. Tavig did not really need to be troubled with that pettiness, however.

Her good intentions were hard to maintain when, barely an hour later, Tavig hurriedly ushered her into the shelter of some large rocks and gnarled trees. This had happened so often in the last two days that she knew exactly what it meant. Iver's mercenaries were near at hand—again. She was beginning to truly hate those men.

"Where are they now?" she asked.

"Not far to the left of us. They have chosen an easy path down the hill," Tavig answered.

"Mayhap we should follow them for a change." She frowned when Tavig stared at her. "'Twas only a poor jest born of my ill temper. I am sorry. I had promised myself that I would cease to plague ye with it."

Tavig laughed softly, giving her a quick, hard kiss. "Ye werenae plaguing me. And this time ye have come up with a truly inspired idea."

"What do ye mean?" Moira wondered if the strain of the last few days had disordered his mind.

"Lass, where is the last place those fools would think to look for us?" When she just continued to stare at him as if he had lost all of his wits, he answered his own question. "They willnae look behind themselves. They would never expect us to follow on their heels. We should be running for our lives, not trailing along the same path they are. Ye dinnae understand what I am saying?" he asked when she still said nothing.

"Oh, I understand. I was just thinking that it could be verra risky. It will put us verra close to them."

"We are verra close to them now, dearling. Any closer, and they could smell us."

"If we do follow them, what happens when they stop? Ye said they wouldnae go near Mungan's keep, that they willnae wish to be seen by Mungan or his men. That means they will stop short of where we wish to be, and we will have to get around them ere we can travel the rest of the way to your cousin."

"I didnae say it was a perfect plan. Howbeit, at least for a little while we will be going in the right direction and we will ken where they are every step of the way. In truth, getting around them shouldnae be much more difficult or different from what we are doing now. We already spend most of our time trying to evade them."

"All right, we will try it. After all, ye have kept us safe thus far."

Tavig gave a short, bitter laugh. "Safe? I have done a cursed poor job of getting us to Mungan's. If ye had any sense ye would avidly question my judgment. I begin to do so."

"Nonsense. Ye kept us from drowning, got us away from the fools who cried us witches because ye saved that poor child, and got us out of that other village as weel. Ye cannae foresee every trouble we face yet ye get us away from them. Aye, and for two long days ye have kept us out of the hands of Iver's men."

"Without me ye never would have faced those troubles at all."

"Weel, arenae we feeling sorry for ourselves."

"I am stating facts here, Moira. Hard, cold facts ye ought to look at more closely."

"Nay, ye are struggling to don a hair shirt and flog yourself for not being able to stop things that cannae and couldnae be stopped." She adjusted Adair more comfortably in his sling. "If those curs are gone now, I think we had best be on our way."

"Aye, now that ye have soundly rebuffed all my attempts at humility, we may as weel start walking again."

Moira laughed softly as she moved to follow him. Her good humor faded swiftly as they started trailing the men who hunted them so intently. It made her very uneasy to be so close to them even though she knew Tavig was taking extreme care to keep them out of sight. She could not fully shake the feeling that at any moment they would walk straight into the arms of their enemy.

The sun was beginning to set when Tavig signaled her to stop. Moira was exhausted. She sank down onto the ground and wondered if they were going to spend another cold, watchful night huddled in the dark. Moira was beginning to fear that sleeping without the warmth of a fire would soon cause Adair to sicken. She waited patiently as Tavig crept down the trail to see exactly where their enemies were. It was not until she felt his light touch on her arm that she realized she had begun to fall asleep. The sunset had already faded into the gray of twilight.

"Is everything all right?" she asked in a hushed voice as he knelt down beside her.

"Aye. In fact, things are looking verra hopeful, indeed."

"Have the men decided to give up and go away?"

"Weel, nothing that good. They have camped for the night and are obviously as weary as we are. One mon has been set out to stand guard, and, even as I left, he was falling asleep."

"Are we going to try to go around them now?"

"Aye. Mungan's keep is but a mile or two away. It will-nae be easy to reach it in the dark, but the moon will rise soon, and that will help us a wee bit. At least we can be sure that if we slip by these fools unseen, they willnae be hunting us tonight." He handed her Adair's goat's milk. "If ye could see to his needs as quickly as possible, we can use the dark time before the moonrise to our advantage."

Moira struggled to regain some semblance of alertness. The thought that they could reach the safety and comfort of Mungan's keep in but a few hours helped a great deal. The promise of warmth, food, and a bed to sleep in provided enough inspiration to help her conquer her exhaustion.

Adair was very cooperative. Yet again Moira got the unsettling feeling that the child was aware of far more than any babe his age ought to be. He drank his milk faster than he ever had before, did not squirm once as she changed his wrappings, and did not even make his soft, happy, noises he so enjoyed as he was fed. It was as if he somehow understood the need to move quickly and quietly. As she secured him in his sling she gave herself a stern scolding. Adair was a bairn, not even a year old. She was allowing superstition to make her foolish and attribute far too much to simple good behavior. Moira just hoped the air the child had to have swallowed as he drank his milk so hastily did not choose to come out as they tried to creep past their enemies.

She struggled to be calm as she followed Tavig down the trail. Each time she put her foot down she feared breaking a stick or dislodging a stone. Although she was confident of her ability to move quietly, she suddenly found it a little difficult to trust in that confidence.

They passed so close to Iver's men she was sure she could hear them breathing. She fought the urge to look. Tavig had tied cloths around the goat's mouth, and she prayed the animal did not know how to make a noise despite the muzzle. When the men's horses shifted nervously and snorted, she felt her heart stop but obeyed Tavig's abrupt signal to keep on moving. She did not release her breath until they were well past the men's camp.

"Ye are doing just fine, dearling," Tavig whispered as he helped her down a sharp incline.

"I would feel a great deal better if the ground we walked over didnae hold such promise of being noisy."

"We will be on quieter footing in but minutes, love."

When they finally reached the rock-strewn base of the hill, Moira breathed a hearty sigh of relief. The feel of the soft grass and moss beneath her feet made her relax even more. At least she no longer had to fear that some misstep would expose them. She looked at Tavig when he stopped to unmuzzle the goat.

"Are ye sure ye ought to do that?" she asked, recalling how noisy the goat could be at times.

"If Iver's men are even able to hear the beast's cries all the way up in those hills, they will assume he is just one of Mungan's. The gag was agitating him, and I decided that could prove far more dangerous now." He looked back toward the hills. "I will confess it now. I really didnae think we would be able to slip away, certainly not so easily."

"I am verra glad ye didnae confess that before we tried it. I was terrified quite enough without kenning it."

He leaned closer, brushing a kiss over her mouth. "Poor wee Moira. Just a wee bit longer, and we will be safe."

"Will ye tell me the truth if I ask ye if ye can find your cousin's keep in the dark?"

"Aye. And soon it willnae be as dark as it is now. Not much longer, and the moon will shed some light on our path. I fear this is all the rest I can give ye for now."

"'Tis enough."

He nodded and started walking. Moira quickly fell into step behind him. She could barely see the ground so she kept her gaze fixed upon Tavig. If she followed his steps exactly she felt she would be all right. When the moon finally came out, she breathed another sigh of relief. She did not like stumbling along in the darkness.

"There it is, lass," Tavig announced a few moments later. Moira looked in the direction he pointed and nearly

gasped. She had envisioned a small tower house. Mungan
Coll's keep was a great deal larger than that. He had obviously taken a few lessons from the larger English and
French castles. Encircled by a thick curtain wall, it also
looked temptingly secure.

"Do ye think we ought to wait for daylight so that he
can see us better as we approach the walls?" she asked.

"It might be wiser, but now that my goal is in sight, I
really havenae the patience to wait. There are only two of
us, plus Adair and the goat. I dinnae think we will appear
as any great threat. I also ken most of Mungan's men-at-
arms so there is sure to be someone on the wall who will
recognize me."

"Let us hope so. 'Twould be verra annoying to be cut
down by the mon we have struggled to reach for a fortnight." She smiled wearily when Tavig chuckled, then fell
into step at his side as he started toward the castle.

"I think I ought to tell ye a few things about Mungan ere
we get to his gates."

"Ye have told me enough for me to ken that he is an odd
sort of fellow."

"Oh, aye, he is that. He is also big, verra big, and he can
look and sound as fierce as any man I have e'er seen. Ye need
not fear him. He bellows and roars, but 'tis mostly air and
noise. What I think ye need to ken is that, while Mungan can
seem almost foolish at times, he can also be clever, even
sly. Aye, there are times when he is truly slow to grasp fact,
but he can also play the fool to gain himself some advantage.
No matter how he acts, remember that he does have a sharp
wit when he feels inclined to make use of it."

"Are ye sure this cousin is truly trustworthy?"

"In some ways, nay. In most others, aye, verra trustworthy. I trust him not to stab me in the back or act as Iver
does and has. Do ye recall the advice Mungan gave Old
Colin on how to regain Craigmoordun?" When Moira
nodded, he continued. "That is the sort of slyness Mungan
can indulge in. 'Tis mostly harmless unless ye hold the

thing he is after. 'Tis verra hard to explain the sort of mon Mungan Coll is. Just keep in mind that he can be sly."

"I will remember, although I cannae see how it will matter to me. I have nothing he could want."

She thought she saw a brief frown darken Tavig's face but could not be certain. It could easily have been a trick of the shadows caused by the moonlight. Tugging the blanket sling more securely around Adair, she concentrated on getting to Mungan Coll's keep and, she prayed, a soft, warm bed.

As they approached the gates of the castle, Moira felt some of her apprehension return. Barricaded against the dark and all the dangers it could hold, the castle did not look very welcoming. The men on the walls watched her and Tavig so closely she could feel the hairs on the back of her neck stand on end. Once inside, Moira became increasingly sure that she would feel safe, but standing in front of the huge barred gates waiting to be judged and admitted was unnerving.

"'Tis Tavig MacAlpin," Tavig called up to the men on the wall. "I have come to see Mungan."

"'Tisnae easy to see who ye are in this light. Why should we take ye at your word?" called down one man.

"Is that ye, Conan? It sounds like you. Come, what enemy approaches with a lass, a bairn, and a goat?"

"There is something to ponder. But what friend or kin comes in the dark of night? Aye, and when has Tavig MacAlpin e'er arrived at these gates without a horse?"

"When he has been sent to his heels by that bastard Iver. Come, ye can see that we are no threat as we stand here. Let us in so that ye can judge us by a stronger light. If ye deem us enemies surely ye can deal with but the two of us."

"Get right up to the gates then so that only the pair of ye can enter."

Moira stood close to Tavig as he waited next to the gates. A moment later a small door opened. Before she could see who was there, she, Tavig, and the goat were dragged inside, the door slammed and barred behind them. A burly gray-haired man walked up and gave Tavig one long, searching look then enfolded the slimmer Tavig in what looked to be a bone-crushing hug.

"Conan," Tavig protested. "Let a mon breathe."

"So 'tis ye, laddie," Conan said, releasing Tavig and giving him a sound clap on the back. "Mungan will be pleased."

"Ah, good, he is here. I wondered if he would be. I need his help, and from what I hear, he has been a busy lad."

Conan grimaced. "Ah, ye mean the lassie. That was a mistake in many ways, but ye ken how Mungan is once he gets a thought in his head. The twice-cursed thing cannae be shaken out." He nodded toward Moira. "Are ye going to introduce me to your lady?"

"Aye. Conan, this is Moira." Tavig smiled faintly as Conan gallantly kissed Moira's hand. "The bairn is my son, Adair, by a woman named Jeanne."

"I think ye have a lot to tell." He waved his hand toward the keep. "Go on in, lad, Mungan is just setting down to a meal. I suspicion ye will welcome some food."

"Ye arenae coming in?" Tavig asked.

"Nay. 'Tis my turn upon the walls. I will hear it all on the morrow."

"Aye, there have never been any secrets kept from you."

A thrill of anxiety snaked down Moira's spine as she entered the keep hand in hand with Tavig. It briefly flared to full life as they walked into the great hall. A huge dark-haired man sat at the head table. She instinctively took a step backward when the man stood up, strode over to them, and enfolded Tavig in his big arms. Moira noticed with some surprise that Tavig's feet were a few inches off the ground as he endured his cousin's hug.

"What are ye doing slipping in here after sunset?" the big man demanded as he released Tavig.

"Fleeing from Iver and his dogs."

"Aye, I have heard a whisper or two that there has been some trouble. Dinnae frown, Cousin. I dinnae believe ye killed those men. My first thought when I heard the news was that Iver didnae have the wit to ken that no mon who kens ye would believe ye could kill any mon in such a cruel way. Still, 'tis odd that ye would come to my gates in the dark, a time ye ken weel as an unwelcoming one."

"I had no choice. Iver's dogs have been nipping at my heels for the last two days. They are up in the hills just south of here." Tavig smiled faintly when Mungan ordered one of his men to get a small troop of soldiers together and go hunt down Iver's men. "I would like at least one live prisoner," he told the man as he strode by.

"And have ye wed, then?" Mungan asked, a hint of disbelief in his voice.

"Nay, not yet." Tavig lifted Adair from his sling. "A lass named Jeanne left me this as her legacy—my son Adair."

"A fine-looking lad. Lass," he called to one of the maids, who quickly hurried to his side. "See to the bairn's care. His name is Adair." The maid took Adair, smiling and cooing to him as she carried him out of the hall. "Ye should have introduced your woman first."

"Aye, in normal circumstances." Tavig clasped Moira's hand in his. "This is Moira Robertson." He grimaced as he watched the expressions on Mungan's broad face. The surprise and delight Mungan revealed confirmed Tavig's growing suspicions.

"Ye rogue," Mungan bellowed, grinning as he clapped Tavig on the back. "Ye have brought me the ransom."

Chapter Fifteen

"Me?" Moira was so shocked the word came out as a hoarse croak, and she had to clear her throat. "*I* am the ransom for Una?"

"I had begun to suspect it," Tavig said, shrugging when Moira turned her horrified gaze his way. "It answered so many questions and puzzles, dearling. The biggest one was, why were ye being taken along at all?"

"Oh, aye? And is that why ye brought me here? To hand me over to him?" She was not sure she believed the look of hurt that passed over Tavig's face.

"Dearling, when are ye going to have some faith in me? I am *not* like your kinsmon. I brought ye here for precisely the reasons I told ye—I need my cousin Mungan's aid, *and* ye will be reunited with your kinsmen here if that is what ye still desire."

The expression in Tavig's dark eyes told Moira that she had disappointed him, even caused him some pain, but she found it difficult to cast aside her wariness completely. "So that my cursed kinsmen can hand me o'er to him."

"Nay, lassie. I would ne'er allow it."

Mungan looked from one to the other several times before walking around Tavig and Moira three times, then pausing to face them. "'Tis indeed strange that the Robertsons would send one of my own kinsmen with the ransom. Ye must tell me how ye became a part of this, Tavig."

"I am *not* delivering Moira for ransom." Tavig put his arm around Moira's slim shoulders, pleased when she did not tense or pull away from him despite the anger still evident in her expression. "Moira is here because she travels with me."

"With you?" Mungan grumbled and began to scowl only to roar a moment later, "Have ye been bedding *my* bride?"

"Mungan, just because ye decided to call Moira your bride doesnae make it so."

"Nay," muttered Moira. "That is a privilege only Sir Tavig MacAlpin can enjoy."

Tavig ignored her remark. To his dismay, his cousin did not. Mungan was choosing to be clever now. There was a look of curiosity and contemplation on his dark angular features as he studied Moira. Tavig knew he was going to have to convince Moira to weigh her words more carefully.

"Cousin, she is *mine*," Tavig said, drawing Mungan's full attention back to him. "She and I are destined."

"Ah, so that is how it stands. Ye have seen this, have ye, Cousin?"

"Aye, I ken it."

"Weel, come to the table." Draping his muscular arm around Tavig's shoulders, Mungan moved toward the long linen-draped table at the head of the hall.

"We *are* a wee bit hungry." Tavig pulled Moira along with him. "When I tell ye all that has happened in the last fortnight, aye, and in the last month, ye will see matters far more clearly." Mungan sprawled in his heavy oak chair at the head of the massive table, and Tavig took a seat on the bench to his right, tugging Moira down beside him.

"Where have ye confined Una?" demanded Moira.

"Confined her? There is no confining that wench." Mungan scowled toward the heavy doors of the great hall. "She is late for the meal again. A verra contrary woman is your cousin," he said to Moira. "She sore tries a mon's temper."

"Ye havenae hurt her, have ye?" Moira was a little surprised at how offended Mungan looked.

"Nay, I havenae laid a hand on the fool lass, save for bringing her here. The women of your family dinnae think too highly of men, do they?"

"They have good reason not to, Cousin," said Tavig.

"What are *ye* doing *here*?" screeched a voice Moira quickly recognized as Una's.

Moira rose to greet her cousin, but the look on the voluptuous Una's face was not a welcoming one. She quickly sat down again. Una did not resemble a distressed kidnap victim. In fact, she looked healthy and was elegantly dressed. Before Moira could answer her cousin's sharp question, Una paled, pressing back against the gray stone wall near the door and looking around.

"Is my father here?" Una asked in a voice carrying a tremor of fear.

"Nay," Moira replied. "I am here alone. Weel, I came with Sir Tavig MacAlpin." Moira nodded toward Tavig.

"The accused murderer?" Una straightened, patted her thick blond hair to assure herself it was still neatly braided, and walked toward the empty seat on Mungan's left.

"Aye," agreed Mungan, "but I told ye that he didnae do it. The lad doesnae have that sort of meanness in him. 'Twas our other cousin, that sly bastard Sir Iver MacAlpin."

"So ye came here with him?" Una looked at Moira and Tavig with narrowed eyes as she sat down.

Moira did not understand Una's belligerance, and it began to annoy her. "Aye, Cousin. I am glad to see that ye are unharmed. And, aye, I, too, am hale and whole despite my recent ordeals. How kind of ye to inquire."

"Now I am certain that Papa isnae here. Ye would ne'er be so pert if he was. Why, ye are almost as pert as ye were when ye first came to live with us. All eyes and impertinence, ye were."

"And your bastard of a father swiftly cured her of that, didnae he?" snapped Tavig.

"He did," replied Una. "I warned her, but she wasnae inclined to listen to me." Una helped herself to a few large slabs of roast as the platter was passed around. "She was a terribly coddled child. Papa soon showed her she would-nae be treated so indulgently by him. A few nights locked in the pit soon curbed your tongue."

"The pit?" Tavig muttered.

"Aye." Una heaped small tender carrots on her plate. "Papa has a pit in the swine pens. 'Tis his favored place to banish impertinent people. It has a grate over the top so the pigs dinnae fall in, but, of course, most everything else seeps into it. I only required one visit. I fear Moira re-quired a great many ere she learned her lesson. I was a wee bit sorry when she did grow silent for 'twas enjoyable to hear her speak so directly to Papa. No one else did."

Mungan leaned forward, staring intently at Una. "Your father put ye in a hole in the ground and left ye to rot in pig muck?"

Una nodded while she chewed on a thick slice of heav-ily buttered bread. "I was only there once. A foul place, and he wouldnae let ye bathe for two days after ye got out." She shuddered. "The smell fair turned your stom-ach." She then shrugged. "'Twas better than most of his other punishments."

"Aye," Moira whispered, shaken by the memories Una was stirring up. "At least ye could see the sky." She started in surprise when Tavig took her hand in his, his clasp almost too tight.

"I am surprised ye werenae frightened half out of your wits when we were tossed into that dark prison in Craig-moordun," Tavig said.

"So am I," Moira replied, sending him a faint smile. "I think I was too concerned about your injuries and, although ye werenae much company for a while, I wasnae alone."

"Ye were put in prison?" Una asked, pausing in her eating long enough to stare at Moira in surprise.

As Moira began to reply, Tavig touched a finger to her lips. "Eat, loving. Ye havenae taken a bite of your food yet. I am near done with my meal so I will tell the tale."

She nodded, glad to give the chore to him. Mungan and Una would undoubtedly ask a lot of questions, and she would be left eating a very cold meal by the time the full tale was told. Although Una listened intently, her eyes wide with interest and amazement, Moira noticed, with some amusement, that her cousin never paused in her eating.

As everyone talked, frequently interrupting Tavig's story with exclamations and questions, Moira studied her cousin. Una was constantly touching Mungan, sitting as close to him as she possibly could. Mungan often patted her hand, somewhat absently at times and the pair constantly exchanged remarks on the story Tavig was telling. By the time Moira had finished her meal, she was sure that the pair were lovers. That explained Una's dismay at finding her here and that strong hint of animosity. What Moira could not understand was why Mungan wanted *her*? She did not compare favorably with her cousin in beauty of face, womanly form, or richness of dowry. Mungan's insistence that she was his bride made no sense at all.

"Weel, Tavig, m'lad, ye *have* worked hard to bring me my bride," Mungan said, then frowned when Una suddenly jerked away from him and slammed some more food onto her plate.

"She isnae your bride," snapped Tavig. "I told ye— Moira and I are destined."

"I will admit that I am a wee bit angry that ye have lain down with her, but ye didnae ken my plans, so I forgive ye. There will be no more of it, however, and I am firm on that."

"Mungan, ye thick-headed oaf—"

"Wait!" Moira flinched when both men stared at her, unsettled by becoming the center of all attention. "Before the arguing and insults begin, mayhap ye can explain why ye are so determined to make me your wife, Sir Mungan."

"It should be quite clear to any fool," he answered.

"Weel, I fear this fool is quite confused and needs it explained."

"An explanation would please me as weel," Tavig said. "Why have ye set your heart on this particular lass?"

"I havenae really set my heart on *her*," Mungan replied. "Truth to tell, she is a skinny wee thing and not much to my taste. Howbeit, I cannae get my hands on her lands without wedding her."

"My land?" Moira shrugged when Tavig looked at her. "I dinnae ken what he means. I have no property."

"Nay? Come look here," Mungan ordered, standing and walking to a window at the far side of the great hall.

Moira scrambled to follow, Tavig and Una right behind her. Mungan tugged her to his right side when she reached the window, pointing to a sturdy peel tower on a hill directly across the loch. Tavig and Una pressed close, looking out and frowning with the same confusion Moira felt. As Moira looked at Mungan, she fleetingly noticed that Una was entwined around Mungan's left arm. Tavig took her hand, tugging her closer to him. Matters were getting very complicated.

"'Tis a verra fine tower house, Sir Mungan," she said. "What does it have to do with me?"

"'Tis yours," Mungan replied, scowling at her.

"Nay, ye are mistaken. I have nothing."

"Ye have that and more, though I cannae say how much more. I was only concerned about that thrice-cursed tower which looms o'er my lands like some carrion bird. I have been trying to get my hands on it since your parents died, but that cur Sir Bearnard wouldnae deal fairly with me. I even offered for your hand though I loathed the idea of gaining something through forcing a lass to my bed. Robertson laughed at my offer. That is when I conceived my plan to just take ye and wed ye. Aye, then that fat swine would cease to laugh."

"I dinnae own anything," Moira said, feeling confused and somewhat desperate.

"Wait," Tavig urged, placing his arm around her shoulders and ignoring his cousin's dark scowl. "Mungan, are ye verra sure Moira owns that tower house? Mayhap her parents didnae own it?"

"I wish I could say they dinnae, but no one kens better than I just who owns it," Mungan grumbled, placing his hands on his hips and glaring at the tower house. "Do ye remember what a whimsical fellow my father was?" Tavig nodded, and Mungan continued. "Weel, he met with the lass's parents once and was so taken with the young couple, he gave them that lump of stone."

"He *gave* it to them? He asked naught for it?"

"Not a farthing. And I was but a wee lad—"

"Mungan, ye were ne'er a *wee* lad."

"Weel, I was too young to stop that as I stopped so many other fancies he was seized with. That old mon would have left us with naught but rags had I let him do all he pleased. That tower was the last thing he gave away. I held tight to everything else or retrieved it later. I think I could have dealt with the lass's parents, but there is no dealing with Robertson, who holds all the lass's properties and coin."

"Coin, too? Are ye sure? The lass was told that she had nothing, not a farthing."

"Aye, Robertson would tell such a lie. His steward can be more truthful, though. It took but a wee bit of cajoling to get that spindly wee mon to tell me all he kenned about Robertson's lands and monies." He gave one sharp bark of laughter. "That coward was verra free with Robertson's secrets."

"But if ye hurt Robertson's steward, then Robertson must be aware of all ye have learned."

"I didnae hurt him." He held his hands out in a pleading gesture when Tavig scowled at him. "I swear it, Cousin. I but hung the wee mon up by his heels for a while over a fire. I cannae help it if the fool believed I was going to roast him alive. God's bones, the fire wasnae even hot enough to singe what few locks of hair he had. Once he told me what I wished to learn, I let him scurry away. There was no reason for Robertson to be suspicious, and that little coward of a steward would ne'er confess what he had done. Robertson would cut his skinny throat."

"I own land and I have money," Moira said, her voice hoarse and weak. "Sir Bearnard has been lying to me for years."

"Ye sound as if ye dinnae believe it." Tavig kissed her cheek, holding her tighter. "It doesnae surprise me, lass."

"Why would Papa keep her if she could keep herself?" Una asked. "She made him so angry, 'twould have made more sense to use her dowry to arrange a marriage for her and be rid of her."

"Aye," agreed Mungan, "it would make more sense if your papa wasnae such a greedy bastard."

"Aha, he wanted what she had for himself. Aye, that does sound like Papa."

"I need to sit down," Moira said, walking toward the table.

She retook her seat at the table and filled her tankard with Mungan's strong mead. Moira drank it all and refilled her tankard as Mungan, Una, and Tavig returned to their seats. Tavig was looking very worried. Moira knew she ought to tell him something to ease his concerns, but she could think of nothing to say. Her emotions were in a confusing tangle. Her thoughts leapt from place to place and back again until they were a knot of half-finished ideas and opinions. She wanted to cry. She wanted to scream. She wanted to confront Sir Bearnard with his deception. She wanted to kill him.

"Are ye all right?" Tavig asked, placing his hand over her tightly clenched fist.

"I dinnae ken." She took several deep breaths, hoping to calm herself for she knew she needed to think clearly. "I think I need a wee bit of time to understand just how many lies I have been told since my parents died."

"Just when did they die and how? I havenae wanted to ask, but it may be of importance."

"They died ten years ago. We were returning from a market fair in a nearby village when we were set upon by thieves. They killed Mama, Papa, and Grandmère, my mother's mother. The men-at-arms with us were also murdered, and I was left for dead. S'truth, I nearly was. An old lady found me and nursed me. 'Twas weeks ere I began to recover. Then she began the search for my kinsmen. Not long after, Sir Bearnard came to take me away." She saw Mungan and Tavig exchange a long look. "Do ye think Sir Bearnard killed my family?"

"'Tis a possibility, lass, but after ten years 'twould be hard to prove. What matters now is that ye do have land *and* ye have money. Ye arenae to let that bastard keep it from ye any longer."

"She doesnae need to worry on that," said Mungan. "Robertson willnae get his greedy hands on what belongs to my wife. As soon as the lass and I are wed—"

"Ye arenae marrying her," yelled Tavig.

"Please," Moira cried. "I have just learned that the last ten years of my life have been a lie. Mayhap ye can give me a wee bit of time ere ye begin to plan my future."

Tavig pulled her into his arms, smoothing his hands up and down her back. "Aye, lass. Ye will have all the time ye need." He glared at his cousin. "Where are we to sleep?"

"We? I told ye there will be no more of that. Ye will not be bedding her here."

"What does it matter?" snapped Una, slamming her tankard down onto the table and sloshing mead onto it. "The two of them have been rutting about in the heather for days. 'Tis a wee bit late to untangle them now."

Moira closed her eyes, letting the argument swirl around her. She appreciated Tavig's efforts to get his obstinate cousin to listen to reason, but she wished they could save all their squabbles until the morning. The journey she and Tavig had completed was enough to exhaust her and make her long for a soft bed. Learning that she was not a pauper, that her cousin and guardian had been cheating her for years, was a hard blow. The wealth of emotion the truth had produced had drained the last of her strength. She wanted to go to sleep. She did not want to think anymore. Closing her eyes, she decided her three companions did not really need her to add to their rousing argument.

It took Tavig a moment to realize that Moira had gone limp in his grasp. Leaving Mungan and Una to squabble between themselves, he lifted the sleeping Moira onto his lap. He had hoped to force Mungan to give up his mad idea of marrying Moira, but the man was clinging to it the way a starving hound clung to a scrap of meat. The way Una kept glaring at Moira made it clear there would soon be trouble from her as well.

"Mungan," Tavig said, interrupting Una's explicit instructions on what Mungan could do with his offer to keep her as his mistress. "Moira and I need a bed."

"I told ye that ye cannae keep bedding down with my bride." Mungan slammed his fist down on the table, sending his half-full tankard of ale spinning onto the rush-strewn floor.

"She isnae your bride yet. Until she declares herself to ye, she is mine."

"Has she declared herself to you, Cousin?"

"She shared my blanket. For a lass like this, 'tis declaration enough until she says otherwise. Now, where are we to bed down?"

Grumbling all the way, Mungan led Tavig to a small room at the top of the east tower. Tavig watched his cousin closely as he gently settled Moira on their bed. Mungan stood by an arrow slit that overlooked the loch, staring morosely at the tower house. Shaking his head, Tavig stood beside his cousin.

"If ye wanted it so badly why didnae ye just take it some when over the last ten years?" Tavig asked.

"I tried a time or two, but the cost was too high. Ye ken that I am not one to waste my men's lives, and trying to take that cursed tower exacted a high toll amongst my men. Yet I cannae leave it sitting there, looming over me, and allow some enemy to mon its parapets."

"Moira would never be your enemy, Mungan."

"She is naught but a wee lass, Tavig. For most of her life she has been in Robertson's hard grasp. She could easily fall under the grasp of another rogue and one who will covetously eye my lands. I cannae put my fate in the hands of a wee skinny lass."

"Then put it into mine."

Mungan scowled. "What do ye mean?"

"Ye ken verra weel what I mean. She is mine. We are fated. We will marry."

"She hasnae said she will wed ye, has she?"

Tavig silently cursed Mungan's insight. "Nay. She fears superstition would be roused to a deadly height if she, a redhead, married a mon with the sight I but need to show her that, at least at Drumdearg, that wouldnae be so. I must convince her that she exaggerates the danger we may face."

"Maybe ye will, but mayhap ye willnae," Mungan drawled, strolling to the door.

"What do ye mean by that?"

"Exactly what ye think I mean. The lass is still free game, Cousin."

Mungan was gone before Tavig could reply. He cursed his obstinate cousin, glaring at the tower house before walking to the bed. Moira was sleeping peacefully, oblivious to the continuing arguments concerning her future. He briefly considered leaving her alone, but knew she would not be comfortable sleeping in all of her clothes.

Moira stirred, swatting at the hands tugging at her, and partly opened her eyes. It took her a moment to realize Tavig was removing her clothes. He was so intent on slipping off her hose he had not yet noticed that she was awake. Planting her foot in the middle of his chest, she pushed, sending him tumbling to the floor.

Tavig stood up, brushing himself off. "Sorry, lass. I tried not to wake ye up. Thought about just leaving ye to sleep in your clothes, but decided ye wouldnae be verra comfortable."

"Oh, nay, I probably wouldnae." Seeing that she was already undressed to her chemise, she yawned and slipped beneath the blanket. "Thank ye," she muttered.

"Lass, we have a wee problem," he said, shedding his clothes and crawling in beside her.

"We have a great many problems. Which one do ye mean?" She cuddled up to Tavig when he pulled her into his arms. "And must we talk about it now?"

"Nay, we need not talk about it for verra long. I just believe ye ought to ken what is brewing about us. 'Twill be there to confront ye when ye open your eyes in the morning."

"I grow weary of confronting things. Ye speak of Mungan and his insistence that I am to be his bride."

"Aye, dearling." Idly unbraiding her hair, he explained, "Mungan has set his mind firmly on getting that tower house and doing so by marrying you. He can be obstinate. I have told him that we are fated but we arenae mon and wife. He says that makes ye fair game."

"Fair game?" Annoyance briefly cut through her exhaustion. "How endearing. And what of Una? 'Tis clear that she and your cousin are lovers, and I believe he cares for her."

"Oh, aye, he does, but she doesnae own that tower house. I fear my cousin willnae be talked out of this as long as ye are unmarried. He means to pursue you. He wants no enemy in that tower house."

"Weel, I can just assure him that I will ne'er be his enemy."

"I already told him that. He feels that, as a wee lass, ye

cannae give such a vow. Dinnae stiffen, he doesnae question the value of your word. He just believes that men can change that."

"And my having been duped by my guardian has only convinced him of that. It doesnae matter. He cannae make me marry him. Ye wouldnae let him, would you?"

"Nay, I wouldnae, but—"

"Ah, the inevitable *but*."

"Aye, Mungan would ne'er harm us, but he might weel use some trick. He can be surprisingly clever. And dinnae forget that by law Robertson is still your guardian. Robertson will be here soon, and ye were to be the ransom for Una. Mungan could still demand that, and ye wouldnae be able to stop it. I would try, but Mungan could easily set me in a secure place until the deed is done."

"And ye cannae afford to be discovered here, either. Ye are still wanted for murder." She looked at Tavig, a chill of fear rippling down her spine. "Mungan wouldnae hand ye over to Iver to get ye out of his way, would he?"

"Nay, never," Tavig said without hesitation, holding her closer and kissing the top of her head. "As I have told ye before, Mungan loathes Iver. Mungan was fostered at Drumdearg, kenned the two men Iver murdered, and wants revenge. Nay, Mungan would cut off his own hand ere he would give me over to Iver. And I swear to ye again, he will ne'er hurt either of us to gain what he wants. There isnae much else he willnae do, though. Howbeit, there is one solution, one thing ye can do that my obstinate cousin Mungan will accept."

"And what is that?" Moira asked, despite the sinking feeling that she knew what Tavig was about to say.

"Ye could marry me."

"And Mungan would honor that?"

"Aye. I would then be the mon in your life, and he kens I will ne'er be his enemy."

"Nay, but everyone else will see us as their foes."

"Lass, ye fret o'er that too much."

"I must think about this." She yawned, wondering how she could be so eager to go to sleep when such important matters needed to be discussed. Her exhaustion ran so deep it could not be ignored.

"Dinnae take too long, dearling. Mungan is determined, and your kinsmen are on their way."

"I will decide tomorrow. I am so tired I cannae think clearly. 'Twould be foolhardy to make such a decision now."

"Sleep then, lassie." He lightly kissed her, then held her close.

Moira closed her eyes, the heaviness of sleep quickly sweeping over her. It hurt that Tavig could speak of marriage yet offered no words of love. She still feared the superstitions they could rouse if they married, but now knew she would face them if she had Tavig's love. She was not sure, however, that she had the strength to be his wife, knowing that he did not love her. Cursing silently, she gave herself over to the hard pull of sleep. Tomorrow she had to make a weighty decision. A good night's sleep could prove vital.

Chapter Sixteen

"Here. These are for you." Mungan thrust a clump of flowers at Moira.

Moira warily took the half-crushed, half-withered daisies. It was late in the year, and she wondered how he had found them. Considering the poor state of the little bouquet, she suspected he had sent one of his men out searching for them. She inwardly sighed. She had only just finished eating her morning meal and was planning to go to see Adair. Mungan's crude attempt at courting her was not something she wished to deal with now.

"Thank ye. They are verra pretty. Now, if ye would excuse me, I should like to find Adair."

"He is being cared for." Mungan grabbed her by the arm, tugging her outside his keep. "My men brought back one of Iver's hirelings, so Tavig is verra busy talking to the fellow."

"Shouldnae ye be with him? After all, if ye are to help Tavig fight Iver ye will need to ken all ye are able to about Iver, his men, and Drumdearg."

"Tavig will tell me what is important. I thought I would show ye my holdings while my cousin is too busy to interfere. The lad hangs o'er ye like a dark cloud. Here is the armorer's shed," he told her.

By the time Mungan finished showing her every part of

his keep, every outbuilding and every person living inside the walls, Moira was completely out of breath. She slumped against the alms table in the front hall where food and drink were set out for beggars and monks. Mungan was wealthy, tall, dark, and handsome in a rough-featured way. It would be flattering to be wooed by such a man, except that he wooed her lands, not her. Because of that, Moira was highly annoyed over being dragged around the man's holding like some puppy.

"So, lass, ye can see that I have a lot to offer you."

"Aye, that ye do, Sir Mungan. Ye have a verra fine holding. Why, ye seem to be doing as fine as some of those grand English lairds." She almost smiled as he puffed out his already impressively large chest.

"I dinnae feel I make too grand a boast when I tell ye 'tis finer and richer than Tavig's Drumdearg."

"That is quite possibly true. Howbeit, I have ne'er seen Drumdearg. There may be something there that pleases me more." She forced herself to stand up. "I thank ye for showing me about. Now, if ye would please excuse me, I believe I shall stagger to my bed and have a wee rest."

Mungan rubbed his big hand over his square chin. "Ye are tired? I thought ye stronger than that since ye survived that journey with my cousin."

Moira paused on the stairs to look at him. "Ah, weel, we *walked*."

Inwardly shaking her head, she made her way toward the east tower. She would have a brief lie-down to restore her strength, then find Adair. Moira realized that she missed the child. He had been taken from her so quickly she was left with the feeling that she had somehow lost him. She also could not stop wondering about the care he was being given.

Moira stepped into the room allotted to her and Tavig, saw Una pacing back and forth, and groaned. She tossed her bedraggled bouquet on the clothes chest. Barely glancing at her glaring cousin, Moira walked to her bed and flung herself onto it, face up.

"Ye have been out walking with Mungan, havenae ye?" Una demanded, standing by the side of the bed and placing her fists on her shapely hips.

"My state of total exhaustion gave me away, did it?"

"I saw ye from my chamber window. I saw him escorting ye about the courtyard."

"Ye mean ye saw him dragging me from pillar to post, most of it done at a near-run on my part."

Una gave a dismissive wave of her hand. "Ye just have to learn how to keep up with him and how to slow him down. He is a big mon and takes monly strides."

"That mon's monly strides could keep pace with a galloping horse."

"I ken how ye were flirting with him and admiring this fine keep."

"Una, I was too busy trying to stay on my feet for I am certain that if I had stumbled, he wouldnae have noticed. He would have just kept on dragging me along. As for admiring his keep, I fear I saw little of it. 'Twas mostly a blur as I sped by."

"He gave ye flowers," she snapped, grabbing up the wilting bouquet and shaking it at Moira.

"If ye admire them so much, ye can have them."

After scowling at the battered daisies for a moment, Una tossed them aside. "Did ye drop them and step on them?"

"Nay, they looked like that when he gave them to me. Sir Mungan doesnae have a skilled hand for wooing. Although, considering he is wooing a lump of stone on the other side of his loch, he isnae doing too badly."

"I dinnae understand what ye are babbling about." Una pushed Moira's leg aside and sat down on the bed. "I am here to tell ye that *I* want Mungan." She glared at Moira. "He and I are already lovers."

"Nay!" Moira placed her hand on her chest "Una, I am shocked."

"Oh, do cease your nonsense. So, ye have clearly

guessed what is between Mungan and me. Why put yourself between us?"

"I fear *ye* dinnae see exactly what is standing between ye and Mungan Coll. 'Tisnae me. 'Tis that thrice-cursed tower house."

"Ah, but I have a solution to that problem. If ye give me the tower house, then Mungan will seek to marry me and leave ye alone. Is that not simple?"

Moira raised herself up on her forearms to stare at Una in disbelief. "Una, listen verra carefully. I have lived under your father's fist for ten long years. More than anyone else, ye must understand what that life was like. I endured it because I thought I had no choice, that I was dependent upon his charity. Now I discover I do have a choice. Worse, I discovered that I have always had it, but your father concealed it from me. Do ye have any idea how angry that makes me?" She could tell by the wide-eyed look on Una's face that it was going to be difficult to make Una understand even part of what she was feeling.

"Weel, I suppose ye have a right to be angry. But what does all that have to do with the tower house?"

"'Tis *mine*. I may ne'er get back the coin that was left to me and which your father stole, but he cannae slip that pile of stone into his purse and slink away. That lump of rock is my freedom. I cannae and I willnae just hand it o'er to ye so that ye can get Mungan Coll to wed you."

"Oh." Una jumped up. "Ye are so selfish. All this talk about freedom is just nonsense. Ye want my mon."

Moira sagged back down onto the bed. "I dinnae want your mon. In truth, I cannae understand why ye would want him if ye must bribe him with that tower house to get him to marry you. Where is your pride?"

"I could ask ye the same thing. Ye have been whoring your way across Scotland with a murderer."

"Tavig didnae murder anyone," Moira snapped, but Una was already striding out the door. She winced as her cousin slammed the door after her. "Give me the tower house, she says. As if it were some child's toy she covets."

Everything Tavig had tried to warn her about was coming true. Mungan had only made his first try at wooing her, but she was sure the man would keep after her. Now Una was angry and jealous. That, too, would only get worse, increasing with every attempt Mungan made at wooing her. Una and she were not friends, and Moira was not sure they would ever be, but she certainly did not want them to be enemies, either. She did feel a bond of sorts with Una since they had both suffered beneath Sir Bearnard's cruel guardianship.

The more she thought about the uncomfortable position she found herself in, the more she realized that Tavig was right. There was one quick, simple, but sure way to put an end to all the nonsense. She had scolded Una for her willingness to bribe a man to wed her yet she was considering marrying a man so that she did not have to put up with any more of Mungan's or Una's foolishness. She had only had a brief taste of that foolishness, but that had proven more than enough.

As she sat up, rested enough to find Adair despite Una's visit, Moira could almost believe Tavig's talk of their being destined. It certainly seemed as if some unseen hand were pushing them along. No matter how hard she tried to cling to her decision not to marry Tavig for his own safety, things kept happening that forced her to remain close to Tavig. Now it seemed as if fate had set her down in the midst of a multitude of reasons why marrying Tavig suddenly appeared to be the safest and the wisest thing to do.

Moira left her room in search of Adair. There was still time to consider more carefully what few choices she had and pick the one that offered the most complete solution to her problems. As she entered the nursery one of the maids had directed her to, she spotted Adair right away. Moira laughed, moving quickly to pick him up as he smiled and crawled toward her. She nuzzled his thick black curls and realized that, despite her best intentions,

Adair would be one strong reason why she might make the risky choice of marriage to Tavig MacAlpin.

Tavig scowled at Mungan, who sprawled in his large ornately carved chair, sipping ale and surveying the others gathered in the great hall as if all were right in the world. Grabbing the jug off the table, Tavig filled his tankard with the hearty ale and took several long drinks in a vain attempt to cool his rising temper. He wanted to make plans to go after Iver and he wanted to convince Mungan to give up his plan to marry Moira. The day was almost at an end, and he had accomplished very little.

"Curse ye, Mungan," he finally snapped. "Are we to play the idle courtiers until Iver sends an army to your walls?"

Mungan looked at Tavig, in feigned surprise. "Ye are a wee bit short of temper today, Tavig, m'boy."

"Ye have a great skill at sorely trying a mon's patience. I thought ye were as eager as I to make Iver pay for the murder of our friends."

"I am and I already prepare to go after that foul kinsmon of ours. There was no need to trouble ye with such preparation. Ye ken what must be done to ready oneself for such a battle, but so do I. Why waste our time discussing such unimportant things?"

"Fine, I could agree with that if we were taking that extra time to discuss something else. I thought the information I got from Iver's mon would help us plot some battle plan. I would have preferred to have gotten my hands on that murdering swine Andrew, but this mon was useful."

"It did help us. Did we not already decide how many men we will need? Ye ken that I dinnae like to make my plans too exact, as matters can change rapidly between the time ye make the plan and when ye must carry it out. Soon the men I sent to gather more information on our traitorous cousin will return. Once we have their reports to add to what Iver's mon said, we can discuss our fight with Iver in more detail. Aye and we hold the added advantage of kenning Drumdearg as weel, as thoroughly, as Iver."

Tavig relaxed a little, annoyed that Mungan was the one to see that and not him. He had become so intensely determined to make Iver pay for his crimes and to get Drumdearg back that he had become somewhat blinded. It would not be easy, but he would have to try to concentrate on his battle with Iver as if it were just another battle and not such a deeply personal one.

"We have another advantage," Tavig said. "Many of the people of Drumdearg will come to our side. Iver surrounds himself with hard men whose loyalty is bought, not given, because he kens he cannae depend on the loyalty of the people he tries to rule. I think he kens they will desert him, turn against him, the moment the chance arises."

"Aye, and my men will be seeing just how much of an advantage that will give us. He will be testing the people's loyalty to you and warning those who can be trusted to be prepared for our arrival." Mungan smiled toward the doors of the great hall. "Ah, the ladies arrive."

Inwardly cursing because he knew that would end any further talk about how they would take back Drumdearg, Tavig turned to look at Moira. Una was several paces in front of Moira, and it was clear to even the most casual observer that there was far more than a physical separation between the pair. He had had little chance to speak to Moira today, but it was clear that she was already suffering some of the troubles he had foreseen. Although he felt bad for her, he could not completely repress a surge of hope and delight over her predicament. Such turmoil would serve to push her where he wanted her—standing in front of a priest saying her marriage vows. He stood up, brushing a kiss over her cheek as she moved to sit next to him.

Una kissed Mungan's cheek as she sat down next to him. "Ye look verra pleased to see me."

"Aye," Mungan agreed. "Now we may eat our meal."

Moira winced, then sighed when Una glared at her. "As if I am responsible for the mon's boorish behavior."

"What did ye say, lass?" Tavig asked, leaning closer to her so that he could speak softly without a scowling Mungan overhearing him.

"Nothing of any importance." She forced a smile. "How has your day passed? Ye have been verra busy."

"Aye. Iver's hired dog was slow to talk, but when he did he was verra helpful. Mungan has sent a few of his men to Drumdearg to gather even more information. When they return, we will finalize our plans."

"And then ye will go to battle." She was not sure she completely disguised her shiver of fear.

"That is how it must be. Iver will fight to hold what he has stolen from me." He took her hand in his, kissing her palm. "Dinnae fret o'er me, dearling. I can win this."

She tugged her hand free of his as the pages and maids set the food on the table. "I wasnae worried about you in particular, Sir Tavig. I but dislike the idea of men hacking away at each other with swords."

"Sometimes men are given no other choice. How did ye pass your day? I ken that ye visited with Adair, for 'tis where I saw ye the last time I was able to exchange a few brief words with you."

"Weel, I was dragged about the keep by your cousin. He wished to show me what a fine life he could offer me." She put some venison on her plate, covertly watching Tavig, who scowled darkly at Mungan.

"So that is why he so amiably allowed me to talk to Iver's mon alone. I sought to keep Mungan from too vehemently questioning the mon, perhaps injuring him too much, so we would get nothing from him. Mungan sought to steal some time to court ye, then?"

"Aye, I suppose ye can call it courting." Moira decided she would not tell Tavig about Mungan's pursuit of her. The man had hunted her down several times during the day until she had given serious consideration to hiding.

"And that is why your cousin is so angry with you."

"Una is certain that I am trying to take Mungan away. There is no talking sense to her. She even asked me to give her the tower house so that Mungan will hie after her. She has plagued me about that all day. In her eyes I am selfish beyond words because I will *not* give away the tower house." She sent him a cross look when he opened his mouth to speak. "If ye say ye warned me about this, I shall hit you."

"Ye would deprive a mon of the chance to boast that he was right?"

"I would. I have no wish to suffer your gloating. That scowling pair at the head of the table is as much as I can bear for the moment. There is no talking to either of them. They are stubborn, and at times during this verra long day I began to think they might be deaf as weel."

Tavig laughed, and her disapproving look did nothing to end his amusement. "Now, sweet Moira, ye must see how funny it all is." When she glared at him, he cleared his throat. "Weel, mayhap not just now."

"Nay, not now. All I wish to do now is crawl into a hole and stay there until our cousins sort themselves out. Mungan may want my lands, but he doesnae want me. He wants Una, and she wants him."

"Aye, 'tis clear to see, although methinks Mungan doesnae ken it. He is too intent upon getting that tower house. I understand what ails him for I have just discovered that I have been briefly blinded by my urgent need to regain my holdings, to avenge myself against Iver. 'Tis all I thought about and nearly missed noting one or two of the advantages Mungan and I have over Iver. Being so intent upon one thing can be dangerous. 'Tis certainly unwise. I now see the danger and will be wary. The question is, how do we get Mungan to see it?"

"After what I have been through today I cannae believe that will be easy."

"Nay, nor quick, and your kinsmen will soon be here."

Moira silently cursed and turned her attention to her

meal. She had a strong urge to scream or bang her head against the heavy oak table. She felt as if she were being pulled in many different directions. Everyone was demanding something of her, but no one was considering her feelings at all. Not even Tavig, she mused, stabbing at a piece of venison with her eating knife. He spoke of marriage as a solution to the problems she now faced, and those problems would disappear if she agreed to marry him, but he had his own reasons, too. She could not believe he would take such a large step to satisfy some whim of fate, but he spoke of nothing else.

It all gave her a throbbing ache in her head. She wished they would all go away and leave her alone. It was not to be, and, glancing at Tavig, she admitted that she did not wish to lose any of what little time she might have left with Tavig, no matter how he might annoy her on occasion. She dearly wished they would give her time to think, however. So much had changed in her life since yesterday, since the moment Mungan had shown her the tower house she owned, that she needed to think about it all. One quick peek at Una, Mungan, and Tavig told her she would not get that time. They all had their own games to play, and for the moment she was little more than a pawn. Such inconsideration on Una's and Mungan's part annoyed her. On Tavig's part, however, it hurt her.

"Ah, another fine feast," Mungan said as the table was cleared of all save the tankards of ale. He sprawled in his huge chair, his gaze fixing on Moira as he rubbed one big hand back and forth over his taut stomach. "Now, Moira, lass, a battle is brewing, so we had best get on with this courting business."

"Oh, weel put, Cousin," muttered Tavig, torn between amusement and annoyance. He did not like Mungan pursuing Moira, but the man was so inept at the art of courtship it was laughable.

Mungan ignored Tavig. "'Tis said by some that a lass likes to have a wee stroll about when the moon is up."

"Aye, 'tis verra nice," agreed Moira.

Tavig watched Una. The woman was so furious her eyes glowed with the emotion, and her cheeks were flushed a deep red. It was highly inconsiderate of Mungan to talk about wooing Moira while he held Una's hand. What troubled Tavig, however, was how Una was directing her fury at Moira and not at Mungan where it belonged. Moira was not encouraging Mungan and did not deserve that anger. Unfortunately, Una would not turn it toward Mungan, for she loved the man.

"Weel, then, I can take ye for another stroll about the inner bailey," Mungan cried.

"Nay," Moira cried, smiling quickly. "I fear I am still weary from our last walk."

"Aye? But that was hours ago." He scowled at her then looked at Tavig, saying, "She doesnae seem to be a verra strong lass. How did ye get her here?"

Moira first gaped at Mungan, then looked so beautifully outraged that Tavig was hard-pressed not to laugh. "She walked, Mungan. Walked, climbed, waded through water and occasionally ran."

"Ah, I see." He nodded then smiled at Moira. "Ye need to rest more from your journey. We can go for a wee amble tomorrow eve. Ye will be recovered by then." He looked at Una. "Do ye wish to go?"

Tavig managed to hold back his laughter until Una and Mungan left the great hall. One look at Moira's face broke his restraint. She looked stunned. As he laughed, she controlled herself and glared, first at the door their cousins had strolled through, then at Tavig.

"I cannae believe she went with him." Moira took a long drink of ale, banged her tankard back down on the table, and shook her head. "He speaks of courting me, tries to take me outside for another swift race about the bailey, and, when I say nay, he asks her. Doesnae Una have any pride?"

"She loves the overgrown fool," Tavig said, laughter still evident in his voice.

Moira sighed and sent him a half-smile. "I ken it. The

question is, does he care for her? Tavig, Una has spent her whole life beneath her father's fists. 'Tis verra odd, considering what Mungan looks like and the fact that he kidnapped Una, but she isnae afraid of him. I am worried about how she will feel or act if—" Her eyes widened when he placed a finger against her lips, stopping her words.

"I swear to you, dearling, Mungan cares for your cousin. 'Tis hard to explain Mungan to those who havenae been with him for years as I have. In his mind 'tis more important to keep that tower house from falling into the hands of an enemy. I also think he strives to eradicate all memory of his father's harmless but obvious insanity. He probably thinks Una will understand this. Recall how directly he spoke to you. He made no secret of the fact that he would try to persuade you to wed him so that he could have that tower house. Ye cannae accuse him of playing ye false."

"That is true enough. Aye, one cannae say he is playing Una false, either. 'Tis probably why she is so angry with me and not him. She loves Mungan, and he is being painfully honest. That leaves her with only me to blame."

"Which is unfair. Her anger concerns me. I cannae help but remember whose daughter she is."

"Oh, I dinnae believe Una would hurt me. For all she has been the victim of brutality and has learned all about it since she was a bairn, she has never even slapped her maids. I think, in Una's mind, such violence is a mon's province. The fact that Mungan doesnae act in such a way makes him nearly a saint in Una's eyes, of course."

"There is a solution to all of this," Tavig began.

She held up her hand, shaking her head. "Ye need not repeat yourself I am weel aware of your solution. 'Tis only our first day here. Mungan already thinks I am a weakling. Mayhap he will decide he doesnae want me, that even that cursed tower house isnae worth taking to wife a sickly lass."

There was such a clear look of doubt on Tavig's face, she inwardly cursed. Even as she spoke of the possibility, she had experienced her own doubts. She had wanted Tavig to ease them. Instead he shared and intensified them. Although she had not known Mungan Coll long, she had the sinking feeling he was the type of man who would need a sign from God Himself to make him change his mind. Moira sincerely hoped they would soon be blessed with one of those.

"One more day," she murmured, scowling into her tankard of ale.

"What did ye say?" asked Tavig.

"I said I will give it one more day. Mayhap things will change." Moira did not find Tavig's short bark of laughter very encouraging.

Chapter Seventeen

"Ye are being a verra stubborn lass," Mungan said, scowling down at Moira.

Moira glanced at Tavig, who stood beside his cousin as she sat down on a little stool by the stable door. She ignored her audience, yanked off her boots, and rubbed her sore feet. Mungan had insisted on showing her more of his lands, including the nearby village. Despite his cousin's clearly displayed annoyance, Tavig had insisted on coming along. His presence had not been much help. Mungan had plunked her on a horse, they had ridden the boundaries of his land, often dismounting to trudge over a spot Mungan felt was of particular importance, and then gone into the village. Once there they had dismounted again and walked all over it at his usual furious pace. For a knight, Mungan Coll did a lot of walking, she mused crossly.

"The lass has the right to consider things," Tavig snapped.

"How much does she need to consider?" demanded Mungan. "I have shown her all I have to offer and told her what I want. 'Tis just a matter of her saying aye."

"Or nay," Moira said, but neither man paid her any heed.

"Why dinnae ye just give this up, Mungan?" Tavig shook his head. "We all ken that ye would rather be wed to Una."

"Una would be a fine wife, but she doesnae own the tower house. And *this* lass," he said and pointed one long finger at Moira, "willnae let her have it." He stared at Moira. "Ye ken that I could just force ye to wed me."

"Oh? And do ye expect me to stand quietly aside as ye drag her before the priest?" asked Tavig, his voice taut as he visibly fought to control his temper.

Mungan cast his cousin one quick, narrow-eyed look. "Ye could be secured until the deed is done."

"Weel, ye cannae force her to the altar. We are hand-fasted."

"What?" cried Moira, her demand echoed by a bellow from Mungan. "What are ye talking about, Tavig MacAlpin?"

"When we were in Craigmoordun I called ye wife, and ye called me husband before witnesses," Tavig replied. "We did the same in Dalnasith. Those declarations make us handfasted. Because of them, the law says we are mon and wife."

"Only for a year and a day," said Mungan. "Then there had best be a child, *and* the lass will have to agree to the wedding before a priest."

"Ye cannae mean ye will torment us for a full year?" Tavig demanded.

Moira barely heard the ensuing argument between Tavig and Mungan. She sat, her hands curled into tight little fists on her knees, and tried not to let the anger billowing inside of her get out of control. It would serve no purpose to yell at Tavig or at Mungan. Giving up the fight, deciding she did not care if she made a scene and that Tavig deserved every ounce of her anger, she leapt to her feet. Cursing softly, she punched Tavig on the arm.

"Moira," he cried, staring at her in shock as he rubbed his arm.

"Ye bastard," she spat. "Ye call Mungan sly, but ye are the cunning one. Ye kenned verra well what ye were doing, but hid your game beneath a cloak of concern, saying we needed to do it to be safe."

"Now, Moira, that isnae exactly the truth," he said in a placating tone.

When he reached for her, she slapped his hands away.

"Nay, dinnae try to smooth over your deceit with pretty words. Ye speak so grandly to Mungan about allowing me a choice, but 'tis now clear that ye never meant to give me one." Unable to think of anything to say that was not simply nasty, she turned to walk back to the keep. "The pair of you can just rot for all I care."

Tavig debated going right after her, but Mungan's laughter diverted him. "What do ye find so cursed funny?"

"Ye." He slapped Tavig on the back. "I ne'er kenned that ye could be so sly."

"I wasnae trying to deceive her," he muttered, yet knew that was not the complete truth. "She believes in my sight yet refuses to accept that we are destined. I kenned we had verra little time. I needed to try to bind her to me in some way. Handfasting allows me a year and one day to convince her that we are mates. The bare fortnight we have had was not enough, although I tried." He combed his fingers through his hair. "Sweet Mary, I have ne'er wooed a lass as diligently as I have wooed her."

"Aye, it must be difficult for a sweet-tongued courtier like yourself to admit defeat."

"I am not defeated." He explained Moira's fears to Mungan. "I kenned 'twould take more time than I had to convince the lass that although the dangers are real, they shouldnae be allowed to control our lives. I also needed to get her to go to Drumdearg. She has to be there for a while so that she can see that she will be safe there. Tricking her into handfasting with me meant that if she wouldnae come to Drumdearg with me willingly, I could press her to honor the bond."

"Clever. I dinnae think she will care much about that bond now. That is one verra angry wee lass. I dinnae ken if even ye have the skill to soothe that temper. So, in a year I can get her to wed me."

"Oh, shut your mouth," Tavig grumbled, scowling at the keep and wondering how long he should wait before he went to try to talk to Moira.

* * *

Moira paced her room as the maids filled a tub with hot water. She knew they watched her warily, but she was too angry to soothe their concerns. As soon as they left, she stripped off her clothes and got into the tub. It took only a moment of soaking in the hot water for her tense anger to begin to wane. She did not like to be so angry and was glad to shake free of the feeling.

She was still shocked over Tavig's deceit, however. As she grew calmer she decided he must have had a good reason for playing such a trick on her. Moira simply could not believe that Tavig would deceive her simply to get his own way. She needed to calm down enough to listen to whatever explanation he had to offer. Although she doubted she would agree with any of the reasons he gave, she prayed they would be good enough to allow her to forgive him.

Just as she left her bath to dry herself, the door to her bedchamber slammed open. A screech of surprise escaped Moira. She scrambled to cover herself, only partly relieved to see that her intruder was Una. Moira winced as Una banged the door shut behind her. The last thing she needed now was another confrontation, but one look at Una's scowling face told Moira that that was exactly what she was going to have to endure.

"I need to talk to you," Una said as she glared at Moira.

Inwardly sighing, Moira continued to dry herself and get dressed. "That doesnae require such an intrusion. I havenae been hiding from you or refusing to talk to you. Ye didnae need to come storming in making demands."

"'Tis difficult to talk to ye privately as ye always seem to have Mungan or Tavig mooning over you."

"Ye exaggerate. Tavig was with me when we arrived here, and he doesnae play the besotted lover. Mungan simply grabs me now and again to drag me about and tell me how much he craves my tower house."

"And that is *all* he wants from you."

"I ken it."

"He will still come to *my* bed. Even if ye do wed him, I willnae leave. Aye, and ye will probably be glad of it. Mungan is far too much lover for you."

As Una began to talk about what she and Mungan shared as lovers, Moira fought to ignore her. That was not easy, for Una kept confronting her, refusing to allow Moira to go about the business of getting dressed undisturbed, and revealing details of her relationship with Mungan Coll that Moira did not really want to know. Finally sitting on a thick-legged stool before the fire the maids had built for her, Moira began to brush out her wet hair. She kept a covert eye on Una, who appeared to be coming to the end of her tirade.

"So, ye see now that ye willnae get much from Mungan," Una said, standing next to Moira and placing her fists on her voluptuous hips.

"I dinnae want anything from Mungan Coll," Moira replied, annoyance sharpening her voice. "And I really didnae want to hear what ye are getting from him. What the pair of ye do between the sheets is of no concern to me."

"Then ye should cease playing this game. Just tell him ye dinnae want him."

"Ye must ken the mon weel enough to realize that that doesnae work."

"Then give *me* that cursed tower house," demanded Una.

"Nay. 'Tis mine. Your father has kept it from me for too long. I dinnae intend to let ye and your lover take it from me now. That tower house is my chance to escape from your father's fists and ye, better than anyone else, should ken the importance of that."

"So escape him by wedding Tavig MacAlpin. He wants you. I dinnae understand why ye keep refusing the mon."

"I have my reasons, verra good reasons, too. They are really none of your concern."

"Ye havenae heard the last of this. I intend to fight for my mon," Una snapped, marching out of the room.

"How delightful," Moira murmured, flinching as Una banged the door shut. "I begin to think I am being punished for something, although I cannae believe I have committed a sin dire enough to deserve this."

She sighed as she tied back her damp hair with a wide blue ribbon. The thought of Una badgering her with more details of her intimacies with Mungan made Moira shudder, yet she feared that was to be her cousin's new tactic. Trying to deter Mungan's pursuit of her was no longer a good plan. It was hard enough enduring his persistence, but if she had to suffer Una's continued anger as well, she would undoubtedly lose her mind.

Standing up and brushing down her skirts, Moira decided enough was enough. She could endure no more of Mungan's wooing, no more of Una's fighting for her man, and no more of Tavig and Mungan arguing over her like two spoiled children over a toy. Until she made herself completely inaccessible to Mungan and made him feel the tower house was no longer a threat, the strife would continue. She would have to accept Tavig's solution.

It made her sad to marry Tavig under such circumstances. She would have liked to accept his frequent proposals with the knowledge that they would be safe and perhaps even happy. What she needed was some assurances that a union between her and Tavig would not be like releasing a wolf into a pen of newborn lambs. She also wished that she had some assurances that Tavig truly and deeply cared for her. And she definitely needed some assurances that if their marriage brought the trouble and danger she feared it would, Tavig would not grow to hate her for it.

"Ye want too cursed much," she scolded herself as she left her chambers to find Tavig.

One thing she would demand was an explanation for why he tricked her into a handfast marriage. She also had to get him to agree that the marriage did not have to be forever, that if she chose to leave, he would let her go. Since the situation with Mungan and Una was forcing them to marry, she did not think that was too much to ask. Moira had to know that she could leave before she and Tavig were seriously threatened by superstitions or—she shuddered as the thought fled through her mind—she caused Tavig to be injured or even killed.

She found Tavig with Mungan. Both men were shirtless and surrounded by Mungan's men-at-arms as they fought with each other. For one brief moment Moira was terrified that the argument over her had become a true battle. She elbowed her way through the men, each crash of the swords making her jump. One look at the two battling cousins told her that it was no real fight. Tavig and Mungan would certainly suffer a lot of bruises and scrapes, but neither man had any intention of hurting the other. They were just teasing each other, showing off their prowess before the men.

Tavig was soon declared the winner, his grace and speed overcoming the admirable skill and impressive strength of the larger Mungan. The audience shuffled away while the cousins stood by a bucket of water, cleaning off the dust and sweat and admiring each other's bruises. Shaking her head over the strange way of men, Moira walked up to Tavig but did not return his tentative smile. She briefly contemplated waiting until Tavig was alone, but decided that Mungan was so involved in their lives at the moment there was no real need to be secretive.

"Ah, ye are still angry with me," Tavig murmured when she did not smile back.

"Aye, but I have calmed myself enough to heed your explanation for such cunning." She crossed her arms and stared at him.

"The look on your face isnae one that promises forgiveness," he said.

"Right at this moment I dinnae feel too forgiving. I was hoping your explanation might make it easier."

He cleared his throat. "I wanted to be sure ye went to Drumdearg with me. All ye keep talking about is the fear and superstition ye and I could stir up. Ye never really listened when I said it wasnae like that at Drumdearg. It was clear that ye didnae even mean to try to see if I was right. So when I first came up with the idea of claiming we were wed to keep us safe in those wee villages, I realized it would be the same as our being handfasted to each other."

"Except that I didnae ken I was declaring myself."

"Ah, weel, aye, there was that. Lass, I just wanted to be sure ye would at least test the truth of what I have been telling ye about Drumdearg. If ye didnae decide to come there with me, then I thought I could use the fact that we are handfasted to make you."

"Aye, 'twas a fine plan," said Mungan, lightly clapping Tavig on the back.

"Oh, aye, verra fine," agreed Moira, giving Tavig a disgusted look. "Verra clever and verra sly. 'Tis clear that 'tis not only Mungan who can be sly in this family."

"Did ye say I was sly, Cousin?" Mungan asked, frowning at Tavig.

"Ye can be, Mungan, and all ken it. Now, will ye hush? This doesnae concern you. I am trying to make amends with Moira, and your interruptions dinnae help that to go smoothly."

"I am not sure anything ye say can make the trick ye played sound any more like a base deceit," Moira said, drawing Tavig's attention back to her. "Howbeit, although I dinnae agree with the reasons ye give in your weak attempt to explain yourself, they will suffice."

"Suffice?" He stepped closer, tentatively putting his hands on her shoulders. "Am I forgiven, then?"

"I wouldnae say ye are forgiven, but I do understand. 'Twas a foolish trick, but I see no real evil in it. So now I may speak of what I have decided with as much ease as one can under the circumstances."

"Ye have something else to discuss?"

"Aye, I will marry you. Ye were right; 'tis the only solution. One more day didnae make any difference. I dinnae think e'en one more year would make a difference." She stared at him, hoping he could see that her next words were not only about Mungan. "Some people can be so stubborn they havenae the wit to give up."

Tavig grimaced as he slowly enfolded her in his arms. "Rebuke accepted. So, are we to be married?"

"Aye, but we need a moment or two of privacy to discuss a few particulars." Moira looked at Mungan, who just smiled, apparently deaf to her hint.

"So, ye and the lad will marry. Weel, 'tisnae as good as if ye married me, but at least I can rest easy kenning that ye hold the land, Tavig. Now," he said as he rubbed his hands together, "I must find Una. I dinnae think she much liked the idea of me wedding Moira. Dinnae trouble yourself, Cousin, I will find the priest, and the whole lot of us can be wed ere the sun sets," he said, picking up his tunic and striding toward the keep. "That swine Robertson will have himself a hearty surprise when he arrives to find his daughter and his ward married."

The minute Mungan was gone, Moira wriggled out of Tavig's light hold. She was still angry because of the way he had tricked her. She was also a little angry because matters she could not control were forcing her to do things she did not really want to do. If she and Tavig were ordinary people, she knew she would be thrilled to have such a handsome, charming, and modestly wealthy man as her husband, especially since she loved him. Even the fact that *he* never spoke of love would not deter her. Now that was just one more difficulty and one that could easily make the other problems they faced seem far worse.

"Ye dinnae act much like a happy bride," Tavig murmured as he tugged on his shirt.

"I have been pushed and pulled about until I am securely cornered. Mungan's head is as thick as his precious walls. He willnae give up. Neither will Una. She has now begun to tell me all about the relationship she and Mungan have, right down to the sort of personal detail I have no wish to hear. 'Tis clear that her newest plan to get me to give her the tower house or put myself completely out of Mungan's large reach is to let me ken, in nauseating detail, just how weel she and Mungan get along beneath the blankets." She frowned at Tavig, who started to laugh. "Ye find that funny?"

"Weel, aye, I fear I do." He continued to laugh for a moment before struggling to control himself. "Sorry, I was just trying to imagine a lass speaking lyrically about old Mungan as a lover."

"I would cease trying unless ye have a strong stomach," she grumbled as she sat down on a rough bench near the well the men had drawn their water from.

Setting his foot on the bench at her side, Tavig leaned toward her, his forearm resting on his raised knee. "Is this what ye needed privacy for? To tell me Una was boasting about Mungan? Lass, Mungan wouldnae have been troubled by that. He would have been annoyingly pleased with himself."

"I suspect he would have been, but that isnae why I asked for privacy."

Tavig reached out to grasp her hair, rubbing the thick swatch between his fingers. "Ye mean to set some rules, dinnae ye, lass?"

"'Tis most annoying how ye can guess what I am about to do or say. Are ye sure ye cannae read a person's thoughts?" she asked, eyeing him suspiciously.

"Nay, I cannae read minds. 'Twasnae so verra hard to guess. There wasnae that many choices."

"Aye, I wish to make a rule or two. To shake off Mungan, we must marry. He will wed Una, and our troubles with him are at an end. This doesnae solve all those problems I mentioned when I explained why I couldnae marry you." She held up her hand when he started to speak, scowling a little when he grasped it, kissing her palm. "Ye wish me to go to Drumdearg. Ye think I will see that my fears are foolish once I am there."

"Aye, loving, I do."

"I willnae argue that with you. What I ask is that if my fears *do* prove warranted, I dinnae want us to think that this marriage binds us so tightly we stand like terrified deer waiting for the arrow to strike."

"Ye want me to agree to let ye walk away if ye ask to go."

Moira flushed a little beneath his steady look. She was unable to read his expression clearly, and that made her uneasy. She had to weigh her words carefully, and she was not good at that. Sighing and wishing she knew what he was feeling, she nodded.

"Simply because I have agreed to this marriage doesnae mean that I now think it is safe or wise for us to be wed," she replied. "This has been forced upon us by necessity. I need to ken that escape is possible if I must seek it. I need to ken that this difficulty with your stubborn cousin hasnae stolen away my chance to make a choice. Aye, and in this case that choice could be one of life or death."

"Ye think far too much about what *may* happen." He sat down next to her, gently pulling her into his arms.

"Someone must. I should like to be proven wrong in my fears."

"But ye also need to ken that ye can end the danger by leaving me."

"Aye, so will ye promise me that ye willnae try to hold me to the vows if I decide I must go away?"

"And what if I dinnae promise? What choices do ye have, then?"

"Not verra many, true enough. Howbeit, I could simply try to wait Mungan out. He has accepted that we are handfasted, so I would have a year. Mayhap after having me as the holder of that tower house for a full year, he will more readily accept that I can be an ally even though I am but a wee lass. I shudder at the thought of enduring his wooing again and Una's unjustified anger, but 'tis far less appalling than the two of us clinging to some sense of honor, to a need to obey laws and vows, as people stack kindling about our feet."

"Ye do fear that kindling."

"As would any sensible person. Weel, do I get that promise?"

"It seems that this time *I* am to be given no choice. Aye, ye have that promise." He did not return her smile. "Ye do reveal a skill at robbing a wedding of much hope."

"Tavig," she began, then saw Una hurrying her way, the girl's face transformed by a huge smile.

As Una hugged Moira, Tavig could not help but compare

the women's moods. Una was so delighted she babbled, whereas Moira smiled faintly, occasionally murmuring congratulations. Una was full of hope and plans for her future with Mungan. Moira looked as if she had just taken one step closer to a scaffold. Tavig tried to be understanding, for he knew the fears she spoke of were very real to her. That knowledge did little to soothe the sting of pain. He was sure it was far more than his vanity that was stung, but decided that, under the circumstances, he would do himself no good at all by delving too deeply into those feelings.

"Mungan says the priest will be here within the hour," Una announced.

"So quickly," murmured Moira as she allowed Una to tug her to her feet.

"Mungan sees no need to wait. And my father could be here at any moment. 'Twould be best if the deed is done ere he arrives."

"Aye, it would be," agreed Tavig. "If naught else, he would wish to keep Moira from wedding me, for the mon will ken that I will take back every farthing he has stolen from her."

"Oh, dear, Papa willnae like that," said Una. "Come along, Cousin Moira. We have only a verra short time to try to prepare for our weddings," she continued as she tugged Moira back to the keep.

Tavig watched the two young women until they disappeared into the castle. Shaking his head, he stood up and ambled along after them. He had one thing he desired— Moira would go to Drumdearg. Unfortunately, getting her to stay there looked to be a very large problem. Tavig could only pray that he had the skill and the patience to ease her fears enough for her to want to face them at his side.

Chapter Eighteen

Moira winced as Una laced up her bodice. There had been little they could do to improve the look of her poor ragged clothes. A good brushing and a few ribbons were not really enough to make her a beautiful bride, but they did help a little. Moira wished they had been allowed more time for preparation. Although she would enter this marriage with little hope that it could last, she would have liked to look better than she did.

"Ye dinnae look much like a bride," Una muttered as she stood back to look Moira over.

"'Tis not so surprising. My clothes are poor and have seen a great deal of wear. Ye didnae have a chance to bring any clothes, and neither did I. Ye have been here a long time, so ye have had a chance to make or obtain clothes." Moira inwardly sighed with a touch of envy as she surveyed Una's lovely blue gown, prettily embroidered at the neck, hem, and sleeves. "I dinnae even have the time to alter anything to fit me."

"I ken it. 'Tisnae just your clothes, Cousin. Ye dinnae appear verra happy. Ye are the mon's lover. I rather thought ye loved him."

"Oh, aye, I do, but if ye tell him so, I shall make ye sorely regret it. Nay, I am not as happy as ye are, but it would take too long to explain it all. There are—weel—difficulties. I am not sure they can be solved, but we arenae going to be given any time to find that out, either. To be honest, Una, I am marrying Tavig so that Mungan will leave me be and your father cannae touch me again. All the rest can be sorted out later."

"Is it because of your special gift or his?"

It took Moira a full minute to fully comprehend what Una had said, then she gaped. "Ye ken about my gift?"

"Of course. Ye have lived with me for ten years. How could I miss it? Ye used it from time to time, swearing the ones ye helped to secrecy, but 'tis verra hard to keep such a big secret from everybody." She lightly patted the stunned Moira on the head. "Both Nicol and I ken about at least a few of the times ye slipped up to our bedsides and used your gift to ease our hurts, the ones our father so often inflicted."

"Oh, and I thought I was being so clever."

"Ye could only keep it a complete secret if ye didnae help anyone. Tavig has the sight, 'tis no secret around here, so why should your healing gift trouble him?"

"It doesnae trouble him because he doesnae ken anything about it. I havenae told him and I dinnae ken whether I ever will. So ye will keep that knowledge to yourself as weel."

"Ye are asking me to keep a lot of secrets."

"Aye—two. I think ye can hold fast to that much. Weel, we had better go down to the great hall." She made one last check on the ribbons in her hair before starting out of the room.

"Moira, what do ye think my father will do when he discovers we are both married?" Una asked as she fell into step beside her cousin.

"Rant, bellow, make threats. Ye need not fear it this time, Una. I believe Mungan Coll is verra capable of dealing with Sir Bearnard. After we say our vows before the priest neither of us needs to worry about Sir Bearnard Robertson again. We will be free of the bastard."

"I think I will be slow to really believe that."

"Aye, I suspect I will continue to look o'er my shoulder for a long time. The kind of fear he breeds in a person is a verra hard one to break free of."

They entered the great hall, and Moira immediately felt uncomfortable. Mungan looked handsomely imposing in his black jupon. Una, who hurried to his side, looking delicate and tiny next to him. Tavig also looked very handsome. Moira wondered where he had gotten a full change of clothes. As he took her hand, she realized the clean, unpatched clothes the other three wore only served to make her attire look even more pathetic. It was not the wedding she had planned in her dreams.

"Dinnae look so woeful, lass," Tavig said, raising her hand to his lips and kissing her palm. "Ye will have Mungan's people thinking I force ye to wed me. 'Twould sorely bruise my vanity to have the lads thinking that."

Moira smiled faintly then impulsively stood on her tiptoes, kissing him on the cheek. "There, now they shall think I am properly besotted with you. Your vanity should be safe from harm now."

"How kind of you." He glanced toward Mungan and the priest, who were deep in converration. "Ye did look sad, Moira. 'Tisnae verra encouraging."

"The sadness ye saw had little to do with you. I but regretted the swiftness of the wedding. Every lass, even one trapped in the poor life I was, dreams of the day she will be married. The few times I allowed myself to dream, I ne'er imagined standing next to my husband dressed in little more than rags."

"Ah, I see. Ye look bonnie, dearling." He lightly touched her hair. "Mayhap I shouldnae have changed into a finer set of clothes, but since I had left a few things here, I saw no harm in it."

"Nay, there is no harm in it. Ye jested about your vanity, but I am the one who suffers from it. All the rest of ye look so fine, I but felt sorry for myself."

He put his arm around her shoulders, tugged her closer and kissed her cheek. "I think ye look verra fine."

"Careful, rogue, ye are disordering my ribbons."

"I have plans to disorder a great deal more than that once we say our vows."

Moira felt the faint sting of a blush, but had to fight a smile. "Do ye think we can go to our chambers first?"

"Ah, ye fear to shock the priest."

"That is a consideration."

"Are the two of you just going to stand there and talk?" demanded Mungan. "Ye havenae changed your mind, have ye?"

"Nay, Mungan," Tavig replied, grasping Moira by the hand again and tugging her closer to the priest. "We but waited for the priest to be ready." He bowed slightly to the round-faced, balding priest. "If ye are ready to begin, we are at your service."

As the priest began the ceremony, Moira battled a sudden panic. She wanted to be married to Tavig. She wanted to live a normal life with him. She wanted to bear his children. And none of that was possible. Tavig kept saying they were destined to be together, but Moira was equally certain that together they were doomed. Kneeling before the priest, she was being tempted with all she needed and desired, but she would only be able to hold on to it for a little while. If this was why fate had thrust her and Tavig together, then fate was a cruel mistress. A bitter laugh echoed inside of her head. By giving her a skill she could use to do good, but one that aroused only fear, Lady Fate had already revealed her cruelty.

The priest declared them man and wife. Before Tavig gently took her into his arms, Moira caught a quick glimpse of Una being heartily kissed by Mungan as his men cheered. Despite the hoots of the men, she readily returned Tavig's kiss. She decided that for just a little while, she would practice a little self-deception. For just a little while, she would pretend that her marriage to Tavig was real and would survive. An embarrassed cough from the priest brought her back to an awareness of her surroundings. Blushing deeply, she wriggled out of Tavig's hold.

"And now we can have ourselves a feast," announced Mungan even as he tugged Una over to the linen-draped, food-ladened table, amiably waving the priest over to join them.

"I wouldnae have thought ye had enough time to prepare a feast," said Tavig as he sat on Mungan's left, pulling Moira down by his side.

"I didnae. This feast was already prepared," replied Mungan as the pages filled everyone's tankard with ale.

"Ye didnae ken there was to be a wedding."

"Nay, but I did ken we would be riding off to do battle with Iver soon. Verra soon. Once my men return and tell us all they have discovered, we will make our battle plans and ride to Drumdearg. There will be no time to set out a feast then, and I like my men to have a hearty round of gluttony ere they ride off to fight. So this fine array of food was already being prepared. 'Tis just that now we have more to celebrate than the imminent demise of our treacherous cousin." He glanced around at his men-at-arms, who were loudly consuming large quantities of food and ale. "Feasting now will also insure that the men arenae suffering from such greed when we ride to Drumdearg."

Tavig laughed, then turned all his attention to Moira. She reveled in being his sole interest throughout the meal. As they playfully fed each other, she decided it was not difficult to cast aside her concerns and fears for a time. She had earned a bit of happiness even if it was stolen. Deluding herself for a few days would not make her forget why she had to leave Tavig or make the pain of leaving him any greater.

It was not long before Mungan and Tavig made it clear it was time to begin the wedding night. To Moira's surprise, Una took her by the hand and pulled her out of the great hall. They both blushed and giggled over the remarks the men made. Moira knew those remarks could get a lot rougher after they were gone.

"I am not sure why we are indulging in this wee show of ceremony, Una," Moira said as they went up the stairs. "'Tisnae as if we shall be doing anything different tonight or sleeping in a different bed. We have all been lovers right up until we stood there saying the vows, and all ken it."

"'Tis part of the game, Cousin." Una grinned at Moira as she dragged her into her chambers. "I also wished to get ye alone for just a moment." She pointed toward Moira's bed. "After all, if ye waited until Tavig brought ye up here ye would ne'er get a chance to wear this."

A gasp of delight escaped Moira when she saw the nightgown spread out on the bed. She hurried over to pick up the white lace-trimmed gown. Afraid it would not be the right size, she warily held it up against herself. She gave a sigh of relief and pleasure when she found it was only a little large.

"Oh, Una, where did ye get it?"

"Weel, once I kenned we were to be wedded to our chosen men, I spoke to the women here. I was certain there had to have been other weelborn ladies who had lived here. Even Mungan had to have had a mother." She briefly grinned when Moira giggled. "Just before I came to help ye tie the ribbons in your hair, one of the maids brought this to me. It was Mungan's mother's."

Moira could not resist one long wide-eyed look at the small nightgown. "Did she die in childbirth?" She smiled a little crookedly when Una giggled. "'Tis just hard to imagine a woman nearly as tiny as I am bearing a child who could reach Mungan's impressive size."

"She bore five sons and one daughter ere she died. All are still alive. I havenae met them, but Mungan insists that his brothers are akin in size to him and that his sister is a big, healthy lass."

"How odd. He willnae mind me wearing this?"

"Nay. His mother's things were put aside for one of the

son's wives to use if they wished to or had a need. I tried to find ye a gown, but most of them have disappeared. Mayhap they were taken to be made into other things. This was still there, though. Weel, I had best hurry to my own chambers. I want to be ready for Mungan."

"Una, do ye truly love the mon?"

"Aye, I thought ye kenned it."

"I did, but then I realized I had never heard ye say it. For a brief moment I feared ye were marrying him for—weel—simply because he doesnae beat you."

"Oh, there is that, and 'tis what first made me soften toward him. It took me some time to ken what I was doing, but one day I realized that I had been pushing the mon, testing him. Since the moment he grabbed me, I tried to make him hit me. I did everything I kenned would have made my father strike me or punish me, and Mungan ne'er touched me. He bellowed a lot, but if I even looked as if I expected him to hit me, he was insulted, even hurt."

"Aye, Tavig is the same."

"That is when I started to fall in love with the man. Now, I must go. I wish to be prepared *before* he comes to our chambers."

The moment Una was gone, Moira began to get undressed. Despite having had a bath earlier, she thoroughly washed herself before carefully donning the nightgown. She smoothed her hands over the soft material and lightly fingered the delicate lace. She had never worn anything so finely made or so beautiful. It was odd, she mused, how a piece of clothing could make such a difference. She and Tavig had been lovers for over a week, yet simply by donning the beautiful nightgown, she felt as if this night would now be special.

Tavig subtly straightened his shoulders before entering his bedchamber. He hated the feeling that Moira did not consider their marriage final, their vows binding. He had detested promising her he would let her go if and when she decided it was necessary. But, worst of all, he had hated speaking that promise knowing he did not intend to keep it. He had lied to Moira and that pained him. It also made him feel uncomfortably guilty. Tavig wanted to be certain none of those feelings would be revealed in his face when he spoke to Moira.

He caught his breath as he stepped into the room and saw Moira standing by their bed. She looked beautiful, he decided, as he shut and secured the door. Her smile was a shy one, a light blush tinting her cheeks. Her thick, bright hair hung in long ribbon-decorated waves almost to her hips. The white lacy nightgown was a little big for her, pooling slightly around her tiny feet and slipping down to reveal one pale shoulder. The light from the fire and the candles shone through the thin material, revealing each slim, tempting curve. He inwardly grinned, certain that Moira was unaware of that.

"Ye look verra bonnie, Moira. So bonnie I cannae think of anything clever and flattering to say." He smiled when she blushed even more, nervously plucking at the lace on her sleeves.

"'Twas Mungan's mother's nightgown. Una had the maids hunt it down."

"I shall see that they are all rewarded."

"When ye reclaim what is rightfully yours."

"Aye." He stepped closer to her, reaching out to slide his hand over her thick hair. "Ye sound as if ye begin to believe I will do it."

"I have always believed ye could do it, just not all on your own." She smiled when he chuckled. "There were times when it seemed ye intended to march to the gates of Drumdearg alone with naught but a sword and boldly challenge Iver. And, of course, all of Iver's men as weel."

"Of course." He lightly brushed his lips over hers, then sat down on the bed to tug off his boots. "He has but four and twenty hirelings, mayhap a few more by now, but I need not worry about them."

"Nay, not at all." She leaned against the bedpost, watching as he undressed to his braies. "They will flee, trembling and wild-eyed with fear, when they see ye striding toward them, sword in hand."

"Aye, they will unmon themselves and leave naught behind but dust as they flee to the hills."

"'Twould be verra fine if that would happen," she murmured as he stood before her.

"'Twould be verra fine, indeed. 'Twould be an almost bloodless battle. Howbeit, sweet Moira, such things are rare." He slowly began to untie the ribbons on the front of her nightgown. "As rare as a bonnie bright-haired lass with eyes like a summer's sky and skin as soft as thistledown. No mon ever had a fairer bride," he said in a soft, husky voice, bending slightly to kiss the hollow at the base of her throat.

Moira could think of no response to his flattery. She met his gaze and was firmly captured, held motionless and speechless by the warmth she read there. Her heart began to beat so fast it ached. She could feel her rapid pulse throughout her body, hear it throbbing inside her head. The look in his eyes told her he was glad she was his wife, promised her far more than passion, and dared her to reach for it. Although the voice of common sense tried to tell her it was foolish to reach for things she could not keep, Moira ignored it. It was selfish, but she intended to grab hold of anything and everything Tavig wished to offer. Soon she would have only memories to cherish and she wanted those memories to be rich and vivid ones.

Tavig held her gaze until her gown slipped from her body to crumple around her feet. She felt a deep blush burn her cheeks as he held her by the shoulders and slowly looked her over. When he met her gaze again, there was so much heat in his look that Moira did not hesitate. She stepped forward until their bodies touched.

She echoed the faint shudder that went through him. A

soft, inviting laugh escaped her when he groaned, caught her up in his arms, and placed her on the bed. Moira wrapped her limbs around him when he shed his braies, easing his body over hers. It was strange, even a little silly, but she could not shake the feeling that this time their love-making was different. Moira could not believe it was simply because a priest had now sanctioned their union.

Her capacity for thought was soon kissed and stroked away. Emboldened by her own desires and Tavig's almost reverential lovemaking, Moira began to match him kiss for kiss, touch for touch. She slid her hands down his back to cup his taut backside. The way he groaned, his lovemaking intensifying, encouraged her to further daring. Slowly she moved her hand over his hard stomach then down, gently, warily, curling her fingers around his erection. He bucked, and she started to retract her hand, but he stopped her. With words and actions he showed her his response had been born of pleasure not disgust. Moira quickly discovered that his pleasure fed her own.

He soon moved out of her reach, his rapid breaths heating her abdomen even as his kisses heated her blood. She shifted restlessly, her passions so strong she could not keep still, as he measured the length of her legs with soft, nibbling kisses. Her heart skipped with shock when his caresses moved from her inner thighs to what lay between. It was only a brief check to her desire. Her cry of shock and denial quickly changed to one of blind pleasure with but one intimate stroke of his tongue.

She squirmed beneath his attentions even as she opened to him, urging him on with the arching of her body and entangling her fingers in his thick hair. When she felt her crest draw near, she pulled at him, calling out to him. A guttural cry of relief escaped her when he fiercely joined their bodies. She wrapped herself around him as he took them to the sweet oblivion they both so desperately craved.

* * *

Moira lifted her head off Tavig's chest long enough so she could peek at him through her tousled hair. He was holding her so closely, so tenderly, she knew he felt no shock or distaste over what he had just done or her enjoyment of it. She relaxed, her uncertainty fading. Murmuring with the warm remnants of sated pleasure, she cuddled up to him.

"I suppose there is no chance of forging a treaty with your cousin Iver," she said quietly, absently toying with the small dark curls encircling his navel.

"Nay. My cousin has been blinded by his greed and envy. In truth, I waited too long to respond to his threat. 'Tis why my friends were murdered and I have lost months in running and hiding. I didnae want to draw a sword on my own kinsmon, didnae want it to come to that between us. He didnae suffer the same qualms. To Iver our blood ties are not binding, they are simply another weapon to use against me. The mon sensed my hesitation, played upon my wish to solve our differences without bloodshed, and used them against me. Those feelings became my weaknesses, and my weaknesses cost the lives of my friends."

"Nay," she said against his skin, idly counting his ribs with her fingers as she kissed his chest. "Ye carry no guilt for those murders. 'Tis all Iver's burden. 'Tis no weakness to expect loyalty from your own kinsmon. 'Tis certainly no weakness not to see that he would kill innocent men just to draw you into a trap." She tentatively caressed his stomach, felt him tremble faintly as he held her a little tighter, and she grew bolder. "I but pray he doesnae succeed in his treachery."

"Ah, so ye would care if I fell beneath Iver's sword." Tavig threaded his fingers through her hair, murmuring his pleasure as she warmed his stomach with kisses, the touch of her tongue against his skin stirring his desire until it was difficult to think clearly.

"Ye do ask some verra stupid questions at times, Sir Tavig." She gently nipped at the insides of his thighs and savored his soft moan.

"A mon likes to ken that he will be missed."

"Ah, ye seek to have your vanity stroked."

"Aye, amongst other things." He shivered with pleasure and the strong bite of anticipation when she laughed against the hollow where his leg joined his torso. "Lass, neither Mungan nor I wish to lose our lives and the lives of our men. Dinnae fret o'er the coming battle with Iver. Aye, it willnae be easy or bloodless but we willnae be hurling ourselves into the fray in senseless fury." He smiled faintly over the thick huskiness in his voice. "The battle facing me isnae of any great interest to me at the moment."

"Nay?" Resting her arms on his hips, she smiled at him as she lightly stroked his groin with her fingers. "What is of interest to you, my fine knight?"

"My wedding night." Tavig did not think Moira had ever looked so exciting as she did now, sprawled between his legs, her breath and fingers teasing his loins. "'Tis custom for a newly wed couple to spend the wedding night in frenzied lovemaking until they are all asweat and too exhausted to move."

"Are ye certain such exertion is good for a mon who must soon go to battle?"

"Aye, 'twill make him stronger." He grinned when she laughed, closing his eyes with pleasure as she encircled his navel with tiny kisses. "Lass, I dinnae think ye ought to torment a mon so," he said, his voice a low groan as she touched kisses all around the place he ached to feel her lips.

"Patience is a virtue."

"I have ne'er claimed to be particularly virtuous. Sweet Moira, if ye dinnae put your mouth on me soon, I shall go mad," he whispered and cried out with pleasure when she obeyed his urgent request.

Tavig fought to control the desire rippling through him. He wanted to savor the pleasure of her lips, her stroking tongue. When she obeyed his silent urgings and took him into the warmth of her mouth, he felt his control rapidly unravel.

Only a moment later, he grabbed her beneath the arms,

dragging her up his body. She settled on top of him, easing their bodies together with an instinctive skill that left him gasping. She needed little prompting from him to move, quickly taking them both shuddering into passion's blinding heights.

He caught her in his arms as she sagged against him, holding her tightly as he released his seed deep inside her. As he savored the way that felt, he suddenly realized he had a way to hold Moira at his side. It was not particularly honorable, even unfair, but he could get her with child. He smoothed his hands over her slim body and decided that if all else failed, he would indeed stoop to that. Reluctantly he admitted that he needed her that badly.

Chapter Nineteen

Tavig groaned, eased out of Moira's lax hold, and rubbed his forehead. It took him a moment to realize that the pounding he heard was not coming from inside his head. As he staggered to his feet and pulled on his braies, he glared at the door. Still struggling to shake off his grogginess, he stumbled to the door, opened it, and scowled at Mungan.

"Why arenae ye still abed with your bride?" he demanded of his cousin.

"Because we are about to have visitors."

"Aye?" Suddenly awake, Tavig muttered a curse. "Robertson is here."

"Weel, he will be riding through my gates in an hour or less."

"'Twas a foolish hope, but I had wished he wouldnae appear for a few days yet."

"All things considered, ye are verra lucky he wasnae here when ye arrived."

"True. I will be ready and at your side ere he arrives. Are the lasses to greet him as weel?"

"Aye, although it wasnae easy to convince Una of that."

Glancing back at the bed, Tavig groaned. Moira was awake. She sat in the middle of the bed, a linen sheet wrapped around her, staring at him with wide eyes. In her eyes he saw a glimmer of the fear he had tried to defeat.

"Nay, it wouldnae be," he murmured as he turned back to Mungan. "Moira will be there."

Shutting the door after Mungan left, Tavig strode to the washbowl. He washed, then fled to the garderobe. Although he knew he was being cowardly, when he returned he was a little annoyed to find Moira still sitting where she had been. He had hoped she would get dressed and be ready to meet Robertson, thus saving him the distasteful chore of forcing her to do something that so clearly frightened her.

"Ye have to be there to greet him, lass," he said as he started to dress.

"Why? Cannae ye and Mungan tell him everything?" She shuddered. "He will be so furious."

"He cannae hurt you," Tavig assured her as he sat down on the bed, taking one of her cold hands between his. "Mungan and I would ne'er allow him to."

"I ken it, or at least a verra large part of me kens it. Howbeit, inside of me is a small terrified child who refuses to see reason. All she keeps saying is that Sir Bearnard is coming, and he will be verra angry. All she wants to do is hide."

"Una undoubtedly feels the same, but she will be there to face her father. Can ye do less? And, loving, she is probably counting on ye to be with her, to stand firm at her side. After all, ye are the only one amongst us who can understand what she is feeling as she faces that bastard and confronts his anger."

Moira sighed. He was right. Una would be expecting her, would need her. And if Una could face her father, then Moira knew she would feel the worst of cowards if she did not do the same.

She slid out of bed to get dressed. The knowledge that she would soon be face-to-face with Sir Bearnard so filled her mind that she was not concerned about washing and dressing in front of Tavig. It was not until she tried to braid her hair that she was fully recalled to his presence. He stepped up behind her to take over the chore. She was grateful for his help as her hands were shaking badly.

"Think of it as finally saying faretheeweel to the mon," he suggested.

"That may help."

Her braid done, he turned her toward him, taking her into his arms and kissing her gently. "I wish I could let ye hide. I dinnae like forcing ye to face something that makes ye turn so pale and has ye shaking like this. Aye, I can deal with Robertson, but I feel helpless against the fear he has scarred ye with."

Despite the fears knotting her insides, Moira had to smile at the frustration darkening Tavig's expression. "And ye really hate feeling helpless, dinnae ye, Tavig?" She reached out to stroke his cheek.

"No mon likes it. Aye, and vain though it may be, I have always considered myself a mon who could fix most anything, solve most any problem." He grimaced, jamming his fingers through his hair. "These last few months have been most unsettling. I havenae solved the problem with Iver and I cannae fix what Sir Bearnard has done to you."

"Nay, ye dinnae have that quite right. Ye *will* solve the problem with Iver and do so verra soon, even if it isnae in the way ye wished to solve it. And I? Nay, ye cannae take the fear out of my heart. Howbeit, ye have taught me to be *less* fearful. That is no small victory. I feel certain that a fortnight ago I wouldnae have been able to face my guardian no matter what ye said or did. I would have heeded that tiny terrified child inside of me and run, then hid, despite being sure Robertson would find me and kenning that I would pay dearly for making him hunt me down."

Moving toward the door, she looked at him. "Now, we had best get down to the great hall ere he arrives and ere I give in to that part of me that is cowering and scrambling to get away."

He smiled, stepping forward to take her hand. "Ye are far braver than ye think ye are."

As she followed him down to the great hall, Moira heartily wished he was right. She was so knotted up with fear, she was feeling ill. That did not seem very brave to her. She could not let Tavig face Sir Bearnard alone, however. There were matters that had to be settled that were between her and Sir Bearnard Robertson alone. If she intended to hold on to her tower house after leaving Tavig, she had to start by letting Sir Bearnard know she would never allow him to keep her birthright from her again. If she could not even face her brutal, deceitful guardian while surrounded by men ready to protect her from him, she would never be able to convince Mungan that she could be a strong ally.

She looked for Una as she and Tavig entered the great hall, finding the girl standing only a few feet to the right of the door. The moment she saw her cousin's wide-eyed, pale face, Moira slipped free of Tavig and hurried to Una's side. Seeing Una so close to collapsing restored a little of Moira's calm. It would help no one and nothing if they both met Sir Bearnard trembling and weeping with terror. The man would thoroughly enjoy that, she mused with a spark of anger.

"Una, be easy," she urged, signaling a page to bring her a tankard of wine.

"I thought I would be calm," Una muttered, snatching up the wine the page brought and taking a long drink. "I have a husband now, a big, strong husband. I thought that would be enough. Instead I feel terrified."

"Big and strong as Mungan is, Cousin, he cannae cure a fear that has been beaten into you since the day ye were born."

"Come, lasses," Mungan called from the head table. "Sit with us."

"If ye dinnae mind," Moira replied, "I think we will feel better if we can face Sir Bearnard on our feet."

"Aye, 'tis easier to run away," muttered Una.

"Then when the time comes, we will stand with ye," Tavig said as he sat down next to Mungan.

Moira nodded before turning all her attention back to a still-trembling Una. "There, that should make ye feel calmer. There shall be two strong men, swords at hand, standing by our side. Aye, and ye ken that ye can count on every one of the other dozen or so men lurking in this hall."

"I ken it. I wish it would make me as brave as ye are."

"Brave? I am so afraid I feel ill with it. When Sir Bearnard enters this hall, I may empty my stomach all over his boots." She smiled when Una uttered a weak, unsteady giggle.

Una sighed, pulling out of her skirt pocket a linen square to dab at her tear-filled eyes. "I feel oddly sad as weel. He is my father, Moira. I havenae seen him in weeks, months. I should want to see him. I should be eager to tell him of my marriage and present my husband. Instead I find myself praying that some disaster will befall him ere he reaches the gates. Is that not sad? I must be the most ungrateful daughter any mon has been cursed with."

Grasping Una by the shoulders, Moira gave her cousin a little shake. "That is exactly what Sir Bearnard would want ye to think. Ye are wed to a mon ye love and a mon most fathers would welcome an alliance with. If there is naught between ye and your father but fear, 'tis *he* who put it there. Ye have naught to be grateful to the mon for, except mayhap that he didnae kill you."

"Aye, a part of me kens that. 'Tis still sad, though."

"Oh, aye, 'tis sad. There is no arguing that." Moira tensed as she heard the sounds of men approaching the great hall and echoed Una's shudder as a chillingly familiar voice reached their ears. "Easy, Una, stand firm," she whispered and knew she was speaking to herself as much as to Una.

Tavig and Mungan reached their sides just as Mungan's men ushered Sir Bearnard and Nicol into the great hall. Moira sent Tavig a look of thanks when he halted Mungan so that they stood a little apart from the women. It allowed them to be close enough to support her and Una yet not so close it would appear to everyone as if the women hid behind their men. It allowed her and Una the face-saving illusion of bravery without all the risks.

She did not feel brave at all when Sir Bearnard looked her way. He looked mildly surprised to see that she was still alive, then irritated over her survival. Nicol beamed at her, but his father stopped him from coming any closer. A familiar wrinkled face appeared from behind Nicol and Bearnard, and Moira smiled at the gaping Crooked Annie. A moment later Moira found herself tightly enfolded in the old woman's bony arms. She grimaced, patting Annie's thin back as the woman wept.

"I thought ye were dead, lass," Annie wailed. "I thought ye were lying cold in a watery grave."

"Weel, as ye can see, I am dry and hale." She wriggled out of the woman's hold and glanced at Tavig. "Some wine?"

"Here, I will get the poor old crone a wee sip of wine," said Mungan grabbing Crooked Annie's hand and dragging her over to the head table. "Ye lasses can share a few greetings with your kinsmen."

"Old crone?" Annie muttered, but said no more after Mungan thrust a tankard of wine into her hands.

"I see that ye have already gathered your ransom, Sir Mungan," Bearnard said, nodding at Moira. "The rest of our business should be easy to deal with."

There was a tight anger in Bearnard's fleshy face, and Moira noticed that even Nicol looked stern. Glancing at the way Mungan's men slouched around the great hall, insolent, amused looks on their faces, also puzzled her. A moment later she understood what was happening. By not immediately offering hospitality to the Robertsons, Mungan was being blatantly insulting, and she was sure that Mungan knew exactly what he was doing. And he was adding to the insult by being so solicitous to Crooked Annie. By refusing to discuss the business of ransom, Mungan was also telling Bearnard that he now had the upper hand. Mungan was right. He held both the kidnap victim and the ransom. Moira could see that Bearnard hated that. He was growing dangerously red in the face. She wished she could enjoy Bearnard's suffering as much as a grinning Tavig did.

When Bearnard fixed his glare on her, Moira could not fully restrain a shudder. Tavig ceased to grin and moved a little closer, but she subtly shooed him back. Matters were tense enough, and Una was close to crumbling. They still had the marriages to announce.

"Ye should have stayed in your cabin, lass," Bearnard snarled at Moira. "If ye hadnae been up on deck whoring with this rogue"—he shook a finger at Tavig—"ye wouldnae have been washed away."

Again Moira waved Tavig back, Bearnard's insult to her causing her husband to grow visibly furious. "And ye should have told me I was to be the ransom for Una. Mayhap I would have been inspired to take better care of myself." She could tell by the way Bearnard narrowed his eyes and clenched his fists that he ached to hit her.

"Ye have your ransom, Coll. Give me my daughter back," Bearnard ordered, glaring at Mungan, who leaned against his huge table with a deceptive idleness, sharing a tankard of wine with Crooked Annie.

"Moira cannae be used as ransom any longer, Robertson," Tavig said. "She is my wife."

"Your wife?" Bearnard stared at Tavig in stunned disbelief for a moment before looking at Mungan. "Ye didnae let this murderer wed her, did ye? Ye wanted her, wanted her so badly ye tried to kidnap her."

"True enough," agreed Mungan. "I wanted that cursed tower house out of your hands. But after some thought I decided 'tis just as safe in Tavig's hands as it is in mine. Besides, I cannae have two wives and I decided to marry Una. She suited me better and all that."

"Ye married Una?" Bearnard was breathing so heavily,

his fury so strong, that his voice became an unsteady squawk.

Moira stumbled a little when Bearnard glared at her and Una, causing Una to take a hasty step backward. That distraction caused her to miss the start of Bearnard's attack. She caught a brief glimpse of his fist just before it hit her. Pain engulfed her head as she was catapulted backward from the force of the blow, taking Una with her.

Dazed, she could not move even though she felt Una squirm beneath her. Una sat up, holding her. Moira saw a slender, familiar figure hurl itself at Bearnard and knew Tavig would not be stopped this time. Although still groggy, she did manage to stop Mungan from grabbing Nicol as both men reached her side at the same time.

"Nicol willnae hurt us," she said, the pain still ripping through her head making her voice hoarse. She eyed the piece of skirt Crooked Annie was using to dab at her bloodied lip. "Ye couldnae find a clean piece?" She was not surprised when Annie ignored her.

"Shouldnae ye help Tavig?" Una asked Mungan.

"He would turn on me if I interrupted." Mungan crossed his arms over his broad chest and watched Tavig throw off Bearnard then leap on the man, fists flailing. "I think the lad will have the bastard subdued soon." He warily glanced at Una. "Sorry, lass. I forgot he is your father."

"No need to apologize, husband. Just dinnae let Tavig kill him."

"Oh, I will step in ere that happens. After all, we have only been wed a day, loving." He winked at Una. "Far too soon for me to be killing your kinsmen." He grinned when Una, Nicol, and Moira were startled into laughing briefly.

Bearnard hit Tavig so hard the smaller man hit the floor, sliding toward them. Moira reached out toward Tavig only to be firmly held in place by Una and Crooked Annie. She did not struggle for she was still light-headed from Sir Bearnard's punch, and Tavig was already back on his feet. Shaking off Crooked Annie's grasp, she turned enough to look at Nicol, a little surprised to see him just sitting there next to his sister and watching his father being pummeled by Tavig.

"Ye have no wish to aid your father?" she asked her cousin Nicol, keeping an eye on Tavig at the same time to be sure he continued to hold the upper hand with Sir Bearnard.

Nicol shook his head. "Why should I halt his being beaten senseless? 'Tis the only time he gets his due."

Although she had always suspected it, Moira was a little shocked to see that Sir Bearnard had succeeded in beating the love right out of his children. Una was saddened by that, but neither she nor Nicol showed the slightest concern about their father being soundly beaten by Tavig. Even though it was now clear that Tavig was going to win, they sat unmoved by Sir Bearnard's plight.

Moira turned her full attention back to the swiftly waning battle. She had watched just enough to make sure Tavig was not losing, but the sight of him being injured, even in a battle he was winning, was more than she could bear. When Bearnard went down and stayed down, she breathed a heavy sigh of relief, smiling at a slightly battered Tavig as he moved toward her.

Her smile froze as she caught the shadow of a movement from Sir Bearnard. Fear for Tavig tightening her throat, she was only able to croak out a warning as Sir Bearnard pulled a dagger from inside his boot, staggered to his feet, and lunged toward Tavig's unprotected back with a speed that astonished her. Tavig turned, but Mungan was faster. He caught Bearnard by the wrist, halting the man's treacherous attack. Mungan wrenched Bearnard's wrist to disarm him. Moira heard the crack of bone, and Bearnard's scream of pain drowned out the sound of his dagger clattering to the floor. With one sound blow to the jaw, Mungan silenced Sir Bearnard's wails, tossing the unconscious man aside when Bearnard went limp in his hold.

"Sorry, Una," Mungan said as he moved to his wife's

side and patted her on the head. "I fear I broke his wrist. 'Tis not a break that heals weel. He could lose all strength in his sword hand."

And his punching hand, Moira thought. Glancing at her cousins, she saw them eyeing a blandly smiling Mungan with the same suspicious consideration she felt. Mungan could easily have disarmed Bearnard without breaking any bones. He had purposely maimed the man. She turned to face Tavig and caught the glance he sent his cousin, a glance that revealed Tavig shared her opinion.

Tavig touched her throbbing cheek, and she managed a smile. "Ye are far more battered than I," she said.

"It looks far worse than it is," he murmured.

"Both of ye need tending," Crooked Annie said as she stood up, grabbed Tavig by the arm, and tugged him toward the head table.

"What about Sir Bearnard?" Moira asked as she followed them, the others quickly falling into step behind her. "He is beginning to stir."

"I must not have hit him as hard as I thought I did," Mungan said, scowling toward Bearnard as he sat down in his huge chair, Una taking her place at his side. "Angus," he called to one of his men. "I think Robertson needs some time in a secure place."

"I need my wounds seen to," Bearnard cried, his voice slurred with pain. "Nicol, why do ye stand with our enemy?"

Nicol shrugged and sat next to Una. "He is my kinsmon now, not my enemy."

"Traitor!" Bearnard screamed as two of Mungan's men started to drag him out of the hall. "Ye are all traitors! I will make ye all pay for this. Curse ye, Nicol, I am your father!"

Bearnard's voice grew stronger as he screamed threats at all of them, struggling enough to impede the men trying to get him out of the great hall. Nicol, Tavig, and Mungan all looked angry, and Moira feared the confrontation would be renewed. She prayed that Crooked Annie's avid attentions to Tavig's wounds would keep him in his seat. Bearnard might be impaired by a broken wrist, but he had already shown that he was not above acts of dishonor.

Just as she began to fear Tavig intended to lunge for the man again, Mungan rose, ambled over to Bearnard, and started speaking to the man in a low, even voice. Bearnard turned the color of cold ashes, all the fight leaving his body until he nearly sagged in the grip of his two widely grinning guards. Not another word escaped Bearnard as he was taken away, his frightened stare never wandering from Mungan until the doors of the great hall shut after him. Whistling softly, Mungan strode back to the table, kissed the top of Una's head, and sat down.

"What did ye say to him?" Tavig asked, half smiling at his cousin as he nudged Annie away and waved her to a seat. "Enough, woman," he told her. "I am fine. Mungan, ye said something to that bastard that sucked all the strength from him. I am curious as to what it was."

"Aye, so am I," said Una, eyeing her new husband with admiration.

Mungan smiled faintly. "First I reminded him that no one will raise an outcry if he just disappears. That was but a guess, yet 'tis clear he believes in its possibility. I mentioned that I dinnae have the sharpest of memories and have, on occasion, purely forgotten I hold a prisoner in the bowels of this keep. Then I remarked on how so much noise can set my head to throbbing so badly I dinnae ken what I do. I expressed my sincerest regrets concerning a few men who fell victim to these lapses of mine. It seems Sir Bearnard found those tales a wee bit unsettling."

"Aye, I wager he did," murmured Tavig. "He will guess your game when naught happens to him."

"Ah, but he willnae be allowed to guess my game. I willnae hurt the cur—weel, not too badly—but he will ne'er be allowed to doubt my tales." He patted Una's hand. "Dinnae worry, lass. He will leave here alive, but when I let him leave, he willnae be the fist-wielding bastard he was when he arrived."

"How can ye do that?" Una asked. "He has been that way his whole life."

"'Tis in his blood, is it?" Mungan asked, eyeing Nicol a little suspiciously.

"Nay, I dinnae think so." Una frowned, looking at Nicol. "It isnae, is it?"

"Nay," Nicol answered. "Our people have always told me that our father was the only one like that. He learned at a young age that he could rouse fear in people. He liked it. His father doted on him, for he was the only son, and so no leash was put on his brutality. When the old laird died, our father grew even worse. Ye will have a difficult time trying to change him," he said to Mungan.

"I can be most patient and stubborn," Mungan said. "What I must question is, where do ye stand?"

"With my sister and cousin. We are kinsmen now."

Mungan nodded. "Accepted. Ye can guard the lasses here whilst Tavig and I ride to battle our kinsmon Iver."

"And when is that to be?"

"On the morrow."

Tavig choked on the wine he was drinking. Moira slapped him on the back to help him clear his throat. He looked furious, and she inwardly sighed. Mungan and Tavig were obviously closely bonded, but they did seem to love to argue with each other. She was beginning to suspect that they thoroughly enjoyed the confrontations.

"We are to ride on the morrow?" Tavig demanded. "When did ye think ye might tell me about this, Cousin?"

"Weel, about now, actually."

"Mungan, curse your thick head. Why have ye decided we should ride against Iver on the morrow? We were waiting for your men to return. I havenae seen them."

"They arrived just before dawn. We had a wee talk, and I sent them off to their beds."

"Mungan, it was your wedding night." Seeing how Una

blushed as she kept her gaze fixed upon her food, Tavig laughed softly.

"Weel, my men didnae ken that I had gotten married. And I cannae fault them for wishing to tell me what they discovered. None of your people stand with Iver. Not a mon, woman, or bairn. He only has his mercenaries."

"Last I kenned, he had four and twenty of them. Not a large force, but each one battle-hardened and safe behind the walls of Drumdearg. They could easily force us into a siege. They have food and water to hold out for months."

"Aye, but we can avoid the slow bloodletting of a siege, Cousin. It seems not all of your men were forced into hiding or killed, *and* many of them never doubted that ye would return. They have been waiting, and my men found them almost too eager to join us. A few of your men have even convinced Iver that they have changed their loyalty to him. They will get us into Drumdearg."

"Then defeating Iver will be easy."

"Easier than if we were forced into a siege. Howbeit, it will still take a battle even with surprise in our favor. Iver has more than fifty hirelings now."

"There was no exact count made?"

"Nay, for Iver has sent a call out for more men, and the number grows a wee bit each day. Word about Drumdearg is that Iver expects another ten men verra soon. I have but eight and twenty men-at-arms prepared to go, no time to bring in or prepare any more of my people, and I cannae take every mon I have."

"Of course not. Ye cannae leave your own lands unprotected. So we face Iver with thirty men—"

"Thirty-one," said Nicol.

"Ye will join us?" asked Tavig.

"We are kinsmen."

"Then welcome, kinsmon." Tavig looked at Moira, smiling and taking her hand in his when he saw the worry in her eyes. "Mayhap ye and Una should leave us to discuss the battle, as it so clearly upsets you."

"Aye, it upsets me, but I will stay. I should like to ken exactly what I am riding into," she said.

Moira smiled slowly when she saw Una nod in agreement. It only took one quick look at the men's faces to know that there was going to be a great deal of arguing. Moira refilled her tankard. Nicol, Mungan, and Tavig would soon discover that she could be as stubborn as any of them.

Chapter Twenty

"A wife is supposed to obey her husband."

Moira smiled at Tavig as he rode up beside her. He was not taking losing their argument very well, but she could forgive him for that. She and Una had used some less-than-honorable means to gain their ends. Neither Tavig nor Mungan wanted to lock them up in the dungeon with Sir Bearnard, and she and Una had made it very clear that that was the only way they would be kept from riding with their men.

"I shall be verra obedient for the rest of this adventure." She laughed softly when he cursed.

"Most men wouldnae tolerate such stubbornness in their wives."

"Ah, but ye are not most men." She glanced toward Nicol and Una, who rode flanking Mungan and were laughing at something he had said. "I cannae believe the change in my cousins."

"That wasnae a verra subtle change of subject, lass." Tavig watched her cousins for a moment. "They feel safe from their father, and it has lightened their hearts. Mungan has become quite the valiant knight in their eyes. I pray he can break Sir Bearnard as he claims he can. Mungan can protect Una, but Nicol would pay dearly if Sir Bearnard is released an unchanged mon. I fear that if Sir Bearnard returns to his old ways, Nicol would soon kill him."

"And have the blood of his father on his hands." Moira shook her head. "He would ne'er be free of that guilt." Shifting a little in the saddle, for the full day's ride was beginning to make her sore, she asked Tavig, "Dinnae ye believe that Mungan can take the brutishness out of my guardian?"

"If it can be done, Mungan can do it. I have heard him speak of the most blood-chilling tortures with a cool amiability that makes even a strong mon sweat with fear. I have kenned Mungan all my life and ken that he would ne'er do as he threatens, yet for that one moment while he speaks, even I shudder.

"Bearnard beat fear into the hearts of those weaker than himself and subservient to him. Mungan also kens the value of fear, but he uses words and plays upon the fears all men hold. Of course, with Mungan ye can beat him at his game if ye use your wits. He wins because some men, like Bearnard, believe he will do all he says and look no further so they never guess that they have been fooled. And, like Bearnard, many a mon who rules with his fists is actually a coward." He shook his head. "Men like Bearnard like to inflict pain, but have little stomach for enduring it themselves."

"I hope Mungan succeeds in terrifying all of the brutishness out of Bearnard, at least long enough for Nicol to gain the upper hand. Aye, and for Nicol to realize that he is no coward, something that oftimes troubles him. I dinnae like kenning that I am a coward, but it must be bitter indeed for a mon who is expected to be brave and honored for it."

"Ye are no coward, Moira."

Moira smiled faintly. "I was nearly mindless with fear when I faced Sir Bearnard. Everyone saw it."

"Aye, but ye faced him despite that. Ah, Mungan wants me. We are nearing Drumdearg and must decide whether to camp and wait until the morning or go in at night."

She nodded, watching him as he rode up to take Una's place beside Mungan. As Una dropped back to join her, Moira thought about what Tavig had said. She *had* faced Sir Bearnard despite her gut-wrenching fear of the man. It was difficult to consider that brave, however, when she had not been alone in doing so and had been nauseated with fear the whole time. She certainly had not *felt* brave while trembling before her guardian.

"Ye have a verra black scowl upon your face, Cousin," Una said as she reached Moira's side.

"I was just concerned about Adair," Moira lied.

"He will be fine with Crooked Annie. She is old, but she is still an excellent nursemaid."

"Aye, except that she did have some sharp words to say about Adair's parentage, men's follies, and wives being forced to care for the fruit of those follies." As she recalled all of Annie's tart remarks, Moira wondered if she should consider them more seriously and not merely shrug them aside as the empty mutterings of an old woman.

"Aye, and all the while ruffling the lad's curls and kissing his cheek. Come, Moira, ye ken better than anyone that Crooked Annie has a sharp tongue, but a loving hand. All the while she wept o'er you after finding ye alive, she cursed you for a fool, called ye reckless for going up on deck in a storm, and branded ye a witless child. 'Tis just her way. Adair may be a wee bairn, but he was smiling at her and gurgling happily. He kens what she is."

Moira laughed softly, a little embarrassed about doubting Annie for even a moment. "Aye, ye are right. And Tavig heard her, yet just grinned. He saw no harm in leaving his son with the woman."

"I must say, ye are verra kindly toward the child. I am not sure I could be so forgiving."

"Tavig didnae even ken who I was when he was seeding Adair. How can I fault him or that bonnie child for things done when I wasnae even a fleeting acquaintance of Tavig's? I was furious for a few hours, jealousy a tight knot in my belly, but it passed. In truth, 'tis fortunate we were too busy running from Dalnasith to talk. It allowed me some time to put aside those feelings."

"And ye can forgive him for how his old lover tried to have ye burned as a witch?"

"As easily as I can forgive Adair for having been born of such a woman. Just as the child couldnae pick his parents, so Tavig couldnae begin to guess how Jeanne would respond when she was set aside. After all, he had given her no promises, no vows."

"And he has given them to you." Una watched Moira closely as she said, "And ye mean to break the vows ye spoke to him."

"I warned him of that ere we knelt before the preacher."

Una sighed. "I wish I was a clever lass so that I could find the words that would convince ye to stay with Tavig Mac-Alpin. Ye love the mon—more deeply than mayhap even ye ken."

"What stands between me and Tavig isnae something that can be talked away with clever words. Now, I really dinnae wish to talk about that. It may be foolish, but for a wee while I want to pretend that our only trouble is Iver."

A grimace twisted Una's pretty face. "And that is the last thing I wish to think about. It means a battle, and men get hurt or killed in battles."

"I ken it, but I just cannae feel that we will lose this battle or any of the men we care about."

"Moira, ye dinnae have the sight, too, do ye?"

"Nay, 'tis just a feeling. Mungan and Tavig ken weel the mon they face, and ken the type of men they must fight. They even ken weel the place they must do battle in. They have the favor of the people Iver tries to rule. With so much in their favor I just cannae believe they will lose. I cannae help but wonder if Iver was always aware of that and 'tis the reason he tried so hard to kill Tavig before he could gather his supporters together."

"I dinnae suppose Tavig has seen anything."

"Not that he has mentioned. He acts verra confident. I would like to think there is more behind that than male bravado. It looks as if they have decided what we will do next."

Moira soon found herself caught up in the business of setting up camp. She overheard snatches of conversation from the men, but not enough to know exactly what was going to happen next. When Mungan sent three men to Drumdearg, she began to get annoyed by her own ignorance. The moment she sat by the fire with Tavig, Mungan, Nicol, and Una, she decided she could wait no longer to be told.

"What are ye planning?" she asked Tavig as the wine-skin was being passed around.

"We stay here until just before dawn, then slip into Drumdearg," he replied, handing her the skin.

She took a long drink of wine and passed it on to Nicol. "Is that a good time to attack?"

"As good as any. We will have light enough to see but shadows enough to hide in. 'Tis a time when men are often less alert. Iver changes the guard at sunrise, so if we plan it correctly, we will catch the guard at the end of their watch when they are weary and concerned mostly with when the new guard will arrive so that they can go to their beds."

"I have sent three of my men into Drumdearg to alert our allies there," said Mungan.

"Are ye certain ye can trust them?" asked Moira. "If any of them reveal your plans to Iver, he will have hours to prepare a trap for you."

Tavig put his arm around her shoulders, tugged her closer, and kissed her cheek. "They can be trusted with our lives, dearling. Even if Iver began to suspect something, he would ne'er pry the truth from these men. They are the kinsmen of the men Iver murdered. E'en if they werenae loyal to me, and they are, they would still do most anything to make Iver pay for those deaths."

"Doesnae Iver ken that his victim's kinsmen could be a danger to him?"

"Aye, but Iver ne'er took an interest in the people he seeks to rule. The ones most closely related to the men he murdered have gone into hiding, but Iver simply doesnae ken that the duty of revenge will be taken up by others. He doesnae think of how the men have more family than a mother, daughter, father, and the like. The lands he took from me teem with the men's cousins, uncles, and others, and he is too blind to see the danger of that."

"And considering that he has no qualms about killing his own kinsmen, he probably doesnae think any of them would trouble themselves to seek revenge. Especially if they are poor men."

"Aye, Iver looks upon all men who arenae knights, wealthy, or weelborn as little more than witless beasts to be worked and used until they die. There is no sense of clan in Iver. He sees the people of Drumdearg as no more than tools to feed him, house him, and gain him coin, to buy more mercenaries. He takes what he wants, including their women, and feels they are all too stupid or cowardly to stop him."

"How can he think such things after living there for so long?"

"He ne'er got to ken the people. He ne'er noticed or thought about them except in how they could serve him. I should have banished the mon years ago, but I was able to curb his worse instincts, and that seemed to be enough. My family isnae a verra large one, and mayhap I feared acknowledging the need to be rid of one of them."

"Ye cannae be faulted for trying to keep a kinsmon from cutting his own throat," said Mungan. "And that is what Iver has done. E'en he has to ken that one of you must now die. He has done his best to insure that that one was you. He failed." Mungan shrugged. "I ne'er liked him, ne'er trusted him, and I willnae hesitate to cut him down, but, as ye said, Tavig, we arenae a large family. E'en I regret the need to lessen our number. Iver has given us no choice."

The men began to discuss the details of the forthcoming battle and, although she dreaded the possible consequences of such a confrontation, Moira could see that the plans were thorough and promised victory—if all went as planned. Once the battle began, Mungan and Tavig would gain more men from the people of Drumdearg. Some of the men who had been hiding would probably return in time to take part in the fight. They had a way to get inside the keep. Mungan had even chosen three of his youngest men to guard her and Una while Tavig had chosen the place they were to remain until it was safe. Her mind told her it would go well, but her heart feared some terrible mishap.

When Tavig stood, pulling her to her feet, and led her to a secluded place within the surrounding wood, she did not resist. Even the knowing looks of the men did not trouble her. In a few hours Tavig would be in the midst of battle, facing a man who desperately wanted him dead. She needed to be alone with him.

"Have ye had any feelings on what is to come?" she asked as he spread out their bedding.

"Ye mean a vision?" He sat down, tugging her down beside him.

"Aye. I was hoping your sight may have come to your aid, warned ye, or given ye some hope. Do ye see nothing?"

"I see Iver dead."

"Ye dinnae sound as if ye believe that prophecy."

"I cannae be certain it *is* a prophecy. I have wanted it to be so since the bastard murdered my friends. There is nothing else, just the image of Iver dying. Usually there is more to my warnings, my visions. Because it is just the one image, I do fear that I myself have put that image into my mind. I daren't act upon what may be only wishful thinking."

"Tavig, Iver doesnae have the sight, too, does he?"

"Nay. Did ye fear he may have seen me planning to attack and is readied for me?" He idly unraveled her braid, combing his fingers through her thick, wavy hair.

"Ye have the sight. Why couldnae another of your kinsmen?"

"True, another could have been given this curious mix of gift and burden. Iver was *not*. In truth, he has always resented me for having it. 'Twas odd, for most people only feared or accepted it. Iver craved it. He envied it even though he kenned that it wasnae perfect, didnae always show me what was to happen, and didnae always show it to me in a way that was helpful." He tugged her into his arms, tumbling back onto the bedding and pulling her on top of him. "I didnae come out here to talk about Iver."

"Nay?" She slid her hand beneath his plaid and stroked his thigh. "Why did ye bring me out here, then?"

"Lass, sometimes ye ask some verra foolish questions."

Moira laughed, but as Tavig kissed her, her amusement quickly changed to passion. She was eager to make love. Although she refused to think that anything could happen to Tavig or that he would fail, she needed to spend what few hours were left before the battle in his arms, passion washing away all her thoughts and worries. Each step closer to Drumdearg brought her closer to the time she would have to leave him. The hours in which she could make some sweet memories were swiftly running out.

The guard yelped with pain, cursed, and hastily moved out of the reach of the whip Iver had just scored his back with. "Why did ye do that? I wasnae sleeping."

"Ye may as weel have been, fool," Iver snapped, looking over the wall and heartily cursing the dark. "Ye were staring at the keep. My cousin willnae be coming from there."

Trying fruitlessly to reach the stinging pain on his broad back, the burly man grumbled, "He isnae coming from out there, either."

"Oh? Ye are privy to my cousin's plans, are ye?"

"Nay, but, curse it, the mon has been running for his life for months. He hasnae had time to raise an army. He certainly hasnae had the coin to buy any soldiers." The man scowled into the darkness as he scratched his softening middle. "Aye, and even if he gets Mungan Coll to aid him, that mon doesnae have the men needed to storm this keep."

"If I heeded your opinion I would decide that I have wasted my coin in hiring you." Iver smiled nastily when the man blustered in an attempt to explain his worth. "My cousin will come. 'Tis but a matter of time. I erred in trying so hard to make his death appear legally warranted. I should have just killed the bastard." Iver rested his bony hands on top of the thick wall, narrowing his eyes as he fruitlessly tried to see into every shadow. "Tavig was a fool to turn his back on me, but I was an even bigger fool to let him escape my trap."

"I still dinnae ken how he did it."

"Fool, did ye forget that the mon has the sight? He kenned what I was doing ere I did it. I was too confident, too certain that he would rush to the aid of his friends. This time his warning must have been exact enough to tell him that it was a trap. Curse it, I should have been the one to get that gift."

"Then ye would ken where and when he is going to try to take his lands back."

"Aye." Iver straightened up, turning to glare at the guard and snapping his whip. "I dinnae have the sight, so ye must be my eyes, and I expect those costly eyes to stay open. Or I may feel compelled to shut them forever."

Iver left the walls, striding into the great hall. He flung his whip onto the large head table, sprawled in Tavig's huge oak chair, and sharply ordered a nervous page to pour him some wine. Tavig was coming. Iver was sure of it. He cursed his inability to know when or where, his visible fury sending the page scurrying away.

"I ken ye are coming here, Cousin," he murmured, glaring into his wine. "I should have killed ye before. No games, no tricks, just simply cut your thrice-cursed throat. Weel, come on, then. Ye have successfully eluded my hirelings for months, but now ye march straight to your death."

* * *

Moira shuddered, sitting up to look around She saw nothing, heard only a soft noise from the camp. The sudden chill of fear that had ripped through her still lingered. After looking around one more time, she settled back down in Tavig's arms. She was not surprised to find him awake, watching her closely.

"A bad dream?" he asked, holding her close and kissing the top of her head.

"I dinnae remember one."

"Ye were frightened. Even in this dim, shadowy light I could see your fear. The cry ye made ere ye sat up was one of fear."

"Aye, fear. That is all I recall. A deep, chilling sense of fear. No dream, no vision, nothing. Just fear. If fear were cold water, then 'twas as if someone crept up and emptied a bucket o'er me. 'Twas that sudden, that complete." She shivered. "Ye dinnae think it means anything, do ye?"

"Do ye mean is it a sign?" Gently clasping her chin, he tilted her face up to his and touched a kiss to her mouth. "Nay. Ye are concerned about this battle, and I ken that ye have been fighting that. Aye, ye have been fighting it since the day we arrived at Mungan's. When ye fell asleep, ye couldnae guard against it any longer and, briefly it overwhelmed you."

"Aye, mayhap that was all it was. I am sorry. I dinnae mean to trouble ye with my worries."

"'Tis no trouble, dearling. At least I ken that ye do worry o'er me and arenae sending me off to battle with nary a concern." He met her look of disgust with a bland smile.

As she smoothed her hand up and down his side, she thought over his explanation of her sudden, violent attack of fear. It made sense, yet it did not satisfy her. Why had she never experienced such a thing before? She had certainly carried a lot of fear during her years with Sir Bearnard, and she had fought it, too, just as she fought her fears now. It did not really make sense that it should suddenly so overwhelm her that she was ripped from a peaceful sleep, trembling and sweating from the force of it.

"Moira, I can see that ye are still puzzled," Tavig said against her throat as he kissed her pulse point.

"Aye, I am." She told him her reasons for doubting his explanation. "Something is different."

"Mayhap 'tis because my life is in danger, or so ye believe."

She heard the hint of a question in his voice, saw the almost sly look in his eyes. He was trying to trick her into declaring her feelings for him—vaguely or directly. It was a little flattering that he was so interested in the state of her heart that he tried such underhanded ways to make her reveal herself.

"Tavig, *my* life is verra important to me. All the time I lived with Sir Bearnard I feared dying at his hands. That fear was almost constant, nearly crippling at times. I fought it, but it never shocked me out of my sleep. Are ye certain ye have had no vision?"

"Nay, and I certainly havenae had one since ye last asked me. If my own life is in danger, the warning can be vague or not come at all. Howbeit, if the battle was going to be lost, I should have some warning of it, for Mungan and ye could also be in danger. That much my gift *would* tell me, and there has been nothing, not a glimpse."

"Ye would think it would have the courtesy to tell you ye are going to win. Doesnae it ever give ye good news?"

"It told me about you."

"Nay, it told you I would drown if ye didnae hurl yourself into a cold, storm-tossed sea. I wouldnae call that good news, and dinnae try to flatter me into forgetting what I was worried about."

"I would ne'er be so sly," he protested, nuzzling her ear as he combed his fingers through her lightly tangled hair.

"Hah! Ye can be a verra sly mon, Sir Tavig."

"Ye wound me, sweeting." He pulled her close, pressing their loins together and savoring the way she instinctively rubbed against him. "I think ye ought to make amends. Ye wouldnae wish to send me off to battle feeling pained, would ye?"

Despite how swiftly passion was clouding her thoughts, she laughed with undisguised amusement over his nonsense. "Ye are such a rogue, Tavig MacAlpin."

"And now she cries me a rogue," he said, his voice heavy with feigned mourning. "Ye shall have to work verra hard to soothe my battered vanity, m'lady MacAlpin."

"Your vanity would rise hale and strong even if all of Scotland's knights ran over it."

He turned, gently pushing her onto her back and sprawling on top of her. Their verbal jousting delighted him. It revealed that she felt at ease with him. She did not see it yet, but she trusted him enough to speak freely, not afraid that he would punish her for her barbed words. It also saddened him a little, for they rarely indulged in any talk other than repartee. She remained elusive, her true feelings hidden from him. It frustrated him to the point where he was tempted to shake her until she confessed what was in her mind and especially in her heart. He always controlled the urge, however, for he knew that to push her too hard would be to push her away, and she was only barely within his grasp now.

As he teased her full mouth with light, promising kisses, he watched passion darken her eyes and soften her features. Tavig had no doubts about her passion, and how evenly matched they were in their desires. Moira was wild and free in his arms, despite her complete innocence. At any other time in his life he would have laughed at a man who said such fierce desire was not enough, but now he knew he needed more. He gave her a slow, deep kiss, enflamed by the way she returned it.

"Moira, bonnie Moira, do ye ken how ye incite a mon's senses?" he murmured as he kissed the hollow in her throat.

"*I* incite a mon?" She smoothed her hands down his back, her long fingers tenderly tracing his spine.

"Aye, incite and bewilder. Ye are innocence from the top of your bonnie head to these wee pretty toes"—he grasped her foot in his hand and touched a kiss to each toe—"but when your passion sparks to life, ye are as wild and free as any creature in this forest. Ye bemoan your cowardice yet squarely face the mon who bred your fears, trudge over the rough trails at my side for a fortnight without faltering, save my life, and now insist on riding to a battle. Aye, loving, ye are verra bewildering. I think a mon would need more than a lifetime to puzzle ye out, and I am nae too sure even that would be enough."

Moira bit back the urge to ask him if he intended to take up that challenge. She did not want to know exactly how willing he might be to stay with her, for the knowledge would only hurt her more when she needed to leave. It would be easier to leave a man she was unsure of than one who already promised her everything she desired.

"I dinnae think I am so verra bewildering," she murmured, sliding her feet up and down his calves as he resettled himself in her arms. "At this moment I think ye ken me verra weel, what I want and what I feel."

She suddenly realized what a dangerous statement that was. It begged for a response. Before he could make one, she caught his face between her hands and kissed him. As she hoped, passion proved to be the perfect diversion.

Moira cried out in alarm when Tavig suddenly pushed her onto her back, sprawled on top of her, and held his sword at the ready. Her heart pounded with alarm. The last thing she recalled was curling up in Tavig's arms, replete from their lovemaking, and going to sleep. Now he was ready for battle.

"Relax, Cousin. 'Tis just me," Mungan said as he stepped out of the shadows.

As Tavig moved carefully, shielding her, Moira quickly covered herself with the blanket. "'Tis time?" she asked.

"Aye, 'tis time," answered Mungan. "I will leave ye to ready yourselves."

As soon as Mungan left, Moira looked at Tavig and found him watching her closely. "Weel, 'tis off to the battle."

"Aye, lass. 'Tis off to victory."

I pray ye are right, she thought, but said nothing, smiling in agreement.

Chapter Twenty-One

Rubbing her arms to ease the bite of the chill predawn air, Moira gritted her teeth against the urge to pace. Tavig and the others had only been gone a few minutes, slipping away to be swallowed up by the shadowy mists curling over the land. It was too soon to feel so tense, so concerned, yet her stomach was tied in knots.

She looked at the three beardless youths who had been left behind to guard the horses, her, and Una. The swords hanging from their slender hips looked too big for them. Their sullen faces revealed that they ached to use them, however, and deeply resented being left behind. Moira knew she ought to feel at least a little guilty for being one of the causes of their unhappiness, but she felt not a twinge of guilt. They were far too young to be going off to battle. She knew their mothers would be delighted because they had been forced to stay behind, safely away from the fighting.

"Moira," Una murmured, only briefly opening her eyes to peek at her cousin from her resting place under a tree, "ye are so taut I can almost feel it."

"I cannae help it. I am worried." She shook her head. "Your serenity leaves me somewhat envious."

"Oh, I am not completely serene."

"Ye certainly look like ye are."

"I am verra tired. Mungan felt that sleeping was a waste of time before a battle. He kept me verra busy."

"That doesnae really surprise me." She blushed a little as she recalled Tavig's sensual greed as well as her own.

"Also, I dinnae believe in getting all twisted up in knots of fear and concern over things I cannae change. I was worried and all the rest while this was being planned. Tried to convince Mungan not to do it. Said he didnae need to help his cousin this much. He just patted my cheek and said it was proper for a wife to worry so over her husband. That was when I might have stopped all of this and I wasnae able to. Now I just have to wait until 'tis all done and over with."

"While I find this waiting the hardest thing to do."

Una snuggled deeper into her cape and murmured sleepily, "They will be back. I just cannae imagine anything happening to Mungan. Nothing truly bad anyway. Mungan was just far too alive last night."

Moira sighed and let her cousin go to sleep. She had not known Mungan Coll long, but she found herself a little suspicious of his need to make love to Una all night long, almost without respite. Even Tavig had indulged in a nap or two. It was possible that Mungan made a habit of such a thing before each battle. It was also possible that he hoped to leave Una just as exhausted as she was, so exhausted that she did not have the strength to worry or succumb to her fears for him and do something foolish. She briefly wished that Tavig had been so clever, then shrugged. It would not have worked. No matter how exhausted she was she would never be able to sleep while Tavig faced a man who wanted him dead and had already gone to great lengths to try to accomplish that.

She wrapped her arms around her knees and hugged them close to her body. Despite the obscuring fog and shadows, she stared toward Drumdearg. Soon the sounds of battle would shatter the stillness enveloping them. She knew she would suffer the fear that each sound could be the one announcing Tavig's death. Moira shivered. This was going to be the longest day of her life.

Tavig whispered a curse as he knelt next to Mungan and the stiff grasses cut into his shins. After a slow, tedious crawl up to Drumdearg's outer walls, he ached with the need to take action. Such stealth was necessary, but he did not enjoy it at all. He waited tensely for the man Mungan had sent off to return with the word that they could begin to slip inside the walls. Above him he could hear the slow movements of the guards, even occasional snatches of conversation. The fear of discovery was a tight knot in his stomach. He was so close that any failure now would be, if not deadly, certainly unbearable.

"Be at ease, Cousin," Mungan whispered, his mouth close to Tavig's ear so that their soft words would not reach the men on the walls. "Soon ye will face that traitorous bastard and regain all he has stolen. Aye, and avenge our murdered friends."

"Being so close is nearly as torturous as not being able to do anything." Tavig saw the flash of Mungan's teeth in the gray light and returned his cousin's understanding grin. "I should also prefer to challenge our cousin directly rather than slipping inside like a thief."

"This place was built too weel for making direct challenges. Ah, here comes my mon Ranald." When the slender dark man crouched beside Mungan, he asked, "Have our allies done as they promised?"

"Aye," replied Ranald, casting a nervous glance upward, obviously fearing they might be overheard. "We must slip round to the main gate. They will be waiting there. The gate has been eased open enough for us to slide underneath."

"A slow way to enter. We could easily be cut down ere we get all the men inside," said Tavig.

"These men are the guards for the gate. We have until

the sun begins to clear the horizon before that guard is changed. It should be long enough to get us all inside. We shall have to crowd into the narrow towers on either side, but once the men are in, we can act immediately."

"Aye, and I think we should first send the men who are to take the walls. They must be able to hie up the stairs to the walls within those towers the moment the last mon is inside."

Mungan nodded. "Aye, the walls must be taken as soon as possible. Tell those men to go now, Ranald." He looked at Tavig as Ranald crept away. "Ye will go last."

"Last? 'Tis my battle, more than any other mon's. If not for the need to clear the walls, I would go in first."

"And if this fails ye would be the first to be captured or killed. Then Iver has won. 'Tis why I will also go in after my men, though it galls me to do so. Iver willnae want me to live long, either, as he kens I will make him pay for his crimes. If this is a trap, 'tis best if one of our men is caught. Then we are free to continue the battle."

"I ken ye are right and I even share your thoughts, but that doesnae mean I must like it." He heard the muffled tread of a guard pass along the wall over their heads, and fell silent until he was gone. "I also ache to see those traitors cast from my walls."

"Ye will soon hold Drumdearg again."

"Aye, ye will," whispered a raspy voice from the other side of Tavig.

Tavig turned slowly, his hand on his dagger. There was no threatening move from the shadowy figures who had managed to creep up to him unseen and unheard. He realized they could have already cut his throat if they had been inclined to. Peering harder through the misty shadows they all huddled in, it was a moment before he could discern a craggy face that was immediately familiar.

"Old Ennis," he whispered in a hearty breath of relief. "Who is with ye?"

"O'er a dozen of your men-at-arms. More men will soon arrive. We were the readiest."

"I thought ye had all been killed or fled."

"Aye, but we didnae run verra far. We kenned ye would return and wished to be near at hand."

"Good, we have need of every mon we can muster."

After pausing to let the guard on the wall pass by, Old Ennis said, "I regret that the mon we fight is your kinsmon."

"As do I, but Iver leaves us no choice. Feel no hesitation to treat him and his hirelings as the enemies they are. E'en if I could reach a truce with Iver, and there is no hope of that, he must pay for the murders he committed." The old man nodded, and Tavig said, "Few believed his claim that I had done it?"

"Verra few. Mayhap folk erred in keeping the truth to themselves, but o'er the years, Iver has done a lot ye dinnae ken about. He was the first one we all suspected when those heinous murders were done. Nothing he has said since has changed our minds."

As he adjusted his heavily padded jupon, Tavig risked leaning away from the walls to look behind Old Ennis. He was sure there were more than a dozen men now. None of them wore armor, either, to maximize the surprise attack, the same as he and Mungan and their men. Tavig was sure Old Ennis had ordered that, as he was a battle-hardened man, knowledgeable in the ways of war. It was good to have such men on his side.

"We best go now, Cousin," said Mungan.

Nodding to the men behind him, Tavig replied, "We willnae be the last in."

"It ne'er hurts to have a few good men at your back."

Mungan began to move along the wall. After signaling Old Ennis to follow, Tavig started after his cousin. He winced at every sound they made even though they were so faint they could never carry to the ears of the guards. As he inched toward the gates he prayed that nothing would go wrong.

The light from the torches within Drumdearg spilled out of the small opening in the gates. Tavig was surprised the guards had not noticed it. Mungan edged through the opening, his large size making it a tight squeeze. There was no warning cry from his cousin, so Tavig quickly followed. Once inside, a heavily bearded man he recognized as Graeme, a distant cousin, quickly grabbed him and shoved him into the tower to the left of the gates.

Even as Old Ennis was shoved in with him, Tavig caught Mungan's signal from the doorway of the opposite tower. Elbowing his way through the tightly packed men, Tavig finally reached one of Mungan's men who was at the base of the narrow winding stairway that led to the walls. He felt and shared the tension of the men so closely surrounding him. They detested hiding in such cramped quarters as much as he did. It felt too much like a trap.

"Pass the word," he ordered. "Ye are to start up to the walls. Ye must try to creep as close as ye can. The moment one of ye is seen, a cry will go up from any guard left standing."

"So we try to cut down as many as we can *ere* we are seen."

"Aye, and stand where that guard was standing. It may work to make the other guards think nothing is wrong. So ye need to slip along the walls one by one. As a guard is taken down and replaced, the next mon slips past ye to take down another. I doubt ye can clear the full length of the walls by that method, but ye need to take as much of the wall as ye can."

"Understood."

Tavig slumped against the cool, damp wall as the man passed his instructions along. Such constant stealth was completely exhausting. He made his way back through the crowd of men as soon as the soldiers on the stairs started to slip up onto the walls. Old Ennis and several of the men he had brought with him were almost pushed outside by the crowd. As Tavig took his place near the door, his distant cousin Graeme stood directly in front of the door, blocking it from the view of the men still on the walls.

"The moment a cry goes up on the walls or the new guard comes out, we move," Graeme said.

"Aye, more waiting."

Graeme briefly grinned at Tavig and returned his watch to the walls and the keep itself. "Ye have only been waiting to start this battle. We have been waiting for ye ever since Iver drove ye out and set his skinny backside in your chair."

"I am sorry I ran, but I could see no other way. At that time my escape was the only way to thwart Iver."

"It was. No one blames ye for leaving. Ye were a dead mon if ye stayed and ye wouldnae do us any good dead. All that surprised us was that ye hadnae seen what was to be in time to halt it."

"Aye, at times when my sight would be the most helpful, it fails me. It told me only enough to keep me alive."

"That is no small thing." Graeme frowned up at the wall. "I just saw one of your men bring a guard down."

"Soon the other guards will see what is happening. Is Andrew MacBain here?"

"Aye. He returned yestereve."

"He is the one who gutted my friends. Aye, Iver ordered it done and carries as much blame as if he wielded the knife, but 'tis Andrew who actually did the killing. I would dearly love to kill him in the same way, but I need him alive, or one of his men, to help prove that I am innocent. Iver had accused me far and wide. I must scrub that slander away and I need proof of my innocence to do that."

"I will do my best to see that at least one of those men survives."

The cry of alarm they had all been tensed for finally shattered the quiet. Tavig moved quickly, but still felt the press of men crowded behind him. He and Mungan paused only long enough to direct the men, then strode toward the keep itself with a small group of men. The clash of swords and cries of men fighting for their lives would be his herald, Tavig thought grimly.

Moira started, crying out softly in fear as the sharp clang of swords disturbed the quiet. She realized that she had been dozing, lack of sleep and the exhausting effects of constant fear for Tavig finally taking a toll. Alert now, she scrambled to her feet and walked to the wooded edge of the small clearing. The sun was starting to rise, and the soft light allowed her to see Drumdearg despite the lingering mists. She cursed the fact that although they were on the edge of the village encircling Drumdearg, close enough to see that a battle was being fought, they were not close enough to see who was doing what to whom.

"It willnae last long," said James, the oldest and fairest of the youths, as he stepped up beside her.

"Ye sound so certain of that. Iver was able to grasp hold of Drumdearg. Why do ye think he will let go of it easily?"

"Oh, he will fight. He has no choice. Howbeit, once the battle begins nearly every mon, woman, and child in the village will rush to Tavig's aid."

"Does Iver have no allies?"

"Only those he has bought." The youth shrugged. "There may be one or two fools who went to his side. No one will miss them when they die."

"I wish I shared your confidence."

"Mungan Coll is the finest knight in all of Scotland. Tavig MacAlpin is verra good, too. Together they can beat a cur like Sir Iver MacAlpin."

She smiled at James before turning her full attention back to the battle. James clearly worshiped his laird Mungan. Moira wished she could share in his blind confidence in the man and in Tavig. Although she had no doubts about Tavig's bravery and skill, she had a clearer view of the type of adder he now faced. At times bravery and skill were not enough to insure victory.

Just as she was about to ask James if they could move just a little closer, the sound of someone trampling through the brush drew her attention. James moved swiftly, drawing his sword and putting himself between her and the three large men who burst into the clearing. Iver's hirelings were already deserting him. Moira heartily wished they had chosen another route for their escape.

When James moved to help his friends fight the men, Moira rushed to Una's side. Her cousin was waking up and rapidly becoming terrified. She reached Una just in time to stop her from running off in a blind panic. Moira grabbed Una around the waist and held on to her until Una's struggles began to ease.

"They will murder or rape us," Una cried.

Moira spun her cousin around and, grasping her by the shoulders, gave her a good shaking. "Remember who ye are now, Una—the wife of Sir Mungan Coll. What would he think of a woman who, at the first hint of danger, ran screaming into the woods?" She saw Una's eyes widen, felt her cousin heave one large sigh, and cautiously released her grip on the woman.

"Ye are right. I must be worthy of Mungan." Una looked toward the three youths fighting the mercenaries. "What can we do, though? We are but two small women."

"We must do something. Those boys cannae fight off those battle-hardened men for much longer." An instant later, her words proved prophetic as one of the lads screamed, a deep wound to his sword arm causing him to stagger. "Find something to use as a weapon, quickly," Moira ordered even as she turned to search the area.

She grabbed a heavy fallen branch. Not waiting to see if her cousin had found anything yet, Moira hurried toward the wounded youth and his opponent. The young man was buckling beneath the hard sword blows of his attacker. Any moment now he would falter so badly he would not be able to fend off a fatal strike.

The mercenary saw her, but could only feint a swing her way. Each time he turned his attention from the boy, the youth went on the attack. Moira heard the mercenary cursing her as he tried to stay out of her reach and hold off the youth, who was still strong enough to be a threat. She knew she had to act fast, however, for the boy's lingering strength was born of hope, the hope that she could stop Iver's hireling from killing him.

Try as she would, Moira was unable to get a clear aim at the man. He kept shifting his body each time she readied herself to strike him. Then she noticed that one part of him was not so easily moved out of the way—his sword arm. He had to keep his sword aimed at the youth. She feinted a swing at his back and, when he moved to avoid the full force of the blow, she brought the stick down hard on his sword arm.

The sound of breaking bone made her feel sick. Iver's man screamed with pain, dropped his sword. He staggered, faltering toward her, fury contorting his face, then turned to pick up his sword with his other hand. The youth struck, his sword entering the man's heart in one clean thrust. Moira echoed the mercenary's groan as he slumped to the ground, dead. She stood staring into his sightless eyes until she heard the young man stumble and fall.

"Help the others, m'lady," he rasped when she hurried to his side.

After a quick but thorough look at the youth, she decided he could wait a moment or two before being tended to. She turned to look at the other fighters. The mercenaries were pressing James and his companion hard. Una darted around the fighters, a heavy branch similar to Moira's held tightly in her hands, but she did nothing. It was clear that Una did not know what to do next. The mercenaries had guessed her inability to act and paid her little

heed. Moira hefted her rough club and crept closer, hoping
to take advantage of their arrogant unconcern.

Just as Moira reached the side of the man facing James,
he finally noticed her. A look of horrified surprise crossed
his square face as she brought her club down on his arm.
Again she heard the horrible sound of a limb breaking.
She saw James move to take quick advantage of her attack,
and decided she had seen enough. Tossing aside her club,
she raced to Una's side and pulled the girl away from the
fighting men.

"I wasnae much help," Una complained as she tossed
aside her club, shuddering as James cut down his opponent and the man's death scream filled the clearing.

"Ye were trying to help, and that is all that matters,"
Moira said, tugging her cousin toward the wounded youth.
"What is your name?" she asked him as she crouched by
his side.

"Malcolm," he said, his voice hoarse from pain. He
smiled grimly when the final mercenary loudly met his
death. "We have won." He managed a weak smile for Una
and Moira. "Ye ladies were a great help."

"Aye, they were." agreed James as he and the third
youth joined them. "I am ashamed to admit that we were
facing men far stronger and more skilled than we."

"Of course ye were," Moira said, shaking her head at
the downcast faces of the three youths. "Those men held
far more years than ye do, years spent fighting and honing
their skills. Once they were just like you. Soon ye will be
like them. Now, Una, rip me a piece or two of your petti-
coats so that we may tend Malcolm's wound. James, fetch
me some water, please."

"Is it bad?" James asked as he returned with the water,
frowning with concern as he studied the pale Malcolm.

"Not so bad it cannae be mended. Please remove his
jupon and shirt."

Malcolm grew even more ashen-faced, despite his
friends' care as he was stripped to the waist. Moira tried not

to think of how she added to that pain as she cleaned his wound then stitched it closed. She had Una place a folded blanket beneath the youth's head as she bandaged him.

When she was done she soaked a small scrap of petticoat in water and gently bathed the sweat from his white face. She could almost feel the pain he was in. It was impossible to ignore. He looked incredibly young, hurt and a little afraid. Moira sighed as she realized what she had to do.

She lightly placed her hands on his arm. She could not heal him, but she could ease a lot of his pain. The youth's eyes widened, and he stared at her with a mixture of astonishment and a touch of fear. Moira knew her skill was already working its magic. She could feel the stares of James and the other boy as they realized she was doing something unusual to Malcolm. When she was done she lifted her hands from Malcolm's arm and slumped, a little surprised to find Una right behind her, ready to give her support.

"What have ye done?" whispered Malcolm, cautiously moving his arm.

"She just took your pain away, 'tis all," said Una as she helped Moira drink some cool water.

"Ye have the healing touch?" demanded James.

For a brief moment Moira tensed, afraid that her kindness to Malcolm would now cause her trouble. Then she looked deeply into each youth's eyes. She saw no fear or condemnation there, only astonishment and curiosity. Moira wondered if their lack of superstitious fear was due to their association with Tavig, even though it would only have been through Mungan, or because of their youth.

"'Healing' isnae really the right word," she replied, slowly regaining the strength she had lost in using her gift to help Malcolm. "I can ease pain, help a person to rest, and even soothe a fever a little. That can lead to a cure. I really dinnae think *I* actually *cure* anyone." Her eyes widened when they all grinned at her, and James, forgetting himself for a moment, clapped her on the arm as if she were one of his fellows.

"Sorry, m'lady," James hastily apologized. "'Tis just wondrous."

"Wondrous? I have ne'er heard it called wondrous before."

"But it is. Do ye not see? Now the MacAlpins, and the Colls, for we are part of the MacAlpin clan, can claim both the sight and the healing touch within our ranks. I dinnae think another clan in all of Scotland can do the same."

"Weel, I am glad ye are so pleased." She stood up, Una hastily doing the same. "I think we had best move into the village."

"But we were told to stay here, to guard the horses and both of you."

"Aye, but that was an order given when it was thought we would be safe here. We are not. 'Tis verra clear that the rats are rapidly deserting their sinking ship, and we stand in their way. There were only three of the men this time, but there will be more if the battle turns in Tavig's favor. Since the people of Drumdearg will take Tavig's side, his enemies willnae risk trying to run through the village."

"That seems reasonable," James agreed. "Howbeit, I dinnae think Sir Tavig will like it."

Thinking of how her secret was no longer a secret and that Tavig would soon know, Moira quietly said, "I suspect that when this battle is over, Sir Tavig will discover a lot of things he doesnae like."

Chapter Twenty-Two

Tavig grimly cut down the guard blocking the entrance to the great hall of Drumdearg. He paid little heed to the pain-ridden scream of the second guard as Mungan swiftly ended his life. His sword held ready for any possible attack, he signaled the men with him to batter the door down. He sighed a little wistfully as they pounded the huge oak-carved door his father had taken such pride in. The thick wooden battering log his men used would seriously damage it.

At the first sound of splintering wood, he tensed, certain that his cousin was hidden inside and eager to get to him. The moment the doors opened, he, Mungan, and the men hesitated, waiting for an attack. When none came, he signaled them to follow as he and Mungan entered the great hall. He cursed when he caught his first sight of Iver. The man stood with a dozen men-at-arms, including Andrew MacBain and his three cohorts.

"Good 'morn, Cousin," Iver drawled. "Your father's spirit will be frowning darkly over the destruction of his prized doors."

"But he will be weel pleased when I cut ye down," Tavig answered, anger tightening his voice.

"Ye would spill the blood of a kinsmon o'er this wee misunderstanding?"

"The blood of two innocent men is on your hands, Iver. That cannae be ignored."

"There is no blood on my hands. I took a knife to no mon."

"Nay, ye ordered it done. 'Tis the same."

"Most of Scotland thinks ye are the murderer." Iver narrowed his brown eyes, twisting his thin-lipped mouth into a sneer. "Ye will ne'er fully remove that stain from your name, Cousin."

"I should have cut your tongue out when ye were a lying, beardless boy," growled Mungan, eyeing his thin cousin with distaste. "Ye were always an envious, dangerous lad. We erred in thinking ye honored the bonds of kinship."

"Come out from behind your minions and face me mon-to-mon," urged Tavig. "Let us end this here and now."

"Do ye think me a fool?" Iver signaled his men to attack.

Tavig cursed viciously yet was not surprised that Iver would not face a simple judgment, but try to take as many men down with him as possible. He had to smile when Mungan gave his distinctive war cry, a sound so loud and bloodcurdling it caused Iver's minions to hesitate a moment. Then the battle began in earnest. Tavig had no clear thought save to cut through Iver's men and get to Iver himself who stood safely behind his hirelings screaming at them to kill him and Mungan and every other man who stood against Iver MacAlpin.

"M'lady, ye said we would come to the village, not go into the keep," protested James, awkwardly grabbing Moira by the arm to halt her advance on Drumdearg castle.

"Look around you, James," she answered, easily slipping free of his reluctant hold. "The battle is as good as done."

Moira joined him in looking at the scattered groups of villagers. They stood talking and keeping an eye on the castle of Drumdearg, but they were relaxed, even hesitantly happy. None of them acted as if their fates were still hanging in the balance. There were even men ambling back into the village from the keep, their swords still sheathed. What had caught and held her attention, however, was the wounded. There were not many—although she suspected she would find more within the castle walls—but they were in pain, their friends and families doing a clearly inadequate if earnest job of tending to their wounds. The art of healing had evidently not been well learned by anyone at Drumdearg.

"The *battle* doesnae sound as if 'tis over," grumbled James. "If ye go too close, ye could be in danger."

"I dinnae intend to march into the midst of fighting men."

"Then ye dinnae need to leave this place. Wait here for Sir Tavig."

"Nay, I am needed, James. Look about you. There are wounded men who have need of my skills."

"Their families will care for them."

"Not weel, and I mean no disrespect when I say that. If there was a healer here, he or she has gone and left no learned apprentice behind. I have the skill these people need and I dinnae refer to my touch, either."

"Sir Tavig will skin me alive if aught happens to ye."

"If it will put ye at ease, stay at my side. Robbie can stay with Malcolm and the horses." She glanced at Una. "Ye can stay behind, too, if ye wish."

"Nay, I will help you."

Moira bit back a smile as she started to walk again and heard a cursing James fall into step behind her. Una kept pace at her side as Moira walked over to a tiny thatched cottage where the wounded men were gathered. There were only five, and none of their wounds would be fatal, if they were tended to properly. She gently but firmly ordered the women to fetch her the things she needed.

As she worked to clean and stitch the men's wounds, Moira tried hard not to listen to the lingering sounds of battle. She could easily imagine Tavig suffering as the men she tended to were suffering. It was also too easy for her to imagine that Tavig would be killed, struck a fatal wound that no amount of skill could mend. Although she had not wanted to say so to Una and the youths, Moira knew she needed to help the injured in order to keep her mind from plaguing her with thoughts of what might be happening to her husband.

Once the men's wounds were cleaned and stitched, Moira did what she could to ease their pain. She saw no scorn or fear upon the faces of Tavig's people as she revealed her gift, only wonder and then the same sort of prideful glee James had revealed. Tavig had been right all along. At Drumdearg she did not need to fear superstition.

Collapsing after tending to the five men, Moira weakly smiled her thanks to the women who gently bathed her sweaty face, made her more comfortable, and helped her drink some hearty mead. Inside she was torn. There was acceptance here just as Tavig had promised there would be, but she did not believe it changed anything. Tavig was a knight. He could not spend all his days cloistered within the walls of Drumdearg, and it was impractical to think he could keep her secured there. Tavig would be expected to go to court, to go to other keeps to treat with other clans, and he would be expected to bring his lady wife, at least some of the time.

And then the trouble would begin, she thought morosely. She could not let the security and welcome of Drumdearg lull her into believing her problems were over. What she did see, however, was that she would never be able to make Tavig believe in her fears. She certainly could not tell him that his love was what she needed to make her stay. If he could not offer it freely, it was no good. Yet it was the bond she needed to feel that they could face the future. There would still be strife, she could not believe that people with their special gifts would live a trouble-free life, but with a shared love they would have the strength to overcome those troubles.

Cautiously Moira stood up, breathing a sigh of relief when she suffered no dizziness. Her strength had returned. She still had to leave Tavig, but she needed to know how he had fared in his battle with Iver. Until she knew the final outcome she would linger and help where she could. Straightening her shoulders, she took Una by the hand and started toward the castle gates.

The moment she stepped inside the gates she met a begrimed but smiling Nicol. "The battle is won," she said happily.

"Not completely," he answered, pushing a lock of sweat-dampened hair from his face. "'Tis but Tavig and Iver who need to settle what stands between them. They battle it out in the great hall." He caught her firmly by the arm when she started toward the keep. "Nay, lass. He doesnae need ye distracting him."

"I am to stand around while he fights for his life?"

"Aye. If ye do anything else ye could cause trouble. Aye, and in this instance, any trouble could prove fatal to Tavig. So, Cousin, busy yourself elsewhere. If it helps ease your fears, not a mon here doubts that Tavig will win."

"Mayhap it should help, but it doesnae." She sighed and ceased trying to pull away from him. "I came to help the wounded."

Nicol frowned. "Ye have decided to reveal your secret?"

"I was given little choice. Ye ken weel that I cannae abide seeing anyone in pain when I ken I can ease it. Where are the wounded men?" As Nicol started to lead her and Una away, she asked, "Did many die?"

"Only a few of Mungan's and Tavig's men. Verra few of Iver's hirelings survive. Many fled when the battle turned against them."

"Aye," muttered James, still keeping close to Moira and Una. "We met three of the dogs." When Nicol looked at him, he related the tale, smiling crookedly when Nicol laughed. "'Twas a bit upsetting to be saved by wee lasses."

"Nay, laddie." Nicol clapped the boy on the back. "Look about ye. Even these battle-scarred men didnae face Iver's dogs without suffering a scratch. Aye, and even the greatest warrior likes to have someone at his back. Ye cannae help the fact that we left ye with only lasses to aid ye. Be glad they had the wit to ken how to help." He stopped before the armorer's shed, pointing to the men scattered around it. "Here are our wounded, Moira. There are one or two of Iver's hirelings here. Ye need not be so gentle with them, but it may prove useful to keep them alive."

"Aye," agreed Moira. "Tavig may have need of them to help prove that Iver's accusations were false."

When she cast a longing glance toward the keep, the need to see how Tavig fared so strong she could taste it, Nicol firmly turned her back to the wounded. Moira sighed and started to work. Nicol was right. Tavig did not need her there. Neither could she help him. He was fighting for his life and only he could wage that battle.

Tavig watched the last of Iver's guard fall to his sword, then looked at his cousin. Mungan's men encircled a wounded Andrew MacBain, insuring that the man stayed alive long enough to prove Tavig's innocence. Mungan stood with his arms crossed, clearly stepping back and allowing Tavig to finish the battle.

Iver stood firm, but his pockmarked face glistened with sweat. Tavig was surprised to realize that Iver feared him. He knew his cousin had strength, despite his bone-thin build, and he had skill. Iver was also fresh, having fought no one while he himself had had to fight several men. It was clear that Iver did not see that he held that advantage or did not believe that it was enough.

"'Tis just ye and me, Cousin," said Tavig.

"And ye expect me to enter willingly into battle with a mon who already kens the outcome?" asked Iver.

"Ye ken as weel as I do that my gift is erratic. I ken only that we must fight," Tavig lied, feeling it unfair to tell his cousin that he had seen him dying. Iver believed wholeheartedly in his gift and Tavig knew such knowledge would only frighten his cousin more, thus weakening him. "I will give ye the chance to surrender."

"Hah! To be hanged? Nay, I think not."

"Ye ken that I have no wish to kill you, but ye leave me no choice."

"Nay, none at all," Iver said and attacked Tavig.

At first, Tavig did little more than fend off his cousin's attacks. It had been years since he had fought with Iver or watched his cousin wield his sword. He needed to study Iver's skill, to search for that weak point.

It did not take long to find it. Iver was a good fighter, but for far too long he had depended upon guile and treachery to get what he wanted. He had ceased to hone his sword skills. Softly cursing Iver for pressing him, for forcing him to take the life of a kinsman, Tavig pressed his attack.

Iver's ability to defend himself was better than his offensive skills, but not good enough. Tavig finally found the opening he sought. Fighting the urge to hesitate, to offer Iver yet one more chance, Tavig drove his sword deep into Iver's thin chest. Iver died with barely a sigh. Tavig pulled his sword free and solemnly watched his cousin fall to the rush-strewn floor.

"A clean strike," murmured Mungan as he stepped over, idly nudging Iver with his foot before crouching to shut Iver's wide, staring eyes.

"I didnae wish to kill him, but since he forced me to it, I decided to try to make it as swift and as painless as I could." Tavig bent to wipe his sword clean on Iver's jupon, then resheathed it. "He could have surrendered."

"Aye, he could have, but 'tis easy to understand why he didnae." Mungan walked to the head table to pour himself a tankard of hearty wine. "This was an easier way to die. Much preferable to hanging." As Tavig walked over, Mungan handed him some wine, then held his tankard high. "To victory." He grinned when his men loudly cheered then took a long drink.

"Aye, to victory," murmured Tavig as he also took a drink.

"Come, laddie," Mungan said, gently clapping Tavig on the back. "The mon gave ye but two choices—his death or yours. Aye, it pains me that one of our own blood had to die at our hands, but he would have felt nothing if he had put us to the sword."

"I ken it. This moment of regret will pass soon." He turned to the men who still kept an eye on Andrew, but were helping themselves to the wine. "One of ye ought to tell the others that the battle is won."

"I will," said Mungan. "Ye set here, Tavig, and I will also find our lasses."

Tavig wearily sat down in his chair as Mungan left. But a moment later his people began to flood the hall. Their exuberance soon infected him. He began to join in the celebration more wholeheartedly and was eager for Moira to join him.

Moira tensed when Mungan hailed them. She waited with little patience as he hugged and kissed Una then amiably scolded them for not staying where they had been put. His talk of victory both pleased and saddened her. She also wanted a few more details.

"Tavig is hale," he told her. "Go and see for yourself. I need a moment to see how my men fare."

She nodded and strode toward the keep. It was not easy to get through the people crowding the hall, but finally she gained a clear view of Tavig. He looked every inch the laird as he sat in his huge chair at the head table, his people gathered around him, celebrating their freedom from Iver's dark rule.

With increasing sadness she looked around the great hall. Signs of wealth were everywhere from the ornate tapestries on the walls to the heavy tankards everyone held. Tavig had said his place was not as grand as Mungan's, but she could see little difference. Although she had a dowry now, it was not a large one. There would be many a bride he could get who would have more and gain him a much-needed alliance. Added now to her feats that her gift would cause him trouble was the knowledge that Tavig could do a great deal better than a marriage to her.

Before he could catch a glimpse of her, she slipped out of the hall. She had to leave and she had to do it quickly, before he could find her and persuade her to stay. By leaving now, she was not only saving him from the trouble a wife like her could bring, but also freeing him to make a better marriage he so richly deserved.

Moira was so caught up in her thoughts that she did not see Mungan until she walked into him. She scowled up at him as she rubbed her nose which had made hard contact with his broad chest. Una was neatly tucked up at his side. Moira wondered why fate seemed so intent on putting obstacles in front of her.

"Why arenae ye celebrating with your mon?" Mungan asked. "Ye can return to the great hall with us."

"Nay. Tavig doesnae need me there."

"Are ye afraid he will chide ye for keeping a secret from him?"

"Ah, someone talked."

"Lass, I heard about little else. Ye cannae display such a gift and expect no one to speak of it. The men whose pain ye eased have done naught but sing your praises. Ye should have told Tavig, lass."

"When ye hide something as long and as determinedly as I have this, 'tis hard to do anything else."

"Weel, no sense in running away and trying to hide now.

Your secret is a secret no longer. Come along, I am sure Tavig will be looking for you."

Moira sighed, knowing she had to speak the truth. Somehow she did not believe Mungan would stop her no matter how much he disagreed with her choice. What she had to do was insure that Mungan did not tell Tavig she was leaving, at least not until it was too late for Tavig to stop her. Although, she mused sadly, Tavig might not even try to find her after she dealt him a two-edged insult—lying to him by keeping her skill a secret and then deserting just as he celebrated his victory.

"Mungan, ye must promise me ye willnae say anything to Tavig," Moira asked.

"Aye, I swear it. What is it I am not supposed to say? If 'tis about your gift, there is little use in tying my tongue. Too many others are clucking about it."

"Nay, 'tis not about my secret. I am leaving Tavig."

"Leaving him—why? Have ye been knocked in the head, lass? Ye arenae making sense."

"I am making perfect sense." She succinctly related all of her reasons and almost smiled at his glowering look.

"If ye kenned all this from the start, why did ye marry him?" Mungan demanded.

"So ye would stop being such a crazy fool and do as ye really wanted to—marry Una." She was a little surprised when Mungan responded to her tart remark with a wide grin.

"Methinks ye arenae as weak as I first thought ye were, either. Weel, I think ye are wrong to leave," he added, growing solemn, "but 'tis *not* my place to try to stop you. Dinnae ask me to help, though."

"Nay, I wouldnae. Ye need not worry about that tower house, Mungan. I would never let it fall to your enemies."

"Oh, I dinnae worry about that at all."

Moira frowned as he walked away, tugging a confused Una with him. She felt a little confused herself. The clash with Mungan had been too brief, too easily settled. It roused her suspicions. She readily recalled how often

Tavig had referred to Mungan as sly. Deciding she might not have much time left, she hurried to the stables.

Tavig frowned, tugging on a clean shirt as he listened to James and Robbie relate the tale of the attack in the wood. He had only been half listening to the youth for, with the help of a page, he had been washing off the worst of the dirt and blood gathered during the battle. When they excitedly told him how Moira had helped Malcolm, he sat up, his whole body tensing with a mixture of disbelief and growing anger. Healing hands? They had to be drunk.

"Moira touched the lad and took his pain away?" he demanded.

"Aye," answered James, eyeing Tavig warily. "She put her hands on his arm, and the pain left him."

"Are ye sure she didnae just put some salve on him?"

"Nay. She had already tended his wound, dressed and bandaged it. We even asked if she had the gift, and she said aye, didnae she, Robbie?" His friend nodded, his thin fair hair falling into his face. "I thought ye kenned it," he added a little weakly.

"Nay, she ne'er told me."

It was easy to tell by the nervous, wide-eyed looks on the youths' faces that he had nearly spat the words at them. Tavig fought to control his anger. His conversation with the boys had been overheard, though, and others rushed to tell him of Moira's skill. As they talked, he recalled the time in Craigmoordun when his aching head had so rapidly faded away. She had been lightly touching his forehead as he had woken up. He cursed himself for a fool for never guessing.

He caught sight of Mungan and Una approaching the table and, somewhat abruptly, waved away a few men, silently commanding them to give up their seats at his side. There was a look on Mungan's dark face that Tavig recognized. It was reminiscent of their childhood. Mungan

was filled with the knowledge that he had information
Tavig did not. The trick would be to get that information
out of Mungan. Tavig was sure it had to do with Moira.

As Mungan sat down, pulling Una down beside him,
Tavig was seized with an odd, chilling feeling. The images
that filled his mind confused him. He stood on the walls of
Drumdearg and watched himself ride away. The wider the
distance grew between his two selves, the emptier he felt.
It was as if he were being torn in two, all the essence of
his life leaving him, the figure on the wall becoming little
more than an empty shell. When he realized that throughout the vision he could smell Moira's delicate scent and that
the image of himself riding away had copper hair not black,
he suddenly understood. Moira was leaving.

"Where is she?" he demanded of Mungan.

"Where is who?" Mungan asked, sipping at his ale.

"Dinnae play games with me, Cousin. I ken she is leaving. I have seen it. Is she still within reach, or must I saddle
my horse and run her down?"

"Weel, if ye go to saddle your horse ye willnae have to
go much farther. I left the lass but a few moments ago, and
she was headed for the stables. I doubt she kens how to
saddle a mount."

"Mungan," Una protested, "ye said ye wouldnae tell
him anything. Ye swore to it."

"I swore I wouldnae *say* anything. I didnae swear not to
answer the mon's questions."

"Oh. Oh." Una took a deep breath and finally said clearly,
"What deception."

"Aye, 'tis a good one, isnae it?" Mungan winked at her
before turning his full attention back to Tavig. "That lass
of yours has some verra odd ideas in her bonnie head."

"Ye need not tell me. I had thought she would linger
long enough to give life at Drumdearg a fair trial. What I
cannae understand is why she didnae tell me about her
gift? *Me?*" he said as he leapt to his feet.

"I would cease discussing it with us and go ask her. She

is a clever lass. 'Tis certain she will soon discover how to saddle a horse."

"Aye, I just hope I can keep from strangling her," Tavig snapped as he strode out of the hall.

"Mungan," Una cried as she watched a stern-faced Tavig leave. "He could hurt her."

"Nay, lass." He draped his arm around her shoulders and kissed her cheek. "He could ne'er hurt that lass."

"But he said he might strangle her and he looked verra, verra angry."

"Of course he is angry. The fool lass has rattled her wits. A good shaking might do her some good. Howbeit, Tavig would ne'er harm the lass. Not only does he abhor men using their greater strength to hold a woman, but that lad dearly loves the fool lass."

"Has he told ye so?"

"Nay, he doesnae need to. I ken that he wants your cousin just as he kenned I wanted you."

"Do ye think he can convince her to stay?"

"Aye, but it willnae be easy."

Chapter Twenty-Three

"And just where do ye think ye are going?"

Moira gasped, whirled around, and gaped at Tavig. He stood in the stable doorway, his clenched fists planted firmly on his hips. He looked a little cleaner than he had when she had last seen him. He also looked furious. She was both elated and saddened to see him. It pleased her beyond words that he had come after her, but now she would have to go through the painful farewell she had been trying so desperately to avoid.

"I was trying to leave, but I seem to be having trouble saddling a horse."

"Good. I should hate to have to hunt down my own wife because she is a horse thief."

"A wife cannae steal from her husband."

"Aye, she can. The law says that what I own is still mine, and what ye own is mine as weel."

"I dinnae think that is quite right."

There was a cold, hard tone to his voice that made her uneasy. She was not sure what emotion he was feeling besides anger. Considering all that had happened and what she was about to do, their conversation was a little silly. It began to look as if he had not come to stop her, just to complain about what she was taking with her.

"How did ye find out I was here?" she asked, suddenly recalling that the last time she had seen him, he was thoroughly engrossed in celebrating his victory. That should have kept him occupied long enough for her to get away.

"I asked Mungan."

Tavig walked over to her horse, gently pushing Moira aside. He removed the saddle she had been unable to secure and tossed it aside as well. His emotions were still running high, and he used the few minutes it took to put the horse away to try to get a firmer grip on himself, on the feelings raging through his body.

It hurt, and the pain made him angry. Frustration also gnawed at him. He had tried everything he knew how to do to make Moira want to stay with him, yet she was trying to leave. Tavig did not know what else to do, and that sense of helplessness also made him angry. Visiting that anger on Moira would not solve anything, however.

Moira softly cleared her throat. "I asked Mungan not to say anything."

"Ye should have been more specific, lass. He didnae *say* anything. He *answered* my question." He turned to look at her, her obvious nervousness giving him some satisfaction. "Ye are my wife now. That means ye stay with me. The law says ye are my property, and I am not a mon who likes to lose his property."

"When I said I would marry you, ye said it didnae have to be forever, that I still had the freedom to change my mind."

"I lied."

"Tavig!"

"Curse ye, Moira. Why are ye running away? I am certain ye care for me at least a little, we share a passion that is sweet beyond words, and I am also certain ye love Adair. So why leave?"

"For the reasons I have told ye again and again, since we first started out on this journey. Now ye ken that there were even more than I told you about. I carry a greater spur to superstition than I can fairly burden ye with."

"Ah, your healing hands. I still puzzle over why ye kept that a secret, especially from me."

"For the same reasons ye are loath to let people ken ye have the sight."

"Ye thought *I* would turn from you?" he yelled. "Me? A mon who understands better than any other the burden ye are carrying?"

"The clever part of me kept pointing that out, calling my fears groundless, but fear can make one unreasonable."

"Aye, ye have shown that often enough."

Moira bit back a sharp response to that casually flung insult. Tavig was angry, which made him nasty. She had known that he would be furious. It was why she had tried so hard to keep her leaving a secret.

"That doesnae matter now," she said. "Howbeit, ye must now see why I have to leave. Mayhap all the other things I mentioned wouldnae be enough to raise superstition to a life-threatening height, but putting a seer and a healer to-gether certainly would."

"When my people saw ye using your skills, did they turn from you?"

"Weel, nay, but the midst of a battle isnae the best place to judge such things."

"But ye arenae staying long enough to see if things will change now that the battle is over."

"Nay, but as we saw in Craigmoordun, things can change so swiftly, become threatening so quickly, ye dinnae have time to get away. I daren't chance that because of me ye may not have a chance to flee."

"So, this is all for my sake. Did it not occur to you that I am mon enough to decide whether or not I wish to face those risks? Did ye even think to ask me?"

She blushed with guilt and some embarrassment. He was right. She had, in fact, never asked him how he felt about facing any possible consequences of their marriage.

The dangers had been clear to her, so she had simply told him how it was to be. Moira knew she had always just said *we cannae*. She had never asked him if he wanted to take the risk.

A moment later she inwardly shook away those feelings. The danger was real. One of them had to have the common sense to do what was needed to avoid that danger. She sternly ignored the little voice accusing her of deceiving herself, that there was far more to her urge to flee than a fear of superstition.

"Nay, I didnae think to ask you," she agreed. "Ye ne'er agreed with me about the dangers, so naturally ye would say ye were willing to face them. Aye, and then ye would convince me. Life will be much simpler for you if I leave."

"Simpler for me?" He stepped over to her, grasping her by the shoulders and shaking her slightly. "How can life be easier for me when half of me isnae here? Mayhap my error was in treating ye so gently, like some poor wounded bird."

"Wounded bird?" Moira pushed aside the hair that had tumbled into her face to scowl at him.

Tavig ignored her protest and continued. "Mayhap I spoke too much of fate and destiny, thus giving ye the idea I was being pushed toward ye by some unseen hand and had no free choice. Do ye really think me so weak-willed?"

He gently held her face between his hands, giving her a slow, heated kiss. Moira tried to resist, knowing that the passion they shared could easily weaken her resolve. She discovered she did not have the strength to turn away from what might be her last kiss. When he ended it, she felt dazed and stared at him through heavy-lidded eyes. He had successfully reminded her of how much she was going to give up, and that saddened her. There was also a soft look in his dark eyes that promised her far more than passion. Moira so desperately wanted to believe there was more; she struggled to fight the strong pull of that look.

"I dinnae ken what more I can do, lass," he said in a

hoarse voice. "Ye dinnae seem willing to heed me, my words, or my actions. I have no words to tell ye how sharply I need you and I dinnae mean just in my bed. Aye, and if ye dinnae ken how much I want you, how ye can make me eager with just a smile, then there is naught else I can do. What do ye think drove me to act like such a crazed mon when Jeanne nearly succeeded in having ye burned as a witch? When Mungan told me ye were leaving, 'twas like a knife stuck in my belly. The knowledge that I have already done all I can do to make ye stay, that there is naught else for me to do, was akin to twisting that knife in the wound."

Moira blinked, too emotional and confused to speak. There was such feeling in his voice that she felt bumps rise on the skin of her forearms and shivered. Suddenly any possible danger they might face because of their particular gifts was unimportant, yet she was afraid to trust her own judgment of what was behind Tavig's words.

"Tavig? Are ye saying that ye really care for me?" She swallowed hard, but her voice was little more than a whisper as she asked, "Are ye saying that ye love me?" His eyes widened, and he stared at her with a look of such total disbelief that she was sure she had overstepped. "Nay, ye need not answer. I shouldnae have asked such questions—"

He suddenly raised his fists and face to the roof of the stable. The yell that escaped him startled Moira. Before she could recover from that shock, he grabbed her, tossing her over his shoulder.

"What are ye doing?" she cried as he carried her out of the stable, striding toward his keep.

"I am going to lock ye—nay, *us*—in a room until I can talk some sense into you. It may take a while as ye seem to have lost what few wits ye had at the start of our journey."

Moira cringed with embarrassment as the people in the inner bailey watched her being carried like a sack of grain. It was little comfort at the moment that they laughed and called out to her, revealing no hint of the fears and superstitions she had worried about. She cursed and pummeled Tavig's broad back, but he took no notice of her.

As they entered his keep, her mortification increased. People were crowded in the wide doorway to the great hall, Mungan, Una, and Nicol to the fore. Una looked shocked and yet amused. Nicol and Mungan just looked amused.

"I see ye found the lassie," said Mungan, starting to laugh out loud.

"Aye," replied Tavig. "I am taking her to my chambers to have a wee talk with the fool."

"Have at her, laddie. We can celebrate this victory without you."

"Have at me?" Moira grumbled, lifting her head enough to glare at Mungan as Tavig toted her up the stairs. "Put me down, ye great oaf," she ordered Tavig, but he ignored her.

He finally paused in front of a thick wooden door that was slightly ajar. She gasped softly when he kicked it open wider, marched into the room, and kicked it shut behind him. Moira got only a brief look at a huge room before Tavig tossed her down onto a wide bed. Breathless, she could only lie there as he latched the door, strode back to the bed, and sprawled on top of her.

As he stared at her, she was torn between annoyance and a strange sense of excited anticipation. He was acting oddly, yet she felt a rich sense of promise in his actions. Only a man seized with strong emotion would act so, and strong emotion was just what she wanted from Tavig. When minutes crept by and he still said nothing, she grew nervous.

"Weel? Ye said ye wanted to talk to me, yet ye just gawk," she grumbled.

"Actually, I was looking for the fear, and it isnae there."

"What do ye mean?"

"Lass, I grabbed ye, tossed ye over my shoulder, and carried ye away. I ken I wasnae hiding my anger weel, either. Howbeit, that fear that so often enters your eyes isnae there. Ye werenae frightened by my actions. 'Tis clear it never occurred to ye that I would not do anything to truly harm you."

Moira stared at him as his words sank into her mind. He was right. She could easily recall the number of times she angered or insulted him with her fears. Yet, despite the slightly rough way he had treated her and despite the anger he had revealed, she had not felt the familiar thrill of fear. She had not cringed or thought of ways to make herself less visible to him. For one brief moment she was so pleased with herself, so elated with her freedom from the fear that had haunted her for so many years, she forgot about the tense discussion she was having with Tavig. She was equally torn between an urge to weep and an urge to laugh with the sheer joy of it.

"Oh, Tavig, this is wonderful. I am sure a few scraps of it still linger, but I am finally free. Those fears no longer rise up simply because a word, a look, or a movement stir memories of Sir Bearnard. And I have you to thank for this."

"And ye thank me by walking away."

"Ah, we are back to that again." She grimaced under the sharp, cross look he gave her.

"Aye, we are back to that again, *and* we will remain with that until I am convinced ye couldnae be happy here with me or I convince ye that ye can be. Happy *and* safe. Why dinnae we start with why ye ne'er told me ye had a healing touch. I should have guessed it. Ye used it when I was knocked on the head in Craigmoordun."

"Aye, I did."

"I noticed that my head didnae pain me as it should, considering the blow I took. And mayhap I would have guessed the truth then, except that I simply couldnae consider the possibility that ye would lie to me."

The accusation in his voice stirred her guilt, and she blushed. "I didnae really lie to you."

"Ye didnae tell me about your gift."

"That isnae lying. 'Tis just keeping a secret." She gave him a weak smile in response to his look of disgust.

"But to keep such a secret from *me*? I am probably one of the few people ye did not need to fear."

"Weel, aye and nay. Ye had the same problem as I so ye should have been the most understanding, but ye were also the last person I wished to see turn away from me."

"And ye were the last person I wished to have turn away from me, but I still told ye about my gift."

"Ye are obviously braver than I am." She sighed, wriggled her hand free of his relaxed hold, and brushed her hair off her face. "Mayhap habit played a hand, too. I think I have needed to keep my gift a deeper secret than ye have had to keep yours. A lot of people in Scotland accept the sight, but my gift isnae so widely revered."

"Nay, true enough. Lass, have ye ever thought that our gifts are the reason fate thrust us together?" He idly smoothed his hand over her hair, which had come undone from its loose binding and was splayed out over his pillow. "Who can better understand us? Mayhap destiny felt we would be happier if we could share our burdens."

Moira studied him, wondering what to do or say. Just before he had carried her out of the stables, he had spoken with strong emotion and said things that held a great deal of promise. She could still feel that emotion in him, but it was no longer coming out in a flood of words. When she had bluntly asked him how he felt about her, questioned the meaning of the things he had said, he had answered with a bellow. She needed a clearer response. If she was to face a future that could be troubled by superstition and the danger it brought, she needed to hear more. There was a chance Tavig thought his one outburst was declaration enough, but she could not let it rest at that.

"Ye must see that my people willnae fault ye for your gift," he continued. "In truth, this is probably the safest place in Scotland for you. Drumdearg has a long history of people with gifts or, weel, odd manners or looks. Ye have to admit that Mungan is no ordinary sort of fellow."

"Not ordinary at all."

"His size and the whimsical way he acts causes as much fear as my sight ever has."

"Ye have convinced me, Tavig. Here at Drumdearg I can set aside my concerns about superstitious fear and the havoc it can wreak."

"Then ye will stay," he murmured in a husky voice, brushing a kiss over her mouth.

"Tavig, we cannae hide here every day of our lives. Ye are a knight. At some time—aye, and more than once—we shall have to leave this place. The dangers will be waiting out there for us."

He cursed, dragging his fingers through his hair. "Lass, I ken ye are no coward. Ye must ken that yourself by now. Why do ye let *this* fear stand between us? What can I do to make ye see that 'tis better if we face whatever danger there is together? We will have more strength, more power." He sighed, shaking his head. "I wish I kenned what ye needed."

"I need more than talk of thrice-cursed fate and destiny," she said in a soft voice.

Now that she had said the words, spoken her needs aloud, she no longer felt nervous and shy. He asked a lot from her. She had every right to ask a few things of him as well. Although she would not demand words of love, did not want them unless they were truly heartfelt, she wanted some of that strong emotion he had revealed in the stable. Moira knew she needed such feelings for him to justify facing the dangers. She needed to know that he held her in his heart, if only in a small way. That was the bond they needed if they were to face whatever the future held without it causing constant, bitter strife between them.

"I have—" Tavig frowned when she shook her head. "Curse it, lass. Ye cannae be that unsure."

"Your tongue loses a great deal of its sweet cleverness when ye get annoyed or agitated."

He gently held her face between his hands, giving her a slow, deep yet tender kiss. "Doesnae that tell ye anything?" he asked, his voice low and husky.

"Aye. It tells me that ye *want* me. It tells me that ye desire me."

"Nay, wee Moira." He gave her another kiss, deep, demanding, and fierce. "*That* tells ye that I want you. That speaks of my passion for you. Ah, lass, mayhap I havenae said what lies in my heart, but I have shown it in many ways. Did I not marry you?"

"Ye have always spoken of that as fate and destiny. And ye wed me so that Mungan would leave me alone."

"If I didnae care for you, I would have let that large oaf have you. Aye, aye, I mutter about the hand of fate a lot, but ye had to see that there was so much more to it." He traced the shape of her face with his fingertips. "I always felt that I could understand women, but ye leave me confused. 'Tisnae easy for a mon who has always kenned what to say or do to find himself uncertain. Now ye ask me to say how I feel and, although I have always found the truth an easy thing to speak, I hesitate.

"Mayhap," he murmured as he lightly traced her lips with one finger, "I would find the courage if ye spoke first. After all, what have ye said to me but nay, nay, and nay again?"

"That is verra unfair of you, Tavig MacAlpin." Although he had said nothing specific, he had said enough to give her hope. It was a little unfair, but if it prodded him to be more forthright, Moira knew she could speak first. "I thought a mon was the one to do the wooing," she said as she slipped her arms about his neck.

"Ye cannae say that I havenae wooed you."

"Aye, ye have wooed me. And won me. 'Tis probably verra unwise of me, but I dearly love you, Tavig."

"Ah, my bonnie, sweet wife, in this matter I thank God Himself for your lack of good judgment."

He kissed her lips before she could speak. It hurt that he

did not immediately respond in kind, but there was such emotion in his kiss, she cast that disappointment aside and clung to him. Her hurt faded even more beneath the strong passion his ardent lovemaking aroused within her. He smoothed it away with each kiss, each caress. As he slowly removed her clothes, he honored each newly exposed patch of skin. Although she did not dare to put a name to it, the deep feeling he put behind his every touch flowed through her, intensifying her passion. He shed his clothes so swiftly she had no chance to regain her senses, his tender onslaught seemingly unbroken.

She cried out in hungry welcome as he eased into her body. It took a moment for her passion-clouded mind to clear enough for her to realize he was not moving. She opened her eyes, blushing beneath his intent stare, yet stirred beyond words by the depth of emotion shining in his black eyes. Moira wrapped her body more tightly around him, trying to tempt him to begin the dance she so craved, but he would not be moved.

"Tavig," she said, a little embarrassed by the plea that tinted her voice.

"Say it again, my Moira. Say it whilst we are as close as any mon and woman can be."

"Bribery. Or mayhap, blackmail."

"Aye, a desperate mon can act less than honorably at times. Say it."

"I love you, Tavig."

"Sweet Mary, dearling. Ye cannae begin to understand how I have ached to hear ye say that. As we age, I wager we will engage in many an argument over whose love is the strongest—yours for me, or mine for you."

Before she had a chance to consider what he had just said, he kissed her and began to move. Moira groaned softly with relief and hearty enjoyment. She clung to him as his movements grew fiercer, their hunger more demanding. Even as Tavig drove deeply, holding himself there and groaning her name as he spilled his seed, Moira's passion crested.

It was not until they were fully recovered, lying closely entwined and catching their breath, that Moira was able to think over the things he had said while passion had clouded her mind. Reviewing his words over and over, she was sure he had said that he loved her. Her heart pounding with a mixture of trepidation and anticipation, she looked at him. He had to cease being so obtuse.

"So, do ye love me or not?" she demanded, a little surprised at her own boldness.

Tavig's eyes widened. "Are ye still uncertain?"

"'Tis hard to be certain when a mon doesnae say it clearly. Plain and simple though the words may be, I think I would prefer ye to say them in the same unadorned way I did. Ye can pretty them up and twist them about all ye like—later. Now, right now, I need ye to tell me what ye feel for me in clear, direct language."

He moved so that he could look directly into her eyes. "I love you, Moira Robertson MacAlpin, now and forever." Tavig frowned when her lips trembled, her eyes brightening with the hint of tears. "Ye arenae going to cry, are ye?"

"Nay." She reached out to brush the hair from his forehead, not surprised to see that her hand shook slightly. The emotions running through her were so intense she was surprised her whole body was not shaking hard enough to move the bed. "'Tis just that I have needed to hear the words so badly for so long it has rather offset me."

"I truly thought ye kenned how I felt, dearling. I was that sure it was there to read in my every touch, my every act."

"Tavig, ye are the first mon I have had aught to do with. In truth, ye are the first mon in many a year I havenae hidden from, cringed from, or feared. Now, I may have become braver, but I havenae become vain, and 'twould

have been verra vain of me to just assume ye loved me."
She smiled when he laughed.

Moving so that he was comfortably sprawled on top of
her, Tavig gave her a slow, tender kiss. "I love you." He
murmured his appreciation when she hugged him tightly
with her whole body. "That is what ye needed to make ye
stay with me, to make ye willing to face all the days to
come?"

"Aye," she said. "We may be blessed, and our lives could
be mostly trouble-free. Howbeit, because of who and what
we are, we could face many a time of strife. To face such
strife we needed to be united by more than passion and
your belief in fate and destiny." She shifted with pleasure
beneath the idle but arousing touch of his hands. "Aye, I
feared superstition and the dangers it could present for us.
Even more, I feared watching that strife push ye away from
me, turn ye against me. Without the tie of love, without the
strength it can give us, that could have happened. That is
what I was trying to escape."

"Then I need not fear that ye will ever try to leave me
again. This is why fate chose us to be lovers and to love each
other. No one could understand what we may face better
than we can. We have the strength to face such fears and superstitions alone, but together we shall be unbeatable."

"I do hope so. I look forward to spending many a long
year with you, husband." She rubbed her feet over his
calves. "Do ye think ye have the strength to face that, my
fine laird?"

"A bold challenge. Ye have thrown down a heavy gauntlet."

"And are ye going to pick it up?"

"Oh, aye, my heart. Pick it up, hold it tightly, and never
let it fall."

Please turn the page for an exciting sneak peek of
Hannah Howell's newest historical romance,
HIGHLAND SINNER,
coming in December 2008!

Scotland——early summer 1478

What was that smell?

Tormand Murray struggled to wake up at least enough to move away from the odor assaulting his nose. He groaned as he started to turn on his side and the ache in his head became a piercing agony. Flopping onto his side, he cautiously ran his hand over his head and found the source of that pain. There was a very tender swelling at the back of his head. The damp matted hair around the swelling told him that it had bled but he could feel no continued blood flow. That indicated that he had been unconscious for more than a few minutes, possibly for even more than a few hours.

As he lay there trying to will away the pain in his head, Tormand tried to open his eyes. A sharp pinch halted his attempt and he cursed. He had definitely been unconscious for quite a while and something beside a knock on the head had been done to him for his eyes were crusted shut. He had a fleeting, hazy memory of something being thrown into his eyes before all went black, but it was not enough to give him any firm idea of what had happened to him. Although he ruefully admitted to himself that it was as much vanity as a reluctance to cause himself pain that caused him to fear he would tear out his eyelashes if he just forced his eyes open, Tormand proceeded very carefully. He gently brushed aside the crust on his eyes until he could open them, even if only enough to see if there was any water close at hand to wash his eyes with.

And, he hoped, enough water to wash himself if he proved to be the source of the stench. To his shame there had been a few times he had woken to find himself stinking drunk, and a few stumbles into some foul muck upon the street being the cause. He had never been this foul before, he mused, as the smell began to turn his stomach.

Then his whole body tensed as he suddenly recognized the odor. It was death. Beneath the rank odor of an unclean garderobe was the scent of blood—a lot of blood. Far too much to have come from his own head wound.

The very next thing Tormand became aware of was that he was naked. For one brief moment panic seized him. Had he been thrown into some open grave with other bodies? He quickly shook aside that fear. It was not dirt or cold flesh he felt beneath him but the cool linen of a soft bed. Rousing from unconsciousness to that odor had obviously disordered his mind, he thought, disgusted with himself.

Easing his eyes open at last, he grunted in pain as the light stung his eyes and made his head throb even more. Everything was a little blurry, but he could make out enough to see that he was in a rather opulent bedchamber, one that looked vaguely familiar. His blood ran cold and he was suddenly even more reluctant to seek out the source of that smell. It certainly could not be from some battle if only because the part of the bedchamber he was looking at showed no signs of one.

If there is a dead body in this room, laddie, best ye learn about it quick. Ye might be needing to run, said a voice in his head that sounded remarkably like his squire, Walter, and Tormand had to agree with it. He forced down all the reluctance he felt and, since he could see no sign of the dead in the part of the room he studied, turned over to look in the other direction. The sight that greeted his watering eyes had him making a sound that all too closely resembled the one his niece Anna made whenever she saw a spider. Death shared his bed.

He scrambled away from the corpse so quickly he nearly fell out of the bed. Struggling for calm, he eased his way off the bed and then sought out some water to cleanse his eyes so that he could see more clearly. It took several awkward bathings of his eyes before the sting in them eased and the blurring faded. One of the first things he saw after he dried his face was his clothing folded neatly on a chair, as if he had come to this bedchamber as a guest, willingly. Tormand wasted no time in putting on his clothes and searching the room for any other signs of his presence, collecting up his weapons and his cloak.

Knowing he could not avoid looking at the body in the bed any longer, he stiffened his spine and walked back to the bed. Tormand felt the sting of bile in the back of his throat as he looked upon what had once been a beautiful woman. So mutilated was the body that it took him several moments to realize that he was looking at what was left of Lady Clara Sinclair. The ragged clumps of golden blond hair left upon her head and the wide, staring blue eyes told him that, as did the heart-shaped birthmark above the open wound where her left breast had been. The rest of the woman's face was so badly cut up it would have been difficult for her own mother to recognize her without those few clues.

The cold calm he had sought now filling his body and mind, Tormand was able to look more closely. Despite the mutilation there was an expression visible upon poor Clara's face, one that hinted she had been alive during at least some of the horrors inflicted upon her. A quick glance at her wrists and ankles revealed that she had once been bound and had fought those bindings, adding weight to Tormand's dark suspicion. Either poor Clara had had some information someone had tried to torture out of her or she had met up with someone who hated her with a cold, murderous fury.

And someone who hated him as well, he suddenly thought, and tensed. Tormand knew he would not have come to Clara's bedchamber for a night of sweaty bed play. Clara had once been his lover, but their affair had ended and he never returned to a woman once he had parted from her. He especially did not return to a woman who was now married and to a man as powerful and jealous as Sir Ranald Sinclair. That meant that someone had brought him here, someone who wanted him to see what had been done to a woman he had once bedded, and, mayhap, take the blame for this butchery.

That thought shook him free of the shock and sorrow he felt. "Poor, foolish Clara," he murmured. "I pray ye didnae suffer this because of me. Ye may have been vain, a wee bit mean of spirit, witless, and lacking morals, but ye still didnae deserve this."

He crossed himself and said a prayer over her. A glance at the windows told him that dawn was fast approaching and he knew he had to leave quickly. "I wish I could tend to ye now, lass, but I believe I am meant to take the blame for your death and I cannae; I willnae. But, I vow, I *will* find out who did this to ye and they will pay dearly for it."

After one last careful check to be certain no sign of his presence remained in the bedchamber, Tormand slipped away. He had to be grateful that whoever had committed this heinous crime had done so in this house for he knew all the secretive ways in and out of it. His affair with Clara might have been short but it had been lively and he had slipped in and out of this house many, many times. Tormand doubted even Sir Ranald, who had claimed the fine house when he had married Clara, knew all of the stealthy approaches to his bride's bedchamber.

Once outside, Tormand swiftly moved into the lingering shadows of early dawn. He leaned against the outside of the rough stonewall surrounding Clara's house and wondered where he should go. A small part of him wanted to just go home and forget about it all, but he knew he would never heed it. Even if he had no real affection for Clara, one reason their lively affair had so quickly died, he could not simply forget that the woman had been brutally murdered. If he was right in suspecting that someone had wanted him to be found next to the body and be accused of Clara's murder then he definitely could not simply forget the whole thing.

Despite that, Tormand decided the first place he would go was his house. He could still smell the stench of death on his clothing. It might be just his imagination, but he knew he needed a bath and clean clothes to help him forget that smell. As he began his stealthy way home Tormand thought it was a real shame that a bath could not also wash away the images of poor Clara's butchered body.

"Are ye certain ye ought to say anything to anybody?"

Tormand nibbled on a thick piece of cheese as he studied his aging companion. Walter Burns had been his squire for twelve years and had no inclination to be anything more than a squire. His utter lack of ambition was why he had been handed over to Tormand by the same man who had knighted him at the tender age of eighteen. It had been a glorious battle and Walter had proven his worth. The man had simply refused to be knighted. Fed up with his squire's lack of interest in the glory, the honors, and the responsibility that went with knighthood Sir MacBain had sent the man to Tormand. Walter had continued to prove his worth, his courage, and his contentment in remaining a lowly squire. At the moment, however, the man was openly upset and his courage was a little weak-kneed.

"I need to find out who did this," Tormand said and then sipped at his ale, hungry and thirsty but partaking of both food and drink cautiously for his stomach was still unsteady.

"Why?" Walter sat down at Tormand's right and poured himself some ale. "Ye got away from it. 'Tis near the middle of the day and no one has come here crying for vengeance so I be thinking ye got away clean, aye? Why let anyone e'en ken ye were near the woman? Are ye trying to put a rope about your neck? And, if I recall rightly, ye didnae find much to like about the woman once your lust dimmed so why fret o'er justice for her?"

"'Tis sadly true that I didnae like her, but she didnae deserve to be butchered like that."

Walter grimaced and idly scratched the ragged scar on his pockmarked left cheek. "True, but I still say if ye let anyone ken ye were there ye are just asking for trouble."

"I would like to think that verra few people would e'er believe I could do that to a woman e'en if I was found lying in her blood, dagger in hand."

"Of course ye wouldnae do such as that, and most folk ken it, but that doesnae always save a mon, does it? Ye dinnae ken everyone who has the power to cry ye a murderer and hang ye and they dinnae ken ye. Then there are the ones who are jealous of ye or your kinsmen and would like naught better than to strike out at one of ye. Aye, look at your brother James. Any fool who kenned the mon would have kenned he couldnae have killed his wife, but he still had to suffer years marked as an outlaw and a woman-killer, aye?"

"I kenned I kept ye about for a reason. Aye, 'twas to raise my spirits when they are low and to embolden me with hope and courage just when I need it the most."

"Wheesht, nay need to slap me with the sharp edge of your tongue. I but speak the truth and one ye would be wise to nay ignore."

Tormand nodded carefully, wary of moving his still-aching head too much. "I dinnae intend to ignore it. 'Tis why I have decided to speak only to Simon."

Walter cursed softly and took a deep drink of ale. "Aye, a king's mon nay less."

"Aye, and my friend. *And* a mon who worked hard to help James. He is a mon who has a true skill at solving such puzzles and hunting down the guilty. This isnae simply about justice for Clara. Someone wanted me to be blamed for her murder, Walter. I was put beside her body to be found and accused of the crime. And for such a crime I would be hanged so that means that someone wants me dead."

"Aye, true enough. Nay just dead, either, but your good name weel blackened."

"Exactly. So I have sent word to Simon asking him to come here, stressing an urgent need to speak with him."

Tormand was pleased that he sounded far more confident of his decision than he felt. It had taken him several hours to actually write and send the request for a meeting to Simon. The voice in his head that told him to just turn his back on the whole matter, the same opinion that Walter offered, had grown almost too loud to ignore. Only the certainty that this had far more to do with him than with Clara had given him the strength to silence that cowardly voice.

He had the feeling that part of his stomach's unsteadiness was due to a growing fear that he was about to suffer as James had. It had taken his foster brother three long years to prove his innocence and wash away the stain to his honor. Three long, lonely years of running and hiding. Tormand dreaded the thought that he might be pulled into the same ugly quagmire. If nothing else, he was deeply concerned about how it would affect his mother who had already suffered too much grief and worry over her children. First his sister Sorcha had been beaten and raped, then his sister Gillyanne had been kidnapped—twice—the second time leading to a forced marriage, and then there had been the trouble that had sent James running for the shelter of the hills. His mother did not need to suffer through yet another one of her children mired in danger.

"If ye could find something the killer touched we could solve this puzzle right quick," said Walter.

Pulling free of his dark thoughts about the possibility that his family was cursed, Tormand frowned at his squire. "What are ye talking about?"

"Weel, if ye had something the killer touched we could take it to the Ross witch."

Tormand had heard of the Ross witch. The woman lived in a tiny cottage several miles outside of town. Although the townspeople had driven the woman away ten years ago, many still journeyed to her cottage for help, mostly for the herbal concoctions the woman made. Some claimed the woman had visions that had aided them in solving some problem. Despite having grown up surrounded by people who had special gifts like that, he doubted the woman was the miracle worker some claimed her to be. Most of the time such *witches* were simply aging women skilled with herbs and an ability to convince people that they had some great mysterious power.

"And why do ye think she could help if I brought her something touched by the killer?" he asked.

"Because she gets a vision of the truth when she touches something." Walter absently crossed himself as if he feared he risked his soul by even speaking of the woman. "Old George, the steward for the Gillespie house, told me that Lady Gillespie had some of her jewelry stolen. He said her ladyship took the box the jewels had been taken from to the Ross witch and the moment the woman held the box she had a vision about what had happened."

When Walter said no more, Tormand asked, "What did the vision tell the woman?"

"That Lady Gillespie's eldest son had taken the jewels. Crept into her ladyship's bedchamber whilst she was at court and helped himself to all the best pieces."

"It doesnae take a witch to ken that. Lady Gillespie's eldest son is weel kenned to spend too much coin on fine clothes, women, and the toss of the dice. Near everyone—

mon, woman, and bairn—in town kens that." Tormand took a drink of ale to help him resist the urge to grin at the look of annoyance on Walter's homely face. "Now I ken why the fool was banished to his grandfather's keep far from all the temptation here near the court."

"Weel, it wouldnae hurt to try. Seems a lad like ye ought to have more faith in such things."

"Oh, I have ample faith in such things, enough to wish that ye wouldnae call the woman a witch. That is a word that can give some woman blessed with a gift from God a lot of trouble, deadly trouble."

"Ah, aye, aye, true enough. A gift from God, is it?"

"Do ye really think the devil would give a woman the gift to heal or to see the truth or any other gift or skill that can be used to help people?"

"Nay, of course he wouldnae. So why do ye doubt the Ross woman?"

"Because there are too many women who are, at best, a wee bit skilled with herbs yet claim such things as visions or the healing touch in order to empty some fool's purse. They are frauds and ofttimes what they do makes life far more difficult for those women who have a true gift."

Walter frowned for a moment, obviously thinking that over, and then grunted his agreement. "So ye willnae be trying to get any help from Mistress Ross?"

"Nay, I am nay so desperate for such as that."

"Oh, I am nay sure I would refuse any help just now," came a cool, hard voice from the doorway of Tormand's hall.

Tormand looked toward the door and started to smile at Simon. The expression died a swift death. Sir Simon Innes looked every inch the king's man at the moment. His face was pale and cold fury tightened its predatory lines. Tormand got the sinking feeling that Simon already knew why he had sent for him. Worse, he feared his friend had some suspicions about his guilt. That stung, but Tormand decided to smother his sense of insult until he and Simon had at least talked. The man was his friend and a strong believer in justice. He would listen before he acted.

Nevertheless, Tormand tensed with a growing alarm when Simon strode up to him. Every line of the man's tall, lean body was tense with fury. Out of the corner of his eye, Tormand saw Walter tense and place his hand on his sword, revealing that Tormand was not the only one who sensed danger. It was as he looked back at Simon that Tormand realized the man clutched something in his hand.

A heartbeat later, Simon tossed what he held onto the table in front of Tormand. Tormand stared down at a heavy gold ring embellished with blood-red garnets. Unable to believe what he was seeing, he looked at his hands, his unadorned hands, and then looked back at the ring. His first thought was to wonder how he could have left that room of death and not realized that he was no longer wearing his ring. His second thought was that the point of Simon's sword was dangerously sharp as it rested against his jugular.

"Nay! Dinnae kill him! He is innocent!"

Morainn Ross blinked in surprise as she looked around her. She was at home sitting up in her own bed, not in a great hall watching a man press a sword point against the throat of another man. Ignoring the grumbling of her cats that had been disturbed from their comfortable slumber by her outburst, she flopped back down and stared up at the ceiling. It had only been a dream.

"Nay, no dream," she said after a moment of thought. "A vision."

Thinking about that a little longer she then nodded her head. It had definitely been a vision. The man who had sat there with a sword at his throat was no stranger to her. She had been seeing him in dreams and visions for months now. He had smelled of death, was surrounded by it, yet there had never been any blood upon his hands.

"Morainn? Are ye weel?"

Morainn looked toward the door to her small bedchamber and smiled at the young boy standing there. Walin was only six but he was rapidly becoming very helpful. He also worried about her a lot, but she supposed that was to be expected. Since she had found him upon her threshold when he was the tender of age of two she was really the only parent he had ever known, had given him the only home he had ever known. She just wished it were a better one. He was also old enough now to understand that she was often called a witch as well as the danger that appellation brought with it. Unfortunately, with his black hair and blue eyes, he looked enough like her to have many believe he was her bastard child and that caused its own problems for both of them.

"I am fine, Walin," she said and began to ease her way out of bed around all the sleeping cats. "It must be verra late in the day."

"'Tis the middle of the day, but ye needed to sleep. Ye were verra late returning from helping at that birthing."

"Weel, set something out on the table for us to eat then, I will join ye in a few minutes."

Dressed and just finishing the braiding of her hair, Morainn joined Walin at the small table set out in the main room of the cottage. Seeing the bread, cheese, and apples upon the table, she smiled at Walin, acknowledging a job well done. She poured them each a tankard of cider and then sat down on the little bench facing his across the scarred wooden table.

"Did ye have a bad dream?" Walin asked as he handed Morainn an apple to cut up for him.

"At first I thought it was a dream but now I am certain it was a vision, another one about that mon with the mismatched eyes." She carefully set the apple on a wooden plate and sliced it for Walin.

"Ye have a lot about him, dinnae ye."

"It seems so. 'Tis verra odd. I dinnae ken who he is and

have ne'er seen such a mon. And, if this vision is true, I dinnae think I e'er will."

"Why?" Walin accepted the plate of sliced apple and immediately began to eat it.

"Because this time I saw a verra angry gray-eyed mon holding a sword to his throat."

"But didnae ye say that your visions are of things to come? Mayhap he isnae dead yet. Mayhap ye are supposed to find him and warn him."

Morainn considered that possibility for a moment and then shook her head. "Nay, I think not. Neither heart nor mind urges me to do that. If that were what I was meant to do, I would feel the urge to go out right now and hunt him down. And, I would have been given some clue as to where he is."

"Oh. So we will soon see the mon whose eyes dinnae match?"

"Aye, I do believe we will."

"Weel that will be interesting."

She smiled and turned her attention to the need to fill her very empty stomach. If the man with the mismatched eyes showed up at her door, it would indeed be interesting. It could also be dangerous. She could not allow herself to forget that death stalked him. Her visions told her he was innocent of those deaths but there was some connection between him and them. It was as if each thing he touched died in bleeding agony. She certainly did not wish to become a part of that swirling mass of blood she always saw around his feet. Unfortunately, she did not believe that fate would give her any chance to avoid meeting the man. All she could do was pray that when he rapped upon her door he did not still have death seated upon his shoulder.

ABOUT THE AUTHOR

Hannah Howell is an award-winning author who lives with her family in Massachusetts. She is the author of twenty-eight Zebra historical romances and is currently working on a new Highland historical romance, HIGHLAND SINNER, coming in December 2008! Hannah loves hearing from readers and you may visit her website: www.hannahhowell.com.